Love By Its First Name

by
Don Hanley

authorHOUSE™

1663 LIBERTY DRIVE, SUITE 200
BLOOMINGTON, INDIANA 47403
(800) 839-8640
WWW.AUTHORHOUSE.COM

This is a work of fiction and not a memoir nor an autobiography; all characters are fictitious although, at times, they are composites of persons I have known. The protagonist, Jerry Haloran, is taller, far better looking, more intelligent and courageous than I ever was – so he is a figment of my wishful thinking. Aberdeen and Paris, Kansas do not exist.

First published by AuthorHouse 10/21/05

ISBN: 1-4208-9590-7 (e)
ISBN: 1-4208-4106-8 (sc)

Printed in the United States of America
Bloomington, Indiana

This book is printed on acid-free paper.

Acknowledgements

I would like to thank all the people who have helped me over the years in writing this novel. At first I was going to name all of you in this space, but there are just too many, but I do think of all of you and appreciate your encouragement and help. I would especially like to thank Mike MacCarthy, my 'book doctor' whose Read and Critique class and editing assistance has been invaluable. My daughter, Micaela Myers, generously helped me with editing and character development ideas and especially by sharing two heart-felt poems that I have incorporated into the manuscript. Jim McErlean shared a portion of his journal that I believe gave a bit more reality to the book's ending. Mina Sirovy, Patsy Gaffney and Gayle Copeland helped a great deal in editing, characterization and plot development. A special thanks to Michelle Durban and Linda Shafer and all those who read one or more of the early, truly awful, manuscripts but encouraged me to continue anyway. I thank Rod McKuen and Montcalm Productions for the beautiful words of the song, Who Has Touched the Sky. One line of that song is the title of this novel. And a thank you to Amanda McBroom and Fox Fanfare Music for the wonderful lyrics of the song, The Rose. And last, but not least, I thank Anne, my wife of 35 years, for helping me discover love by its first name

Thank you all for blessing me with your time, talent, energy, and love.

CHAPTER 1

God is love and he who lives in love, lives in God and
God lives in him.

1 John 4:6

What am I doing here?

Jerry Haloran knew what he was supposed to do, but that didn't mean he had no other choices. He slowed his faded Pontiac to a halt in front of the white clapboard building—Peterson's General Store. He parked beside a rusting camper, then enjoyed the car's air-conditioning for a moment, weighing his options. Picking up the keys would be a sign he'd taken the assignment. In all his twelve-plus years as a priest, he'd always looked forward to each new mission, but not this time.

He had almost gotten his spirits up for this new venture, but when he entered the small Kansas town with half its buildings boarded up, his despair returned. It was just about the ugliest burg he'd ever seen. If he simply backed his old clunker out of the dirt driveway and kept driving north, he'd be on Interstate 70 in an hour; then he could go anywhere he wanted.

Sure thing, dimwit. With your leg and this heat, you and this heap would last maybe another twenty minutes, tops. He switched off the engine, took a deep breath, and opened the car door. He moaned quietly and eased himself out of the hissing machine; the back seat was crammed with clothes and the rest of his "worldly possessions." The humid summer air struck his aching body like a blast from a jet engine; the pain in his right leg throbbed as if he were being shot all over again. He balanced himself with one sore arm, pulled a cane from the front floorboard, and straightened up as best he could. If only I hadn't been such a coward and had really helped poor, pregnant, fifteen-year-old Melanie, none of this would have happened. He fought off a sudden attack of tears. You sure talk a good game, Haloran, talk, talk, talk—that's about all you're good for these days.

Jerry and his cane made their way toward the store. A sign on its cluttered wooden porch read: "Welcome to Paris, Kansas, Elevation 612, Population 931. We're smaller but friendlier." A thermometer on a porch post read 102 degrees. He glanced across the road to a run-down clapboard church and a bungalow that needed paint. That, he was sure was his new Catholic 'parish plant'. He winced, shrugged his shoulders and again, almost regretted the sermon he had given that lost him the new, large ultra modern church in Aberdeen and had him exiled to this godforsaken place.

He hobbled into the country store. A distinguished-looking gray-haired man, waiting on a couple with two young children, was apparently the owner of the store. Even dressed in jeans and a freshly ironed short-sleeved shirt, he looked more like a senator or bank president than a clerk in a dinky store in the middle of nowhere. It reminded Jerry of a well-kept 7-11, except it sold hard liquor, half an aisle's worth. A stiff scotch on the rocks would do wonders for his attitude right now.

Jerry waited for the family to leave before making his way to the cash register. "Excuse me, I'm looking for Mr. Peterson."

"That's me," the gray-haired man said. He had a wrinkled, ruddy face and an easy smile. "What can I do for ya?"

"I'm Jerry Haloran. I've come for the keys to St. Patrick's."

Peterson raised two bushy eyebrows, "And why should I want to give the keys to our only Catholic Church to a complete stranger?"

"I'm the new pastor."

"You're a priest?" Peterson studied the tall stranger. "What happened to your leg?"

Jerry ran his hand through his thick black hair. The demonstration in May and the pain of his own blood oozing through his pant leg and onto his fingers flashed through his mind. "… I had a little accident, I guess you could say."

"The way you're gimping around here, it doesn't look like a 'little accident.'" Peterson smiled and held out his hand. "Welcome to Paris, Father. It'll be nice to have a full-time priest for a change."

They shook hands. Jerry said, "Thanks. Good to be here."

"Yeah?" Peterson looked skeptical. "You all right, Father? You look a bit pale."

"No, I'm fine," Jerry said. "But I could use some water."

Peterson opened a refrigerator door and handed him a plastic bottle of cold water. "Here. I keep these ready all the time. This heat's rough on everyone."

"Thanks." Jerry gulped down a few swallows.

"How'd you mess up so bad they sent you way out here in the middle of nowhere?"

Jerry shrugged. "The Bishop thought I needed lighter duties."

Peterson chuckled, "Getting used to Siberia is an acquired taste."

"Isn't Siberia supposed to be cold?"

The older man laughed, "Nice to meet a fellow exile."

Jerry laughed with him and then joked, "Did the Bishop decide you needed lighter duties too?"

"Oh, I exiled myself. Used to work in Kansas City. Big corporation. Bad situation. Alice, she's my wife, grew up here, so we moved back some years ago. It's quiet; we kinda like that." Peterson opened the cash register, plucked out a set of keys and tossed them to Jerry.

The priest snagged them with one hand like a first baseman catching an errant throw. "Thanks a lot, . . . Mr. Peterson."

"Call me Sy. If you call me Sylvester, I'll kick your other leg. And don't go jumping to any conclusions; wife's the only Catholic in our marriage. Want to meet her?"

"Sure." Despite the air-conditioning, Jerry ached now, almost head to toe.

Sy ushered him through the back door into a spacious and pleasant living room. Family pictures adorned the redwood walls and bookcases. The room had the medicinal smell of a hospital.

"Alice." Sy said gently, "Meet your new pastor, Father Haloran."

Jerry half-expected a robust farm wife and almost gasped when he saw a small, emaciated woman with only wisps of hair left on her head. She had hazel eyes, a narrow nose, high cheekbones and full lips, all indicating she had once been a beautiful woman. He glanced at a picture on the wall, and wondered if it was their wedding picture. The room was far from cool, but the old woman sat wrapped in a colorful afghan.

Alice turned off the television, and slowly turned in their direction. She grimaced, attempted a smile, and haltingly extended her hand.

Jerry knelt beside her recliner, placing his cane on the floor. Pain shot up his leg with the ferocity of a thunderbolt, and through years of practice, his face showed no pain. Gently taking her hand, he said, "How nice to meet you, Mrs. Peterson."

"Call me Alice." Her voice was almost a whisper, but her eyes glowed. "It will be wonderful to have a full-time priest again. The one from the Abbey last summer used to bring me communion every Sunday. He was a nice young man. Will you bring me communion?"

"Every day, if you're not too much of a sinner."

Her eyes twinkled. "Oh, you like to make jokes? That's good, but I'm afraid my sinnin' days are but a dim memory. The cancer's taken most of the fun out of me."

"Oh, I don't know about that. Your eyes tell me that you have some mischief in you yet."

Alice smiled and looked over at Sy. "I like this fella." She turned back to Jerry. "I don't know why you've been sent way out here to our poor little town, but I'm glad. Are you a drunk?"

Jerry had always liked the way the old and dying said what was on their minds. He winced, thinking of the times he'd over-indulged on alcohol since last May, but he gave Alice a soft, "No, I'm not a drunk." She could not know how much her enthusiastic "I like this fella" had meant to him. He felt something warm awakening in him.

"Had to ask. We've had our share at St. Patrick's. Poor Father Blaise was such a kind, shy man but couldn't stay away from the bottle." She stopped herself, as if ashamed of talking negatively about Father Blaise. She gave Jerry a thorough once over. "So, what did you do to that pompous old Bishop to get yourself sent to sleepy old Paris, Kansas?"

"I guess he figured I needed some peace and quiet."

She nodded. "And you've kissed the Blarney Stone too. I heard a new priest was heading our way back in June. What took you so long?" She looked down at his cane on the floor. "That leg keep you away all this time?"

Jerry smiled. "About three weeks worth, but I also needed to finish my Master's, so I took a little detour to Loyola University in Chicago."

"Master's in what?" Alice asked.

"Education."

Alice's eyes sparkled brighter. "Think we might need a little education out here on the prairie, do ya?" She squinted her eyes and extended her hand again. "What did you say your last name was?"

"Haloran."

"An Irishman, eh? Well, I hope you won't get bored with our little parish, Father. And you really will bring me communion?"

Using his cane, Jerry stood up. "You count on it." He bent down and took her hand. "I'll see you in the morning, Alice. A delight to meet you."

When he and Sy were back in the store, Jerry asked, "How bad is her cancer?"

"Petty bad, it's eating up her whole body. Doctors told her a year ago she had about three months to live. But she hangs in there and suffers in silence. Docs want her in the hospital, but there's not much they can do. She's had chemotherapy and radiation about all she can stand. Now, well …"

"I'll see her every day." In more ways than one, Alice reminded Jerry of his mother. He gave a little wave of the keys toward Sy and said, "Thanks for these. Nice meeting you, too."

When Jerry was nearly through the door, Sy shouted after him, "Oh, Father, the church is across the street, if you didn't already know. And there's a young dog over there. Father Blaise kept him, called him Pluto, I think. Been giving him food and water every day. He's friendly."

As Jerry limped toward his car through the searing heat, he glanced at the church and rectory across the road. The clapboard-sided buildings looked like they hadn't been painted in years. The top of the steeple was missing and its tarpaper-covered stump barely rose to the roof ridge. The little rectory, some fifty yards north of the church, had a front porch that sagged so much it looked ready to collapse. At least the repairs will give you something to do—for a few months anyway, he told himself.

When Jerry finally pulled his car onto the gravel drive and parked, a big, gold, brown, and black dog, complete with dirty, matted fur, came running to the car wagging his tail. Collie-shepherd mix, he guessed.

The priest reached out and got his hand licked. Taking the dog's head in both hands, he petted him and studied the animal for a moment. "You have intelligent eyes, buddy. But, you're not a 'Pluto,' you're a philosopher. From now on your name will be Plato." The dog pushed against Jerry's leg, as if agreeing to the name change.

The cornerstone of the church caught the priest's eye; it read 1921. "Well, Plato, let's see what this place looks like inside."

Maybe between Alice, Sy, Plato, and the repair work that needed doing, he could dredge up enough spirit to stay for a year. After an hour inspection of his new run-down assignment, sweat poured down Jerry's face and back. He hobbled from the church and re-joined Plato, now quietly panting in the shade. "Good thing God invented air-conditioning, right Plato? Without it, we could probably give away free money on Sundays and no one would come."

He decided it was time to start meeting the rest of the town. He remembered the Cozy Café from when he'd driven through Paris, no more than a few blocks away. It was one of the few buildings that wasn't boarded up.

"What do you think, Plato, want to go for a walk

with me?" The collie wagged his tail. "Got to do something to get rid of this limp and these sore muscles. Nothing worse than a middle-aged priest who looks like he's ready for an old people's home."

Only one old pickup passed him on the way. He thought of the saying, "Only mad dogs and Englishmen venture out in the noon day sun." He saw no one else. Sweat poured out of him and soaked his white T-shirt and jeans.

His leg throbbed worse than ever as he entered the restaurant door. Inside, the café didn't look too cozy, but it was cool and clean. Six tables with oilcloth covers and worn wooden chairs filled the space in front of a counter with seven stools. The only customers were four men sitting at the largest table nearest the counter. Two empty chairs at the table had dirty dishes in front of them, and the four men were drinking beer. One man was without a hat, but a line across his forehead indicated where a hat usually sat. One sweat-stained straw hat, a DeKalb, and a John Deere baseball cap remained atop the other three.

The four locals watched as Jerry limped to the counter. He nodded to them and sat down on one of the middle stools. Immediately, a heavyset woman emerged through the swinging saloon doors in back. "What'll ya have, hon?" Seeing Jerry looking up and down the counter, she pointed to a whiteboard above the coffee maker. "There's the menu." From the look on her face, she probably wanted to add, "stupid."

The menu was limited to chicken soup, chicken-friend steak, hot beef sandwich, and a hamburger. "How about a hamburger and fries?" he asked.

"Ain't got no fries. How about some chips?"

"That's fine and ..." he glanced over at the round table and decided to imitate the others, ". . . a bottle of Coors."

The four men hadn't said a word, even to each other. Rather than introduce himself, Jerry folded his hands on the counter and waited for the food. He could hear the hamburger sizzling on the grill.

The waitress brought his beer without a glass and plopped it down in front of him. She didn't say a word. Maybe the sign about this Paris being friendlier was a lie.

His hamburger arrived along with a small bag of Fritos. The waitress stepped back and folded her arms across her ample chest. "You just passin' through?"

"No, ma'am, I'm just moving here."

"In that case, my name's Mabel." Her face softened into a smile, and she extended her hand.

He shook her hand. "I'm Jerry Haloran."

"Ain't had anybody move in here for some time. What do ya do?"

"I'm the new pastor at St. Patrick's."

"Oh, so it's Father Haloran, is it? I figgered they'd just close the place down after Father Blaise left. He weren't worth much, but he did hold services, I guess. So, what do you think of our poor little rundown burg?"

One of the men spoke up. "Aw, Mabel, don't give ol' Paris a bad name."

Jerry looked toward the speaker, who said, "Padre, why don't ya join us? We'll fill ya in about our paradise here. Mabel, do yer job and clean off this mess and make room for our newest resident."

The town's new priest picked up his plate and beer, and stood for a minute while Mabel picked up the dishes and wiped off the table. The men appeared to be in their forties and fifties. As he sat down, the speaker touched the brim of his straw hat and put out his hand. "I'm Joe Gaffin."

Jerry gave him a firm handshake.

"This here's Paul Gilbride." He pointed to the one with the John Deere hat, "Over there's Carl Johnson." Carl was the one with the De Kalb hat. Each man nodded toward Jerry. "And sitting next ta ya there is Bill Cochran. You'll want to talk to him 'cause he's a bootleg Catholic. Needs some goosing about religion, I think." Joe chuckled, took off the straw hat, and ran one hand through his hair.

Jerry shook Bill's hand, the only one he could reach without stretching across the table. "Glad to meet all of you." He looked at Bill. "What's he mean by 'bootleg Catholic'?" He nodded toward Joe.

Before Bill could respond, Joe blurted, "That's somebody who goes to church only at Christmas, Easter, and when out-of-town relatives show up. Ain't that right, Bill?"

Bill looked at his beer and mumbled something like "I guess."

Jerry turned to Joe. "So, Joe, are you a bootleg something, or are you a regular something?"

Carl chuckled. "Naw, Joe ain't something, he's a nothing." Paul and Joe laughed with him, and even Bill smiled a bit.

The easy camaraderie was noticeable and pleasant.

Again, the feeling of sadness came over Jerry as he thought of the comfortable way he and his closest friend, Wayne at St. Gabriel's, had always gotten along. He wondered how long before these men would accept him as one of them, or if they ever would.

"How did Paris get its name?" Jerry wondered out loud.

That opened the floodgates. For half an hour, the four men talked about themselves and quite a bit about Paris, the town and county. Joe did most of the talking. Carl had a farm west of town. Paul was the mayor, lived in town but farmed south of town. Bill ran the ramshackle lumberyard across the street.

"Keep telling him to fix that damn heap of a lumberyard up 'fore it falls down," Joe said.

"Yep, Father," Paul finally piped in, "yer sittin' among the big-wigs of Paris. Joe here is the county sheriff."

Joe pulled a badge out of his shirt pocket to verify the statement.

Seems that Paris was named after "ol man Paris" who, at one time, owned "damn near" the whole county. It is the county seat and once had nearly 2,000 people. That was before World War II, when there were lots of small farms and people didn't travel a hundred miles to get their supplies. Paris even had a daily passenger train until 1948. Now the only industry around was an egg ranch and large dairy—both owned by some out-of-town "fellers." The town of Paris now had a little over 900 people, and Paris County had around 3,000 people, "all told."

The priest noticed the men had been studying him

all through the discussion, but he already felt at home with them, like going back in time to the small plains town, where he spent most of his childhood.

The new arrival's comfort level evaporated when Carl asked, "Ain't I seen you on television some time ago? Can't remember what it was all about, though."

Jerry looked around the group, and Carl seemed the only one interested in the question. Maybe he could buy some time. "Yes, I was on television back in May. I'll tell you all about it one of these days."

One of the things he appreciated about small towns was that people seldom pried into other people's affairs, at least to their face. Suddenly he remembered poor Plato outside in the heat. Looking outside, he saw the dog watching him expectantly. "Excuse me a minute. I need to get my dog some water; I didn't know I'd be in here so long." He asked Mabel for a pan of water and took it to Plato, then retuned.

Joe asked, "You a city boy?"

"I've been a city boy since I was 16. Paris reminds me of Henning, Nebraska, where I grew up. Might have been even a little smaller."

"Henning's up there in the corner near Wyoming, ain't it?" Paul said.

"That's where it is. Haven't been back there in over twenty years."

"I'll be damned!" Paul took off his hat and ran a hand through his balding hair, then replaced the hat. He looked at Jerry, deep in thought. "Ya know, I was up in Nebraska last week, visiting the wife's kinfolk. One of her uncles told a story about a young fella, just a kid I guess, who killed his pa while the old man was beating up his ma. Think he said it was some twenty-five or thirty years ago." Paul scratched the back of his head. "I'm pretty sure the guy said it was Henning. The uncle said the kid was one of the finest youngsters he'd ever known. Damnedest thing I ever heard. Didja ever hear anything about that?"

A chill went down Jerry's spine. "Yes, I remember it." His voice was soft as he studied his empty beer bottle for a moment. He looked around the table. Sadness, anger, shame, all welled up in him at once, almost more powerfully than he was able to handle. "I was that young feller," he said, almost in a whisper.

CHAPTER 2

But tell me, where does wisdom come from? Where is understanding to be found? The road to it is still unknown to man, not to be found in the land of the living.

Book of Job, 28, ll:13

Rebecca Brady had mixed emotions about volunteering as a writing mentor to abandoned or abused teenage girls, but a promise was a promise. The truth was Helene Walker, her closest friend and director of the young women's shelter, could sell snow to Eskimos, and besides, it was a good cause.

Helene was waiting for her in the lobby when Rebecca burst through the front door, late as usual. "Sorry," the tall journalist said out of breath, "I thought I had enough time, but I forgot about St. Louis morning rush-hour traffic."

"Don't worry about it. After all these years, if there's one thing I know about you and time; there's regular time and then there's 'Becky-time.' I told the girls to expect you about 9:15, so technically, you're right on time."

Rebecca scowled and took a deep breath, stuffing keys into her purse. "That's really embarrassing— 'Becky-time'? How long has that been going on?"

Helene smiled. "It's not a big deal. Come on." She hurried across the lobby. "To Rene and Denise you're a big-time reporter and role model who's taken time from her busy schedule for them." She entered a set of numbers into a computerized door lock, opened a set of double-doors, then waited for Rebecca.

"Are those their names?"

"Yes. Just remember, they're kids—despite how tough they may try to act. Rene is sixteen, both parents dead; she's here because she's under arrest for prostitution. Denise is also sixteen and came here after her father shot and killed her mother and baby sister."

Rebecca closed both eyes and shook her head. "Are you sure I'm the person for this job? I have to tell you that right now I feel about as inadequate to help these two girls as Ann Sullivan must have felt after her first day with Helen Keller."

Helene stopped in front of a single door. "You'll be fine, Rebecca." She turned and gave her friend a quick hug. "You're always putting yourself down. Trust me, I wouldn't let just anyone spend time with these girls. You have so much more going for you than you even realize." Helene walked to the door. "I'll introduce you, get the three of you settled in, and then I'll leave. If things go badly, just push the buzzer on the inside door jam of this door. Someone will be there within ten seconds."

*   *   *

As Rebecca drove back to the downtown St. Louis offices of *Women Today*, she shook her shoulders to rid herself of some of the sadness that seeped into her bones from listening to Rene and Denise's stories. She had a hard time holding back the tears but chuckled when she remembered how Rene kept challenging her to talk about her love life. "Tell us about yer fuckin'," the sixteen-year-old had said. "You do fuck, don't you?"

Rebecca realized her embarrassment was indicative of how uptight she had been with the girls. She wished she could have laughed or at least smiled, instead of being outraged at Rene's goading. The two girls had definitely touched her, and they were going to teach her a lot more than she would ever teach them.

Women Today occupied the entire eighth floor of an attractive glass and steel building that also housed attorneys and high-tech companies. The upscale magazine had been creeping up in the women's magazine market, closing in on the fifth spot in circulation and paid subscriptions. Rebecca felt personally proud that it had more articles of substance than any of the other mainstream women's magazines.

Before entering the office, Rebecca made a detour to the women's room. She brushed her shoulder-length black hair and touched up her makeup. She stood back from the mirror and straightened her light rose summer suit, wondering if Denise had been admiring her or her clothes when she said she was beautiful.

Rene then scolded Denise, "Quit staring at her clothes, Midget, she ain't gonna give 'em to ya." Almost anything would have been better than the faded old print dress Denise wore. Rebecca made a mental note to ask Helene if it would be okay to take the girls shopping one day soon.

Sitting down at her computer, she pulled up her

article on the children's conference in Washington. Just as it appeared on the screen, Gayle Matthews, the editor, entered, dressed in a dark green suit with matching earrings. She was a bit overweight, but it only added to her commanding presence. She plopped down on the chair next to Rebecca. "I've been looking for you. You're late."

"I told you I'd be late on Monday. Getting forgetful in your old age?"

Easy banter was the way these two women communicated and one of the many things that made Rebecca's job pleasant. "So, why have you been looking for me, other than to chew me out?"

"How's your article on the children coming?"

"Pretty well. I should have it wrapped up this afternoon, tomorrow at the latest. Then, I'm supposed to do that article on the so-called 'demise of women's liberation.' But I can tell you have something else in mind."

"Of course. We have to keep you out of mischief, you know." Gayle handed the folder to Rebecca.

Rebecca opened it and saw a number of newspaper clippings. "So what do we have here?"

Gayle chuckled. "A trip to Paris."

Rebecca only smiled, waiting for the other shoe to drop. "Now that does sound interesting. I've never been to Paris."

"This Paris isn't in France, it's in Kansas."

Her smile faded. "Kansas?"

"Oh, Kansas isn't so bad. Remember I grew up and went to college in Lawrence, so be careful what you say about my home state."

The reporter put the folder on her lap. "It's still not France. So what's the big deal in Paris, Kansas?"

"I don't know how big 'the deal' is, but it's about a Catholic priest. Read these articles and I think you'll agree he'll make a great story. One of the main themes will be the abortion issue."

"Come on, Gayle, we've been over this before a 100 times. Remember I turned down the trip to Florida when they had the shootings down there. I'm too pro-choice to be objective on abortion."

"The priest will be the main focus, not abortion. Remember what happened two years ago? I went against my better judgment and sent little Miss Eager-Beaver; she brought back a superficial piece not worth spit. I want something about this guy that has depth and scope and a personal angle, and you're just the one to do it. You're a professional and know how to put your biases aside and write a good story."

"Isn't there anyone else? How about Sheila Vernon? She's a good writer and a Catholic to boot, so she'd know something about priests. I've never even talked to a priest in my entire life."

Gayle reached over and touched Rebecca's head. "Hello? Sheila is eight months pregnant."

Rebecca gave her editor a resigned look; a moment from her childhood flashed through her memory. "Okay, Gayle, for you—only for you."

"You look like I just stole your Easter basket. What's the matter? "

She couldn't look her boss in the eye. "Nothing."

"So, are you going to do it or not?"

"I suppose," Rebecca answered without enthusiasm.

After lunch Rebecca finished the article on the children's conference and put it on Gayle's desk. She then decided to look over the papers in the folder Gayle left, even before beginning her research on the women's movement. The first one was from a May issue of the Aberdeen, Kansas, *Daily News*. The headline read, "PRIEST SAVES LIFE OF ABORTION DOCTOR" and described how Father Gerard Haloran, age 42, had saved Dr. Justin Breen from being shot by a woman from Oklahoma. The priest sustained multiple gunshot wounds in one leg and was in serious condition in Aberdeen's Mercy Hospital. Two pictures accompanied the article: one showing the assailant behind the priest, a middle-aged woman carrying a sign: "Dr. Breen is a Baby Murderer." The other picture showed a grimacing priest wrestling the woman to the ground.

According to the article, the demonstration was one of the largest ever held in the United States. Dr. Breen was the target because he was one of the few physicians in the entire Midwest who performed third trimester abortions. The *St. Louis Post-Dispatch* and even the *New York Times* had articles on the incident. Rebecca couldn't believe she'd missed the original articles in the St. Louis papers. Three weeks after the shooting, the Aberdeen paper had a second article about Father Jerry Haloran. The headlines read, "HERO PRIEST BLASTS HIS CHURCH." The lengthy article outlined how the priest gave an impassioned sermon, contradicting Catholic teachings on masturbation, birth control, homosexuality, and abortion.

On the last subject, the priest didn't seem to be

pro-abortion but believed it was not immoral under certain conditions—not such an outrageous stance as far as Rebecca was concerned, but maybe it was for a priest. She'd have to look into that. Evidently, it was newsworthy enough to deserve small articles in the *Chicago Tribune* and *New York Times* as well as the St. Louis papers.

Rebecca re-read the Aberdeen article, noted the Jeff Heathcote byline and circled the name; the article sounded as if the reporter had been there to hear the priest. He noted Haloran enjoyed a reputation as one of the outstanding priests of the diocese—on track to become a bishop, according to sources. But, according to Heathcote, the May speech ended such talk. She made a note to look up the reporter.

The last article in the folder was a small notice from an inside page of the Aberdeen paper, "DISGRUNTLED PRIEST EXILED." The piece stated that Father Gerard Haloran had been "re-assigned" to Paris, Kansas, a hamlet over one hundred miles northwest of Aberdeen. The notice had been dated one week after the sermon.

So, Rebecca thought, the sermon outraged the church authorities enough to get him sent to the boondocks. What had happened with the priest? What turned him from one of the fair-haired boys to an outcast? Why did he risk giving such a sermon? He appears at an anti-abortion demonstration, then, three weeks later, blasts his church on that very issue, as well as other church teachings having to do with sexuality.

She returned to the first article and studied the two pictures. This Father Haloran doesn't look too happy as he studies the lady with the sign. In fact, he looks almost as tormented in this first picture as he does in the second one after being shot. He's obviously a tall man and well built, but she couldn't really tell from all his facial expressions what he looked like.

"Well, Gayle Matthews," she muttered to herself, "I think we might just have an unusual story here."

Chapter 3

If you bring forth what is within you, what you bring forth will save you. If you do not bring forth what is within you, what you do not bring forth will destroy you.

Gospel of Thomas

Jerry took a deep breath to hold down the panicky feelings that arose in him when the man named Paul, sitting at the Cozy Café in Paris, Kansas, mentioned that "a young fella, just a kid I guess, killed his pa while the old man was beating up his ma" twenty-some years ago. It was an accident and only his mother and the parish priest knew he had anything to do with it.

Even without closing his eyes, he was fourteen years old and helping his dad finish a big remodeling job on one of only three nice houses in Henning. His dad had quit drinking a year after he and Jerry's mom divorced. At the time of the divorce, she moved with his two youngest sisters to Crawford, Nebraska, a town twenty-five miles away. His four older siblings, two brothers and two sisters, were married, struggling and living in four different western states. In the two years since the divorce, his two younger sisters had never visited their dad, but Jerry had gone to visit them about every two weeks. Jerry stayed with his dad because he felt sorry for him, at least that was what he thought at the time. As an adult he realized that, even though his father was often a mean drunk, he loved him and needed a dad.

The owner of the house they were working on, knowing of the previous drinking problem, agreed to pay the eight thousand dollar remodeling bill only when the job was complete. Dad had not been able to send a child support check for the three months, so when he received the paycheck, he was happier than Jerry had ever seen him. "Now, I can send your mom some money, and some extra. You clean up here, and I'll deposit this and send her a check." Jerry wanted to holler or clap or do something to celebrate, but that kind of show of emotions was always greeted by a comment like "don't get too excited." Just the previous weekend his mom and sisters bawled him out for not bringing money with him when he made the trip from Henning. He wanted to catch a bus and head back to Henning right after he arrived in Crawford, but there was no bus scheduled that day. After cleaning up, he found himself skipping as he made his way home. Arriving at the little bungalow, even through the closed door, he could hear his mom's voice. That in itself was unusual, as she was usually quiet as a mouse. Evidently, she had taken the bus to Henning. She was yelling, "You're drinking again, aren't you? You're a no good selfish bastard!" Her yelling frightened him as it always did because it always led to some kind of violence from his dad. Jerry had often reflected on the fact that the only times he had ever seen his dad touch his mother was when he hit her. He opened the door just as she slapped his father. Dad grabbed her by the neck and began choking her. Without thinking and with a rage building in him, Jerry ran and caught his father's arm. Dad backhanded him so hard, blood spurted from his nose and he went sprawling to the floor. Jerry wiped his face with his shirtsleeve and jumped back up. He was not going to give up. This time he took hold of his dad's shirt collar and pulled as hard as he could. He could see his mother grasping at dad's hands, turn blue, and gasp for air, making short gurgling sounds. Jerry couldn't seem to get his father to let go. He put both hands on his collar and yanked as hard as he could. His father lost his balance and fell backward. Jerry jumped out of the way. It seemed like his dad was falling in slow motion and hit his head on the edge of the cast-iron cook-stove; he appeared to bounce slightly away from the stove and then thudded to the floor. Blood flowed from a wound on the back of his head. Jerry fell to his knees and cried, "Daddy, Daddy!" Seeing a dish towel over the back of a chair, Jerry grabbed it and tried to stop the flow of blood from dad's head, not heeding the blood still pouring from his own nose. Dad didn't move a muscle. Mom knelt on dad's other side and took his hand, feeling his wrist. With tears flowing down her cheeks she said quietly, "He's dead, son." He began bawling like he had never bawled before.

He didn't know how long he knelt there, but after a while Jerry realized he was stiff and holding a handkerchief to his nose. The bleeding had stopped, and his mom had her arm around him. It was the only time he ever remembered his mother holding him. Jerry whispered, "Mom, I didn't mean to kill him. I just didn't want him to hurt you."

"I know son, I know."

The town marshall reported the incident as an accident. Neither Jerry nor his mother had told another soul the whole story, other than the parish priest. Jerry did tell Father Wayne Cameron a few years ago. Although his mother and the priest assured him it was an accident, he could never quite get rid of the haunting thought that he had killed his father. He did not cry at dad's funeral. Jerry only recently realized that it was then that he began to numb himself whenever he had strong feelings—positive or negative.

He snapped out of his unpleasant reverie and looked around at the quiet and thoughtful men at the Cozy Café in Paris, Kansas. He didn't know, or care, if they could see the tears forming in his eyes.

The man named Carl chuckled as he said, "Don't suppose you killed someone else and that's what got ya sent to Paris, huh?"

Father Jerry just looked at Carl and then slowly pushed his chair back and stood. Without saying a word, he went to the door, picked up the empty water pan and returned it to Mabel. When he paid for his beer and meal, he left an extra dollar tip for the dog's water.

"Don't s'pose I hit a nerve, do ya?" The priest heard Carl ask as he approached the door.

Joe Gaffin responded, "That's one of the most stupid-assed things I've ever heard. Carl, sometimes I think you've got shit for brains!"

Plato waited patiently for him at the Bank of Paris, where he found out the parish had a bank balance of over $300,000. The only son of ol' man Paris had donated $600,000 to St. Patrick's over twenty years ago, when he sold the land to the egg and dairy people. The Sunday collection never quite paid for expenses, not even the priest's salary, and so it had dwindled over the years. It was made clear in making the gift that the parish priest was to have sole control of the money and that the Bishop of Aberdeen could not touch it. Jerry wondered why they never fixed up the church. At least he wouldn't have to go begging to the Bishop.

When he got back to the house, the air conditioners had done their job. He closed the windows, then began lugging in the boxes and suitcases. Plato followed him back and forth from the car. "You know, Plato, I think you're going to be a life-saver."

Opening a box of books in the office, he held up a card he'd thrown in when he packed up his stuff at St. Gabriel's that morning. The card had a rainbow-colored crescent moon and a star on the front. He opened it and again read the printed message, "Everyone whose life you touch is blessed." Below it as a hand-written message, "Dear Jerry, the above message is true. Thank you for 'touching me.' Love, Kathy." In parenthesis, she added, "I haven't signed 'Kathy' to anything for years—feels good." He started to throw the card away, paused, then placed it carefully in the center drawer. He mumbled to himself, "I'm going to miss you, Sister Kathleen." He shrugged his shoulders as if to shake off the self-pity to which he was beginning to succumb.

Returning to the box of books, he found a picture of himself and Melanie Kurtz at St. Gabriel's eighth-grade graduation. Even in the eighth grade, Melanie looked older and more mature than her years. The picture was clipped to a piece of paper. He detached the picture and turned it over and read his own written words, "Father Jerry, please help me. You are the only one!" On the paper was the poem he had read at Melanie's funeral. He read it again, and he could feel tears forming. As he placed the picture and poem in the drawer, he mumbled, "I'm so sorry, Melanie, that your life wasn't blessed by my touch." He sat there for he didn't know how long before resuming his unpacking. He completed emptying the rest of the boxes, randomly putting books on the bookshelves.

As the sun moved to the west, he decided to do something physical to try and subdue the despair creeping up on him. Dragging a lawnmower from the garage, Jerry guessed it had been about sixteen years since he'd mowed a lawn. He got it started after several pulls of the cord. Starting on the road edge of the 'lawn,' he noticed that under all the weeds was a good stand of Bermuda grass just waiting for water. For some strange reason, that cheered him up a bit. He was half-finished with the area between the church and the rectory when a young girl, holding something, headed his way. The red-haired, freckled-faced girl said, "The man at the store asked me to bring this to you." She held out a can of beer.

Jerry took the can from her. It was icy cold, and he placed it against his forehead before popping it open. "Well, thank you, sweetheart. That's really nice of you." He wiped his hand on his jeans and held it out to the girl. "My name's Jerry, what's yours?"

"April O'Conner."

He guessed her to be about seven. "April's a pretty

name. You live around here?"

"No, we live in Aberdeen. We're going to camp and water ski on Lake Paris. Mommy and me think it's too hot, but Daddy says there are shade trees. Is that true?"

"You known, April, I really don't know. I just moved here today. I haven't seen the lake yet."

"Are you a gardener?"

Jerry looked down at his sweat-soaked tee shirt and dirty jeans. "Yeah, I guess I am."

A man called from a camper with a boat hitched to the back. "April, we're ready to go."

"Thanks for bringing me the drink, April."

"You're welcome." She ran to the camper.

Jerry wondered what it would be like to go camping with a family. In his many years as a priest in Aberdeen, he'd never thought about doing anything with a family. Hmm, too busy he guessed and wondered how many more "new" and disturbing thoughts he'd have out here on the lonesome prairie. He mowed for a while longer and then found a hose and sprinklers. His back and leg were killing him as he limped over to the store. He thanked Sy for the beer, bought bread, cheese, and lunchmeat for sandwiches and food for breakfast. Before he left, he said, "Looks like there's a lot to do over there. What happened to the steeple?"

"Tornado took it off before we moved back here." Sy stroked his chin. "I'd say over twenty years ago. They've replaced the tarpaper a couple of times, that's about all."

On Saturday Jerry toured the town and lost count of the number of run-down and boarded up houses and other buildings. The high school was the largest and nicest building in town. A sign proclaimed, "Paris Unified High School—Home of the Wheatshockers." The discouraging tour of the town took all of fifteen minutes. He took a look at the county's 'pride and joy,' Lake Paris. It did have shade trees and several nice camping areas.

After a dinner of sandwiches, beer, and self-pity, Jerry called Father Wayne Cameron. Wayne picked up the phone after the first ring. "Hi Wayne, Sitting there trying to figure out how to inspire the people tomorrow?"

"Hi, Jer, ol' buddy, how's the new parish?"

"Forlorn, I'd say."

"And you with it, I suppose?"

"No, I'm just pitiful. How'd the meeting go with his Excellency?"

"Good and bad, I'd say."

"Tell me the good first."

"The good is that I told him I wouldn't change my stance. The bad is. . . I guess it's bad, don't know yet. I'm ordered to leave St. Gabriel's for a smaller parish September first."

Jerry knew Wayne did not want to add to his misery, but his words made him even more depressed than he'd been all day. All he managed to say was, "You don't know where yet, huh? Wayne, I'm sorry I've put you in such a bind."

"Don't be sorry. You said what needed to be said." They chatted a few more minutes and closed with Wayne telling him that he'd keep him posted about the new assignment.

The one Mass scheduled for 9:00 Sunday morning was the dreariest celebration Jerry had ever had—no alter boys or girls, readers, flowers, or music. The only thing that could possibly be positive was that there were more people attending than he had been led to expect. After Mass, he greeted all who stayed to the end of the service. Bill Cochran, the 'bootleg' Catholic, was there with his wife and three teenage children. The boys had the same depressed countenance and limp handshake as their father.

April O'Conner, holding her mother's hand, approached Jerry and said scoldingly, "You lied to me!"

"Now April." Her mother appeared shocked at the girl's outburst.

Glancing at the mother, Jerry put his finger to his lips. He knelt down in front of the little girl. "I did?"

"Yes, you did. You told me you were a gardener."

"Um…" Father Jerry stroked his chin. "I did, didn't I? Well, I was a gardener when I met you, April, wasn't I?"

April wrinkled up her face. "Yeah, I guess so. But you're really a priest."

"Can't I be a priest and a gardener, too? I'll bet you're a student and a daughter and a helper to your mom." He winked at April's mother. She smiled.

"Okay." April looked up at her mother and then blurted out. "Can you come to dinner with us today?"

He looked at her parents and they nodded their heads yes. The father introduced himself as Bob O'Conner, his wife, Linda, oldest son, Al, and younger son, Steve. "You're welcome to join us if you don't mind camper grub."

"We'll barbecue." Linda seemed happy with the idea. They set a time and gave directions.

After taking communion to Alice, he returned to the rectory and began figuring out how to avoid having another such dismal Sunday Mass. At 6:00 p.m. he headed for Lake Paris. As he approached the small grove of cottonwood trees, he spotted Bob and April O'Conner standing near the road in back of the camper. Bob motioned him forward and Jerry unrolled his window to ask where he should park. April smiled, but her father looked grim.

Bob approached the priest's car and said to his daughter, "April, please go back to the table and join your mother, she needs your help." The girl waved and left. O'Conner put his hands on the car door. "Father, uh…, oh…, ah…, you can't stay for dinner with us. I'm sorry."

"Is someone sick?"

"Uh, no Father, that's not it. Oh, hell, sorry Father. It's uh, well, Linda talked to her sister this afternoon and, uh, well, she said that you were the priest who gave the sermon about…, well, you know, that was in all the papers. Is that true, Father?"

Jerry had to muster all the control he had to take a deep breath and simply say, "Yes."

"Well, I'm sorry about all this. Linda and I had a big fight this afternoon, and I finally gave in, I…."

The priest cut him off by rolling up the window, putting the Pontiac in drive, and without saying a word, he drove off. Back at the rectory he opened a fifth of Chivas Regal someone had given him for Christmas and poured himself a water-glass full. Jerry looked at the drink and thought of Alice Peterson dying of cancer across the street and asking him if he was a drunk. After another moment of hesitancy, he muttered, "To hell with it!" He put the glass to his lips.

CHAPTER 4

My heart is ready, God
--I mean to sing and play

Psalm 108: 1

Kathy Olson was nervous as she drove her old, battered Toyota down Paris's so-called main street. God, what a dreary place. It would be a dreary place even if it wasn't raining.

She wasn't sure how Jerry would receive her. He sounded a bit cold when she told him that she wanted to come to Paris and visit with him.

She immediately felt disappointed when she saw Father Wayne Cameron's car parked in the driveway next to the rectory. She liked Wayne but she wanted a private visit with Jerry. Parking the Toyota behind Wayne's car, she turned the rearview mirror towards her and brushed back her shoulder-length blonde hair with her hand and checked to see if her lipstick was okay. Jerry had never seen her with lipstick; in fact, he had never seen her when she wasn't a nun. She glanced down at her bare legs. She would look stupid wearing white shorts in the rain. It wasn't raining when she left Manhattan, Kansas; it was a beautiful, warm September day that looked like it would get hot. She mumbled, "Oh, well. " as she opened the car door, poked the umbrella out and popped it open.

A big brown and gold dog jumped off the porch

and greeted her with a wagging tail. Kathy pushed his nose away from her crotch and ran for the porch. She was up on the porch before she saw Jerry standing in front of a lawn chair. He said, "Hi, Kathy. Welcome to Paris!" He put out his hand as if to shake hers but she rushed past his hand and gave him a hug. It seemed like five minutes before Jerry put his arms around her and then she squeezed him tighter than he did her.

Kathy let go of him, stood back and held his hands. "It's so good to see you, Jerry."

"Good to see you too, Kathleen."

"It's Kathy now. Kathleen makes me think of being a nun. Is that Wayne's car there."

"Yes. He's in the house taking a nap."

Wayne pushed open the screen door and bounced out. "He is not! Hey, Kathleen, you're a sight for sore eyes." He held out his arms and gave her a hug, a better and closer hug than Jerry had. That surprised her.

Jerry held the screen door open. "Come on in. Kathleen... oops, Kathy, you can tell us about your new adventures in college."

After she and Wayne sat down at opposite ends of the couch and Jerry sat stiffly on the recliner, Wayne said: "Well, Kathy, what do you think of Jerry's new metropolis?"

"Rather dreary, I'd say." She tucked one leg under the other and noticed that Jerry watched every move she made. Trying to sound relaxed, she asked Jerry, "What do you think of your new parish?"

"Oh, it's great, lots of time to meditate, play carpenter and painter, counsel people."

"Counsel people? From around here?" Wayne

asked, incredulously. "You've got what? Twenty families?"

Jerry chuckled and sounded indignant as he said, "I'll thank you to know I have twenty three families, counting a divorcee and an old bachelor south of town. But they are all pretty self-sufficient. My counselees come mostly from around Aberdeen and guess what their problems usually involve?"

Almost simultaneously, Wayne and Kathy said, "Sex!" They both giggled.

"Yes. Mostly about birth control, pre-marital sex, permission to have an abortion. I'm sure that my client load will diminish when they realize I don't tell them what they want to hear. I tell them to follow their consciences but they want permission. When will people begin to think for themselves?"

Wayne answered, "Oh, about the same time the majority of priests do."

"What about bishops?" Kathy asked.

"Hell, they wouldn't even be bishops if they thought for themselves," Wayne said.

"Take our friend here, Kathy, when he was first ordained, he wouldn't utter a word unless he was sure a bishop or pope or the Bible said it first. He talked like he just had breakfast with God. And now he tells me that the ministers of Paris won't even let him join their ministerial council because, and I quote, "He's not Christian enough!"

Sounding hurt, Jerry asked, "I wasn't that bad, was I?"

Kathy looked at each of them with a bit of amazement and was glad that they seemed to include her in their banter. "So, Wayne, when did you notice Jerry began to think for himself? Before you answer, I had lunch already but you know what I would really like?"

She couldn't keep from giggling.

"I'm sorry, I should have asked. Would you like something to drink?"

She giggled again and asked softly, "How about a beer?"

"Hey, Jer, she really has changed! Kathy, I often offered you a beer when we were at St. Gabriel's but you always refused."

"It was against the rules." Kathy squirmed as she added, "Now, I don't have any rules." She noticed that both men glanced at her legs as she kicked off her sandals and put both feet under her. She could feel herself blushing. "I mean, I don't have anyone ready to tell a mother superior every little thing I do."

As Jerry headed for the kitchen, Wayne shouted, "Bring me one, too, Jer."

"Jer, Jer? I never heard you call him Jer, before."

"I only do that in private."

Jerry called from the kitchen. "And don't you start, Kathleen."

"I will, if you don't start calling me Kathy."

When Jerry returned with three bottles of beer, he asked, "So, Kathy, what are you doing at Kansas State?"

"Right now I'm working on a Masters in education although I might change it to counseling." She went on to tell them how exciting she found college life, so different from her undergraduate years when she was still a nun. When she finished, Kathy asked Wayne how things are going at St. Gabriel's parish in Aberdeen.

"As of two weeks ago, they were fine. Now I don't know. As you know, I was transferred to St. Mary's in Lakeside."

Kathy looked shocked as she said, "No, I didn't know. What happened? Why were you transferred?" She looked at Wayne and then at Jerry.

"Well, the Bishop asked me to give a sermon condemning everything that Jerry said in his now infamous sermon. I refused and so I'm now a pastor on the other side of the diocese. It's not bad. A really nice parish with about 200 families and Lakeside is a wonderful metropolis compared to this little hellhole."

"Don't you dare call my city a 'hellhole'!" Jerry acted like he was going to jump out of the chair and attack. He relaxed back and added, "It's only hot in the summer."

Kathy ignored Jerry and said, "Wayne, I'm glad you didn't give in to the bishop. I didn't hear Jerry's sermon, but I read about it and I definitely think he said some things that needed to be said."

They continued to discuss the Church, their new assignments and complaints about the Bishop of Aberdeen. Around six they decided to have dinner at Le Restaurante de Paris. Kathy was relieved when Wayne indicated that he would have to head back to Aberdeen after dinner. She changed clothes in the spare bedroom, exchanging the shorts for white slacks. When she came back into the living room, she winked at both priests and said, "We don't want to scandalize the faithful, do we, gentlemen?"

Wayne stood up and asked Kathy to turn around. She hesitated for a moment and then, with only a little self-consciousness, put her hands on her hips and turned slowly as she thought a fashion model might do it. "How's this?" She gave them a coquettish smile.

"Won't do, you look too delicious." Wayne gave her a hug. He let her go and turned to Jerry. "Your turn."

"Nope, she's too, uh, delicious." Jerry turned away.

Kathy didn't know if he was upset, embarrassed or what. Part of her wanted to apologize to him, but she didn't know for what. After pondering a moment, she blurted out: "How come he can hug me but you can't?"

"Because..." Wayne hesitated and then went on, "I'll tell you, if you promise to keep it confidential, okay?"

What in the world is he talking about? She put a finger on her chin and said, "O...kay."

"Because I'm gay and he's not."

"You're kidding? Wayne, you're gay? Really?" Wayne nodded solemnly and Kathy threw her arms around him and kissed him on the cheek. "Wow! That's wonderful!"

She had no idea why she said that. She looked at Wayne as if it was the first time. He was about the same height as she, five feet eight inches, muscular and a classically handsome masculine face only a little diminished by a receding hairline. In no way did he look effeminate or gay. She then realized that she had no idea what a gay man was supposed to look like.

Anyway, he didn't look like the stereotype she'd imagined.

Wayne held her at arms' length. "What's so damn wonderful about it?"

"I don't know really...I guess because you'd tell me about it. Who else knows?"

Wayne turned his hand with his thumb pointing at Jerry. "And now you."

"And that's all?" She put her arms around him again and kissed his cheek.

"I'm sure glad I didn't tell you when you were at St. Gabriel's. If you'd been that affectionate toward me then, we really would have scandalized the faithful." They all laughed.

Kathy suddenly looked serious and put her hands in front of her in a prayerful manner. "I would have been very proper and respectful, just as I always was. And I always was, wasn't I, Jerry?" It would have been wonderful if they had this kind of banter back then.

*   *   *

"Definitely." For the life of him, he couldn't figure out why she was so excited about Wayne's gayness. Maybe she's gay, too.

Le Restaurante was pleasantly full and Jerry introduced Wayne and Kathy to Joe Gaffin, "our esteemed county sheriff", and his wife, Miriam, then to the couple who owned the restaurant, and several other people he had met in the five weeks he had been in Paris.

When they sat down, Kathy said, "I'll bet that by

Christmas, you'll know everyone in town."

"I'm sure everybody believes they already know me."

Despite its name, Le Restaurante was a typical small Midwestern café'—steak, pork chops, or chicken; mashed potatoes and gravy, green beans or peas, and salad. It did have tablecloths and linen napkins, and the food was well prepared.

Wayne left for Aberdeen as soon as they returned to the rectory after dinner. Kathy and Jerry went into the house. She petted Plato as she sat down on the couch. Jerry sat opposite her on the recliner. She seemed very serious as she said, "Jerry, I'm glad I can have some time to talk to you alone."

"How much time do we have? Do you have to get back to the university tonight?"

"No." She broke into an impish grin. "I was hoping I could stay over. I notice you have an extra bed."

"Kathy, you know better than that. You were raised in a small town. Ashland, isn't it?" She nodded. "I'll bet you that someone already knows that you and I are alone together right now, and half the town will know by tomorrow. If you stayed overnight in this house…"

"Yes, I know. That's all you'd need to really scandalize everybody, right?" She didn't wait for an answer. "I really hoped I could stay in a motel or bed and breakfast, but I didn't see anything like that when I drove in. I was hoping I could spend some time with you tomorrow." She looked away as if scolding herself for being stupid. The serious look returned, not serious, but sad, as if she were about to cry.

Jerry snapped his fingers and Kathy looked over at

him, startled. "I've got an idea.

There's a wonderful woman who lives with her ailing father a couple of miles outside of town. I'll bet she would love to have some company. I'll call her." He stood up.

"Are you sure it wouldn't be too much trouble?"

"I really don't think so. She rattles around a big, old farmhouse. I'll find out, okay?"

He went into the office and called Marge Woerner. Returning to the living room, Jerry said, "Marge said, and I quote, she would be 'delighted' to have you. I told her I would lead you out there at nine. How's that?"

"That's fine, thank you. What's she like?"

"Her name is Dr. Marge Woerner but she doesn't like to be called 'doctor' except by her students at Northwestern University. She is a doctor of chemistry and now is on leave to take care of her father, who is terminally ill."

"She grew up around here?"

"Yes. She's very down-to-earth and unpretentious. I'm sure you'll like her." He started to tell Kathy that he had gone horseback riding with Marge but changed his mind. "Kathy, you wanted to talk to me about something. What is it?"

"Well, first, I want to thank you for the sermon you gave about sex. You know I wasn't there that day because I was on retreat, but I read about it. I thought of just calling you, but I really wanted to say what I have to say in person. You know that when you are on retreat, you're not supposed to read newspapers or magazines. Anyway, not all the nuns at the Motherhouse were on retreat and I heard two of them talking about the scandalous article in the paper and your name was mentioned. I snuck into the parlor and when I saw the headlines, 'Hero Priest Blasts His Church', I nearly fainted. I read the article and well, I was so relieved."

Jerry leaned forward in the chair. "Why's that?"

"Remember when I first met you. I came to you for confession about two years before I was assigned to St. Gabriel's?"

"Yes, I remember." He sounded calmer than he felt. Her confession had haunted him for the past six years and as she sat there with her legs folded under her, it still did. He guessed that she had been about twenty-one at the time. She had heard a talk he had given at a religious education conference and thought he would understand her "problem." Then, as now, she was beautiful with natural blond hair and a peaches-and-cream complexion. Many people would say that she was "drop-dead gorgeous", even without makeup. Her "problem" was masturbation and the chaplain at the Motherhouse had told her that because of it, she should leave the convent. A problem like that, he said, was a sure sign that she did not have a calling to the religious life. She was in tears. Two times previously, nuns had confessed the "sin" of masturbation but that was in the confessional box and he did not know them and they sounded older than Kathy. Remembering this beautiful young woman in front of him confessing that she masturbated nearly every day excited him beyond belief. He remembered crossing his legs and calmly telling her what he had told the other two nuns, teenage boys, and everyone else with the "problem." In his view, masturbation was not a sin and his basic message was to enjoy it and forget it. He gave her a couple of book-references by Catholic moral theologians who agreed with him, as well as other publications.

"Well, at that time, your telling me that masturbation wasn't a sin actually saved my life." Evidently Kathy saw the puzzled look on his face and added. "Really it did. I was so down on myself that I was thinking about suicide. I even had a plan. So thank you, again. The books you recommended helped too. And believe it or not, I did quit masturbating compulsively, I guess you'd say. The book, *For Yourself*, really helped. You did read that one, didn't you?"

"Yes." He wasn't being entirely honest. He had read parts of it but reading intimate details about how women can and should pleasure themselves to orgasm was just too much. He agreed with the book, but it still disturbed him. "So, how did my sermon help you this time?"

"You came right out and said what you believe—publicly."

Jerry chuckled. "And you see where it got me?"

Kathy did not smile. "I'm surprised it got you anywhere except out of the priesthood. My brother, the Jesuit, said he was surprised the Bishop didn't defrock you. Why didn't he?"

"He threatened to, but I told him that if he did, I would sue him for violating my rights."

Kathy laughed. "You didn't!"

"I did. I knew it was an empty gesture because it has been tried before and was thrown out of court. Bishop Mazurski knew that too, and told me so. I said, 'I know, Bishop, but with the press I've been getting, it would make headlines for a few months.' He's very publicity-shy, you know? Anyway, he said I should come here and be a good boy, not talk to reporters or make any more public statements about sex. He called it 'human reproduction.' If I'm a good boy for three years, I may be re-assigned. You know, Kathy, I really like it here."

"You do! Jerry, this is an awful place. I thought Ashland was bad, but it's a bustling metropolis compared to this."

"Anyway, I'm glad that the sermon was helpful."

"Obviously, I didn't complete the retreat. It was in preparation for my final vows, you know."

Jerry crossed his legs. The damn jeans are too tight. He wasn't about to let Kathy know how uncomfortable this conversation was making him. He was sure the Church fathers who first began to make nearly everything about sex a sin did it because they were protecting themselves from what he was feeling this very moment. "I thought you made final vows a couple of years ago."

"I was supposed to, but I put it off. Now, I'm glad I did."

He really wanted to drop the whole subject but thought to himself that it was time to be a little more courageous. A little arousal wasn't going to kill him or force him to do anything that he didn't want to do. He wasn't going to tell Kathy what he discovered, looking back, about his own masturbation. At the time, believing it was sinful, was what kept him from being a complete holier-than-thou jerk in the seminary and the early years of the priesthood. He had religiously kept all the rules and only did and said what was "proper", but he just couldn't overcome the "sin" of masturbation. Thank God for old Father Fisher, who said to him what he has been saying to Kathy and others.

Kathy pushed her hair back. "You know, Jerry, you were always kind of aloof from me. Did you know that you always gave Sister Martha a fuller and longer hug than you ever gave me?" She gave him a rather sad and questioning look. When he did not respond right away, she looked away and added, "That sounds rather childish, doesn't it?"

Jerry wasn't sure where she was going with this or how his sermon had made her feel free, and couldn't, for the life of him, figure out how hugs had anything to do with it.

He decided to be straight forward about the aloofness issue. "Okay, Kathy, I guess it's about time I was more honest with you. The reason I deliberately kept some distance from you is, uh, well, I, uh, was bothered by you."

Kathy, looking hurt, interrupted him. "Bothered by me? Why? My personality, lack of knowledge, looks, what?" She bit her lip and again looked away.

Jerry chuckled, "No, no, none of that. You have a wonderful personality, an excellent mind, and, of course, you are very beautiful." She looked startled—disbelieving. He went on, "Kathy, it was that confession. Every time I saw you or thought about you, I thought of you as a sexual person. Of course, everyone is a sexual person, but every woman doesn't bother me. Now, I'll sound childish, or at least immature, as my seminary professors would have said, you were 'an occasion of sin' for me." He was sure he was blushing, at least his face felt like it.

"But I never flirted with you or was disrespectful to you, was I?" Her face showed her confusion.

"No, you were always very proper, pleasant, easy to be around. It was something in me, something that I just couldn't get rid of."

Now Kathy seemed irritated. "Are you saying, Jerry, that you saw me only as a sex object?"

He looked at the ceiling. God, how could he get out of this one? "No, er, well, I only but, well, I was trying not to and I guess I thought that it would help if I kept some distance from you."

"If that newspaper article was accurate, you said in your sermon that sex is natural. Is it natural for everyone else, but not for you? Is that it?" The anger in her voice had not gone away.

Jerry rubbed his hands together in front of him nervously. He felt himself redden again as he said, "Kathy, this vow of celibacy is really difficult. I, uh, do, uh, practice what I preach, I guess you'd say, because I do masturbate." He had never told another soul that outside of confession. "I'm sorry." Why in hell did he say that? Sorry for what?

Kathy mirrored his thoughts, as she asked, "Sorry for what? That you're human? Anyway, thanks for telling me that. I suspected it but, well…" She stood up and, in a rather hesitant voice, asked, "Would you give me a Sister Martha kind of hug?"

"Sure." He got out of the recliner and put his arms around her and held her tight. To his surprise and relief, he didn't get too aroused. "I'm sorry Kathy if I seemed cold to you all these years."

"That's okay," she said into his shirt.

*   *   *

When they were about a mile outside of town, on their way to Marge Woerner's place, Kathy honked her horn and flashed her lights to get Jerry to stop his car. He stopped his car on the side of the gravel road and she pulled her car up behind him and turned off the lights. As she got out of the car, she shouted, "Jerry, would you turn off your lights and join me for a moment."

He joined her beside the road and asked, "Is something wrong?"

She looked up at the moonless sky. The rain had cleansed the air and the stars sparkled wondrously. The few lights of Paris were only a faint glow. She said, "No, there's nothing wrong. I just wanted to look at the stars. She hesitated only a moment before moving next to him and putting her arm around his waist. Without taking her eyes off the stars, she said, "You know, Jerry, when I was young, I used to go outside like this and look at the stars. It made me feel closer to God. I really missed that when I was in Aberdeen." She was glad he didn't push her away. She couldn't remember when she felt so alive and close to someone. It was a romantic setting and, in a way, she hoped Jerry felt so too—maybe even feeling a bit sexy. She wondered if she should feel guilty for thinking that and, maybe, a little guilty for not feeling guilty.

Jerry surprised her by saying, "I'm sorry to say that I haven't noticed the stars lately. You know what,

49

Kathy?" She looked up at him and he added, "You are wonder-filled, you know that?" She felt warm all over when he put his arm around her and rested his hand on her shoulder.

She squeezed him with one arm and whispered, "Thank you."

They stood there for a few more minutes and she was disappointed when Jerry said, "I'm afraid Marge will wonder what happened to us."

Marge was waiting on the front porch when they arrived. Jerry gave her a Sister Martha kind of hug and Kathy was instantly jealous of the statuesque, very sophisticated-looking, and beautiful woman with brunette hair who looked to be in her early forties. She had a wonderful smile as she took Kathy's hand in both of hers and said, "Welcome to my home, Kathy." She sounded like she meant it.

*   *   *

Jerry started Saturday morning by taking Communion to Alice Peterson and two other elderly shut-ins in the parish. He spent two hours with a Mexican-American family learning conversational Spanish and working with them on a sermon for the Sunday Mass. He had begun having Mass near the shanties at the dairy and egg ranch on sunny Sundays. He hoped to entice them to attend Mass in the church as soon as possible.

Kathy came back to the rectory in early afternoon and told him that Marge wanted them both to join her for dinner. After about half hour of uncomfortable conversation, Jerry took Kathy across the street to meet Alice Peterson. He excused himself and went back to the house to work on his English sermons. One for the youth Mass that evening and another for Sunday morning.

At dinner, Kathy managed to make him uncomfortable by telling Marge about all the wonderful work he did at St. Gabriel's and at the Diocesan Religious Education Office.

Jerry left at six-thirty and the two women said that they planned to see him at Mass.

Sy and Alice Peterson's youngest son, an amateur guitarist, had formed a rock band with three of his friends: two boys and a girl. They had a lot of spirit, if not developed talent, as they warmed up for the second youth Mass at St. Patrick's. Only about twenty young people had attended the previous week. By 7 p.m. between forty and fifty youths and a few adults were in attendance. During Mass, Jerry noticed that Kathy, an accomplished musician, winced several times as the band struggled through their numbers. She had played the guitar at the youth Mass at St. Gabriel's.

After Mass, Marge and Kathy joined Jerry in the rectory. They talked a little about the Mass and the music. At the end of the discussion, Kathy said, "You know, Jerry, I was thinking. I could help out the kids with their music if you would want me to and, of course, if the kids are open to it."

"How could you do that? K-State is a long ways from here and you'll have lots of studies and all." He was really more worried about how he would handle her presence. It was bad enough at St. Gabriel's when he saw her only briefly, once or twice a week. And, damnit, he was not as lonely then.

"Oh, it's really not that far, about two hours. And it would be a way for me to keep up with my music and do some good." She looked like she wanted to add something serious, but she only added, "What do you say?"

He knew the trip was over three hours unless she drove a hundred miles an hour and she couldn't do that on the two-lane country roads. "If you did this, we should really compensate you for your trouble and contribution, and we really couldn't give you very much. Maybes fifty dollars a week and that's an insult."

Marge jumped in, and to Kathy's delight, said, "It certainly is, Father. What if I make an extra fifty dollars a week donation to the parish and you earmark that for Kathy?" She turned to the younger woman, "Would a hundred dollars a session be helpful?"

This was like a dream come true, not only would she get to visit Jerry every week, she could now feel that Marge didn't have any designs on him, and she could make a little extra money too. Of course, she couldn't say all this. "I could do it for free but the money would really help. I'm going to school on a government loan, so, well, things are really tight. So, Jerry, you really want me to do this? I wouldn't play with the kids at Mass— just give them some lessons. It should be their show, don't you think?"

"Okay, let's do it. As you saw, they really need the help. I'm sure the boys especially, will love to have a beautiful teacher like you, don't you think so,

Marge?" But in himself, he could find only fear and trepidation.

"Definitely! And you can stay with me when you come here. I'd like the company."

Marge glanced at her watch. "Kathy, we better get back to the house, my neighbor lady said she could only stay for two hours."

Before leaving on Sunday morning, Kathy stopped by the rectory. Jerry told her that the four teens thought it was great that she would lend them a hand. Jim Peterson, the organizer, said, "Yeah, we really need some help from someone who knows what she's doing. I saw her at the Mass and she's a real looker!" The girl in the quartet punched him in the ribs. As Kathy drove away, he muttered to himself, "Well, Haloran, ol buddy, you've done it. You don't have to worry about God leading you into temptation, you are already in it – deep. You better ask for His help on this." He wiped his hand down his chest as if to wipe off the effects of Kathy's "Sister Martha-like hug".

CHAPTER 5

*Make sure that no one traps you and deprives you of
your freedom by some secondhand philosophy based
on the principles of this world instead of on Christ.*
Paul to Colossians, 2,8

It was mid-morning on a sunny October Friday
when Rebecca stopped at the only service station in
Paris, Kansas. The station had a gravel drive and four
pumps. A young man with a straw stuck in his mouth
leaned against the doorjamb and gawked at her as she
asked, "Could you tell me where St. Patrick's church
is located?"

He took the straw out of his mouth and drawled,
"Sure, ma'am, jist follow the main street ta the edge
of town. You'll see a sign that says 'Lake Paris.' Turn
right and it's jist about a quarter mile." He hadn't
moved but asked, "Need some gas?"

"Not right now, thanks. And thank you for the
information."

"Yer welcome, ma'am."

She drove down the short main street. God, what
an awful place, she thought. How could anyone live
in a town like this? For the first time she realized that
she had seen similar towns only from the vantage point
of an interstate or looking down from thirty thousand
feet in an airplane. She had never driven through such
a place, let alone stopped. She was sure she'd find

this Father Haloran sitting in some dumpy little house feeling sorry for himself.

She saw a small white church on her left. A half dozen cars and trucks were parked nearby and several people were working around. Three men were on the newly shingled steeple putting up a large white cross. Four or five men were pouring concrete for a walkway, and three women were scraping paint on the side of the church. Two young fellows were working with shovels. Rebecca drove into the gravel driveway between the church and a small white house with peeling paint. After parking behind a dusty Pontiac, she got out and approached a young man wearing a straw hat who had stopped using his shovel the minute she drove in. He and his baseball-hatted companion stood there starring at her. Rebecca looked down at her jeans and bulky white knit sweater to make sure she hadn't spilled coffee or something. Maybe it was her sweater, a little heavy for such a warm day, it had been cooler in Aberdeen. "Good morning, could you tell me where I could find Father Haloran?"

The two lads kept looking at her as if she were some kind of apparition. She was about to ask them again when one said, "Oh, sure, he's up there." He pointed at the top of the steeple.

Rebecca shielded her eyes from the sun with one hand. She guessed the priest to be the one in the broad-brimmed hat. One was too short and the other too fat. Or perhaps the priest had gained thirty or forty pounds since the pictures were taken. "Do you know when he'll be back down?"

"Naw. Lemme call him." The young man cupped

his hands around his mouth and yelled, "Hey, Father Jerry, somebody here to see ya."

The tall one with the straw hat turned their way and seemed to study the scene for a moment. He yelled back, "If you're a reporter, you can go home. If you are not and are willing to wait, I can see you in a while, may take us an hour up here."

Without hesitation, Rebecca called back, "I'll wait." She wasn't about to drive all the way out here and then turn right around and go back. Jerry's friend, Father Cameron, said that he probably would not be very receptive to an interview, but she hadn't expected him to be so rude. Of course, she didn't expect him to be playing carpenter on a steeple, either. She turned to the young men. "Is that his house?" She nodded toward the bungalow with the peeling paint.

"Yep."

"Do you think he'd mind if I waited in the house?"

"Nope, he wouldn't care."

The boys kept looking at her as she stopped at the BMW and picked up her laptop. She thought that perhaps she could get some writing done while she waited. She started to close the car door and then picked up her camera. A picture of the priest working on the steeple would be good for the article. She knew she would look like the reporter he didn't want, but was willing to take the risk. She was going to have to deal with that fact sooner or later anyway. She moved around and got several shots. If the priest noticed her, he didn't say anything. As she headed for the house, she heard one of the boys say, "Man, is she ever a looker!"

"Man, I guess! Wonder if she's a movie star."

A big, mostly gold-colored dog ran toward her, tail wagging. Rebecca froze. She had never spent much time around dogs. She had read somewhere that if they didn't growl or bare their teeth, they wouldn't bite. She tentatively held out her hand. The dog licked her hand and then put his nose in her crotch. Rebecca glanced around, embarrassed. Pushing the dog away, she headed for the house; the dog followed.

The interior of the house was a pleasant surprise. Too masculine for her taste but impressive despite the clutter—magazines, books, and newspapers strewn about and dog hair on the carpet. After finding the bathroom off one small bedroom, she glanced around the rest of the house. The kitchen had been remodeled but a stack of unwashed dishes, at least a day's worth, was piled randomly near the sink. He's definitely no housekeeper. Going back to the living room, she thumbed through his collection of CD's. Nearly all of them were classical, jazz, or show tunes. There was no country and western music in the collection—one thing in his favor. There was little that would help her with her article about the priest.

Rebecca began to feel more than a little panicky. "What do I do if this jerk refuses to talk to me?" She asked herself. She decided to call Gayle Mathews, her editor. She walked into the little office and sat down at the desk. First she tried to use her cell phone but there was no connection. She muttered to herself, "Boy, talk about being in the middle of nowhere!" Picking up the house phone she told herself to be sure to pay for the long-distance call. Gayle answered the phone after only two rings. "Gayle, I've got a problem. My subject is up on the church steeple and yelled down that if I was a reporter to go away. I said I'd wait. When he comes down, I doubt if he'll talk to me."

"Rebecca." Gayle sounded like a patient and loving elementary school teacher.

"You've been in this kind of position before, you can get through it. If you've got time, look around for any kind of information that will help. Where are you now?"

"I'm sitting at his desk in his dinky little house."

"Well, good. That's a great place to find information. When he comes down convince him that your article will help him get his message out to the world, beyond Kansas. And it's the truth isn't it? Use your feminine wiles."

"I don't like doing that, but I'll do my best."

"You do that, sweetheart. I'm relying on you. Gotta attend a meeting with the publisher. Bye and good luck."

Rebecca looked around the paneled office and decided that there might be some information she could use that would make the trip useful. A small card with a picture of a lamb in front of a cross sat on top of the desk in front of her. Turning it over, she read:

Gerard D. Haloran

Ordained a Priest

May 23, 1984

Several spaces below, she read:

No matter what great things
A man may do in life
Unless he become a loving person
His life is a failure

Rebecca wondered if the priest had written that and if he considers himself a loving person. Loving person? She tried to think of someone she knew whom she could call a loving person. Helene Walker, for sure. The only male she could think of who would fit the description would be Paul Brady, her stepfather she hadn't seen since she was seven years old. She doubted if she was one.

On top of a pile of papers was a greeting card with roses forming the words, "Thank You." Rebecca hesitated a moment and then opened it and read: "Dear Jerry, Thank you for the wonderful time last weekend. You are a rose in the thorn bush they call Paris. I had a hard time getting back to the books after my hours with you. Looking forward to seeing you on Saturday. I love you, Kathy." She folded the card and put it back exactly where she found it. Hmmm, she thought, so there's a woman in his life. She wondered what Kathy was like and how they spent their time together. Father Jerry Haloran is looking more and more interesting.

She opened the middle drawer and picked up a photo of a very attractive dark-haired girl shaking hands with a smiling Father Haloran. Without the grimacing, Rebecca thought, he is a good-looking fellow. She turned the picture over. On the top, in a neat girlish

hand, were the words: "Thank you Father Jerry, for all
your help the past few years. Love, Melanie" Below
that, in a hurried masculine scrawl was: "Father Jerry,
please help me, YOU are my only friend!!!" followed
by a large question mark. The picture was clipped to
a poem entitled, "Why Must Young Souls Die?" The
poem was by Melanie Kurtz. She began reading:

Why must young souls die?
Are they taken
Or mis-taken
I see the tears in your eyes
I hear you cry
I, too, wonder WHY
Children give so much good
Why, oh, why must they die?
Is there something to learn about love?
How much we can give before we are gone?
Whenever we think of her
We'll think of a soul so strong
And her love will linger on
Long after we are gone
The question will rage on
Why, why, must young souls die?

Rebecca had a difficult time holding back the tears
as she finished reading the poem.

She tried to remember where she had heard the
name, Melanie. Someone in Aberdeen had mentioned
it. Just as she put the photo and poem back in the drawer,
she remembered her conversation with Sister Martha
at St. Gabriel's. Sister Martha was one of the most

pleasant people Rebecca had ever met. She glowed as she described Father Haloran and how well he got along with all the kids in school and how inspiring he was in his sermons. The nun turned sad when she described the anti-abortion demonstration. "Father Jerry was very down that day. He had been down for over a week. One of our young parishioners, Melanie Kurtz, was hit by a truck and killed right in front of the rectory. Father Jerry was there and anointed her poor broken little body." Tears formed in Sister Martha's eyes as she told Rebecca that Melanie was only fifteen and everyone was certain she had committed suicide. "Poor Father Jerry. For some reason, I think he felt responsible for her death, like there was something that he should have done to prevent it."

Rebecca wondered what the priest's relationship was with the girl who committed suicide. Considering all the publicity about priests molesting children, she wondered....

She winced, hoping that this priest was not one of them. God, she thought, that would make this interview impossible. With more than a little guilt, she again opened the drawer and took out the picture and poem. Opening her camera case, she then took a photo of both the front and back of the picture as well as the poem. She also photographed the 'loving person' card. After replacing the items in the drawer and closing her camera case, she looked around the small office. Two ceiling-high bookcases filled one wall. Like everything else in the house, there was no order to the books. Theology, education, psychology, and other non-fiction books were scattered on every shelf, mixed in with paperback novels by various authors. She was surprised to find Gloria Steinham's *Revolution from Within* along with a number of other 'feminist' authors. This guy is a complex character. She hoped he would talk to her. She glanced at her watch, it was eleven fifteen.

She decided it might help if she made herself useful. Washing the dishes would be something he wouldn't resent. She was sure it wouldn't fit Gayle's idea of using her "feminine wiles." Copying those personal papers probably would. She headed for the kitchen in hope of ridding herself of some guilt. There was no dishwasher, but finding dishwashing soap and a dishtowel, she rolled up her sleeves. She was just drying the last plate when she heard the front screen door slam and a deep voice say, "Do I have a visitor in here?"

Still holding the plate and towel, Rebecca appeared at the doorway to the living room. He was even taller than she had envisioned, six foot, two inches, at least. His penetrating blue eyes seemed to look through her as he stood there in his blue cotton work shirt and jeans, holding his straw hat in his left hand. She set the plate down and headed his way, drying her right hand and smiling. "Hi, I'm Rebecca Brady." She held out her hand and said, "You must be Father Haloran." He did not smile as she took his surprisingly hard, callused hand.

*   *   *

Jerry didn't know what to make of this alarmingly attractive woman. She had raven hair and facial features that reminded him of an older Melanie Kurtz, about twenty years older, he guessed. Her smile seemed somewhat forced and there was a certain hardness in her eyes that made him uncomfortable. For some unfathomable reason, he found himself wondering, if Melanie had lived to adulthood, would she have had a similar look? "Yes, I'm Father Haloran. And what can I do for you? Sorry for keeping you waiting."

"That's okay. I, uh, saw that you hadn't had time to do the dishes, so I thought I'd make myself useful."

"Thank you. I appreciate it. As you see, I'm not much of a housekeeper. So, again, what can I do for you? It's not a very good time for me." The woman seems nervous. He felt sure that she was a reporter.

"Well, I came here to talk to you, but it looks like I picked a bad time."

He raised one eyebrow and tilted his head to one side. "I am going to take a guess. You are a reporter, aren't you?"

She gave him a sheepish smile. "No, technically, I'm a journalist."

"And a master semanticist, right? If I had yelled from the steeple, 'If you are a reporter *or a journalist*, go home,' would you still have waited?" He smiled a little.

The woman looked down at the floor and then back up, this time with a genuine smile. "Yes, I would have. After all, I came all the way from St. Louis to talk to you and I had to, at least, give it a try."

"When I first got here in August, a few reporters came by. I sent them away. It's been over two months now and what they wanted to talk about is ancient history. What do you want to talk to me about?"

"I have been assigned to write an article about you. Are you willing to talk to me?"

"No." He put his hat back on his head and turned toward the door.

"Wait! Father Haloran, please? I've already spent two days in Aberdeen learning about you. I already have enough material to write an article but I'd like to include what it's like for you here in Paris." Her words tumbled out rapidly, as if she had to get them out before he bolted out the door.

He turned around and looked at her intently. Damn, she did remind him of Melanie. "Here's the deal. I will talk to you but anything I say is strictly off the record. Okay?" He could not figure out why he was giving in so easily. Was it because she reminded him of Melanie? Or was it a way of somehow, passive-aggressively, letting the Bishop know he was not willing to fade away into the woodwork?

She rolled down the sleeves of her sweater. "If that's the best I can do, I guess it'll have to be okay. But why?"

Jerry headed for the office and she followed. Sitting down at a dated Brothers word processor, he said, "If you'll sign a little agreement for me, I'll tell you." He began typing rapidly as she looked over his shoulder.

To Whom It May Concern:

I, Rebecca Brady, will not quote Father Gerard Haloran in any way in any article I write for...

He looked over his shoulder. "Who do you write for?"

"*Women Today* magazine."

Jerry continued writing: "*Women Today or any other publication. Nor will I indicate in any way, in my writing, that I have talked with Father Haloran by making such statements as 'he seems to believe', etc. If, I, Rebecca Brady, violate this agreement, I do understand that Father Gerard Haloran has the right to take legal actions against me in a court of law.*

Rebecca Brady   *Date*
Witness, Fr. Gerard Haloran   *Date*

Jerry printed the agreement and handed it to her. Now we'll see how serious she is, he thought.

"Wow! You mean business. This is kind of harsh, don't you think?"

"It's a harsh world sometimes."

Rebecca picked up a pen from the desk, signed and dated the statement. She handed the pen to Jerry and he did the same. He then put the paper in his fax-telephone, and gave her the copy. "Okay, now we can talk—a little now and perhaps more later."

"I signed it, so tell me what this is all about."

"If you spent some time in Aberdeen, I'm sure you've learned about my now 'infamous' sermon." Rebecca nodded. "Well, part of the agreement I made with the Bishop, so that I would not be kicked out of the priesthood, was that I would not talk to any of the news media. So, officially, I will not talk to you—*everything* I say is off the record. You want to go home now?"

"As your boys out in the yard would say, 'Nope.' I'll work around it. Is it okay if I talk to people here, like your workers?" Before he could answer, she added, "Oh, and is there anything I can do to help?"

Jerry looked at her expensive sweater, designer jeans, and expensive white running shoes, and thought that she wasn't dressed for manual work. "Yes, you can run down to the Cozy Cafe and pick up some food for my crew. I've already called it in. Mabel will have it ready."

"Where's the Cozy Cafe?"

"You saw the boarded up theater?"

"Yes."

"It's right next door. If you have to wait, you can talk to some old codgers, they're about my age. They'll be sitting at the round table in the middle of the place. They can tell you about the fair city of Paris. While you're gone, I'll go across the street and get some beer and pop."

"Pop? What's that?"

He deliberately drawled, "That's what they call soda in these parts." For the first time, they both laughed.

*   *   *

As Rebecca stepped into the cafe, four men at the center table stared at her. Three of the four had their hats on and continued looking at her as she approached the counter. A stout woman, Rebecca guessed to be Mabel, looked at her suspiciously until she told her she was there to pick up an order for Father Haloran.

"It's almost ready. Gimme ten more minutes. Need a cup of coffee?"

"That would be nice." She didn't "need" coffee as she was already too keyed up, but she thought it might help break the ice.

Mabel sat the coffee down in front of her. "Need cream?"

"No thanks." Rebecca looked over at the men at the table. Not one of them had as much as whispered since she entered. She rather relished this new experience as the men didn't look anything like the business and professional men she was used to talking with. She bet that damn priest was sure she wouldn't talk to them. She picked up the coffee and a bit nervously approached the table. "Hi, I'm Rebecca Brady. I'm visiting Father Haloran to do a story on him and St. Patrick's. He said if you have time, you might be able to give me some information about the town and all?"

The one without a hat or a smile, said, "I'm Joe Gaffin, ma'am. Sit down and join us." Joe introduced Carl, Bill, and Paul and then asked, "So what would you like to know about our fair metropolis?" He chuckled and two of the others joined him. The one named Bill scrutinized the middle of the table.

Carl, the one with the John Deere hat, spoke. "Joe here can tell you the most—he's the county sheriff and knows all the dirt about nearly everybody around." He smiled.

She couldn't tell if the men were being serious. She decided to play along as best she could. "Are you really the sheriff?"

Joe pulled his badge out of his pocket. "Sure am

m'am."

"Well, Joe ... or should I call you 'Sheriff'?"

"Joe's fine. So you were going to ask me something."

"Tell me how Father Haloran has been accepted here in your fair city?" Rebecca smiled.

Joe ran his hand thorough his hair. "I reckon that he's been accepted pretty well. What do you think, fellas?"

"I'd agree. He's a real regular fella. Works hard, doesn't put on any airs. Think people kinda like him." This from Paul. The way he said "regular fella" made it sound to Rebecca like a very high compliment.

Joe prodded Bill to speak by saying, "Bill you're the only Catholic in this bunch, what do you think?"

Bill studied his coffee cup. "I guess he's okay. Our kids like him, 'specially the Saturday night Mass. My wife thinks he's just entertaining the kids when he should be teaching them some religion. I dunno, I guess he's doin' some good."

Rebecca said, "I notice he has quite a crew helping out over at the church. Was it pretty run down?"

Joe, obviously the spokesman for the group, exclaimed, "That's putting it mildly! The top of that steeple was blown off when I was a kid and this is the first priest that's done anything about it."

"Hell, they've had three or four priests there since you were a kid, Joe," Carl added.

"Six," Bill said, still looking at his cup.

Mabel called out, "Hon, yer food is ready."

Rebecca stood. "Thank you, gentlemen, it's been nice talking with you. Sheriff, since you know everyone, if I have time, could I talk to you again about Paris?"

Joe got a bit red and stammered, "Sure, Ma'am. The Padre has my number. Give a call."

Rebecca picked up the box of what looked like hamburgers and french fries. When she got to the door, she heard one of the men say, "Well, Joe, I think you made quite an impression on the pretty little lady." They all chuckled.

Mabel called out, "Tell Father Haloran that if he doesn't come in and pay that bill tomorrow, he'll be washing dishes fer me fer the next two years!" Mabel chuckled and the men joined her.

"I will." She had to admit, that the informal way they talked was refreshing.

When she got back to the church, the crew was seated at three picnic tables under the trees. Father Haloran took the box from her. He gave her a flicker of a smile when he asked, "Get a chance to talk to the codgers?"

"Yes. They were very nice. They reckoned you were okay."

"Hey, you all. I'd like you to meet Rebecca Brady. She's a journalist and is here to write an article about me. I don't know why. She might want to talk to you. If you do talk about me, only say nice things 'cause I cry easily." They laughed. He began introducing all the people at the tables. Rebecca remembered most of the names as they introduced themselves. Some smiled to her, a few waved, and others were too busy getting their hamburgers and fries to notice her when they were introduced.

The priest motioned to an empty space for her. "You want a beer, Coke, Sprite, or root beer?"

Rebecca noticed that two women at her table were drinking beer, so she said, "Beer, please." He sat next to her and shared a bag of fries. She felt out of place in the group but noticed that Father Haloran seemed very much at home.

The two women sitting at the table studied Rebecca for a few moments and then one said, "So, Miss Brady, this article you're writing. Does it have anything to do with what happened back in Aberdeen?"

Rebecca wasn't sure how to respond. If she said it had a lot to do with Aberdeen, the priest would close her down. "That will be part of it, I'm sure, but it will be mostly about his work here and the kind of person he is." She figured that her reply was vague enough to give her some space. The direction of the article was still vague in her own mind.

The other woman, older than the first, smiled. "Well, the kind of person he is, is this: He's done more around here in two months than all the other priests did in twenty years. I think he's liked by everybody."

Rebecca glanced at Father Haloran who seemed to be blushing.

A man on her right swallowed his bite of hamburger. "Well, he ain't received well by everybody. I heard a couple of people call him the anti-Christ. I think the articles about what went on in Aberdeen had somethin' ta do with it."

"Will you people quit talking about me as if I'm not here? Hank, I haven't heard of the anti-Christ bit. Who's saying that?"

"Well, it ain't among the parishioners. I ain't at liberty ta say who said it."

Father Haloran grimaced. "That really makes me feel sad."

The older woman looked disgusted. "Oh, pay it no mind. There are always people who think if you say something that isn't in the Bible, it shouldn't be said at all. Keep up the good work, Father." The discussion went back and forth among them and everyone present seemed to be on the priest's side.

Father Haloran stood up. "Okay, back to work, you all. You're not getting paid to sit around and philosophize."

One young fellow piped up, "We ain't getting paid, Father."

"Sure you are. You're working for your reward in heaven." He chuckled.

"I can't deposit that in the bank."

The priest folded his hands in front and attempted to look pious. He rolled his eyes toward the sky. "It's being deposited in your name in the bank of heaven." They all laughed or, at least, smiled.

Rebecca helped him clean up the food wrappers, beer, and soda cans and wipe off the tables. "It looks like you're going to be tied up for a while. Are you sure there's nothing more I can do?"

He stroked his chin and smiled. "You aren't dressed to help with the paint-scraping and my clothes won't fit you." He snapped his fingers. "You know what you could do that would really do some good for someone?"

"No, what?"

"Mrs. Peterson, across the street, is a wonderful woman and could use some cheering up. She's dying of cancer and is confined to a chair or bed. She's conscious and very intelligent. She'd appreciate talking to someone like you, someone outside of Paris. Are you game?"

Rebecca hesitated for a moment and then said, "I've never spent much time around dying people."

"Alice is different from anyone you will ever meet. You'll like her, I'm sure. I find her a real inspiration. Come on, I'll introduce you to Alice."

They crossed the road. "I notice that you're limping," Rebecca said, "Is that from the shooting at the demonstration?"

"Yes. I used crutches and a cane for a while. The leg is better but it hurts a bit now and then, like when I crawl around on steeples, I get a catch in my gitalong."

"Catch in my gitalong?' Is that another Kansas term in these here parts?" She looked up at him and smiled. He chuckled. For some reason, he'd lost his grumpiness. That's good.

When they entered the store, Father Haloran introduced her to Sy Peterson and asked if Alice was up for a visit. She was. The thin, weak-looking woman was watching a show on television when they walked into the comfortable living room. In a low voice Jerry said, "Alice." The frail lady switched off the television and looked their way. The priest went over to her and knelt down beside the recliner. "Alice, I have a lost soul here who needs an injection of wisdom." He looked up at Rebecca and winked. "You are just the person to give it to her. I'd like you to meet Rebecca Brady. Rebecca, I would like you to meet my spiritual director, Alice Peterson."

"Father Jerry Haloran, get yourself out of here and take that Blarney Stone with you. Sy tells me you have a crew to run over there." Alice looked up at Rebecca. "Nice to meet you, young lady. Pull up a chair and sit where I can see you without craning my old neck. Good to have you. Damn television is such a bore."

Rebecca pulled up a chair in front of Alice and willed her heart to stop pounding. The priest told her to just be herself. "I'm glad to meet you Alice. Are you in a lot of pain?"

"Yes, all the time," Alice spoke softly but clearly. "Relax, my dear, I'm going to die, but not right in front of your eyes. You don't have to be afraid of me." Alice opened her mouth. Nearly all her teeth were gone. "Can't bite you, either. Damn chemotherapy and radiation did more than the damn cancer to rot my body. My mind is okay though. Might be better off if I lost it. Do you suppose?" Alice's eyes sparkled.

"No ... I don't think so. I think Father Haloran was being sincere when he said you were his spiritual director. He tells me you have been a real inspiration for him."

"Well, my dear, he has been a Godsend. The other priests have been kind but they were always playing the role of priest. He is himself first and priest second. That is wonderful. So what brings you to Paris?"

"I've been asked by my editor to write an article about your Father Haloran."

"Call him 'Father Jerry—everyone else does. I

think he'd prefer just plain 'Jerry' but is afraid it would put off too many people. Your writing assignment, is that a result of his getting shot at that demonstration and that sermon he gave in Aberdeen?"

"Yes it is. He got a lot of publicity in May and June, as you probably know."

"Yes. We get the Aberdeen paper and I read all about it. I'm sure that sermon is the reason he's been sent to poor Paris. It's our gain, though. Usually we get the priests who can't handle their liquor." Alice studied Rebecca closely, and then added, "Tell me a little about yourself. It might help me get a clue as to how best to talk to you. First, let me take a guess. You're not married and never have been and you don't have any children."

How in the world could this lady guess that? She had never met Rebecca before and could know nothing about her. The younger woman felt the muscles in her neck tighten, a sure sign that she was getting defensive.

Alice smiled. "You aren't used to being talked to that way, are you, my dear?" Rebecca shook her head. "The only advantage being old and dying is that I don't much worry about what people think about me or what I say. And, I'm guessing you are wondering why I said what I said."

Rebecca was irritated, but even more curious. "Why, yes I am. You don't know me at all. You are right about marriage and children, but how did you know?"

"You want to know the truth?"

Rebecca nodded.

"It's your eyes, dear."

The tension that was about to leave returned. "What about my eyes, Alice?" She didn't want to let Alice know how concerned she was about her comment. Everyone had always commented on how beautiful her brown eyes were. What did Alice see? Rebecca wondered.

"Now, don't get defensive. Oh, I guess you can if you want. Anyway, your eyes tell me that you have been hurt rather badly in your life. I kind of see a bit of hardness in your eyes, like you're not going to let anyone hurt you again. Am I all wrong?"

Rebecca tried to distract herself by looking around the room. One would never guess a room like this existed behind the store. She counted the photographs on the wall—twenty. Okay, Rebecca told herself, quit avoiding the issue. Alice's words hurt her and she never wanted anyone to see through her façade so easily. But this old woman held a fascination like no one she had ever met. "No, you're not wrong, Alice. Are you psychic?"

Alice gave out a little chuckle and coughed. "Oh no, dear, when someone sits around as much as I do, you think a lot and notice things. So, would you tell me a bit about your hurt? I've never known a person who didn't have pain and if they were worth their salt, they owned it."

"I like that, may I quote you?"

The little lady chuckled again, "Not unless you're worth your salt. So tell me about yourself."

Rebecca had never met anyone quite like this woman. The priest obviously has great faith in her, she thought, so maybe she could tell her a little about herself. Rebecca began by telling her about growing up in New York City and the man she always thought of as her real father, Paul Brady. This time she included the fact that he was her first stepfather. She found herself relaxing completely when she saw Alice had tears in her eyes as she told about how, when she was seven, her mother ordered Paul Brady out of her life. Rebecca, herself, teared up as she recalled holding onto Paul's leg and cried, "Don't leave me, Daddy." Her mother had yelled at her, "He's not your father, you stupid little shit. Your father died before you were born!" It was the first time Rebecca had ever heard that Brady was not her biological father. She had never told anyone about all this except her therapist.

"I never saw Paul Brady again." Rebecca said to Alice. "My mother told me he had died. She remarried soon after." Rebecca told her about the next three stepfathers—all rich, handsome, insensitive men. Rebecca thought that ought to be enough. "So that's a little about my childhood."

"Thank you, Rebecca. I find myself not liking your mother very much."

"I don't either. I haven't spoken to her in more than seventeen years."

"Because of what she did to you and Mr. Brady?"

Rebecca looked down at her hands folded in her lap. "Yes." She just couldn't tell her about the rape and abortion.

Alice leaned her head a little to one side. "You know, you're eyes seem a bit softer now"

"Alice, you know, you would make a wonderful

counselor. Were you a counselor earlier in your life?"

Alice gave out a delighted little chuckle, "Thank you. Before I was married and before Sy and I had children, I taught primary school for a few years. Oh, how I loved those students."

"I'll bet you did. I will tell you one more thing that might help explain my eyes. And, Alice, this can be confidential, can't it?"

"Of course, dear, if you would like. I am not a gossip anyway."

Not wanting to talk about the rape, Rebecca told her that her fourth stepfather had been abusive and that she ran away from home when she was fifteen. She lived with a wonderful childless couple name Grace and Al Ripen. "You know, Alice, you remind me of Grace. She was so kind and gentle. Maybe that's why I'm willing to tell you all this." Rebecca hesitated, part of her wanted to be more truthful but…

She saw only compassion and understanding in Alice's eyes. "I've never told anyone this before, outside of therapy."

Alice gave her a little smile. "Thank you for telling me all this, Rebecca. It is a gift. You definitely are worth your salt." The frail lady chuckled. "Our Father Jerry, too, has experienced a great deal of pain, and it has nothing to do with his being sent to Paris."

"Do you know what it is?"

"Some of it. I hope that he will tell you. I would feel like I was violating his confidence if I told you what I know." Alice looked over Rebecca's shoulder, then added. "I do wish he had a wonderful woman to share his life with. I believe he is lonely. This celibacy business is nonsense." Alice smiled mischievously. "I sometimes think those bishops have little peckers that are so shriveled up they can't think straight."

Rebecca couldn't help but giggle. "Alice, I really like you!"

"That's mutual, my dear. It doesn't take weeks to get to like someone, just openness, don't you think?"

"Yes, definitely. What more can you tell me about Father Haloran, since he is my project?"

"He is very intelligent, hard working, kind, sensitive and, I hate to say it, wasted in Paris. He brings communion to me every morning and always stays and chats with me about his life and his ideas. He should be a bishop, I think."

"Is he well received by the people here?"

"By most, I'd say." Alice put one frail hand next to her mouth. "I probably shouldn't say this but I understand that the local ministers told him he wasn't Christian enough to join their little association. Please ask Father Jerry if you want to include that in your article. Hell, in my book he is more Christ-like than those boobs will ever be."

Rebecca looked at the pictures on the wall and asked about them. Alice told her at length about her six children and eleven grand children. The children ranged in ages from thirty-five to seventeen. "Sy and I have been married thirty-seven years and they have been wonderful years. I am dying prematurely, I guess you'd say, but I have had a grand time. Rebecca, I have genuinely enjoyed talking to you. Right now I am very tired and need to take my medicine. I do hope you can stop by again. And I hope your article is a good one. What magazine do you write for?"

"*Women Today.*"

"I'm sorry to say I've never heard of it."

"I'll make sure you get a subscription." Rebecca bent down and kissed the older woman on the cheek. "Alice, thank you so much for talking with me."

"I hope you can stop by again."

As Rebecca crossed back over the road, she felt very relaxed and alive. Alice had injected something, maybe not wisdom, but something. She didn't get any particulars about Father Haloran but she did get more than an inkling of his attitude and spirit. That would definitely help her story. She wondered how much detail he would share with her.

Stepping up to the rectory porch, she noticed that all the cars and trucks were gone except her own and the dusty Pontiac. The cross was up, the side of the church, facing the house, shone with new paint, and a new sidewalk connected the church to the house. She glanced at her watch, it read 4:45. Oh my God, poor Alice. She had no idea.

Rebecca knocked on the screen door. There was no answer. The main door was open and she went in. She had to pee so bad that she could hardly stand it. The dog greeted her at the door. The larger bedroom door was closed and she could hear water running. Not remembering if there was another bathroom in the house, she looked in the kitchen and the smaller bedroom. The dog followed her. She went back to the closed door and not hearing any water, she knocked. "Father Jerry, are you in there?"

"Yes, who is it?"

"Me, Rebecca Brady."

"I'll be out in a minute, hold your horses."

"I don't have any horses but I really need to use your bathroom!" Rebecca was nearly screaming. She pushed open the door. The priest stood there with only his boxer shorts on and a tee shirt covering his head. He quickly pulled the shirt down. She rushed to the bathroom. "Sorry, I got to go bad." She slammed the door.

When she came out, he was dressed in black pants and a blue plaid short-sleeved shirt. His jeans and work shirt were in a pile on the floor with the dog on top of it all. He asked pleasantly, "Have a nice visit with Alice?"

"Yes, definitely. She is a wonderful person. You know, I was just thinking that even if you refuse to talk to me anymore, it was worth the trip just to meet and talk with her. I feel better than I've felt in days or maybe months. She's dying but has more life than most people I know. Alice has quite a sense of humor, too. You know what she said about your priestly celibacy and your bishops?"

"No. But I wouldn't be surprised at anything Alice would say. Tell me."

"That celibacy is nonsense and is probably due to the fact that the bishops' little peckers are so shriveled up they can't think straight."

The priest doubled up with laughter then stood straight and said, "Well, that's our Alice. You know, Miss Brady... It is Miss, isn't it?"

"Yes, but please call me Rebecca."

"Okay, Rebecca. Anyway, what I was about to

say is that Alice and Sy are two of the most authentic people I've ever met. They are one of the reasons I truly find living in Paris a joy.

"I can understand enjoying them but I'm not so sure about enjoying Paris."

Father Jerry headed for the living room. "I'm going to have a beer. Join me?"

"Sure, why not?" She seated herself on the couch, assuming the recliner was reserved for the priest.

He came halfway across the living room holding two bottles of Coors. He stopped suddenly. "Oh, would you prefer a glass?"

She would, but "going native" would probably mean drinking out of the bottle. "The bottle is fine," She said, hoping she didn't sound phony.

He seated himself on the recliner. "So, are you going to head back to St. Louis this evening?"

Before answering, Rebecca looked around the room and noticed that he had picked up the newspapers and magazines and even vacuumed the floor. The dog was at his feet. "What's your dog's name?"

"Plato." He reached down and stroked the dog behind the ears.

"As in the philosopher Plato?" Plato looked at her quizzically.

"Yes. Fits him, don't you think?"

"I guess. I've never had a dog."

"Where did you grow up? I'd guess back east somewhere."

"Yes, New York City, until I was twenty-two."

"Then to St. Louis?" Rebecca nodded. "And you still haven't answered my question about heading back there this evening."

"Well, I was hoping to stay over another day, get a little better feel for the place." She still was hopeful that she could have a real talk with him. "As I drove in I didn't see anything like a motel, hotel, or bed and breakfast."

"There aren't any."

"I notice you have an extra bedroom."

* * *

Surely she's joking, Father Jerry thought, but it doesn't look like it. Two beautiful women telling him the same thing in a little over a month floored him. If he were an ordinary bachelor, probably neither of them would even suggest it. Or would they? He was sure he didn't know anything about women. Maybe Kathy was more than teasing; she was sort of flirty that first weekend. He smiled. "You're not serious?"

"Why not? Are you planning to have company?"

"Let me ask you something. Have you ever asked a man if you could stay over in his house before?"

"No. But I've never been out in the middle of nowhere or in a place where there wasn't a hotel."

Maybe she's serious! "And, I gather you don't know much about priests and small towns."

She looked startled. "You mean I wouldn't be safe with you?" Then she smiled, a rather coquettish smile, it seemed.

"Right this minute, someone or several someones, know that you are in this house with me. That's okay because I have a number of visitors during the day, but

83

if you stayed overnight..."

Rebecca laughed, "The shriveled-up-pecker rule, huh?"

Jerry had to laugh. "It's related. It's the scandal rule. It would be scandalous even if you were fat and ugly and my maiden aunt. Seriously, you must have enough for your article. You heard the people at lunch, you've talked to Alice Peterson. And you've seen the fair city of Paris."

"Seriously, I could go with what I have but there is still something missing. I don't really understand some things. Isn't there some place I could stay?"

He didn't know if Marge would be interested in having another overnight visitor. He was afraid she would think he was trying to turn her place into a hotel. She was going to put Kathy up tomorrow night. He could give her a call and knew that she would be honest with him. On the other hand, it would probably be better if Rebecca left town. Jerry asked himself why in the world he would want to accommodate her. Was he flattered that such a beautiful woman was being so interested in him? Perhaps, but he found himself, almost involuntarily, saying, "There is one possibility I can think of. I'll call her." He went into the office to make the call. He knew Marge's number but was afraid that the reporter would get the wrong idea if she saw him punch in her number without looking it up.

Marge answered on the second ring. "Marge, this is Father Jerry. I want to ask for another favor. Please be brutally honest with your answer, okay?"

"Aren't I always brutally honest?"

"Yes, I think so. Anyway, I have another unexpected

visitor who showed up today and needs to stay over."

"I'm going to start answering the phone, 'Marge Woerner Hotel'."

"That's what I'm afraid of."

"I'm teasing, Father. I really look forward to Kathy's visit every Saturday. She's sweet on you, you know?"

"Marge!" He sounded truly exasperated. They'd gone over this before. Kathy was fifteen years younger; she was a very beautiful and nice young woman but, he kept insisting to himself, she was not sweet on him. But he would not tell Marge that saying these things just encouraged too many fantasies in his prurient, and probably sinful, mind. She probably already knew it and just liked to see him squirm.

"What's this visitor like? A woman, I suppose."

"Yes. She's a journalist from St. Louis and has been asked to do a story on me for some reason."

"Is she nice?"

"I've been pretty busy today so I haven't talked to her much, but I'd say so."

"Well, I was going to entertain Bill Cochran this evening. We're having an affair you know?" She giggled. "But I could put him off. Is she more interesting than Bill?" Marge and Bill had gone to school together and she once said that he was as dull then as he was now.

Jerry pictured the sullen Bill Cochran sitting at the Cozy Cafe table. "My dog is more interesting than Bill Cochran."

"I'll put her up on one condition."

"What's that?"

"That you'll both join me for dinner. I'll make my famous lasagna. Oh, one other thing. I have to have your permission to give her the real low-down on you."

He laughed, "You don't have the real low-down on me, so you can tell her whatever you want."

"You might be surprised what I know. See you around six-thirty, okay?"

"Thanks, Marge, you're wonderful." He walked back to the living room. "It's all set, dinner and a bed. Only one catch."

"What's that?"

"I have to join you for dinner."

"I have no problem with that. I could hear your end of the conversation. This Marge sounds quite interesting and humorous. What does she do?"

"Right now, she is taking care of her father, who's terminally ill with emphysema. He's in a sort of coma most of the time. She's on a leave of absence from Northwestern University near Chicago. She teaches chemistry."

"So she doesn't have the 'low-down' on you. Who does? That's who I want to talk to."

"No one really. Perhaps Father Wayne Cameron."

"I met him—he was moving some stuff out of the house in Aberdeen. He's nice. He took some time off and invited me to lunch. He told me a little about you but I wouldn't call it the 'low-down.'" Rebecca touched her chin thoughtfully. "When we got back to the house, rectory, I guess you call it, I helped him put some boxes in his car. I talked to the new pastor of St. Gabriel's but he gave me only a few minutes. I got the impression he didn't like either one of you. He said something about you both being radical-liberals."

"He would. To give you some idea of his mentality, I was once having a discussion with him about some church teaching. I quoted a few modern theologians and he looked perplexed. I asked him if he had ever read any of them. He looked me in the eye and said, and I quote: 'Listen here, Haloran, I went into the seminary when I was fourteen and I haven't had an original thought since then. I let the Church do my thinking for me!' He was so proud of himself."

"You're not kidding, are you?"

"No."

"Are there many priests like that?"

"A few, not many, thank God. So what did you learn about me during your stay in Aberdeen?"

Rebecca glanced at her watch. "What time do we have to be at Marge's?"

"Six-thirty, we have a few minutes."

Rebecca leaned forward and folded her hands on her knees. "I got most of my information from Father Cameron, because most everyone else either made general comments like: 'He's very nice,' or, 'He's very kind and intelligent,' etc. A few said you were too liberal and were extremely unwise to give that sermon and that the Bishop was very tolerant to let you stay in the priesthood." She stopped to see his reaction to the last remark.

His only reaction was to ask, "What did Wayne tell you?"

"Wayne? ... Oh, Father Cameron. Let's see, he said you grew up in a large, poor family, seven children, in

Nebraska. That you came to Aberdeen as a teenager after your father died." Rebecca sat back against the couch. "You know, Father Cameron sort of hesitated about your father's death. When I asked about that, he just said there was a tragic accident. Can you tell me more?"

This woman is sharp, doesn't miss much, Jerry thought. If he told her about his dad's death, she would put it in the article. "I just as well tell you because if you nose around a bit, you'll find out anyway." He saw Rebecca stiffen but she didn't say anything. He went on, "My dad was choking my mom and I pulled on his shirt. Pulled him over backward and he hit his head on a stove." Jerry looked out the window for a moment and then added, "He died. I was fourteen."

Silence reigned between them for several moments before Rebecca said, "That must have been awful."

He looked at her, and she seemed to understand his anguish. "Yes, it was."

"I'm going to take a wild guess. You decided to become a priest right after that."

The reporter was far more perceptive than he could ever have imagined. "Yes I did. What made you guess that?"

"In my interviews with people, I've often found that many make momentous, life-altering decisions, after a tragedy."

"Do you? Or maybe you never had a tragedy in your life."

The question seemed to take her aback, for she sat thoughtfully for some moments before answering. "I've had my share of tragedies, I think. But Father

Haloran, you are the subject of the article, not me." She looked at him with what he thought was defiance. She sounded more than a bit haughty and a hard look had returned to her eyes.

Jerry waited a moment and then said, "You can find out about my father's death elsewhere but I ask you not to say I killed my Father."

"Have some people said that?"

"Only once to my face, back in Henning, Nebraska, where I grew up. A kid and I got in an argument and he said it."

"What did you do?"

Jerry gave her a grimace-like smile. "I gave him a black eye. I was suspended from school for two days." He looked at his watch. "I think we better head out to Marge's."

*   *   *

As Rebecca followed Jerry's Pontiac out of town to Marge's farmhouse, she reflected on their very personal exchange. There's some experience he's keeping to himself, she thought. And it doesn't have anything to do, at least directly, with the death of his father. She found herself liking him and thinking that he really could not be a child molester, but then she wasn't a psychologist and really didn't know what the profile would be on such a person. Anyway, he was nothing like any man she had ever dated, especially the egotistical Sam Hawkins. For a moment she thought that it was too bad he was a priest and living in podunkville.

Although the priest drove slowly, his car created a

minor dust storm and she had to stay back a hundred yards. He pulled into a long dirt driveway and parked next to a large two-story white house with a porch all along the front and one side. The lawn had only a little green left in it and the flowerbeds were bare except for a few late-blooming roses. She parked behind his car and Father Jerry quickly moved to open her door for her. A tall, dark-haired, slender woman in her late thirties or early forties came out on the porch. University professor or not, Rebecca had expected to see some kind of dowdy-looking farm-wife type. This poised woman was wearing a stylish yellow dress and had intelligent blue eyes and a welcoming smile.

As they approached the stairs, Marge said, "Father Jerry, I'm glad you called. I hope we keep you at St. Patrick's. As long as you're here, my life will not be dull." They climbed the stairs and Jerry gave Marge a full hug. Rebecca wondered if he gave all his parishioners hugs like that.

"Marge, I'd like you to meet Rebecca Brady. She's a city slicker, but a nice one."

Marge shook her hand and said, "Welcome, Rebecca. I'm glad you can stay with us." There was no trace of the Kansas drawl she'd encountered with everyone else around Paris, except Father Jerry. "Do come in."

The living room was comfortably furnished with a blue couch, matching chair, and love seat. The walls had recently been covered with a pleasant light beige paper with small blue and pink flowers. Marge ushered them into what was usually the dining room, now turned into a convalescent room. It had the medicinal smell of a medical ward. She motioned toward an old, thin man lying quietly on a hospital bed. "This is my father. Unfortunately he spends most of his time sleeping. He will probably wake up while you're here but he won't be able to talk or recognize you. Much of the time, he doesn't even recognize me." She turned toward Jerry. "I do wish God would take him, Father. He is in such pain all the time. He was always a lively, hard-working man with a great sense of humor. I keep reminding myself to see him that way. Sometimes, it's hard."

Rebecca wondered how she would cope with a dying parent. She was pretty sure she could do it for Paul Brady, but never for her mother. Marge led them into the large, spotless kitchen. A white linen tablecloth covered a table that was set with fine china. A bouquet of roses was in the center. Marge served lasagna, salad, and garlic bread—a meal that would be difficult to match in a fine Italian restaurant. During dinner Rebecca learned that Marge was forty-five, received her doctorate from the University of Chicago, was divorced, and had no children. She had a younger sister who had six children and a brother with two children; both of her siblings lived in Aberdeen. The thousand acres her father had once farmed were rented to a neighbor. Marge kept busy editing a professional journal, taking care of her father along with three horses and a garden on the half-acre where the house stood. She is beautiful, intelligent, charming, available, and obviously at ease with the priest, Rebecca thought. It had nothing to do with her article but she wondered if he was ever tempted to make a pass at this woman.

She really did want to know what made this handsome, intelligent man tick.

Only once did Marge's father interrupt them. Marge excused herself and took a bowl filled with something that looked like baby food along with some medicine to the man. Their conversation went on until around ten, then Father Jerry asked Rebecca what she would like to do on Saturday. Marge volunteered the idea that the three of them could ride the horses in the morning, providing she could get the neighbor to sit with her father.

"I've never been on a horse in my life. Do you ride, Father?"

"I rode a little when we lived in Nebraska. I've taken a few rides with Marge since the weather turned cooler. I'm still a tenderfoot."

Marge laughed. "I hadn't ridden a horse since I went away to college. We've kind of been re-learning together. He's a natural with horses. All three horses are creampuffs, especially Daisy, the one you would ride."

"Gosh, I don't know. The very idea scares me to death." It would be something to tell the gang back at the office, though. Perhaps she could get a picture of the priest on a horse, which would be great for the article. "Okay, I'll do it—or try to."

Father Jerry stood up. "I'm going to have to leave you ladies. I'm beat. Marge, thanks for the great dinner, it was delicious. In the morning, how does nine o'clock sound?"

Rebecca and Marge stood. "Nine is fine with me. Is that okay with you, Rebecca?" Rebecca nodded.

The priest turned to leave. Marge put her hand on his shoulder. "Well, aren't you going to give us a hug?" He gave each of them a hug; the kind clergymen give family members at a funeral. Rebecca wondered if it was different from the initial hug he gave Marge because he was obliged to give one to her. They walked out to the porch with him and waved as he turned his car around and drove off.

When they were inside, Marge asked, "Would you like a nightcap? I have some lovely brandy. Or white wine? I didn't offer any after dinner drinks because Father Jerry says he is on the wagon."

Does he share everything with this woman? Rebecca thought. "Brandy sounds good. He had a beer this afternoon."

"He says he gives himself permission if he's been working hard. I hope that's all. St. Patrick's has had its share of alcoholics."

Marge poured an inch of the amber liquid in large snifters and sat down at the kitchen table across from Rebecca. Marge sloshed the brandy around the glass and held it under her nose. After smelling the strong drink, she tasted it. "So, Rebecca, how is the article coming along on our Father Jerry? What do you think of him?"

Before responding, Rebecca mimicked Marge's gesture with the brandy, smelling it and then taking a small swallow. "This is good! I really don't know what to think of him. He's so different from what I expected a priest to be, not that I've known that many. In some ways he seems so out of place here and yet he seems so at home. Tell me about him from your perspective, you seem to know him pretty well."

"In some ways he's easy to know, in others he seems inscrutable. He's intelligent, obviously, but troubled. I honestly think he won't last long here."

"Why do you say that?"

"I'm not sure but I don't think it'll be challenging enough after he gets done with all the projects he has outlined for himself."

"What kind of projects?"

"Remodeling the church, of course. He's also working with the Methodist minister on remodeling one of the boarded-up buildings on Main Street for a teen center. He hopes to raise enough money to help the Hispanic farm-workers build some better housing. Knowing him, he's probably thinking up some other things in addition to these."

"What does he do for fun?"

"I asked him that once. He said 'work.' And I think he means it. He said there was a tribe in Brazil that uses the same word for 'work' and 'play.' Then, he added, jokingly I'm sure, that he was probably a member of that tribe in a previous life. You should stay for the Youth Mass. It's on Saturday evening at seven. I went to it once. You'll find it interesting. You'll see how much he really does enjoy what he's doing."

"Could you put me up for another night? I'd hate to head for St. Louis at night."

"Sure, no problem, there's plenty of room. A former nun that Jerry worked with in Aberdeen will be here, too. She's an accomplished musician and comes over from Kansas State to help the kids who play in a sort of rock band at the Mass. I really think she comes over so she can spend time with Father Jerry."

"He's a good-looking man. He would be a most eligible bachelor in any other profession."

Marge chuckled, "I really don't think he has any idea of how good looking he is. Another person you might want to speak to is Alice Peterson—a wonderful woman who is dying of cancer. Father Jerry talks to her a great deal."

"I met her this afternoon. We had quite a talk. She is, indeed, a wonderful person—happier than most people I know—cancer or not."

The two of them talked a while longer and then Marge showed Rebecca to an upstairs bedroom. It had faded wallpaper but, despite a slight musty smell, was very clean. A solid oak chest of drawers, bed, and chair were its only furniture. The bathroom was down the hall. Rebecca got to take a bath in a claw-footed bathtub, similar to ones she had seen before only in the movies.

As she climbed into bed, she thought of how the day had been far different from what she had expected. Thinking of the morning, she wondered if women still rode sidesaddle like in the Western movies she had seen as a child.

CHAPTER 6

A man who lacks intelligence cannot be taught,
but intelligence can increase a man's bitterness.
                                        Ecclesiasticus 21:12

Marge held the reins of one horse and Rebecca was sitting astride another when Father Jerry drove up. It was a beautiful day without a cloud in the sky. Marge had coached her on horsemanship and Rebecca had taken a practice ride around the yard. She felt like she was ten feet off the ground when she first mounted Daisy, but she got used to it and was actually enjoying it. Daisy, a brownish-red color Marge called "sorrel," was indeed a creampuff.

Dressed in jeans, faded plaid shirt, and straw hat, the priest walked over. "Mornin', ladies." He touched the brim of his hat, just like in western movies. He sauntered over to Daisy and peered out from under his hat. "Looks like you're right at home up there, Rebecca."

"Wey-all, pardner, Marge has been hepin' me get the hang of this here critter."

Marge laughed. "She's a fast learner, even sounds like a cowgirl."

Father Jerry caressed the larger gray horse's nose. "Good mornin', Jack. Ready for a ride?" He turned to Marge. "Where's your horse? Or are you going to ride Jack? Do I need to go saddle up my own?"

"I'm afraid I can't go with you. My neighbor couldn't come over this morning, so I better stay here. You have a good time."

He climbed on the horse effortlessly. "Well, pardner, ya'll wanna take a ride over by the lake?"

"I guess, as long as we don't go too fast."

"Thanks for saddling up Jack for me, Marge."

Marge said, "No problem. I'll have some lunch ready for you when you get back. Oh, I almost forgot. I want to take your picture." Rebecca had asked her to take pictures of the priest on horseback. Rebecca was afraid that if she took them, Jerry might object, thinking she would use them in the article, which she planned to do. Over the years, Rebecca had gotten used to what she considered a little deception to get what she needed for a story. Marge took several snapshots from various angles. "Okay, cowboys, you can go now."

They waved to Marge as they headed down a two-track trail behind the barn. A narrow grassy ridge separated them as they proceeded at an easy walk. They hadn't gone far when Rebecca said, "Marge is a very nice person. Thanks for introducing us."

"You're welcome. How do you like being on a horse?"

"So far, really good. I was a bit scared at first but I like it. How far is the lake?"

"About three or four miles."

They came to a barbed-wire fence with a strange-looking gate. The priest got off the horse and handed Jack's reins to her. "After I open the gate, lead Jack to the other side and I'll fasten the gate." He put one arm around a post that held strands of barbed wire and pulled up a wire loop attached to the stationary post. He pulled the limp gate away from the horses.

Rebecca loosened the reins on her horse and said, "Let's go, Daisy." She didn't move. "Come on, Daisy, let's go." She reflected on how the simple acts involved in taking a horseback ride made her aware of how different this man was from all the other men she had known. And how different she was when she was with him.

Father Jerry laughed. "I guess Marge didn't teach you everything. Give her a little kick with your heels and say, 'giddy up'."

"I can't kick this nice horse!"

"It won't hurt her. She's used to it. Think of it as stepping on the gas."

Rebecca did as she was told and Daisy walked through the entrance with Jack following.

"Now say, 'Whoa there'."

She did and Daisy and Jack stood patiently until he fastened the gate.

As they rode along side-by-side, Father Jerry said, "This reminds me of a story. Want to hear it?"

"Sure."

"There was this Texas rancher who wanted to show off his ranch to his new bride. So they saddled up the horses and were riding along looking at things when his horse stumbled. He said, 'that's once.' They went on for a while and the horse stumbled again and the rancher said, 'that's twice.' The young bride, of course, wondered why he said this but didn't say anything. They went on and the horse stumbled a third time. The Texan got off his horse, pulled a rifle from the saddle, and said 'that's three times.' Then he shot the horse. The young woman couldn't believe it and let him know it. She called him the cruelest man she ever knew and really cussed him out."

The Texan calmly looked up at her and said, 'that's once!'" The priest chuckled.

Rebecca didn't even attempt a smile. "Is that supposed to be funny?"

"Well, I thought it was. I guess you don't."

"No, I don't. I'm surprised you think so because it seems to me to be demeaning and sexist." The story made him sound like a chauvinist and she didn't want to think of him that way.

*   *   *

Jerry looked over at her and saw the hurt and anger on her face. He always thought it was a pretty tame little joke, but looking at it from a woman's point of view, it wasn't. He had told it several times before but the audience was always Catholic. He guessed they were obliged to laugh at the priest's jokes. His mind wandered back to the first and only priests' poker party he had attended the summer he was ordained. Six priests sat around a table and told "dirty" jokes as they played cards and drank too much. He had never considered himself a prude but the jokes were raunchy, more demeaning and insulting to women than most of the jokes he had heard on construction sites. Or maybe it was because he expected so much more from his new priest-colleagues. It was a very disillusioning moment and he vowed not to repeat it.

They rode on in silence until they arrived at the top of a little knoll. They stopped and Jerry waved his arm toward a surprisingly large body of water. "And this is Lake Paris, the county's pride and joy." A number of colorful little sailboats and fishing boats dotted the lake. "I apologize for the joke," He said. "It was a bit chauvinistic, I'm sorry."

Rebecca met his gaze. "Yes, it was chauvinistic-- and more than a 'bit.'"

*   *   *

They rode down to the lake. Rebecca refused his assistance in dismounting and awkwardly climbed down, nearly falling. Jerry laughed and, reluctantly, she did, too. They tied the horses to a tree and sat down at a picnic table. Jerry took off his hat, set it on the table and ran his hand through his hair. "I took communion to Alice Peterson this morning. She said you were a lovely young lady."

"Is that all she said?"

"No. She also said you were intelligent, beautiful, charming, and thanked me for introducing you to her. She hopes she can see you again."

"She really didn't say all that, did she?"

"Well, not exactly in those words but close, I'd say."

"My guess is, that is part of your Blarney Stone act. Maybe I can see her this afternoon." She gazed at the lake.

He studied her face for a moment. Yes, she does look like Melanie, a bit darker complexion but similar, classically beautiful features. "Yesterday you didn't finish telling me what Wayne said about me."

Rebecca looked at him. "No, I didn't, did I? One thing sticks in my mind. He said that you changed rather dramatically around the time you were shot. Something about the death of a high school girl you knew quite well. Sister Martha also mentioned it. From what I gather, she committed suicide." Rebecca squinted and wrinkled her forehead. "I think her name was Melanie somebody or other."

"Melanie Kurtz."

Rebecca, thinking of the possible molest issue, was more than a little hesitant and nervous as she said, "Yes, that's it. Father Cameron said he didn't know her well but you did. How did her death change you?"

"I got to know her quite well. I still grieve her loss." Jerry looked out over the lake and thought of the last contact he had with Melanie.

*   *   *

It was a Saturday afternoon in May. Suddenly he was there in the confessional and could hear Melanie's voice, "Father Jerry, is that you?"

"Yes." Melanie was a fifteen-year-old parishioner. He had been hearing her confessions about once a month for two years. In the eighth grade, Melanie was one of the brightest and most delightful students in the class, always asking penetrating questions. She was social and cheerful. But soon after entering high school, she changed--she was no longer cheerful. She looked sad and stopped going to communion at Mass.

She then began coming to him for confession. She resumed receiving communion but continued to look like all the life had gone out of her.

"Bless me, Father, for I have sinned..." She caught her breath, sobbed once, and blurted out, "Father, I'm, I'm ... pregnant."

Jerry felt his neck and shoulders tighten. He bit his lip, sat back, and breathed heavily. Many times he had begged her to talk to him outside the confessional and she refused every time, saying, "He said that if I ever told anyone, he would kill me and Mom and my little sister. And I know he would. In here I'm safe, cause you can't tell anyone, right, Father Jerry?" He repeatedly assured her that he could, under no circumstances, violate the seal of confession.

Melanie pounded the plastic grate between them, almost breaking it. "Father Jerry, did you hear me?"

"Melanie, was it your stepfather again?"

Still crying, Melanie paused, then quietly whispered, "Yes."

He wanted so badly to strangle Ralph Kurtz with his bare hands.

"Father, please help me, I have to get an abortion! Please, Father Jerry, you're the only one, please!"

Still clinching his fists and working hard to sound calm, he asked, "Melanie, are you sure you're pregnant? Have you seen a doctor?"

"Yes, I'm sure!" She blurted out impatiently, "and, no, I didn't see a doctor! He would tell and you know what would happen. Please, Father Jerry, will you help me?"

She sounded so sad and desperate. He wanted to

get out of the confessional and hold her, absorb some of her pain. That bastard! That stupid, insensitive, evil bastard! For two years, he hadn't been able to think of her stepfather without wanting to beat the hell out of him, and now this. "Melanie, I could help you find a place to stay, a place that would be safe and nice. You could...."

"I won't have my stepfather's baby! I won't!" She was sobbing almost hysterically. "He's evil! He's mean? Father, help me." Her sobbing was heartbreaking. Melanie pleaded, "Please, Father, you have to help me."

"Melanie, abortion...." He swallowed hard. "Abortion is wrong. I can't help you arrange an abortion. Please, let me help you find...."

"You're the only one who can help me. I thought you were my friend." She was screaming now. "You won't help me. God won't help me. Nobody will help me." She slammed the confessional door and he could hear her steps echo in the empty church as she ran toward the exit.

Jerry remembered sitting there trembling for a long time. He fumbled with the door handle, finally realizing his hands were clenched. He stumbled out of the confessional. The church was empty. He ran to the front doors, threw them open, and looked up and down the street. There was no sign of Melanie.

All through that weekend Melanie Kurtz's voice kept ringing in his ears, "Please, Father Jerry, will you help me?" He needed to talk to someone but his usual confidant, Father Wayne Cameron, was out of the question. Wayne might guess who he was talking about and he couldn't risk violating the seal of confession. He had finally decided on Dr. Resa Candelaria, a psychologist to whom he had referred several parish families. He admired her wisdom and understanding and as a former Catholic, she was familiar with the Catholic position on abortion and the seal of confession.

The first thing Monday morning, he met with Dr. Candelaria and presented a "hypothetical" case of a girl who found herself pregnant by her stepfather and was seeking an abortion. The psychologist stated clearly that anyone who really cared about the girl should immediately help her obtain an abortion. No question! And, by God, she would help! She added, "And what kind of God would condemn this girl?" Even then, Jerry wasn't worried about God. He didn't believe in a condemning God. His anguish was over his own long-held conviction about the sanctity of life and the unborn child Melanie was carrying.

Dr. Candeleria looked at him accusingly and said, "If your hypothetical friend will talk to me, give her my number."

When he returned to the rectory, he noticed that the light on the answering machine was blinking. He pushed the button and heard Melanie's angry voice, "Father Jerry, what color is your heart now? I think it's yellow." He heard the receiver crash down.

"Color of my heart? Where did she get that?" he murmured aloud. He sat down in the desk chair and thought. After a few moments it dawned on him that she was referring to a song he taught the kids when Melanie was in the eighth grade. He softly sang the words as he remembered them:

> Who has touched the sky?
> Who has caught the wind as it goes rushing by?
> None but the few, the few who knew the color of
>   the moon
> The sun by its first name.
>
> There have been those who walked among us
> Those who knew love like a child's smile
> They touched the sky, met it eye to eye
> Just by loving one another for a little while.
>
> Who has touched the sky?
> Who has caught the clouds as they go drifting by?
> None but the few, the few who knew
> The color of the heart
> Knew love by its first name.

Who has touched the sky? What is the color of my heart? Melanie obviously thought it was yellow--the coward's color. He wondered if he was a coward. And he was quite sure that he did not know love by its first name.

All day Monday, he thought of going to Melanie's high school and trying to talk her into meeting with Dr. Candelaria, but he couldn't bring himself to do it. Stepfather or not, she was carrying human life in her body, sacred human life. More than once he murmured to himself, "And Melanie, I'm not a coward." It was as if he had to convince himself over and over.

He awoke Tuesday morning with the thought

that Dr. Candelaria was right, no loving God would condemn Melanie if she got an abortion. He felt lighter as he ate a normal breakfast for the first time in days. As he fastened his clerical collar and put on his black suit-coat, he began formulating a plan. He would call the psychologist and find out if she could see Melanie during the lunch period. He would pick Melanie up at the high school and take her to Dr. Candelaria's office. He wasn't completely sure that this would be the best course of action to take, but he knew he had to do something.

He was still pondering all this and its implications as he picked up his briefcase and walked down the rectory's long hall. He needed to finalize some teacher-training plans at the diocese's Religious Education office. He would call Dr. Candelaria from there.

As he passed the front door, he heard the blast of a truck's air-horn, followed by the screech of brakes. He quickly opened the door and saw a red-and-yellow cement truck with its huge mixer turning over and over. My God, he thought, it's hit someone! He could see the plaid skirt that the Trinity High School girls wore.

Dropping his briefcase and running into the street, he shouted to the frightened and shaking driver, "Go into the house and call 911!" Getting down on all fours and looking under the truck, he saw that it had stopped before the rear wheels ran over the girl. Blood and other fluids trailed from the front right wheel that crushed her lower torso. Her body was mangled.

Trembling, Father Jerry crawled under the truck, unmindful of the blood. Lookingdown at the swollen face with blood oozing from her eyes, nose, and mouth, he was still able to recognize her. "Oh my God, Melanie! Oh my God!" Shaking uncontrollably and tears rolling down his face, he laid down near her, put his arm around her and pulled her close, as if to breathe life back into her. Resting his face next to hers, he whispered, "Oh Melanie, why didn't you wait? I was going to help you today. Oh, Melanie, I'm so sorry. Please forgive me." With a wave of emotion rolling through him, over and over, he kissed her bloody face, repeating, "Oh, Melanie, I'm so sorry."

He was still lying with her when the truck driver came back and squatted down near his feet. He, too, had tears running down his face. "I called 911," he said, "Father, she ran right in front of me, I couldn't stop in time."

Lifting his now bloody head, Father Jerry looked at him and yelled, "Go away."

Kneeling as best he could under the truck, the priest looked down at Melanie, pushed her dark hair from her once-beautiful eyes and stroked her forehead. Her skin was warm as if there was some life still there. He wanted the driver to turn off the cement mixer but he was gone. The loud noise and constant turning seemed to echo the waves of emotion that continued to course through him.

Knowing that her soul had already left her body but wanting to do something, the priest began the words of the Sacrament For The Dying. With trembling hands and tears streaming down his face, he made the sign of the cross on her forehead, and prayed: "Through this holy anointing, may the Lord in His love and mercy…."

He paused. "Oh Melanie, I'm sorry I didn't show you that love and mercy."

He haltingly continued the anointing. "May He, in His love and mercy, help you with the grace of the Holy Spirit." Her skin was turning cold and felt like fine parchment where it wasn't covered with blood. He made the sign of the cross on her hands, saying, "Through this anointing, may He free you from your sins and raise you to life." He added, "Melanie, you don't have any sins to be forgiven; but have no fear, you will have a new and more wonderful life."

He then whispered, "Oh, Melanie, I'm so sorry, I'm so very sorry," and gently attempted to lower her eyelids over her brown eyes, eyes that still seemed to be pleading with him. He could not close her eyes because they were too full of blood.

He remained at Melanie's side, even while the police questioned him, unashamedly letting the tears run down his face. He did not think of his own bloody appearance. He didn't move until Melanie's broken body was placed in the ambulance.

He told the police he would notify her family and have someone identify the body.

*   *   *

Jerry shook a little as he remembered where he was. He took a deep breath and turned to look out over Lake Paris. His left lower arm and hand was resting on the table. He felt a soft hand touch his. Rebecca's eyes were soft and he could feel his own tears. He hadn't told anyone the whole story of Melanie's death because so much of it was a matter of the confessional. For months, he felt a deep desire to tell Melanie's story to someone, for Melanie sake. He knew it was really for his own sake. Maybe Rebecca could be the one. He knew, intuitively, that she would not tell anyone else, if he asked her. An added incentive was that she would be off to St. Louis and he would never see her again.

"Where did you go just now? It must have been a sad place."

Without looking at her, he answered simply, "Yes, it was."

"Did it have to do with the young girl's suicide? Sister Martha said something about you feeling responsible for her death."

Jerry turned toward Rebecca. Her eyes were as soft as her voice. "Yes, I was responsible."

"Will you tell me about it? I will keep it confidential if you prefer and not put it in the article."

"Why would you want to do that? I mean, what good is it to you, if you can't write about it?"

She sounded a bit angry as she said, "Besides being a journalist, I'm also a person, a person with feelings!" Rebecca evidently saw some kind of pain on his face and so she softened her voice and added, "You seemed so…so hurt when you were reflecting. I just want you to know that I care." She looked puzzled and confused as if she was wondering why she said that.

Something in him believed her-maybe it was only his need to unburden himself. He decided to take the risk of sharing the story with this stranger. "Okay, it might help me to share the story with you. And thank you for not sharing this with another soul. It is extremely confidential." And so, slowly and with tears, he told Melanie's tragic story with a woman he had known for less than twenty-four hours. He hoped he would not regret it.

By the time he was finished, Rebecca was crying and, Jerry was surprised to notice for the first time, holding both his hands in hers. She let go with one hand and reached in her pocket for a tissue. "Thank you for telling me this story, Jerry. Is it okay if I call you Jerry?"

*   *   *

He nodded and looked around self-consciously, hoping no one saw them touching. He quickly withdrew his hands from the center of the table. "Thank you for listening. I haven't told anyone else about all this."

They both let the silence reign between them for some time. Rebecca was the first to speak. "Jerry, I'm wondering about the younger girl. Julie, isn't it?" The priest nodded and she went on. "Do you think the stepfather will molest her, too? Shouldn't the child protection people be notified?"

"I've been worrying about that for months. I can't report it because it would be a violation of the seal of confession, and I'm still afraid that what Melanie said could be true, Kurtz would kill her and her mother." His face was wrinkled in pain.

"I can understand the second part but not the first. Surely you wouldn't let a church rule prevent you from protecting a child from rape?" Rebecca looked at him for an answer.

"It is more than a church rule, it is a sacred trust. Most of the time it works very well." He wondered if Melanie's case was one of the exceptions. The thought added to his feelings of guilt.

"Have you heard from her mother and sister?"

"No, not directly. I understand from Father Cameron that they are okay."

Wanting to take the focus off himself, Jerry said, "Yesterday you said that you had some trauma in your younger years—want to talk about it?"

*   *   *

Rebecca squinted as she looked at the priest. She was thinking about her own trauma when she was fifteen. He said that she was the only person he had told of Melanie's molest and suicide. Rebecca had told only Dr. Marilyn Fisher, her therapist, about her own rape and abortion, and then she had only mentioned that it happened. She had never told anyone the whole story, ever. She looked at the man, a priest, across the table from her. She found herself wanting to tell him about what she considered to be the most traumatic event in her life. Up until that moment, she was sure that she would never tell a man about what had happened to her as a child. But this man, sitting across from her at a picnic table out in the middle of nowhere, would understand her, perhaps better than anyone she had ever met. The emotions he had expressed as he told Melanie's tragic death made Rebecca feel a kind of trust that she had not felt since she was seven years old.

Rebecca told Jerry about Paul Brady and her devastation when he left and how the devastation was compounded when she learned that he was not her biological father. She told him about the next two stepfathers, nondescript men about whom she remembered very little except that they were wealthy and each one moved she and her mother into more lavish apartments in Manhattan. "The fourth one was the real bastard," she said, looking over at the priest to see his reaction.

"Tell me about him."

Rebecca seemed to lose some of the courage she had when she began telling the story. She looked at the table and blurted out, "He raped me." Without raising her head, she peeked up at the priest.

Jerry started to reach across the table and take her hand but changed his mind when he saw a car approach. He simply said, "That's horrible. I can understand if you don't want to talk more about it, but sometimes it can be helpful."

There was more than a touch of bitterness in her voice as she said, "Confession is good for the soul, isn't that the way it goes?" Her smile was not really a smile but more of a grimace.

He whispered, "Like I said, sometimes."

Rebecca took a deep breath and exhaled loudly, "Okay, here goes. I couldn't stand him the minute my mother first introduced us. He said something like, 'Well, aren't you the pretty one, just like your mom.' He had this leering smirk that made me sick. I avoided him as much as possible. Several times he patted me on the bottom when I passed him. I complained to my mother, but all she said was, 'Don't pay any attention— that's just the way men are!'" Rebecca paused and thought for a moment, that in many ways, her mother was right. She again scrutinized the priest to see if she could, in any way, detect if he was like most of the men she had encountered in her life.

Seeming to notice her hesitancy, Jerry asked, "Something bothering you—about me, I mean?"

"No, not really, I was just thinking about the way my mother regarded men. So, anyway, after my mother and that jerk were married about six months, she was out for the evening. It was the first time the jerk was left alone with me. I stayed in my room and went to bed about ten. I was almost asleep when I felt someone sit on the bed. There was no lock on the door or I would have used it. It was the jerk. I yelled, 'Get out of my room!' He just sat there and said, 'Rebecca, why are you always so unfriendly toward me?' He had pulled the sheet and blanket off me and grabbed my arm as I moved to the other side of the bed. I was terrified. The asshole kept saying things like, 'Rebecca, I just want to be close to you. We can be friends. I do love you.' And all the while, he's pulling me back to his side of the bed. I screamed until he put his big hammy hand over my mouth. I bit his hand and he started ripping off my pajamas, snarling, 'You little bitch, now you're really going to get it!'"

Rebecca couldn't hold back the tears. It took her a few minutes before she continued. "So he raped me." She looked away.

Jerry waited several moments and then asked, "Then what happened? Did you tell your mother?"

"Yes, and you know what she did?" The priest shook his head. "She slapped me and said that I must have seduced the bastard."

Jerry sighed resignedly. "I would like to say that I'm surprised, but I've heard of that kind of thing too often. So what did you do?"

"I slapped her back and then I ran away. First I went to a girlfriend's house and then to an old couple's house. I helped them out for room and board and worked at a pharmacy after school."

Rebecca looked at Jerry defiantly and was surprised when he said, "I don't know why, but I somehow think there is more to the story." He tilted his head to one side in a quizzical way.

She shrugged her shoulders and said, "Yes there is. I found out six weeks later that I was pregnant."

"And?" Jerry made a cranking gesture with his right hand.

"And I got an abortion." With a certain amount of pride, she added, "And I paid for it twenty-five dollars a month out of my drug-store earnings." She wondered what the priest would think of that, despite his sermon. This was a real-life case, and to her that made a difference.

"Any regrets?"

Rebecca was surprised by his response. It was a simple question and she could not find any trace of an accusation in his tone. "None at all."

He stared at the table with a worried look on his face.

"Jerry, tell me what you're thinking. Are you condemning me?"

"No." He looked into her eyes and continued, "I was thinking of Melanie Kurtz and wondering why you had the courage to take care of yourself and she didn't. And I was wondering if it could have something to do with how we in the Church teach children to always obey, and to doubt themselves. I'm sorry. I do that a lot. Someone tells me something very personal and profound and I go off on some philosophical or theological tangent. Thanks, Rebecca, for sharing all that with me. It means a lot to me that you trusted me enough to tell me about that time in your life. How do you feel right now?"

Rebecca smiled. "You sound like a therapist. I feel surprisingly good, really. Thank you for listening." Again, she reached over and took his hand. He gave her a reassuring squeeze. She felt like giving him a hug but….

They sat quietly for sometime and then Rebecca said, "I keep wondering why you became a priest. Yesterday you said you decided on it after your father died when you were fourteen. Father Cameron said you worked a few years after high school, so you had a lot of time to think it over. How old were you when you were ordained?"

"Thirty."

"So you had sixteen years to think about it, to assuage any guilt you might have had for, uh, contributing to your father's death. So what was your later reason?"

"For many reasons. I believed, and still believe, that Jesus' message of love, justice and peace is what the world, families, communities, and nations, need. And I believe that the Catholic Church, with all of its faults, has the longest history and best organization to promulgate that message. I also wanted to do good in the world, to help people. And I wanted to have a peaceful life. The old priest in Nebraska was one of the most peaceful and spiritual persons I've ever known. His name was Father Groel. Being with him, serving Mass and all, was so pleasant compared to the people in my family. I never saw him angry, humiliate anyone, or be anything but kind." For the hundredth time he thought of how unlike Father Groel he was the day Melanie died and how furious he had been, and still was, toward Ralph Kurtz. He winced.

"You just made a face. What were you thinking?"

"I was just thinking of how enraged I have been toward Melanie's stepfather. I don't believe I have the patience of old Father Groel. I guess I have a long way to go before I can be as kind and thoughtful. But back to my reasons for being a priest, I honestly believe that the Catholic Church has done some wonderful things for people, inspiring, charitable, life-giving things. I'm happy to be part of it even though it has done, and continues to do, many harmful things. And some priests do some horrible things, like molest children. I'm sure you have heard of that."

"Yes, I've read about that. Do you know of any priests who have been accused of molest?" Rebecca couldn't tell him how relieved she was that she could no longer think of him as one of those priests.

"Yes. We have had one priest who was arrested last year for molesting two girls when they were pre-teens. I have to admit that I didn't know him very well. Chose not to, really. I didn't care for him. He seemed phony to me. He's awaiting trial now. Oh, and there was another one but he left the priesthood before I was ordained. Don't know much about that case."

"Why do you think these men do these things?"

"First, because they are humans. I'm guessing that the number of priests who molest children is not as high or higher than men in general – which is too high. It gets publicity because of the hypocrisy. Another reason, is that, I'm convinced, the Church's attitude toward sex is so screwed up."

"As you know, I read all about your sermon. You said that the Church's teaching was unnatural and inhumane. What do you mean?"

"Unnatural because of the way it's treated—it's essential beauty is never mentioned or mentioned only in the most abstract way. Too often it is mentioned only in the context of sin. Over all my years, most of the sins I've heard in the confessional have to do with sex. Rarely is it in other areas of loving or not loving, or justice or injustice, or malice or other kinds of hurt. Sex and sexual organs are a natural part of our being human. Hmmm. Sounds like a sermon, huh?"

Rebecca chuckled and said, "That sermon got you exiled to Paris. Are you angry for being sent out here to the boondocks? Remember, I saw that beautiful new St. Gabriel's church that holds over a thousand people."

He met her penetrating, deep brown eyes. "I was at first, but now I think it was one of the best things that could have happened to me."

"Why?"

"For the first few years I was a priest, I was too busy telling people how to live their lives to really get to know and care for them. Then I was appointed to the religious education office and was too busy to spend real time with people. Oh, I worked with people at St. Gabriel's, but still, there was not enough time. Here, I can really get to know people. I'm better off for it." After saying all of that, he looked at his watch and said, sheepishly, "Speaking of time, we better get back, Marge will have lunch ready for us."

Rebecca stiffly got up from the bench. "Riding that horse has done something to my legs and my, uh, butt. Can we walk around a bit before we get back on?"

"Sure." They walked down to the edge of the water, where Jerry taught her how to skip rocks. After plunking one rock into the lake without a single skip, Rebecca asked, "Wayne said you grew up in a big poor family. How poor was it?"

He chuckled. "About as poor as that throw you just made. If you really want to know, I can show you an example this afternoon in Paris." They headed back to the horses.

After lunch, Jerry told Rebecca and Marge that he had an appointment with one of the Mexican families who helped him prepare his sermon in Spanish. "Rebecca, I'll show you a bit of poverty when you come into town. And I have one other person I would like you to meet while you're here in Paris. If you come by the rectory at about two-thirty, I'll take you around. If you want to see Alice Peterson again, give Sy a call to see if she's feeling up to it. Marge has the number."

As he drove into town he wondered if he would spend as much time with a male journalist, or even a female one if she were homely? Oh hell, Haloran, you agreed to it, so make it worthwhile for her, he thought. Another little voice said, "Get off your holier-than-thou horse. You enjoy spending time with her because she's beautiful."

CHAPTER 7

How happy the poor in spirit;
theirs is the kingdom of heaven.
Gospel of Matthew, 5:3

Rebecca did visit with Alice and met two of her children, their spouses and children. She wanted to include Alice in the article, as the priest's inspiration and 'spiritual director.' Looking for an opportunity to get a picture that would show the older woman's exceptional spirit, she had taken one perfect photo of her with her four-year-old granddaughter. Alice had such a wonderful attitude and the children and grandchildren seemed to accept her infirmity very easily. Rebecca realized that she hadn't given much thought to family life, ever. Helene, with her fourteen-year-old daughter, was the closest to family she had spent any time with. And she and her mother's life were as far removed from family as they could get. No man she had ever dated ever mentioned children. She was pondering all this as she left her car in front of Peterson's store and walked across the road.

Again, the main door was open. She knocked on the screen door and called out, "Anybody home?"

Jerry emerged from the office, smiling. "Come on in. I saw your car over at the store. Have a nice visit with Alice?"

"Yes, and I got to meet part of the family. They

seem like very loving people."

"And it's not just outward appearances, they really are. Ready for a little jaunt around Paris?"

"Sure. Oh, Marge asked if we could join her for dinner. She says Kathy drops by before she meets with the kids at three and she asked me to ask you about time."

"I hear confessions from four to five and the Youth Mass begins at seven, so the schedule is a bit tight, but I'll give her a call when we get back to see what we can do."

Rebecca guessed that he didn't often have anyone ride along in his dusty Pontiac, as he removed a bunch of books and papers from the passenger seat. He threw it all in the back seat with what looked like a bunch of trash. He brushed off the seat with his hand. His carkeeping is worse than his housekeeping.

She climbed in and put her purse and camera on her lap. "So who are we going to meet?"

"A wonderful young man."

As they crossed the railroad tracks, Jerry said, "We are now entering Paris' slums."

"I thought all of Paris was a sl--" She looked over at Jerry and he gave her a disapproving look. About a dozen dilapidated little houses surrounded by weeds, broken fences, and old cars lined the dirt road.

He pulled up in front of a run-down little house, a shack really, with a yard covered with old tires and other junk amidst the weeds. "This place always reminds me of the house we lived in, in Nebraska. We did keep the yard better, though."

Rebecca noticed that the house was the third from

the end on the right. Before leaving town she planned to get a picture of it. If she did it now, he would probably object or at least question her. She wanted to keep the good rapport they had been having. Deception had become as natural as breathing in her years as a reporter.

Just as Jerry was about to put the car in gear, she saw a teenage boy awkwardly moving toward them in a low, wagon-like cart. He was propelling himself forward, with his ungloved hands pushing against the dusty road. Jerry got out of the car. "Hi, Ricky! Just the man I want to see. I'd like you to meet someone."

Rebecca reluctantly joined him in front of the car as the boy continued slowly toward them. He was dressed in a yellowed white tee shirt with a faded Kansas City Chief's logo on the front, worn blue jeans and sneakers. His face was contorted in a crooked smile.

A shiver went down her spine as she looked at this dirty, unpleasant looking boy. And this is the "special person" Jerry wants me to meet.

Ricky stopped a few feet in front of them and in a tortured voice said, "H, h, hi, Fa, Fa, Father Je, Je, Jerry."

Jerry knelt down on the road and leaned over and gave the boy a hug. "Ricky, I'd like you to meet Rebecca Brady. She's a writer who's visiting Paris to do a story. I'm introducing her to some of my favorite people. Rebecca, this is Ricky Alexander."

Ricky seemed to blush and awkwardly rubbed his right hand on his tee shirt. His very callused hand wavered in the air and Rebecca bent down to shake it. "Gl, gl, glad t, ta, me, me, meet y, y, you, Re, Re,

Rebecca."

"I'm glad to meet you, too, Ricky." What a pathetic child, she thought. She had to refrain herself from wiping her hand on her jeans. She chided herself for being repulsed by the dirty, crippled young man. Get a grip, she told herself, where is your compassion?

Ricky looked rather intensely at her and then over at the priest. "Sh, sh, she's ve, ve, very." He clumsily flopped his hand over his face, reddened, and went on, "pr, pr, pretty." He sheepishly looked out from under his hand.

Jerry stroked his chin with one hand and smiled at Rebecca. "By golly, Ricky, I think you're right. I hadn't noticed. She is pretty, isn't she?"

The lad waved his hand in Jerry's direction. "Y, y, yer f, f, f, full o, o, of sh, sh, shit!" This time he flopped his hand on top of his head as if expecting to get hit.

Jerry, still kneeling beside the cart and obviously pretending, said sternly, "Now, that's no way to talk to a holy man of the cloth." Ricky screwed up his face, trying to say something more but the priest cut him off. "Now don't tell me I'm full of shit again-- even if I am." They both laughed.

"Let me get your picture together." Rebecca put her camera to her eye and snapped a photo.

"Hey, Ricky, let's sing a song for her." The boy's eyes lit up. "What would you like to sing?"

"N, n, n, notes."

"From the *Sound of Music?*"

Ricky nodded.

Jerry began the song in a wonderful baritone voice, "When you know the notes to sing...."

Ricky joined him without a trace of a stutter. "You can sing most anything..." His eyes were shining. Rebecca kept taking pictures of the two as they finished the song. She was glad the camera covered the tears forming in her eyes. She had to figure out how she was going to get the event in writing.

When they finished their song, Ricky said, "Fa, Fa, Father, I, I wa, want t, ta, sh, sh, show ya so, so, something."

Rebecca found herself tensing up as she inwardly struggled with a desire to help the boy speak. She noticed that Jerry's lips moved as Ricky talked as if trying to help him out. She and the priest walked slowly beside him as he paddled his way past three houses.

The boy turned up a dirt walkway, crawled off his cart and up two old wooden steps across a weather-beaten porch. Jerry leaned over as if to help him move up the stairs, then caught himself and straightened up and put his hands in his pockets.

Ricky sat awkwardly on the porch and began struggling with the screen door. Before he could open it, a stern-looking woman in a faded dress hanging below her knees angrily pushed the door open. She looked contemptuously at Jerry as she said to Ricky, "Well, Rick, it looks like you found Father Holyjoe."

Rebecca saw that Jerry tensed up as he tried to ignore the woman's manner. "Hi, Mrs. Alexander. I'd like you to meet Rebecca Brady. She's a writer and I wanted her to meet Ricky."

The woman looked at Rebecca and uttered, "Humph." She didn't invite them in. Ricky, in his stuttering speech, asked her if she would get his tablet from his room. With another "humph" she disappeared and returned quickly with a tattered Red Chief tablet, handed it to him, slamming the door. Ricky clumsily turned the pages until he found what he was looking for. He smiled as he handed the tablet to Jerry.

Jerry studied the page for a long moment and looking rather sad and serious, said, "Ricky this is great! May I show it to Rebecca?" The boy nodded.

Rebecca read the poem, which was titled *Suffocating*:

> confusion reflected
> things lying about
> scattered
>
>
> my mind
>
> looking into someone's eyes
> i know what i see
> i can't say it
>
> asking myself
> i know what i want
> fogginess
> heaviness
> i cannot BREATHE
> i cannot speak
>
> i try to cry and cannot
> if i stack things
> pile them high
> will it become clear?

floating now
in an air tight box
unable to reach anything
or anyone
watching things float by
trying to breathe
this body
these hands
not even me

i'm gone

you don't know me
you don't know where i am
you don't even begin to understand
don't pretend you do

my eyes are not just glass windows
they can see
if i can clear them
and find me
like the rag doll you know has a soul
but don't hesitate to twist
throw, or stuff in the closet
i just lie here
making a noise to hear it
looking at something to look
my tears are eating me up
from the inside out

trapped

When she finished reading, Rebecca noticed that Ricky was looking at her intensely— questioningly. The tears she had been holding back refused to obey. "Ricky, I don't know what to say; this is a beautiful poem, very moving. Would you..." She choked up. "Let me publish it in my magazine?"

Ricky looked at Jerry, who said, "I believe she's serious, my man. If you like, I can take it home and copy it and return the original to you this evening. What do you say?"

The boy grinned from ear to ear. "O, o, o, okay."

Jerry knelt down on the porch and took Ricky's hand. "I don't know if it helps any, but I think everyone feels that no one really understands them. And, I know that you have a greater challenge with that than most people. I hope you keep letting me get to know you. It's a very deep and wonderful poem."

The boy seemed embarrassed and jerkily looked away.

"Are you coming over to Mass this evening?"

Ricky nodded.

"Need a ride?"

He shook his head.

Jerry gave him a hug. "See you tonight."

Rebecca bent down and kissed Ricky on the cheek. The boy turned scarlet and stammered, "N, n, ni, nice t, t, to, meet, yo, you, Re, Re,Rebecca. Gl, gl, gl, glad yo, yoo, you, li, like, m, m, my po, poem. Wi, wi,.will I s, s, see yo, you a, a, at Ma, Ma, Mass?" Rebecca nodded.

*   *   *

When they got back to the car, Rebecca said, "Wow, what an experience. I've never met anyone like him. He does write extremely well--a bit hard to read, but his imagery and insight are fantastic. Is he able to type or use a computer?"

"He's learning. Marge had an old computer and gave it to him. I think he'll pick it up pretty well. It will take time, as you can see his co-ordination isn't too good. He's self-taught. He reads voraciously. I think he's ready for college."

"How did you meet him?"

"He paddled his way over to the church soon after I got here. He'd read about my sermon and wanted to talk to me about masturbation. His mother had caught him masturbating and told him he was going to hell if he didn't stop." Jerry hesitated a moment, and then remembered that Rebecca had mentioned that she read all the newspaper accounts about his sermon. He went on, "He wanted to know if that was true and if what the paper reported was what I really said. I assured him it was. He's been coming over a couple of times a week ever since. He will let me take him with me when I go places but, well, like tonight, he'll take a half hour to paddle over to the church. He likes to feel independent."

"What's with his mother?"

"She's angry at God. She was Catholic at one time. When she found out Ricky had cerebral palsy, she said that if there was a God and he would punish an innocent child like that, He was not a God she could put any faith in."

129

Rebecca looked over at him and asked, "What do you tell people about that? I have to admit, I feel the same way. How could a caring God do something like that?"

Jerry drove into the driveway and turned off the engine. "I tried to speak with Mrs. Alexander once, but she wouldn't talk to me. I wanted to tell her: first, I don't know why there is this kind of evil in the world. And second, that her question has bothered me since I was a kid. As far as I can tell, no one knows the answer. I don't believe in a puppeteer kind of God who is somewhere up in the sky randomly pulling people this way and that, nor sprinkling misery here and good fortune and health there." He reached for the door handle.

"Wait a minute." Rebecca grabbed his sleeve. "What kind of God do you believe in?"

"A God that I cannot explain nor describe, and never will be able to."

"That's not a very good answer. You are dedicated to preaching and teaching about God, but you don't know anything about him?"

"The best description of God I can think of is the Biblical passage that says 'God is love and he who lives in love lives in God and God in him.' So God is love and Ricky and his mother and you and I must live in love to find God. I think we have to experience God, know God through experience and not from abstract words."

"So, are you living in love and now have found God?"

"I'm in the process ... I hope." He bit his lower lip

and thought of the song's words, "those who know love by its first name" and how he still had a long way to go before he knew love like that. He looked at his watch. "I better change clothes and go hear confessions. Maybe, if I'm kind enough, I can help someone find God. Please tell Marge that I'll be out between five-fifteen and five-thirty."

Rebecca walked back to her car thinking the priest had dodged her question. She wondered what his definition of love was.

*   *   *

Rebecca sat next to Marge near the middle of the church, and watched Kathy Olson with the five young people near the altar. Rebecca and Marge were wearing jeans and sweaters as was Kathy and the band members. "This is jean-wearing country," Marge had said. The teens were arranging their instruments, a set of drums, two rather large amplifiers, two guitars, and a bass. One pretty young girl adjusted the microphone while another girl and boy tuned up their guitars. When they turned on the amplifiers, the little church seemed to vibrate.

Kathy Olson was a very pretty, natural blond young woman. Rebecca had studied her as she interacted with the priest at dinner. The young woman seemed to try hard to have a studied nonchalance but often looked at Jerry, in what Rebecca could only interpret as, adoringly. She would also often glance at Rebecca as if sizing her up as a possible rival for Jerry's affection. Marge smiled several times as if knowing what was going on. If the priest was uncomfortable in the company of three attractive women, he didn't show it. He was less spontaneous than at other times, however. Their conversation revealed nothing of a personal nature: Kathy's graduate studies, Marge's journal, Jerry's projects and Rebecca's work with Denise and Rene at Helene's home.

Rebecca glanced around the church and guessed that there were over a hundred people, mostly children and teens, present. Jerry had told her that before he came to St. Patrick's, there were usually only about thirty people attending one Sunday Mass. Now there were more than that at each of three Masses, the Youth Mass, a Spanish Sunday Mass, and the regular ten o'clock Mass.

Hearing a bit of commotion behind her, Rebecca turned and saw Ricky paddling himself up the side aisle. The boy stopped next to her pew and held up a wavering hand.

Rebecca reluctantly reached out and shook it. "Hi, Ricky, it's good to see you again." He blushed and smiled broadly. Rebecca again scolded herself for being so squeamish.

The band began playing a fast rendition of "Kumbaya" and, led by the young woman, the congregation sang along. Jerry entered the church from the back. He was dressed in a gleaming white garment with a bright multi-colored piece over his shoulders and hanging down the front. He positively radiated warmth and color, even with his scuffed black loafers. A young man and woman carrying books and two girls dressed in red robes partially covered by white lacey garments preceded him down the aisle. Rebecca could hear Jerry's baritone voice and Ricky's tenor next to her over all the rest. She hurried around to the center aisle near the communion rail and took three pictures of the advancing procession.

Rebecca returned to her seat as the robed girls and Jerry came up to the altar and stood behind it while the book-carriers went to small lecterns on each side. The two readers alternated reading, one from the Bible and the other from Kahlil Gabran's *The Prophet*. Jerry asked everyone to stand as he read the Gospel. It was a passage with lots of 'blesseds' in it--'blessed are the meek,' 'the poor', and so forth. Again Rebecca left her place and took several pictures of the priest.

Jerry began his sermon by reading a little story from a book with a colorful cover. Rebecca tried to get a glimpse of the title but all she could see was "Chicken Soup." The story was about a little boy who wanted to buy a crippled puppy. The pet store owner wanted to give the boy the dog because he wasn't worth much and nobody else wanted him. The boy protested that he wanted to pay for the puppy, fifty cents a week, because the puppy was worth just as much as any of the others. When the owner asked him why he wanted that particular puppy, the boy pulled up his pant leg and displayed a heavy leg brace. "That puppy needs someone who'll understand," he said.

Jerry had glanced at Ricky once, as he read. The boy had tears in his eyes and shook his head. Looking around, Rebecca noticed that there were tears in many eyes, including the priest's.

After a brief silence, Jerry said, "I've read that story

a dozen times and every time, I cry. I think I identify with that little boy. Do you ever feel like you need to find someone who will truly understand? If you feel like it, would you share a time with us?"

A girl began to speak in a near whisper, "My grandmother is dying of cancer. I ... I...I'm sorry." She began to cry. It was Alice's granddaughter! A girl next to her put an arm around her. Several others shared a time in their lives when they were sad or lonely.

Marge whispered, "When I was here a few weeks ago, no-one would say a word."

Ricky clumsily waved his hand and Jerry called on him. "I, I, li, li, like th, that b, b, boy," Ricky said loudly.

Rebecca heard several snickers as the boy stammered through his simple sentence and was embarrassed for him. When she looked down at him, he seemed to be smiling. "I do too, Ricky," Jerry said.

One young man in front of Rebecca turned and shook Ricky's hand and a girl behind him patted him on the shoulder. Ricky grinned and seemed to shake all over. Rebecca hoped he was not hurting himself. One exception to the good feeling was a young fellow in a pew behind Rebecca. He wore a baseball cap on backward and attempted to look cool and disinterested. She wondered why he was in church.

The robed girls brought water and wine to the altar and Jerry announced, "This is the offertory of the Mass. We will pass a basket around. If you have any spare money you can give to the parish, it is appreciated. We do need to buy more paint and fix up the parish hall. If you cannot afford it, that is okay, too."

The girl who led the singing announced, "Kathy Olson has been helping us with our music and she has a beautiful voice. She says that the music should be ours and she is only a coach, but tonight we have talked her into singing our offertory song."

Kathy stepped up from the front pew with guitar in hand. "I would like to sing one of my favorite songs for you—'The Rose.' If you know the words, please join me." Rebecca immediately positioned herself to take pictures.

Some say love is like a river that drowns the
    tender reed
Some say love is like a razor that leaves the
    soul to bleed
Some say love is an endless, aching need
I say love is a flower and you its only seed
It's the heart afraid of breaking that never learns
    to dance.
It's the dream afraid of waking that never takes
    the chance.
It's the one who won't be taken that cannot
    seem to give.
And the soul afraid of dying that never learns
    to live.
When the night has been too lonely
and the road has been too long
and you think that love is only for the lucky and
    the strong.
Just remember in the winter far beneath the
    bitter snow,
lies the seed that with the sun's love in the
    spring becomes the rose.

No one joined Kathy in the singing and there was silence in the church as she finished the song. Kathy smiled at the congregation and then turned to Jerry. The soulful look on her face would melt the hardest of hearts, Rebecca thought. Her expression seemed to say that the love she sang about was her love for him. He appeared to be embarrassed as he smiled in return. If this priest isn't moved, and maybe even very disturbed, by the obvious feelings of love of this delightful and beautiful woman, he has to be dead.

Rebecca hoped she had captured Kathy's smile on film. She wished she had a camcorder for the event. The radiant young woman cradled the guitar in her arms and returned to her seat. A loud applause broke out and lasted for a full minute.

After the offertory, Jerry invited some of the young people to gather around the altar. About fifteen of the younger ones did, forming a half-circle to the sides and back of the altar. Soon after, the band began a rock version of the Lord's Prayer. Everyone began singing and joined hands. The young man a few feet from Marge hesitantly moved his hand in her direction. She quickly moved toward him and took his hand. Marge extended her other hand to Rebecca. Rebecca had to stretch a bit to reach Ricky's hand.

After the lively Lord's Prayer, Jerry said, "Now is the time for the 'Greeting of Peace.' Let those around you know you are someone who wants to understand, in any way that is comfortable for you." Jerry turned and gave each of the young people a gentle handshake. Some of the girls hugged one another and a few couples gave each other a kiss. As Marge gave Rebecca a hug, the reporter noticed a girl step out of a pew and approach the teen with the backward cap and extend her hand. He slapped it away. What an insensitive little bastard! He isn't little, though, she thought as she bent down and kissed Ricky on the forehead. He turned pink and grinned.

Jerry held up a large gold cup, took out one of the small white wafers and held it in front of him. "We Catholics believe this is the body of Christ. We eat this as a sign of our union with Him and with one another. We believe that through this communion we gain strength to love and understand one another. I have not seen some of you before. If you are not Catholic but do wish to dedicate yourself to loving and understanding others, then feel free to join us in our Communion."

Rebecca was impressed with his easy manner. He did not talk down to the young people. He began to give the wafers to those near the altar and then came around to the opening at the communion rail. Rebecca positioned herself near the door close to those receiving communion. Young people lined up in the center aisle but before attending to them, Jerry came over to the side aisle and gave Ricky communion. She got what she hoped was another memorable picture. Jerry held up a wafer and looked questionably at her. She shrugged her shoulders and he nodded. As others had done she took the wafer in her left hand and put it in her mouth with her right. It didn't have much taste but she guessed it wasn't supposed to.

She was surprised Backward Cap was standing in the line behind her and Marge.

Nearly everyone was singing a song with a refrain that included, "They'll know we are Christians by our love, by our love, oh, they'll know we are Christian by our love."

When Backward Cap came to the front of the line, Jerry whispered something to him. The fellow was as tall as Jerry, and heavier. He seemed to stagger a bit as he stood there. Jerry held the wafer in front of the teenager and said, "Okay?"

"Fuck you, man!" Backward Cap lurched forward and thumped Jerry hard on the forehead. The priest reeled from the blow. "Take your Jesus-bread and shove it up your ass!" Quicker than Rebecca could imagine possible and before she could get her camera ready, Jerry handed the chalice to the girl next in line, turned the fellow around, pulled his arm behind him with one hand, grabbed his hair with the other, pulling his head down.

"Open that door!" Jerry nodded toward the side entrance.

Marge pushed on the crash-bar just as Jerry heaved the fellow out the door. Breathing hard, Jerry pulled up his robe and took out a set of keys and calmly selected one. "Marge, would you please go over to the house and call the sheriff. Tell him what happened. Number's by the phone. Better go through the front door." He pointed toward the entrance.

"Do you know the boy's name?" Marge asked.

"Kenny Gaffin, sheriff's son."

As Marge made her way down the aisle, Rebecca heard Jerry ask two of the fellows to see if Kenny was okay. Nearly everyone in the church appeared shocked by the incident. Jerry apologized for being so "unkind" to the young man and then proceeded with the service.

At the end of the Mass, Rebecca followed the others outside the church and found a grim-faced Jerry standing near the door, greeting people as they came out. One girl was saying to him, "Father, you didn't have to apologize for what you did. Kenny is a bully—he's that way at school, too."

"Thanks, Susan. I could have handled it better, though."

"Please don't let it stop our Youth Mass!"

A big round-faced kid came up to him and attempted a 'high-five.' Jerry reached up and took his hand and shook it. "Way to go, man, er, Father. Didn't know you were such a tough dude."

"Joe, I really don't like being a tough dude. I hope I can find a better way next time, if there is one."

"Aw, Father, don't worry, you did good." He gave Jerry a big smile and left.

The greetings continued in this vein until Kathy, Marge, and Ricky, the last ones to exit, joined them. Rebecca gave Marge a hug and took Kathy's hand. "Kathy, your singing was beautiful. I love that song."

"Thank you, Rebecca. I like it, too."

"It shows! You sang with such feeling." Even in the dim light, Rebecca could see that Kathy was blushing.

Ricky, sitting on his cart near the top of a new wooden ramp, stammered, "I, I, li, li, like, y, y, your so, so, song too."

Kathy took Ricky's hand, "Thank you, Ricky. I'm glad you liked it."

Marge addressed the priest, "Well, Father Jerry, that was quite a show. I haven't been here for weeks, is it this exciting every Saturday?"

"Oh, sure, I stage a special event each time. Speaking of special events, Kathy, your song was beautiful. Thank you!"

Kathy whispered, "You're welcome."

"I'm glad you joined us, Marge, but I'm sorry I lost my temper with the boy."

"What do you think he'll do now? I heard him tell the two boys with him that he was going to 'get you.' I told Sheriff Gaffin that."

"I don't know what he'll do." The sheriff drove up. "That's the boy's dad. I'll talk to him. Hey, Ricky, I'm sure the sheriff will give you a ride home. Want me to ask him? Ricky smiled, shook his head, and quickly went down the ramp.

"Will you ladies wait for me at the house?"

They nodded.

* * *

When they entered the rectory, Marge headed for the kitchen. "I don't know about you two, but I need a drink. Let's see what our boy has around here." Rebecca and Kathy watched as Marge opened the refrigerator. There wasn't even a beer in it. She began opening cupboards and finally found a sealed bottle of Christian Brother's brandy. "How about some brandy?"

"Fine with me." Kathy said. "Do you think he'll mind?"

"Not if we tell him we're celebrating your performance."

Marge sure feels at home around here, Rebecca thought. She wondered how much time the professor spends with Jerry.

Not finding any brandy snifters, Marge poured the brandy into four ordinary drinking glasses. Kathy and Rebecca picked up their glasses and Marge took two and headed back to the living room. Marge answered Rebecca's question by saying, "He's got this fixed up quite nicely."

Kathy sat down opposite Rebecca on the couch. "I understand his predecessor did it, or more likely, had it done. I think he was more interested in his creature comforts than in the parish. Fixing up the rectory for himself would be the last thing Father Jerry would do."

Rebecca's focus changed and she began wondering how much time this pretty blond spent in the rectory. Rebecca looked at Kathy and Marge. "I have a question I'd like to ask you two. I hope you won't be offended but you both are very attractive and I was wondering if, uh, Father Haloran has ever made a pass at either of you?"

Kathy reddened and looked embarrassed. Marge smiled and said, "If either of us said 'yes,' would you put that in your article?"

"Oh, god no. I was just wondering. It must get lonely here for him and well ... he is human." She turned to Kathy.

"He sure hasn't made a pass at me and I've known him for nearly six years. Of course, most of that time

I was a nun." Kathy chuckled. "He uses that vow of celibacy of his like a wall."

Rebecca wondered if Kathy wanted to jump over that wall.

Marge laughed as she said, "Shall we see if we can make the wall come tumbling down?" They all laughed.

They were still giggling when the door opened and Father Jerry entered still dressed in his black cassock. "Sounds like fun in here. What did I miss?"

Marge got up from the recliner and held out a glass of brandy. "We were just talking about you."

Without smiling, he took the glass from Marge and sipped the brandy. "I'm funny, huh?"

For some reason, Kathy felt it necessary to come to his rescue. "No, Marge was just trying to be funny."

He paused a moment than added, "Let me get out of this thing. I'll be right back." He stepped into the bedroom, closed the door, and only a couple of minutes later came back out wearing another faded blue plaid short-sleeved shirt. Rebecca thought she should send him a new shirt or two as a thank-you for seeing her over the weekend.

Marge got up from the recliner and held up her glass of brandy. "A toast to Kathy and her wonderful performance."

Father Jerry picked up his glass from an end table. "I'll drink to that."

Kathy held up her glass. "And to our tough-dude pastor of St. Patrick's."

"I won't drink to that." He slumped down in the recliner, looking troubled.

Kathy sat forward on the couch. "Father Jerry, you look terribly worried. How come?"

Jerry looked at the floor and sounded sad. "I wish I had handled the boy differently— not lost my temper and been so rough with him."

Rebecca spoke up, "I noticed you said something to him before he lashed out at you. What did you say?"

"I said, 'Will you receive this Body of Christ as a sign that you want to learn to love and understand? If the answer is yes, please take off your hat as a sign of respect.'"

Marge looked stunned. "And he hit you for that?"

"Probably more because he was the only one I said anything to, I humiliated him. He was half-drunk, too." He glanced at each of them, then smiled.

Rebecca asked, "What are you smiling about?"

"When I told my mother I was planning to become a priest, the only thing she said was, 'Son, I think you're too impatient to be a priest.' I guess she was right."

Marge said, "Oh, I don't know. I thought of Jesus chasing the moneychangers out of the temple. I guess he was impatient, too. Tell us what happened with Sheriff Gaffin."

"First, he was glad you called, Marge. I guess he's had quite a time with the boy. He's the youngest of four. Joe thinks he's got both a drug and an alcohol problem. He told me that you heard him say that he was going to 'get' me. Joe said if he did anything stupid, he'd lock him up, son or not. He'd try to keep an eye on him."

"So what happens now?" Marge asked.

*   *   *

"Being the great know-it-all, Mr. Fix-it, I volunteered to counsel young Kenny if he'd see me. Joe said he'd make sure he kept appointments. He'll be a tough case, I'm afraid."

"Think he'll talk to you?" Kathy, Rebecca was sure, was more worried about Jerry's safety but didn't want to say anything.

"Don't know. I've had some luck with kids before. I always assume that underneath the anger is a lot of fear and hurt. We'll see. I'm sorry that the incident detracted from your performance, Kathy." The look he gave the young woman definitely showed he was fond of her, if not something more, Rebecca noticed. He quickly changed the subject by saying, "Well, Rebecca, what does the city girl think of our Youth Mass?"

"I have to say that I was really moved by the spirit of the young people, the music, the dialogue at sermon time, and just about everything, except Kenny. Except for Kenny, the kids were so respectful toward each another. If I can find a church like this in St. Louis, I might start attending."

"Thank you. I'm sure there's one somewhere in St. Louis."

Marge looked serious as she said, "Jerry, oops, I'm picking up Rebecca's habit. I can call you 'Jerry' if Rebecca can, can't I?"

"No! She's not a Catholic, so she's free, you're a loyal daughter of the Church, so you can't." He looked serious for a moment, then chuckled.

"Well, I'm not so loyal and I'm afraid you're not, either. Aren't you afraid you'll get into trouble for giving communion to non-Catholics?"

"A little, but what more can he do? In the Bishop's mind I'm already in Siberia. Besides, I think it's the right thing to do. In my opinion, a church based on laws is the opposite of what I think Jesus was all about; he wanted a movement based on compassion, and that is inclusive, not exclusive."

Rebecca thought Kathy sounded almost hopeful as she said, "I don't know if it's right or wrong, but he could kick you out of the priesthood!"

Rebecca looked a bit shocked and said, "He wouldn't! Not for such a small thing?"

Marge stood. "This Bishop is a complete numbskull. I wouldn't be surprised at anything he did. Let's not get into this." She glanced at her watch. "I'm afraid I'll have to get back home. I told my neighbor lady I'd be back in two hours. I'm already late."

Kathy put her glass down. "I've had a long day, I better get going, too."

Jerry gave both women a hug and then shyly looked at Rebecca. She opened her arms and he hugged her, too, a much better one than the night before. He gave good hugs. Rebecca couldn't remember when she'd ever had a non-come-on hug from a man. Probably not since her stepfather, Paul Brady—when she was seven.

Jerry asked, "Are you planning to attend the masses in the morning? The Spanish Mass has a pretty good Mariachi group playing."

"Thank you, but I'll need to head back to St. Louis early." She had enough religion for one weekend.

CHAPTER 8

If I have the gift of prophecy, understanding all the
mysteries there are, and knowing everything ... but I
am without love, then I am nothing at all.

First Corinthians 13:2

As Jerry straightened up the living room and began
vacuuming the floor, he reflected on the weekend. He
was more than a little apprehensive about the article
Rebecca Brady would write about him. However it
turned out, he was sure it would infuriate the Bishop.
And he was bothered by the feelings that came over
him as he thought of Rebecca. He wasn't sure what
it was that made him so nervous, besides her obvious
beauty and charm. One thing that could be a factor was
that she seemed to be interested in him as a person and
not as a priest. Or was she putting on an act? Relax,
Haloran, he thought, you'll never see her again. He
smiled as he thought of his friend Wayne once saying,
as they watched a love scene in a movie, "Don't race
your motor, ol' buddy, if you're not going anyplace."

Hearing the doorbell ring, he quickly put the
vacuum away and went to the door. The principal of
Paris High School had called on Friday and asked if he
and his wife could talk with the priest. The kids called
him Mr. Grumpy. Jerry didn't know his real name. He
had seen the principal's wife at the Youth Mass several
times and noticed that she did not receive Communion.

Once or twice a man was with her and Father Jerry assumed it was her husband. If it was, he seemed to match his nickname. It was his practice not to wear clerical garb when he talked to people at the rectory. His only concession to formality was to wear black slacks and a clean sport shirt.

As he opened the door he noticed that Plato's neck hair was raised and he was eyeing the principal suspiciously. Plato was usually friendly. "Welcome. Do come in." He held out his hand to the man. "I guess you know me, I'm Father Jerry Haloran."

The principal, a ruddy-faced short, thin man in his mid-thirties, took his hand without a smile. "Robert Grumble. Nice to meet you. And this is my wife, Sandra." Sandra had reddish-brown hair and freckles, a beautifully sculptured face, and looked to be about eight months pregnant. She held out her hand and smiled.

Jerry motioned to the couch and sat opposite them on the recliner. He leaned forward and said, "I've seen you in church. So what can I do for you?"

Robert turned toward his wife as if to say, "This is your show." Sandra began, "I don't know if there is anything you can do for us, but, we did want to talk with you. You see, Father, both of us were raised Catholic." She looked at the floor for a moment and then back at him. "Well, I was married before for two years when I was eighteen." She went on to tell him that she got married because she was pregnant. It was a Catholic wedding. She miscarried right after the wedding. The fellow was an abusive alcoholic and womanizer six years her senior. When she got pregnant again, she decided that she would not raise a child with a man like that. She got a divorce, was a single mother for four years, and then met Robert, a fellow teacher at her school. They had been married for six years and had one child of their own. "And as you can see, we are expecting another," she said.

Robert picked it up from there. "Sandra wants to get her first marriage annulled. We talked to some priest in Salina about it and he said that it was impossible." The man sounded bitter as he added, "The asshole said that if we wanted to continue to live together, we would have to live as brother and sister." He did not apologize for his crude language but Sandra gave him a disapproving look. Then he chuckled and sneered as he looked at Sandra's abdomen. "As you can see, we didn't follow his advice."

Jerry found himself disliking Robert, seeing him as a bitter man who appeared sour to the core. "I take it, Robert, that you're not very interested in this annulment business, is that right?"

Sandra looked a bit surprised at Father Jerry's comment but didn't say anything. Robert said, "Honestly, I think it's a lot of bullshit." Again Sandra gave him the look. "No priest or bishop can tell me whether or not my marriage is okay."

Jerry agreed with him, that only the married couple could make their marriage okay, but he wasn't about say that to this jerk. He had told five or six couples, who really were working to make a loving and life-giving marriage, that they should just begin receiving the sacraments and participating in the Church, because they are the ones who "bless" the marriage through their love. So far, he didn't think that the couple in front of him had a marriage "blessed" in love. "So, Robert, you came today because Sandra asked you to."

"Yeah, she thinks our marriage isn't working as she would like because it isn't 'blessed' by the Church."

"You know that's not true, Bobby." For a moment Jerry was afraid Robert would hit Sandra as he scowled at her and raised his right hand slightly. He guessed "Bobby" was the wrong word. Sandra went on, "I know you dislike the Church because of things that happened to you when you were a kid. I happen to love the Church and I want to participate as fully as I can. I want to go to Communion."

"Well, why'n hell don't you go? Father here is giving out Communion to everyone— just go! He doesn't give a shit!" Robert was nearly yelling.

Jerry unconsciously made a fist. The man reminded him of a younger and skinnier Ralph Kurtz. He began wondering how many people thought like Robert about his giving out Communion when he wasn't sure whether or not the person was Catholic. "You've been to the Youth Mass, Robert. Do you honestly believe I don't give a shit about who goes to Communion?"

"How in hell would I know? You sure don't sound like any priest I've ever heard before. That old fart I grew up with would call you the devil." He paused a moment, then added, "Yeah, you mouth something about understanding and compassion and love. What the hell does that mean?"

Jerry looked at Sandra, who had leaned away from her husband and seemed to want to put even more distance between them. "So, Robert, are understanding, compassion, and love just meaningless words to you, or is it that you just don't like my saying that they are a condition for receiving Communion?"

Robert gave him a challenging grin. "Would you give me Communion if I came up for it?"

"If you had come up before this evening, I would have assumed you were doing so in good faith. After listening to you now, I wouldn't. From what you've said so far, I see you as a rather callused and mean-spirited person who is really short on those three virtues." Sandra turned away from her husband and smiled.

The young man continued to give Jerry his challenging smirk. "And what about St. Sandra here, would you give her Communion?"

"I probably would. Living with you, she obviously has a lot of patience. And I would guess love, compassion, and understanding. Tell me, Robert, would it take a lot of understanding and patience to live with you?"

Sandra frowned and then smiled. "Well, Bobby, somebody's finally telling you what you need to hear!"

Great! She has more gumption than he first thought. If looks could kill, she'd be dead. Robert seemed like he was about to explode. Jerry said, "Right now, Robert, I'm concerned that you are going to make Sandra pay for what she just said when you leave here. Is she in danger?"

"You sure are a know-it-all, you know that? It's none of your damn business what I do after I leave here."

"I think it is. After all, you are the one who came here to see me." The young husband glared at him. Acting more calmly than he felt, Jerry turned to Sandra. "Do you feel you are in danger, Sandra?"

Sandra seemed to be in pain as she straightened up, glanced at her husband, and then, looking Jerry in the eye, said, "Yes."

Jerry moved to the edge of his chair: the look on the young husband's face spelled danger. The priest placed his hands over his knees and asked softly, "Sandra, has Robert physically hurt you in the past?"

"Uh, yes, but, ah, not since I've been pregnant this time."

Jerry could only guess that Sandra was staying in the marriage because she would be too ashamed to face her family if she were to divorce a second time. He turned to the husband. "Robert, I am sure that you are an intelligent man; otherwise, you wouldn't hold the position you do. And I can guess that you do love Sandra, or, you wouldn't be sitting there." The words seemed to have the desired effect as Robert sat back on the couch. Jerry went on, "As you know, many men have a problem with anger. If you would, please tell me some of the things you have done to control your anger."

"Well, I'm controlling it right now."

"Are you angry at me or at Sandra?"

"Hell, I'm angry at both of you! You think you're so much better than me."

"We are."

Robert appeared shocked by this.

Jerry smiled and went on, "At least we are better

than you at showing that we are compassionate and understanding. Seriously, Robert, do you honestly believe that you are as loving a person as Sandra?"

Robert sat silently for a full minute. "I don't think anyone is as loving as Sandra." He smiled weakly as if he feared showing some kind of positive emotion.

Sandra made an attempt to reach out to him by saying, "Bobby, oh, I'm sorry, Robert, you can be very loving sometimes. You just need to do it more often." He scowled back at her.

"Robert, right now, I am just concerned that Sandra is safe when you both leave here. Will you agree not to hurt her in any way when you leave?"

"Of course, I won't hurt her and I don't need you to act like you're threatening me about it."

"I can see that you are very angry at priests and the entire Catholic Church. Whatever happened in your life, or the life of your family, must have been something pretty devastating."

Again, Robert looked at the floor. "Yeah it was.... Okay, I'll tell you. I haven't even told Sandra this. When I was twelve, my sister, who was fourteen, told me that the priest in our town molested her. Shit! That's putting it too politely—he raped her. Before she told me this, she made me promise never to tell anyone. I told her to tell our mother. And, you know what?" Jerry shook his head. Sandra had her hand over her mouth as if stifling a scream. "My sister did tell our mother, and you know what our mother did?" Again Jerry shook his head. "Mom slapped her and told her never to tell such lies ever again." Robert looked at Jerry defiantly.

Jerry had to work to overcome the rage that had built up in him. As calmly as he could, he asked, "Did that priest ever get reported for the crime he committed?"

"Yes, in a way, but not for what he did to my sister. He did it to another young girl and her parents reported it to the Bishop and I think he was sent away to some hospital or rehab center or something."

"And how is your sister today?"

Robert let out a bitter little laugh. "Oh, she's fine, she's a prostitute and drug addict in Chicago. And I won't apologize for saying that I hope that priest burns in hell!"

Jerry sat back in the chair and let out a deep breath. "I hate to say it, but right now, I'm thinking the same thing. And I can understand it if you've hated priests ever since. And hated the Church for brainwashing your mother so thoroughly that she wouldn't believe her own daughter."

"Brainwashed, yes! That's exactly it. I fear that Sandra is brainwashed and wants to brainwash our children."

Sandra looked at Jerry with tears in her eyes and shook her head.

"I can understand that. And I can understand your being bitter toward the Church. Tell me, Robert, with all that going on inside you, why did you agree to come see me tonight?"

"I like what you are doing for the kids with your Saturday Mass." He looked over at his wife. "And believe it or not, I do love my wife and, well, she's been happier since you've come to Paris. And I came tonight to see if you are for real."

Jerry smiled. "And?"

Sandra took Robert's hand. "Of course he is."

Jerry did not wait for Robert's response. "I would like to meet with you again." He addressed Sandra. "We cannot expect Robert to make a decision about me or the Church with one meeting. Will you meet with me next week?"

"Definitely!" Sandra nodded vigorously and Robert added a weak 'okay.'

Jerry had a hard time going to sleep that night— thinking of that priest. Damn! And damn that celibacy rule that forces men to live unnatural lives. But that damn priest was not forced to do what he did. Damn!

*   *   *

At nine on Wednesday morning, Rebecca sat down in the office of Dr. Marilyn Fisher. She had been seeing Dr. Fisher, a clinical psychologist in her mid-fifties, once a week since her breakup with Sam Hawkins. When she began therapy she thought her problem was choosing the wrong men. She had dated and slept with Sam Hawkins for three years and finally broke it off when she fully realized that Sam was "a male chauvinistic egotistical bastard." Rebecca had used those exact words at their first session and was surprised and pleased that the psychologist was neither shocked nor put off by her remark.

With gentle and respectful prodding from Dr. Fisher, she began to realize that her childhood issues of abandonment by Paul Brady, the succession of stepfathers and the rape by one of them had made her

155

fearful of intimacy. Sometimes Rebecca wondered if she was even capable of having an intimate relationship. She seemed to choose men who were equally incapable. She was anxious to hear what Marilyn would say when she told her therapist about Father Jerry Haloran.

"Well, Rebecca, how has your life's journey been since last week—Tuesday wasn't it, because you had to go someplace on Wednesday?"

Rebecca nodded. "Well, since our last meeting I went to Paris and met the man of my dreams!" She smiled broadly.

Marilyn turned her head to the side and looked at her questioningly. "And you're putting me on, right?"

"Nope, as they say in Paris. That's what I did."

"Nope, as they say in Paris? I thought they spoke French in Paris."

"Not in the Paris I went to."

"Okay, Rebecca. Tell me where this Paris is located and then tell me about your dream man."

"I went to Paris, Kansas, a little burg of less than a thousand people. If you would have told me ever before in my life that I would enjoy spending three days in a little run-down farm town like that, I would have said you were crazy. But, honestly Marilyn, it was one of the most enjoyable and eventful weekends of my life." Rebecca decided to wait to tell her about Father Jerry and went on to describe Alice and Sy Peterson, Marge Woerner, Ricky Alexander, and Kathy Olson. "Those five people are some of the most real people I have ever met."

"And who is the man of your dreams? Is he in Paris, Kansas, too?"

Rebecca gave her a wistful smile. "Yes, he is."

"Rebecca, stop playing games. Tell me!"

"He is the reason I went to that godforsaken poor little town in the first place." She reached down, picked up her purse from the floor, and took out a small stack of photos. She picked out two pictures—one close-up of Jerry with his straw hat and faded plaid shirt and the other of him astride the gray horse. She grinned as she handed them to the psychologist.

Marilyn looked puzzled. "He looks like the Marlboro man."

"He does, doesn't he?" She chose two more pictures. First she handed Marilyn the one showing the priest with Ricky Alexander. "That's the boy, Ricky Alexander, with the cowboy." Rebecca smiled as she handed Marilyn the picture of Jerry giving his sermon.

Marilyn studied the picture for some time. "So, Rebecca, the man you met is a priest? A Catholic priest?"

Rebecca relaxed back in her chair. "Yep!"

"Yep, as they say in Paris, Kansas?"

"Yep." They both laughed.

"So tell me about this priest. Is he the one who turned you into a comedian?"

"He didn't turn me into a comedian but he and they helped me take myself less seriously, Alice Peterson especially. My assignment was to write an article about the priest. He was wounded at an anti-abortion demonstration a few months ago and then gave a sermon condemning his Church's position on all kinds of sexual issues."

"I think I read about him. In Aberdeen, Kansas, right?"

Rebecca nodded and went on to tell Marilyn her impressions of Father Jerry Haloran, his work, and people's reactions to him. Marilyn put a hand to her chin. "Do you know, Rebecca, you sound like someone who is talking about a boyfriend or at least a potential boyfriend?"

Rebecca felt her face flush. My lord, she never thought of it like that but ... that does explain the way she had been feeling. She left Paris feeling high, then down, then up, then...

Marilyn interrupted her reverie, "Where are you going, Rebecca?"

She shook her head as if in a daze. "I don't know."

"About what?"

"About what you just said—that I'm talking about Jerry like he was a potential boy-friend. I, I like him but."

"He's a priest? You just called him 'Jerry.' Why is that?"

"We had a number of talks and at one point I asked him if I could just call him 'Jerry.' He was okay with that."

"So what is it about him that you like?"

Rebecca was sure she looked as confused as she felt. "I'm not sure. I think he reminds me of Paul Brady.

"Your first stepfather, the one man you truly felt close to. What is it about this priest that reminds you of him?"

"I'm not sure. Maybe it's his gentleness."

"It sounds like you felt very comfortable with the priest. I wonder if part of the comfort was due to the fact that he isn't available?"

"Maybe. Anyway, I'll probably never see him again. But it is a nice dream. I know there is one man in the world I could relate to, now I just need to find a second, huh?"

"Have you written the article about him?"

"I finished a rough draft yesterday. I should get it finalized this week. But there's something about the man that I can't quite capture."

"Like why a man like that would be celibate?"

"Yes, I wonder about that, too. But there's something else. He seems so dedicated to doing good, like he's driven by something. Or, maybe, he is just good in a way I find hard to believe."

Dr. Fisher stroked her chin and smiled, "Well, I think that somehow this Paris experience has done something for you. Let yourself think about it and ... well, there's some kind of message for you in all this. Next week you can let me know what it is. I'm looking forward to reading the article."

*   *   *

Kathy stepped out of the shower and looked at herself in the mirror. She disapproved of her figure, as usual. Her sister, growing up, called her 'flubber butt', and called her fat. Her breasts definitely were too large. She always looked at pictures of models in newspapers and magazines and they were all so thin.

The only ones that seemed to look like her at all, were the ones showing off 'full-figured' bras and panties. She couldn't tell for sure but she was almost sure that the reporter doing the article on Father Jerry was built more like a model than she was. And what a beautiful face and that long black hair. Jerry had to notice how beautiful she is. He was really paying attention to her. And Marge let it slip that they had gone horseback riding together. That skunk had never gone riding with me, damn it!

She stung her tongue out at herself and vowed to talk to Jerry about that witch when she got back to Paris on Saturday. She looked at the digital clock on the dresser and told herself to get dressed in a hurry, skip breakfast and get to her first class, psychology. Yeah, some psychology. It was mostly about rats and pigeons. It sure wouldn't help her understand herself or that priest. He wasn't the right kind of rat.

CHAPTER 9

Pull me out of this swamp; let me sink no further
let me escape those who hate me; save me from deep
water!

Psalm 69:14

On a cold first Saturday of November that hinted of snow, Jerry entered the rectory and took off his black suit coat and clerical collar. He had worn his clerical attire to look 'official' for the Methodist Church council meeting. They wanted to know about his and 'their' Reverend Johnson's plans for the teen center that they hoped to open in an abandoned building downtown. There were three men, including Sheriff Joe Gaffin, and four women present, plus Reverend Bill Johnson and himself.   Jerry had been put on the defensive immediately by one of the men asking about his Saturday evening "service." Was he trying to lure their children away from the Methodist faith, he wanted to know. Jerry wasn't sure he had convinced them that he had no intention of doing so and even had encouraged them to participate more fully in their home church.

Even after the sheriff assured the group that he would make sure there were no drugs or alcohol in and around the center, they thought that they needed to study the matter further. One council member implied that perhaps working with Catholics on the project would harm the church. Jerry hated feeling defensive as well as the suspicious reception he had received—with the exception of the minister and Joe Gaffin.

He threw the mail he had picked up on the way home on the desk without looking at it. It lay atop Thursday and Friday's mail, also unopened. Hearing a car pull into the driveway, he looked out the window and saw Kathy's Toyota. He always looked forward to her Saturday visits, even though he still struggled with the sexual feelings that arose in him. Two weeks ago, before she left to go to Marge's, she had given him a different kind of hug. It had a seemingly desperate kind of feel to it. She held him tight for over a minute and then pushed him away. She sounded sad as she said, "I wish it could be different between us, Jerry." He didn't know what to say, so he didn't say anything. Maybe today he could ask her what she meant.

Someone was with her. A young man with long hair pulled back in a ponytail got out of the car and waited for Kathy to come around to his side. When she joined him, he took her hand and headed for the house. Who the hell is that and what is he doing holding her hand? Jerry thought. He couldn't figure out if he was feeling jealous or more like a concerned father. He couldn't be her "boyfriend" and, damnit; he didn't want anyone else to be either. The young man looked around and said something to her that Jerry couldn't hear.

He opened the door and went out on the porch, attempting to look cheerful. "Hi, Kathy." He gave her his customary hug but more perfunctory than usual.

"Jerry, I'd like you to meet Dylan Bradford. Dylan, this is Father Jerry, the one I've told you so much about."

Dylan, not much taller than Kathy, wore a baggy unbuttoned shirt over a white tee shirt. He gripped Jerry's hand almost hard enough to make him wince and said, "Nice to meetcha, man. Kath talks a lot about you."

Jerry withdrew his hand and resisted the urge to shake off some of the pain. Already he found himself disliking the little weasel—with his pretentious handshake, hippy look, calling Kathy, "Kath," and the smarmy smile. Did Kathy dredge him up in the past two weeks? Or was he somehow in her life before her last visit?

"Dylan is a music major at K-State and has volunteered to help me with the kids. Isn't that wonderful?" Kathy looked star struck at the young man.

"Sure, that's great. Welcome to Paris, Dylan." Yeah, Haloran, be the all-loving, kindly pastor, he thought to himself. The little jerk has no interest in the kids' music; he just wants to be with this beautiful young woman.

Of course, Kathy noticed his lack of enthusiasm and frowned. "We stopped by Marge's on the way. She said she would cook dinner for us and would like for you to join us. Could you?" She sounded like a teenager asking good ol' dad to join her and her date. "Oh, and Jerry, would it be okay if Dylan spent the night in your spare room? I told him I was sure it would be okay."

He wondered how he could say "no" to these requests without coming across as an old grouch or offending her. He didn't want to eat with the little creep or have him in the house. He wondered if her request that he sleep in the rectory meant that she wasn't sleeping with him, or was it just a way of not looking bad to Marge and him? He kept all this to himself and, without smiling, said, "Sure, I'll join you for dinner. Dylan, you can use the spare bed. You can bring your stuff in now, if you like." Put some warmth and enthusiasm in your voice, Haloran, Jerry commanded himself. Don't be such a prig, she isn't your daughter or girl friend, just a friend, so be friendly.

After Dylan brought in his small overnight bag and scowled at the dinky guestroom, he and Kathy went over to the church to join the kids. Jerry went into the office and stared at the mail. He sat down and wondered why he was so upset with Kathy bringing a young man with her? How would he feel if someone else had brought him? Was he jealous? Of course not! Another voice entered his head, Come off it, Haloran, you want to be Kathy's one-and-only even if you won't admit it. He told the voice to shut up and that she was just a friend who was free to do whatever she wanted.

More to distract himself than from any genuine interest in the mail, he took out a letter opener and began to slit the envelopes. The bottom item was a large manila envelope with *Women Today* letterhead and "Rebecca Brady" written underneath. He opened it and pulled out the magazine.

"HOLY SHIT!" he shouted as he looked at the cover, a full-color picture of himself sitting astride Marge's gray horse. In bold white letters across the bottom of the picture were the words: NOBLE KNIGHT OF THE PRAIRIE.

A post-it note was attached: "Hi Jerry. I hope you enjoyed the gift I sent you for hosting me over that weekend. This is an early copy of the mag.—it will probably go on sale next Monday. Hope you like it— note: no quotes. Rebecca." Gift? Early Copy? He looked at the envelope. It was postmarked the previous Monday. He remembered that there was a card in his post office box notifying him that he had a package. Each morning he had picked up the mail before the window had opened. He meant to go back and get the parcel but kept forgetting, until today.

Well, let's see what the little lady said about me, he thought. Noble knight! He wondered who came up with that. He opened the magazine to the article. First he glanced at the pictures. A smaller version of the cover picture appeared on the first page of the story. The caption read: "No, he's not the Marlboro man, he's Father Jerry Haloran." Oh, Lord! At the bottom of the page was a picture of him giving the sermon on that Saturday evening. The following page had a picture of the house-shack near where Ricky Alexander lived. The caption for that picture stated: "The house where Father Haloran grew up in Henning, Nebraska." Damnit, Rebecca, that's a lie! On the same page, he was atop the steeple putting up the cross: "The cowboy-priest is a carpenter!"

He hoped the article was better than the stupid captions. He started reading. The article digested his now-infamous sermon criticizing the Church's teachings on birth control, masturbation, homosexuality, abortion, and his plea for more comprehensive sex education. He turned to page fifty-six. More pictures, starting with a picture of the two houses in Aberdeen, one he had bought when he was eighteen and the one behind it that he had built when he was twenty-one. Where could she have learned about that? The center picture was the one from the Aberdeen paper showing him grappling with the woman with the gun. The blood from his wound covered his pant leg. His hands shook as he saw a picture of himself with Melanie Kurtz. He quickly scanned the page to see what Rebecca had said about Melanie and himself. He breathed a sigh of relief as he noticed that she only mentioned that the teen's tragic death had affected him deeply, another tragedy only one week prior to his being shot at the pro-life demonstration. He opened the desk drawer and took out the picture of Melanie. Yes, it's the same one. How did Rebecca get a duplicate? Surely she didn't get it from Angela Kurtz. He then noticed that Melanie's poem was in a sidebar at the bottom of the page. And where did she get this? He wondered. On the same page was a picture of Kathy singing at Mass. The caption read: "The beautiful music coach at St. Patrick's." She was mentioned only in the lively description of the Youth Mass, including the priest's throwing Kenny Gaffin out of the church for being 'disrespectful.' Rebecca described the incident including the hat, the thumping and the 'f ... you' remark.

Turning the page, he saw a picture of Ricky and himself obviously singing. He had forgotten that Rebecca was taking pictures at that time. Ricky's moving poem appeared on the same page. The last page showed pictures of the ultra-modern and large St. Gabriel's church as well as Paris' little church. He read the text near the pictures: "Was Father Haloran transferred to the small parish as punishment for his rather unorthodox sermon? A few people indicated that this was the case but no one would go on record stating it was so. An element of fear seemed to prevail when questions about the internal workings of the administration of the Diocese of Aberdeen were raised. The Bishop of Aberdeen, John Mazurski, refused to be interviewed for this article."

The article concluded: "Father Jerry Haloran wrote on his ordination card: 'No matter what great things a man may do in life, unless he become a loving person, his life is a failure.' In observing him and talking to those who know him well, one cannot help but applaud the wonderful work he has done, and is doing, as a priest. He is, indeed, a noble knight and loving person."

Jerry looked at that last sentence for sometime. He muttered, "Am I a loving person? Rebecca, I'm not so sure you haven't jumped to conclusions." He glanced at his watch and realized he needed to get over to the church for confessions. As he headed out the door he thought that the cover alone would be enough to get him an audience with the Bishop. Some of the tension drained from him as he walked to the church.

Kathy and Dylan were pouring over the *Women Today* article when Father Jerry arrived at Marge's house. They both looked up and grinned. Dylan said, "Hey man, you're a celebrity. Good article, huh?"

He doesn't look too pleased, Kathy thought.

"I don't know—haven't decided yet," Jerry answered non-committedly.

Marge entered from the kitchen. "So, you've read

it. I think Rebecca has captured your story pretty well." She smiled. "Maybe she portrays you a little too saintly but other than that... What do you think?"

"Like I said, I don't know yet." His tone was rather accusatory as he said, "Marge, Rebecca asked you to take those pictures of me on the horse, didn't she?"

She smiled, "Yes. Pretty good for an amateur, don't you think?"

Kathy chimed in, "Marge, they're marvelous! Did you know you were taking a cover photo?"

Marge continued to look at Jerry questioningly and answered, "No, and I don't think Rebecca did, either. Jerry, give us an honest opinion about the article."

"It worries me a bit."

Kathy thought he looked more like he was about to have a panic attack.

"I'm sure I'll get a call from the Bishop on Monday—as soon as that rag hits the stands."

"Rag, *rag*?" Kathy feigned outrage. "I'm going to tell Rebecca on you. So what more can the Bishop do to you? He's already sent you to the dinkiest parish in the diocese."

"I don't know. We'll see."

Marge took Jerry's hand and pulled him toward the kitchen. "Come on, children, we have to eat fast, our Noble Knight here has to get back for the Youth Mass."

Kathy stood. "Yes, mother. Don't forget, Dylan and I have to be there too."

Marge sat at the head of the table, Jerry on her left and Kathy and Dylan on her right. Kathy wanted to scream at Dylan when he put his hand on her leg but was sure that would only make things worse. She glanced at Jerry to see if he noticed and then began eating awkwardly with her left hand. Kathy felt like a teenager as she smiled and giggled at the young man's inane comments about religion, music, and nearly everything. She wanted to shout, "Don't be such a jerk and quit making me look like an idiot!"

Jerry ate only a little and then excused himself, saying, "I still have some work to do to get ready for Mass. Thanks, Marge, for the dinner." He acted as if she and Dylan weren't even there.

He's mad at me, I'm sure, Kathy assumed.

Dylan said, "See you at Mass, man." Kathy smiled.

Following Jerry to the car, Marge asked, "Are you upset about the article? More particularly, are you upset that I took the picture?"

Jerry backed up and leaned against the car. "No, Marge, I'm not upset that you took the picture, more upset that they put it on the cover. And I'm upset with myself that I let Rebecca stay around and get information for it. When did you get your copy of the magazine?"

"Thursday, I think. I thought of calling you but thought that you would talk about it when you were ready. When did you get yours?"

"Don't know. I opened three days' mail this afternoon—the first time I've seen it."

"I talked to Rebecca yesterday. She asked me how you took it. I had to tell her I didn't know. Are you going to call her?"

"I don't know. I'll have to think about it."

Marge put her arms around him and gave him a hug. "Jerry, I hope you won't worry about it too much. I do think it is a good article, gives voice to your message, a message the world needs. Call Rebecca. She doesn't want to hurt you."

Between his thoughts about the article and Kathy's disappointing behavior with the Dylan character, Jerry had a difficult time concentrating on what he was doing at Mass. He was rather infuriated when Dylan, after sitting through the Mass with a smirk on his face, had the audacity to receive Communion. After Mass, Kathy and Dylan drove out to Marge's. Marge could not find anyone to stay with her father, so she had stayed home. Dylan would drive Kathy's car back to the rectory "later." Jerry wondered if he was supposed to wait up for the little creep?

After taking off his cassock, Jerry searched for the card Rebecca had left him. He didn't know what he would say to her if she answered the phone. She probably wouldn't answer on a Saturday evening. He punched in her number. The phone rang four times and the answering machine intoned her delightful voice, "This is Rebecca, please leave..." The message was interrupted by her live voice. "Sorry about that, I was in the other room. Who is this?"

"Hello Rebecca, this is--"

"Jerry, it's so good to hear from you!" She sounded genuinely glad. "I was hoping you'd call. How did you like the article?"

"Ah, the cover."

"Isn't that a great picture? Marge took some great shots, don't you think?"

There's only one, Jerry thought. What is she talking about? "Why did you put the picture on the cover?" He sounded angrier than he intended.

"It wasn't my idea. It was the editor's, but I think it's a great break from the usual cleavage-revealing bimbos. So, did you like the article?"

"Not really. Rebecca, where did you get the picture of Melanie Kurtz and me? Oh, and of course you know that the caption under the little old house is a lie." He just couldn't get the anger out of his voice.

Rebecca lost her initial cheerfulness. "A good reporter never reveals her sources and on the second point, my caption read: 'A house similar to...' The editor changed it because she said it made it more dramatic, and who would know the difference, except a few people in that dinky little town. By the way, Marge herself didn't recognize it and she's lived there all her life."

Jerry didn't know what to say, so he remained silent. "Jerry, why are you so angry? I honestly thought the article was very positive and reflected you and your message quite well. So please tell me."

How could he tell her that he was in a near panic about facing the Bishop over it? "I, uh, just think it is, oh, a bit too much exposure." The anger had been replaced by an overwhelming feeling of weariness.

"Don't you want the world to hear your message?"

Again he remained silent.

"Jerry, what the hell is wrong with you? Let me guess, you're worried about what that Bishop of yours will think when the magazine goes on sale on

Monday, aren't you?" Now Rebecca was the one with the anger.

He hated to admit it but finally uttered a weak "Yes."

"Well, you tell that old goat that five people who call themselves 'fallenaway' Catholics have already read it and said if they could find a priest like you around here, they'd go back to church in a minute. So there!"

He smiled a little as he could picture her sticking out her tongue when she said "so there." "I don't think that would help with this Bishop."

"Well, I think it is a good article and I pictured you as a courageous man. That, I'm now thinking, was a lie! You gave a wonderful sermon and are doing great work in that little backwater town. You are afraid of what some stuffed shirt thinks about an honest article about you and your message? Jerry Haloran, I think you're a coward!" With that, she hung up the phone.

He sat staring at the telephone and muttered aloud, "You're right, Rebecca, but you really don't understand." He was startled as the phone rang. He reluctantly picked it up and said a weary "Hello. "

Rebecca, still sounding angry, said, "I talked to Alice Peterson yesterday. I sent her an advance copy like I did you and Marge. She thought the article would stir up a hornet's nest, as she put it, but that it was a wonderful piece and that the nest needed to be stirred. I respect her opinion more than yours." Again she hung up.

All day Sunday, he felt like a huge axe was hanging over his head. He had his usual Sunday dinner with the

Rev. Bill Johnson and his wife but didn't discuss the article; he'd wait to see what their reaction would be. Maybe they wouldn't even buy a copy.

When he returned to the rectory, he fed Plato and tried to get lost in a mystery novel but kept thinking alternately of Kathy with her new friend and the damned article.

Around ten, he let Plato out for his evening break. He again sat down and tried to get into the novel. He heard a couple of cars drive by and one seemed to have backfired.

It made enough noise to startle him a little. He looked at his watch: it was ten-twenty. Time for Plato to come back in. He turned on the porch light and opened the front door. He called, "Here Plato. Here Plato, come on boy." Usually the dog responded immediately. He called again and then stepped out onto the porch. He thought he heard some kind of noise over by the church. Because of a coming storm, there was no light from the moon or stars and the porch light didn't reach very far. Although the visibility was low, he saw what he thought was the outline of a pick-up truck.

He hurriedly walked to the kitchen and got a flashlight and went back to the door. He stepped outside just in time to see the pick-up spin its wheels and speed away. Still wondering what had happened to Plato, he headed toward the church with the flashlight moving back and forth in front of him. He had gone only a few steps when he saw the lettering on the side of the church: BEWARE THE ANTI-CHRIST WHO HATES THE UNBORN! HE'S GONNA DIE! The lettering was in red and large enough to take up nearly the entire length of the building. Strangely, Jerry was not nearly as upset by the message, as he was about messing up the newly painted church, and his worry about Plato. Where was the dog?

He frantically beamed the flashlight all around, and finally seeing a movement over near where the pick-up had been, he headed that way. Plato was lying on his side. The dog whimpered as Jerry knelt down near him. He touched his head as he moved the light over his body. Plato was bleeding from a wound on the upper right, back leg. "Oh my God, Plato. They hurt you!" Tears came to Jerry's eyes as he examined the leg more closely. The dog had been shot! He quickly pulled a handkerchief out of his pocket and wrapped it tightly around the leg—over the wound, just as had been done for him at the abortion protest.

Jerry stood up and said, "I'll be right back, ol' boy. I'll get the car." Plato whimpered as if he understood. Although Paris did not have a medical doctor, it did have a veterinarian (Animals outnumbered people about a hundred to one in Paris county.)

Jerry grabbed an old plastic tarp from the trunk and placed it over the back seat, and then backed the car up to near where Plato lay. He figured the less he moved him the better it would be. Plato weighed about seventy pounds and it was quite a struggle getting him into the car. Just as he was about to pull out of the yard, he thought he better call the vet.

Again he addressed the dog, "I'll be right back, big fella."

As the mild-mannered man examined Plato, Jerry continued to stroke the dog's head and unabashedly let the tears fall. As he had done so many times in the past six months, he realized how easily he cried since Melanie's death.

The vet straightened up, after cleansing and bandaging the wound, and said, "Well, Father, he's lost a lot of blood, but his heart is good. He's gonna make it. I'll need to keep him overnight and then, if you like, you can take him home. He'll have to stay in the house for a couple of weeks." Bud looked at Jerry and smiled. "He means a lot to you doesn't he?"

"Yes he does. He's been my lifesaver."

The vet looked puzzled but Jerry didn't try to explain. Plato was asleep from an anesthetic, but Jerry patted him on the head and said, "See you in the morning, ol buddy." He was very relieved that Plato was going to make it. He wasn't sure what he would do if the dog had died. It would be like losing a child. He wondered if he would be able to tell anyone how much Plato meant to him and wondered, too, if anyone would understand if he tried.

* * *

On Tuesday morning, Jerry sat down on one of two stiff-backed chairs in the outer room of Bishop John Mazurski's office. The summons from the Bishop came on Monday afternoon. Father Tom Preston, the vice-chancellor, was the messenger. "Father Haloran, the Bishop has received numerous calls today on the scandalous article about you that appeared in some women's magazine. His Excellency wants to see you tomorrow morning at eleven." Wanting to rub Preston the wrong way, Jerry had asked if the Bishop would be coming to Paris to meet with him. Preston officiously answered as if he was serious, "In the Bishop's office at eleven."

He was more relaxed about this visit than he had been earlier, immediately after his now infamous sermon. Plato's near-death, changed something for him, like whatever the Bishop's reaction would be toward the magazine article, it wasn't nearly as serious as Plato's life—or, or course, anyone else's.

When he took Communion to Alice Peterson on Tuesday morning, he told her that he had been called into the Bishop's office. She had taken his hand and said, "It's about that article, isn't it?" He nodded and she went on, "Now, Father Jerry, don't you apologize for that article nor criticize Rebecca. It is a good article and you should be proud of yourself! I am proud of you." For a moment there, he felt tears well up in him. He always wanted his own mother to use those words.

Bishop Mazurski, short, nearly bald, and overweight, appeared in the doorway and said solemnly, "Come in, Father Haloran."

Jerry was sure that it was going to be a repeat of their meeting in June. He sat down on the chair in front of Mazurski's oversized desk. He loosened his shoulders and relaxed his mind by smiling inwardly as he wondered if the Bishop's penis was truly shriveled up.

Mazurski's hands shook as he picked up *Women Today*. "Now tell me, Father Haloran, what do you have to say about this?"

"It tells me, Bishop, that we still have freedom

of the press in this country." Much as he disliked the publicity, he wasn't going to give an inch to this pompous ass.

"It was our agreement, was it not, that you would not talk to any member of the press or the media?" Mazurski sounded like he was about to explode.

"If you read the article, Bishop, you would notice that there is not a single quote from me."

The Bishop thumbed through the magazine. Jerry would bet that he hadn't read it, just heard rumblings from his conservative cronies. "Well, the writer does have a great deal of information about you. Did she visit Paris, Father Haloran?"

"Yes she did." Jerry again stifled a smile and added, "When she refused to leave I thought of having her arrested ... but I couldn't think of any grounds to do so."

The chubby little man looked at him as if he were serious. "And what were her sources for all this, this, uh, garbage?"

Feeling more than a little angry, Jerry wanted to ask, "So, the story of my life and my work is garbage?" Rather than fan the flames, he simply said, "Bishop, I wasn't too pleased with the article. I called Ms. Brady and asked her about her sources. She gave the stock answer that a reporter does not reveal her sources."

"Well, I will have to take your word on this. It does go against the spirit of our agreement, wouldn't you say?"

"No, I wouldn't say that, since I gave no interview nor made any speeches."

"Well, hmmmph. Father Haloran, another matter

has come to my attention and it is this: I understand that you are giving Communion to non-Catholics at some kind of rock-concert Mass you are having out there. Is that true?"

Jerry would have liked to tell him that he truly believed that Communion should be a sign of love and unity among all people, but the Bishop would not agree and that would lead to even more conflict. The priest decided to hedge. "Bishop, since I have been in Paris, over thirty people who had ceased attending Mass for years, have returned. Should I give them the third degree to make sure that they were practicing Catholics at one time?" He was telling the truth as far as it went, but knew that many more who were not Catholic did receive Communion.

"Well, be vigilant on this matter. You know the Church's teachings on this subject. I would like to return to the article. I want you to explain to your people at St. Patrick's that you no longer hold the views given in that sermon that was quoted in that article."

"That would be a lie, Bishop. I do still hold those views. I will not give such a sermon."

Bishop Mazurski turned almost purple. "And I suppose that if I insist that you do or be suspended from the priesthood, you, again, will threaten to hold a press conference and announce to the world what has happened."

"Yes, Bishop, I would do that. I believe I am a very dedicated priest who is doing the work of Jesus Christ and I will do all in my power to continue to do so."

"You may be dedicated, but I'm not sure to what. Father Haloran, you are a *free thinker!*"

He was so loud, Jerry was sure the secretary could hear him. "Thank you, Bishop."

"Thank me, for what?"

Jerry got up from his chair. "For calling me a 'free thinker.' I think that is why God gave me a mind. Good day, Bishop."

CHAPTER 10

Happy the man who discovers wisdom, the man who gains discernment.

Proverbs 3:13

On Sunday evening as Jerry sat at the dinner table in the home of Rev. Bill and Gail Johnson, he thought about how different his life would be if he had a wife and two young children to share it with. He stared at Gail but averted his eyes as soon as he realized he was staring. He sometimes wondered if he looked forward to Sunday evenings so he could gaze at the beautiful minister's wife rather than engage in the stimulating conversations he had with her husband. The priest hoped his look was not lustful, even if, he was ashamed to admit, it was.

After dinner, Jerry dried the dishes after Bill washed them while Gail took care of the kids. They spent an hour and a half in Bill's tiny 'den' working on plans for the teen center. Jerry found himself dreading going back to the empty rectory when they were finished. Gail didn't help much when, just before he left, she asked, "Isn't it lonely going home to an empty house?"

He mumbled, "Yeah, sometimes." That definitely was an understatement. He thought of Kathy, Marge, and even Rebecca and mentally chided himself for it. As he drove back to the rectory, he felt lonelier than he had felt in weeks. It had been a hellish few days.

Rebecca had sent a hundred copies of the magazine with his picture on the cover to Sy Peterson, and the storekeeper had beamed when he told Jerry that it had sold out in three days. "Never made so much off a magazine before. Father Jerry, you've put ol' Paris on the map."

From what he could tell, the article was generally well received by most of the townspeople. Two of the ministers called and told him he was a disgrace to the "cloth." A few old people had refused to greet him at the post office, but more were like Sy, congratulating him for making the news. He guessed most people had accepted his history months ago and so the magazine article wasn't such a surprise.

Marge was visiting Alice Peterson when he returned from his meeting with the Bishop. He told them about the meeting, including his threat to hold a press conference. He smiled to himself as he thought of Marge clapping and Alice attempting to join her with her frail little hands and arms when he told them he thanked the Bishop for calling him a 'free thinker.'

Jerry slammed the car door and locked it, a habit he had begun only after last Sunday's vandalism. He had painted over the graffiti that night before sunrise. He glanced over at the church and was relieved to see that there were no new words painted on its side.

He had begun keeping Plato in the house while he was away. The vet had said, "He'll be a bit lame for a few weeks, so he should take it easy." The poor dog needed to be protected from whomever had shot him and he needed time to heal. As Jerry opened the rectory door, Plato greeted him at the door with his tail wagging so rapidly he nearly fell over. Jerry knelt and held the dog's head in both hands, "You're a great guy, Plato. Who would want to hurt a fellow like you?" Since the first week in Paris, he had been talking to the dog as if he understood every word he said. He headed for the bathroom. "Well, Plato, it's been a week since those jerks came by. Think they'll try again?" He patted him lightly on the head.

As he was washing his hands, he glanced in the mirror at his long-sleeved, button-down shirt with vertical green and medium blue stripes. His trousers matched the blue in the shirt. He smiled as he thought of Rebecca's note in the package, "Just thought you needed another shirt, and pants to go with it. My donation to Holy Mother Church. Blue looks good on you. Love, Rebecca." He frowned at himself as he thought of the many times Rebecca entered his mind since her visit. When Bill Johnson saw his blue pants, he called out to his wife, "Hey Gail, look at this, blue pants! Maybe we'll make a normal human being out of him yet."

Jerry went into the little office, sat down at the desk, and picked up his Breviary to pray Vespers and Compline, the last 'offices' of the day. The first few years of his priesthood, he had 'read' the Divine Office religiously, as a moral obligation. He had angrily dropped the practice when he read that he could be 'excused' from the Divine Office if he sent a certain minimum donation to some Catholic mission society. Since his arrival in Paris, he had gone back to it, not out of a sense of duty but as a spiritual exercise. He found it helpful in a way he had not before. Before he opened the prayer book, he saw the letter Rebecca had sent with the shirt and pants. He was surprised, he rarely, if ever, left a personal letter open on his desk. He started to put it in a drawer and decided to read it again.

Dear Jerry:

I hope you like the shirt and pants, a token of appreciation for your kindness during my stay in Paris. I really enjoyed my brief visit there, especially my time with Marge and Alice, and with YOU, of course. At least once a day, I'm sitting at that picnic table near the lake and horses and talking to you.

It is near midnight and I thought of calling, but knowing that you get up with the chickens out there on the prairie. I thought that I would write. I like to receive letters—hope you do, too. I can't re-read a phone call.

I'm really getting to enjoy Denise and Rene, my mentees, you know. I gave them a tour of the office and then took them home for dinner. They were properly impressed. I think I'm planting a seed for them to think about college.

I had dinner tonight with a wonderful man I met. He is an attorney, but   one with a conscience! He works for the American Civil Liberties Union and is on a mission for human rights and social justice. He talks like you! I think you'd like him. We talked till midnight. It would be wonderful to speak with you again.

Love, Rebecca

He wondered if he would have talked to her differently if he had read the cheery letter before he called her about the article? No wonder she was ticked off at him. He frowned as he, again, felt a bit jealous of the ACLU attorney. He mumbled to himself, "That's pretty stupid, Haloran."

He put the letter in a drawer and picked up the Breviary. The first Psalm was Psalm 69 and began:

Save me, God! The water is already up to my
　　neck!
I am sinking in the deepest swamp, there is no
　　foothold;
I have stepped into deep water and the waves
　　are washing over me.

He put the book down and leaned back in the desk chair. He thought about what the Psalmist was experiencing when he wrote his poem. What did the water symbolize to him? And what was the swamp? He mumbled to himself, "I am up to my neck in confusion and loneliness. Is it a swamp?" He shook his head as if to clear it and began reading again. When he was finished, he watched the ten o'clock news and went to bed.

He awoke with Plato growling. Jerry glanced at the digital clock, 3:30 a.m. "Oh hell, not the graffiti artists again," he said. He jumped out of bed, put on his pants and shoes and headed for the door without turning on the light. He put on his windbreaker and picked up the flashlight. Someone rang the doorbell. The vandals wouldn't ring the bell, surely. Most of the farm workers didn't have phones. Maybe someone was very ill out at the dairy or egg ranch. He turned on the porch light and looked through the miniblinds. It was a disheveled little woman all bundled up like a babushka. He opened the door.

Recognizing Angela Kurtz and seeing her bruised face, Jerry quickly opened the storm door. "My Lord, Angela! Come in, come in." Angela limped into the room. Jerry offered to take her coat but she sadly shook her head. He gently took her arm and directed her to the couch. Angela winced as she gingerly sat down.

Jerry pulled up a chair in front of her and Plato sat down beside him. "Angela, tell me what happened? May I get you anything?"

The poor woman began to cry as she looked at the floor. "Oh, Father, I'm so sorry to disturb you in the middle of the night." She looked up at him and he could see her face clearly for the first time. One eye was swollen nearly shut and her forehead and cheeks were purple and red. Her expression seemed to beseech him to understand. "I, uh, oh, just didn't know what to do or where to go. And, I, uh, thought of how kind you were to my Melanie and I came to you. I'm sorry."

He winced when Angela mentioned his so-called kindness to Melanie. She was too preoccupied to notice. He reached out and touched her hand. "Please don't apologize, Angela. I'm glad you came." He knew she needed some kind of medical attention but there was no doctor in Paris. He wondered how she managed to drive the hundred and more miles from Aberdeen. He wished he knew more about first aid. "Let me get you a cold cloth for your eye." He stood and said, "I'll be right back."

He gave her the cold cloth and a glass of water. Haltingly and with many tears, Angela told him what had happened. She had gone to bed at ten and soon after heard her daughter, Julie, scream. She ran to Julie's room and found Ralph attempting to rape her. Angela screamed and headed for the telephone to call the police. Ralph intercepted her and knocked her to the floor where he kicked her face, ribs, and hips. Julie had tried to stop him but he hit the girl so hard she passed out. He told Angela that if either of them reported him to the police, he would kill them. She ended by saying, "Father, I, we, couldn't stay."

The same rage he had felt when Melanie was killed boiled inside him, but he said softly, "Where is Julie now?"

"She was asleep in the car when I drove up."

"I'll go out and check on her." Jerry put his coat back on and picked up the flashlight. Before he opened the door, he turned back to the battered woman huddled on the couch. "Angela, I'm glad you got out. We'll find some real help for you." She looked up and attempted a weak smile.

He kept the flashlight low as he approached the car. As quietly as possible, he opened the door where Julie, slumped in the seat, was sleeping. She jumped when the cool air hit her. She quickly put her hands over her face and crawled to the other side of the car. "Don't hit me."

Julie, too, had bruises on her face. Jerry whispered, "Julie, it's Father Jerry. You're safe now."

She slowly opened her eyes. Jerry moved the flashlight so she could distinguish his face. She moved a little closer. "Father Jerry? How did we get here? Where is my Mom?"

"She's in the house. She drove here. Why don't we go in and get out of the cold? Okay?" Julie got stiffly out of the car. She was able to walk, but Jerry held her arm as they made their way into the house.

After Jerry fixed hot cocoa for them, they talked about what they could do. They ruled out calling the police in Aberdeen because Ralph would make bail. Both Julie and Angela were convinced he would kill them if he could find them. Jerry learned that Ralph had switched to the midnight to eight a.m. shift at the warehouse. He had gone to work with another fellow after the attack. Immediately after he had left, they had begun packing clothes and whatever else they thought the car would hold and headed for Paris. Both of them had severe headaches. Jerry wondered if they had concussions.

"Angela, do you have any relatives who could help you?"

"My parents live in Lawrence, you met them at Melanie's funeral. Father, I can't involve them. I'm sure Lawrence will be the first place Ralph will look. There's no one else. Ralph wouldn't let me visit them. At the funeral, that was the first time I'd seen them in years. Neither one of them are well."

Jerry wanted to shout, "Angela, this is the twentieth century; women don't need to get permission from their husbands to visit their own relatives!" He realized he would have to notify Angela's parents and encourage them to get a restraining order against Ralph. He began thinking of people who could help. A seminary classmate of his was Director of Catholic Charities in Denver. That would be far enough away. Jerry ruled him out as too much of stickler for rules, he'd want to go through legal channels, even if Julie and Angela's lives were at stake. He might find someone in the parish that would help but then Ralph might think of him, just as Angela did. After mentally going over everyone he could think of, he remembered that Rebecca had mentioned a friend who was a social worker in St. Louis. He glanced at his watch, four a.m. He turned to Angela as she stared at the floor. "Angela, would you be willing to go to St. Louis if I could find a place for you there?"

She looked at him sadly. "Father, I don't have any money."

"If I can find a way, would St. Louis be alright? How about you, Julie?"

Julie was leaning back on the sofa with a washcloth over her forehead and eyes. She mumbled, "I don't care."

Jerry went into the office and quietly closed the door and dialed Rebecca. The phone rang three times and then her answering machine came on. "You have reached..." Rebecca's voice came on over the recorded message. "Just a damn minute while I turn this damn thing off." After a few knocks and screeches, Rebecca was back on, "This better be good, it's four a.m.!"

"Rebecca, this is Jerry Haloran."

"So you're going to start harassing me at night, is that it?"

"No. I need some help. Sorry for waking you. It's important."

"It better be important. The chickens aren't up yet are they?"

"This one is. I've got someone here who needs help." He told her the basic story and then asked, "Could your social worker friend help? I can't remember her name."

"It's Helene. She probably can, she's pretty well-connected around here. I'll call her and call you right back. How will they get here, if Helene can find a place?"

"I thought I would drive them over."

"Are they able to make such a long car trip?"

"I don't know, but I don't know how else I can get them there. Do you know what to do for bruises, black eyes, and possible concussions?"

"God, they've been hurt bad, huh? No, but, of course, you have someone there who does. Remember, Marge was a nurse before she went for her doctorate in chemistry."

"To tell you the truth, I'd forgotten that. I'll call her and take them over to her place. Call me there." He woke Marge up and when she heard a bit of the story, said, "Jerry, get them over here now! I'll see what I can do."

Jerry bundled Angela and Julie into his car and headed for the farm. While Marge was ministering to their wounds, Rebecca called to let him know that Helene was sure she could get them into a safe place in St. Louis. She knew of three shelters that were for women and children in their situation. Rebecca asked him to stop by her place first and she'd give them directions or let them stay overnight if they had to wait until Tuesday. She'd take off work by noon to make sure she would be there to meet them. She gave him directions to her house. After he got off the phone Marge took him into the kitchen and informed him that both Julie and Angela looked like they might have broken ribs and possibly concussions, and that they should see a doctor as soon as possible.

"Marge, time is a real problem. Here's what I'm thinking: Ralph Kurtz, the perpetrator, will start looking for them as early as eight-thirty this morning. I thought I would load up their stuff in my car and have Angela follow me to Aberdeen in hers. We would park her car in the long-term parking at the airport and then head for St. Louis. Could they make it that far and that many hours okay?"

"I'm not sure. If Julie could stay lying down, I think she'd be okay. You'd have to wake her every two hours to make sure. Angela's right eye is so swollen, she can hardly see. And with at least a severe headache and those broken ribs, I don't know how she drove to Paris. She couldn't drive back." Marge stopped and then said, "I've got an idea. I have a cousin near here who has two boys, twenty and seventeen. I'll bet I can get them to drive Angela's car to the Aberdeen airport tomorrow. One can follow to bring the other back. How would that be?"

Within half an hour Jerry, with his car packed nearly to the ceiling, Angela riding shotgun and Julie lying on top of all the luggage, led a procession through, and out of, Paris. Not a soul saw the parade. Dale, one of Marge's two cousins followed in Angela's car and Daryl, the second cousin, followed him in the pickup. Jerry glanced at his watch, it was five-thirty. He was sure they would make the airport by eight. Dale and Daryl were very shy and even seemed sullen. They drove a light colored pick-up. He shook his head at the thought that they could be the graffiti painters, but Plato hadn't growled at them, so he dismissed the thought. Jerry led the boys to the airport and to the long-term parking lot. He gave each of them twenty dollars for gas and for their trouble, thanked them, and asked them to keep their mission "in the family." They wouldn't, of course, this would be a big event in their lives. All Paris would know by the time he got back, so he told the boys he was putting the woman and girl on a plane, but he didn't say to where. They had made it by seven forty five. He waited a few minutes until he was sure the boys were out of the parking area.

Julie woke up and said she was hungry. Jerry was, too. "How about you, Angela, ready for breakfast?" He tried to sound cheerful.

"I guess I should eat something."

He didn't want Julie and Angela to be seen, nor did he want to explain what he was doing riding around with a car packed to the gills and a woman and teenager in the car with him. He headed for a McDonalds' drive-through.

Julie slept easily and Jerry was often sleepy himself

and had to work to stay awake. Once, the powerful blast of an air-horn startled him and, glancing at the dash, he noticed he was going only forty-five miles an hour. The horn startled Angela and Julie. Julie put her head back down but Angela stayed awake as they drove through Kansas City.

The traffic was lighter east of the city and they made good time for over an hour. He began to worry about Julie and was relieved when he heard, "Father Jerry, I'm hungry. I need to go to the bathroom, too."

Jerry glanced at the rearview mirror and saw Julie's bruised face and pained expression. "A sign just said, 'Odessa, three miles,' we'll stop there." Odessa had a Burger King. As they entered, Jerry wondered what kind of picture the three made, a tired but obviously unhurt man with a teen-age girl with a black eye, and a battered, limping woman with a bruised face. Several people looked their way, probably thinking he had beaten his wife and daughter and now was making up for it by taking them out to Burger King. He winced and a cold chill ran down his spine as he thought of Ralph Kurtz.

When he picked up their food and sat down at the table, Julie asked, "Father Jerry, you okay?"

He tried to smile. "Sure I am, sweetheart, why do you ask?" He was glad that she felt well enough to think of him.

Julie gave him a weak smile. "Oh, you just seemed kinda sad."

He leaned across the table and whispered, "I thought some people here..." Jerry looked around, "probably think I beat you and your mom up and now I'm taking you out to eat."

Julie looked startled. "You wouldn't do that! You know what Ralph did once?" She didn't wait for his reply. "He knocked Melanie around and then said he would take us all out to dinner. Melanie wouldn't go and he beat her some more."

Angela, looking very fearful, whispered, "Julie, people will hear you!"

"He did! I hate him! I don't care who knows!" She had lowered her voice, however. Leaning toward Jerry, she asked, "Father Jerry, have you ever beaten anyone up?"

Jerry hesitated a moment. "Sort of. I knocked your stepfather's head against the bricks in front of your house the day Melanie was killed."

Julie's eyes widened in disbelief, then she smiled. "You did? ... I'm glad you did! I wish you woulda killed him."

"Now, Julie, please don't talk like that. It's a sin to think that way." Angela shook her head.

"I can understand her feelings, Angela, and I think God can, too. That day and last night when you told me what happened to you and Julie, I have to admit I wanted to kill him." Because Angela looked so puzzled, he went on, "I'm quite sure I won't but the thought and feelings were there just as they were when Melanie died. So I can understand Julie, and God is more understanding than I am."

Jerry vividly recalled that day. When Ralph Kurtz heard that Melanie had been run over by a truck and that she was dead, he had muttered, "What a stupid little shit. That ain't even the way to the school." Jerry had jumped up and pulled Ralph up from the chair and demanded that they go outside. He told the chubby man not to talk negatively about Melanie and to support Angela. When Ralph said, "You talk like Melanie was your own, Holy Man. Were you diddling my little girl?" Jerry lifted him up by the collar and bounced his head against the bricks and hissed, "Listen here, you evil little bastard, you go in there and take care of your wife. And you go to the city morgue and identify the body—Angela can't do it."

He shook his head as if to get rid of the thoughts and feelings that went with that awful day.

Only a few minutes after they were back on the road, both Julie and Angela fell asleep. Jerry began to think of how Ralph Kurtz resembled his own father. If he had gotten married in his twenties, instead of becoming a priest, would he have been like his dad and Ralph Kurtz? Maybe. His brother Scott was a lot like them. Jerry glanced over at Angela. She looked, even in sleep, tired and sad, just like his own mother did. His thoughts turned to his own family and why he had chosen to become a priest. Maybe he became a priest in hopes that people would love him. They respected his hard work and encouraging words, maybe even respected him, but love him? Probably not. He was just a role to everyone. Maybe not to Wayne. He wondered if he could share any of this confusion with Kathy or Marge or Rebecca. No, Wayne was the only one who might understand, Jerry concluded.

Julie began to feel better as she was awake as they approached St. Louis. Interstate 70 had turned into an eight-lane expressway and the evening rush-hour traffic was bumper-to-bumper, and fortunately most of it was heading west to the suburbs. Julie kept saying, "Wow!" She had never been to a city larger than Aberdeen. She had slept through Kansas City.

"Well, Julie, you think you could like St. Louis?" He could see only part of her face in the rearview mirror.

"Gosh, I don't know, it's sure big."

Jerry glanced over at Angela. "What about you, Angela?"

She shook her head wearily. "Any place has to be better than Aberdeen."

He found Rebecca's address fairly easily. It was a little after four when he found her number in the midst of a huge condominium complex. He parked in the visitor's parking area nearest Rebecca's number. As he got out of the car, he said, "I'll be right back,"

*   *   *

Rebecca jumped when she heard the doorbell. She was sure it would be Jerry but she looked through the viewer to make sure. He stood there in a black jacket, fidgeting and looking tired. Taking another glance at her appearance, jeans and a St. Louis Cardinals sweatshirt, she unchained the door. "Jerry, it's so good to see you."

"Thanks, Rebecca, it's good to see you too." He made an attempt at a smile.

"Come in, come in, and give me a hug." Rebecca kept her smile and opened her arms to him. She would not let him know that she had spent the last hour nervously cleaning house and putting things in order. She also did not want him to know how uncertain she was about how to be with him, knowing his negative reaction to the article.

Jerry slowly entered and put his arms around her. He held her more tightly than he had in Paris. "Thanks, Rebecca, for helping us out."

"Isn't that what friends are for?" She had to work to make it sound casual. She stepped back before he had a chance to push her away. "Where is the rest of the 'us'?"

"They're still in the car. I wanted to make sure you were home and, uh, that I had the right place. Rebecca, they're tired and afraid."

"I'll try to be nice." He seemed to miss the sarcasm as he silently led her to his dirty Pontiac. Julie was sitting in the driver's seat. "Jerry, you didn't let that little girl drive, did you?"

"Why not? She's a good driver." Now it was Rebecca who missed the sarcasm. When she looked up at him, he was smiling. She punched him lightly on the arm. "She climbed down from her perch in back," he said as he opened the door. "Julie, I'd like you to meet my friend, Rebecca Brady. Rebecca, I'd like you to meet one of the bravest girls in the world." Julie smiled weakly and gave Jerry a 'come off it' look.

Rebecca took Julie's hand. "Hi, Julie. Welcome to St. Louis."

Julie's "thank you" was that of a scared mouse.

Jerry bent over and looked at his other passenger. "And this is Angela, the brave mother who drove over a hundred miles when she could hardly see."

Rebecca, too, bent over and saw a woman whose face was so bruised, she could hardly see out of either eye. "Hi, Angela. Welcome."

Angela said 'thank you' in a voice even weaker than her daughter's.

Jerry went around the car to open the door for Angela as Rebecca held the door for Julie. He asked them which bags they would need for the night. They pointed them out to him while Rebecca led them to her townhouse. She noticed that Angela had a difficult time making it up the steps.

"I'm afraid that the bedrooms are on the second floor. I hope that's okay," Rebecca said apologetically. Angela wore faded brown slacks and an old out-of-style coat. Julie was in jeans and a denim jacket that had seen better days. Both of them looked at the living room as if they were on a strange planet.

Rebecca hoped they would be able to make themselves somewhat comfortable. Jerry arrived with two small suitcases and a plastic bag full of clothes. Rebecca took one of the suitcases and said, "If you'll follow me, I'll show you your room. We'll let Father Jerry sleep on the couch." The four slowly went up the stairs. Jerry set the suitcases down in the guest room and quickly went back downstairs.

Rebecca left the mother and daughter upstairs to take a shower and change clothes. As she descended the stairs, she saw Jerry slouching on the couch with his legs extended out in front of him, his lanky frame seemingly taking up half the room. "Nice place you have here, Rebecca." He looked around, taking in the whole room. Rebecca followed his eyes as he looked over the off-white walls, chairs, and white plastic-and-glass tables.

She could tell by his expression that he really didn't like her taste in furniture. But she was more interested in how Angela and Julie came to be dependent on Jerry for their safety. He had told her only that he had a mother and teenage daughter who needed a place to stay to get away from a vicious and violent husband and father.

"Jerry, how did Angela and Julie come to be in your charge? Do they live in Paris?"

The priest pulled his legs in and sat up straight. He said in a soft voice, "Rebecca, you remember me telling you about Melanie Kurtz?" Rebecca nodded. "Well, Julie is the younger sister you were worried about, and, of course, Angela is her mother."

Rebecca put her hand over her mouth, stifling a scream. She sat down on the other end of the couch and whispered, "Oh, my God. Jerry, did the stepfather rape Julie?"

Jerry whispered, "He tried to, but Angela tried to stop him and he beat her. Julie tried to help and he hit her so hard she was knocked out. I hope that it was his first attempt at the rape. Of course, I haven't asked her yet." Jerry went on to tell her as much as he knew about what had happened.

"I don't know about you, but I need a drink. Want one?"

"Got something strong?"

"Red wine, white wine, brandy and I think I have some scotch." She had bought all four this afternoon.

"Scotch on the rocks sounds good, if you have it."

She headed for the kitchen feeling very sad about her poor guests.

Rebecca gave him his scotch and held up her glass of white wine and, attempting a smile, said, "May all visitors to St. Louis enjoy a new beginning in life!"

Jerry looked puzzled for a moment. "I'll drink to that." They touched their glasses.

Rebecca whispered, "Jerry, Julie and Angela look so awful. They have been through so much."

"Yes they have. Rebecca, Marge said they might have concussions. Marge was worried about them making the trip. You think we should get them to a clinic or emergency room?"

"I don't know. Let's ask them when they come down. I don't think they'd want to have a doctor poke around at them tonight. But then--"

Julie came down the stairs, followed by Angela, who took each step very slowly and carefully. She held on to the rail with both hands. Julie had on clean but wrinkled jeans and Angela wore an old cotton-print dress that drooped below her knees. She had on the same scuffed brown loafers she arrived in. At least this woman had the good sense to run away. Rebecca wondered why she ran to Jerry? Wasn't there anyone else in her life she could turn to? She couldn't be much older than Rebecca herself, but looked decades older.

When Julie reached the bottom of the stairs, she looked at Jerry and smiled. She said to the reporter. "Nice place you have, Rebecca."

"Thank you, Julie."

Angela seemed exhausted when she reached the last step. "I hope we're not causing too much trouble,

Miss Brady."

"Not at all. And please call me 'Rebecca.'" She meant it. "I'm fixing lasagna for dinner, is that okay?" They both thought it was fine. Jerry got up and said, "I'll help out Rebecca. Kitchen's aren't just for women anymore."

"They are in our house." Julie sounded bitter.

As they sat down to dinner, Rebecca announced that the lasagna was made from a recipe from one of Jerry's parishioners, Marge Woerner. This prompted Julie to exclaim about what a great priest Jerry was and how they missed him at St. Gabriel's. "You remember, Father Jerry, how you used to have us all sing that dumb song about the old lady and the fly?"

Jerry looked at the ceiling as if to say, "I don't know anything about that."

"You know, you'd lead us all in it and then the nuns would get mad at all of us." Julie laughed a delightful, little girl, laugh. "Father, sing it for us! Please!"

Jerry hesitated then smiled. "Okay, maybe we all need a little laughter." He began, "I know an old lady who swallowed a fly, I don't know why she swallowed a fly, perhaps, she'll die."

It was a dumb song, but delightful. Rebecca watched Julie as she looked admiringly at Jerry. She wondered if it was Julie's idea to go to Paris when they ran away. Julie joined Jerry in the singing and after three verses Rebecca joined them each time they got to "She swallowed a spider that wiggled and jiggled and tickled inside her. She swallowed the spider to catch the fly, I don't know why she swallowed a fly, perhaps she'll die." Jerry and Julie made all kinds of shaking movements as if the spider had crawled down their shirts. Rebecca laughed as she joined them. Even Angela smiled weakly. They all laughed at the end.

"I can see why the nuns got angry at all of you. Was Father Jerry always upsetting the nuns, Julie?" Rebecca was only partially serious. Julie showed no signs of having a concussion.

"Mostly Sister Mary Agnes. She's an old fussbudget."

Angela spoke for the first time. "Now Julie, you mustn't talk like that."

"Well, she is." Julie turned to Rebecca. "There's one song Father Jerry taught us that Melanie and I really liked. It wasn't dumb. Melanie and I used to sing it all the time."

"Would you sing it for me?" Rebecca asked.

"If Father Jerry will join me. Would you?" Julie gave him a cocker-spaniel pleading look.

"I don't know what song you're thinking of, Julie." Jerry didn't look like he was in much of a mood to sing another song.

"*Who Has Touched the Sky.* You remember, Father, don't you?

Jerry looked a bit shaken when he heard the name of the song. "Yeah, I remember. I didn't know it was yours and Melanie's favorite." He seemed reluctant but said, "Okay."

Julie had a beautiful soprano voice to go with Jerry's baritone. It was indeed a touching song. Rebecca clapped loudly and Angela joined her.

Julie was smiling when she said, "You know, Melanie and I used to argue about the next to last line—

'Knew love by its first name.' I said it was someone who had fallen in love with someone special and Melanie said no, it was someone who just knew how to love, like Father Jerry! What do you think Father?"

Jerry seemed to be embarrassed or puzzled or even hurt by the simple question. Rebecca told herself to ask him about it later. He said, "I really don't know, Julie. Maybe it's both. I'm glad that Melanie thought of me that way."

"Well, Father, do you know love by its first name?" Rebecca asked lightly, hoping to perk him up.

He surprised her by simply saying, rather grumpily, she thought. "I don't know." And obviously wanting to change the subject asked Julie and Angela how they were feeling. They said they were tired and felt a lot of pain here and there but they were sure they could wait until morning to see a doctor. Their heads still hurt but they were convinced they did not have concussions.

Jerry helped Rebecca with the dishes and then asked her if she would like to take a walk. He needed to limber up after the hours in the car. They were still in the kitchen when he whispered, "I'll invite Julie, hope she says no." Rebecca did, too. Not surprisingly, Julie declined. Rebecca showed her how to use the remote control on the television. Rebecca put on a down jacket and Jerry his black windbreaker.

It was quite cold as they walked about a block with their hands in their pockets. Jerry kept looking around at the complex. "This place is huge. I'll bet the whole town of Paris could live here."

Rebecca chuckled. "Probably. There are four hundred units. Not many children though, at least I don't see many." She led them to a cinder running-path that was still inside the complex walls. "I run here most mornings, once around is one and a half miles. I usually do two rounds."

"If you want to run, please do. I'm too tired to do it myself."

"Me, too. Want to walk all the way around?"

"Sure. So, how're things going with your ACLU fellow?"

She looked up at him and smiled. "Why do you want to know? You jealous?" It would be nice if he was, she thought.

"No, just wondering." He sounded nervous and maybe a bit defensive.

"Are you still angry about the article?"

"No, I've gotten over that. I'm sorry I was so grumpy on the phone when I called. It's been a hell of a week."

"In what way?"

"As expected, I was called into the Bishop's office. He ordered me to give a sermon retracting everything I had said in my sermon in June and which was repeated in your magazine. I refused and had to threaten to call a news conference again to keep from being thrown out of the priesthood." He chuckled.

"What's so funny? It sounds kind of serious to me."

"The Bishop called me a 'free thinker' and turned purple when I thanked him for it." He chuckled again.

"I take it that he meant it as an insult or condemnation."

"The latter. That was the lesser of evils for the week.

Plato was shot the day before your article appeared."

Rebecca stopped in her tracks and put her hand over her mouth "Oh, no, is he, is, is he, uh, dead?"

Jerry looked down at her and said, "No. He was shot in the back right leg and it didn't break the bone. He's limping around a bit, but he's okay." He hesitated a moment and then added, "They... Rebecca, you won't put this in the magazine will you?"

It must be important for him to ask that, she thought. "Whatever it is, I'll promise not to, okay?"

"They painted big letters on the side of the church saying: 'Beware the Anti-Christ who hates unborn babies. He's gonna die.'"

"My God, Jerry, that's awful! What did you do?"

"I called Joe Gaffin, the sheriff, in case there had been other incidents or would be more. We took pictures and I painted over it. We decided not to tell anyone so that whoever it was wouldn't get any publicity from it."

"Are you worried? I would be."

"A little. I keep the door locked more often now and keep Plato in the house."

Rebecca reached out and took his hand. "Jerry, I'm sorry to hear about Plato, and the threat, of course."

He continued to hold her hand and responded, "Some kind of nut was sure to throw a kind of fit sometime. I'm surprised it didn't happen sooner."

She wanted to continue holding his hand, but he let go and as they resumed their walk. Rebecca told him about St. Clair's home, a shelter for women and children in danger. When they returned to the condo, both Julie and Angela were nearly asleep on the couch.

Rebecca gave Jerry a sheet; pillow, and blanket for the couch and the three women went upstairs. Rebecca really wanted to give Jerry a kiss but only waved as she followed the two up the stairs.

CHAPTER 11

*You are a refuge for the poor, a refuge for the needy
in distress, a shelter from the storm, a shade from the
heat...*

Isaiah, 25:3-4

Jerry was standing in a room next to a church
sacristy. There was a bed in the room and a dark-haired,
naked woman was lying on it. He didn't know the
woman. She was quite beautiful and he was aroused.
He started to take his jeans off and then remembered
that he was supposed to concelebrate a Mass with the
Bishop in a few minutes. The woman spread her legs
and began to stroke her pelvic area. He didn't have
any black pants and he was sure the Bishop would be
angry if he went out on the altar with jeans beneath
his vestments. Maybe he could find a chasuble long
enough to cover the jeans, he thought. The woman
said something to him. He took off the jeans and then
his shorts. He climbed onto the bed. There was a loud,
impatient knock on the door. "Father Haloran, are you
in there? Are you ready for the Mass?" The "Father
Haloran" was repeated again and again and a woman
began to say "Jerry" and again, "Jerry." The female
voice was pleasant but wasn't the voice of the woman
on the bed. He was sweating; he didn't know what to
do. He heard "Jerry" again and felt a woman touch
his hand. Her hand was soft and sensual. He was

mumbling something. What was he trying to say?

He opened his eyes. Rebecca was kneeling beside the sofa, holding his hand. She was wearing a rose-colored robe. He was sure he looked lost as he ran his free hand across his forehead. He looked at his hand. It was wet with sweat. Rebecca smiled. The blankets were bunched around his middle. Thank God. He raised himself up on one elbow and shook his head.

"Bad dream?"

"Yeah, pretty bad."

Rebecca put a finger to her lips, made the "shh" sound and pointed at the top of stairs.

Jerry lowered his voice. "Good morning."

"You were sweating up a storm and shaking your head and mumbling, 'No, I can't. No, I can't.' I was afraid you would wake up the girls. Do you remember what you couldn't do?"

"Yes, er, maybe." He felt shaky. Was it fear? Shame? He wasn't sure. He'd have to wait to see if he could talk about it. He sniffed. "Do I smell coffee?"

"Yes, I'll get you some." Rebecca got up and headed for the kitchen.

He quickly got off the sofa and pulled on his jeans and shirt. He nearly knocked the cups out of Rebecca's hands when he got to the door. "Oops, sorry. Let's sit in the kitchen, okay?"

The table was round with a clear glass top and white legs. Rebecca sat down and scooted a chair out with her foot. Jerry sat down and put the cup to his lips. The coffee was very hot. He sipped it, watching Rebecca over the rim, attempting to distract himself from looking at her legs under the table. The robe was open enough that one leg was visible a few inches above the knee.

Her deep brown eyes looked at him expectantly. "Well, about the dream? What can't you do?"

Jerry fiddled with the cup. "It's a bit embarrassing."

"For you or me?"

"Probably me. Promise you won't laugh."

Before he was finished describing the dream, Rebecca had her hand over her mouth, attempting to stifle her laughter. When he finished, she did laugh. She was trying not to make too much noise.

"So, what's so funny? You promised not to laugh."

"I—I—I couldn't help it." She continued to smile, chuckle, and stifle more laughter. "It's hilarious."

Jerry could feel a surprisingly intense anger arise in him. "What's so hilarious about it?"

Rebecca finally got back in control of herself. Her eyes sparkled and she was grinning ear to ear. "What couldn't you do? Climb in bed with the woman? Or celebrate Mass?"

"It's just a dream, damnit." He knew better, but didn't want to say so.

"Oh, no, it isn't! I think it's very serious, seriously symbolic. And it must have been very emotional. You sounded like you were in pain when you said, 'No, I can't!'"

"So it probably means that I'm afraid of sex or that if I have sex with someone, I can't celebrate Mass. So what's so funny about that?"

"Put that way, it isn't funny. In fact, I find it terrible

that your out-of-date church puts you in such a bind. But when you were telling it, I could picture you in the church, not knowing whether or not to take off your pants." She chuckled and picked up her coffee. Her eyes were smiling in a knowing sort of way as she peered over the cup at him. After a lengthy silence, she put down the cup. "Want to take a jog this morning?"

He did. He thought it might help him get over the dream and stupid anger.

*   *   *

Jerry looked at the handwritten map Rebecca had given him. Julie climbed into the back of the car and Angela gingerly got into the front. He pulled his dusty Pontiac onto the street. "Well, how did you two sleep?"

Angela did not look at him but said, "Alright, I guess."

Julie was in a more up-beat mood. "Super. I really like Rebecca. Father Jerry, is she your girlfriend?"

"Now, Julie, you know better than that. Priest's don't have girlfriends." Angela looked genuinely shocked.

"Well, she looks at him like he was her boyfriend. Doesn't she, Father Jerry?" Julie responded.

"I don't know. She's a friend and she's a girl. Does that make her my girlfriend?"

"You know what I mean! You want to marry her?"

"Julie, now you just quit pestering Father like this. You know priests can't marry."

"Yeah, and I think it's dumb."

Jerry chuckled.

St. Clair's Home was a large, white, turn-of-the century house in a working-class neighborhood. There was no sign or any other indication that it was anything other than a family dwelling. Jerry pulled into the driveway and noticed it led to the back of the house. There was parking for eight cars. He pulled into one of the two remaining spaces. He opened the door for Angela. Julie climbed down from her perch atop all their belongings. They walked around to the front door.

Rebecca told him to look for an attractive redheaded woman in her early thirties. That would be Helene. Just such a woman was waiting at the top of the porch stairs wearing jeans and a turquoise sweatshirt. "I'm Helene Walker, Rebecca's friend, and you must be Father Haloran." Looking at his companions, she added. "and you must be Angela and Julie." She shook each of their hands. "Welcome to St. Louis. Come in." She held the door and ushered Angela and Julie through. Jerry motioned for her to go ahead of him. "You arrived at the right time. The doctor comes to the home every Tuesday morning. He is seeing someone right now but he'll be available soon. Sister Claire will be arriving shortly, we'll wait in here." She led the way to a small parlor.

Jerry wanted to talk to Julie alone before he left. When he mentioned this to Helene, she suggested that she show Angela around and leave him and Julie in the parlor. Jerry moved to a chair close to her. "The reason I want to talk to you, Julie, is, well, when you and your mom arrived in Paris on Sunday night, she told me what had happened and why you left Aberdeen." Julie met his eyes and then looked at the floor. "Did Ralph Kurtz rape you, Julie?" He asked this as softly and gently as he could.

Julie continued looking at the floor. "No, but he was going to. I hate him. I know I shouldn't say this, but I hope he burns in hell."

"Was that the first time he tried to do something like that?" She remained silent. "Julie, you don't have to tell me. If it helps, we can treat this like confession, so you will know I can never tell anyone what you tell me."

The silence continued for some time and when Julie looked up at him, tears were running down her cheeks. Jerry was sure he detected some kind of accusation in her eyes as she looked at him. Her voice was soft, but angry as she said, "Yes, it was the first time for me." She hesitated. "But I know he was raping my sister." He must have looked surprised as Julie went on, "That's the reason she killed herself. You know she killed herself, don't you, Father?"

"I believe she did. What makes you so sure?"

Julie looked away and then back again. "I heard noises in the middle of the night. They came from Melanie's room. Her room is next to mine. I think the bastard made her pregnant. She killed herself because she didn't know what to do. I hate Ralph Kurtz. I suppose that's a sin. I don't care—I hate him."

"I can understand that and I believe God can, too. Julie, did Melanie say anything about all this before she died?"

"On Saturday she cried a lot. In the afternoon she said she was going to go over to the church." Again, Julie gave him that accusing look. "Did she talk to you then?"

Jerry's stomach tied up in knots. "If she did, she did it in confession. I didn't talk to her any place else."

"And if she did talk to you in confession, you couldn't tell me, huh?"

"No I couldn't."

"What difference would it make? She's dead."

"It's still the seal of confession." Jerry looked at the floor and felt ashamed that he had told Rebecca part of the story. There was nothing he could do to ease the child's pain about her sister but he would do everything he could to make sure she never had to see Ralph Kurtz again. He looked up at her tear-streaked face. "Julie, they have a counselor here. You have been through a lot. I hope you will talk to her when you get a chance. Will you?"

"Will it do any good?" She looked sad and lost.

Jerry took one of her hands in both of his. "She can't erase what has happened to you, but talking about it with someone who understands often helps. I hope your mom will see her, too."

"Mom's worried because we don't have any money."

"I gave her a little and the home here will help you with your basic needs." Jerry had gotten three hundred dollars from his own account that morning.

"Will I ever have to see him again?"

"No, you will not." Jerry hoped he sounded more certain than he felt.

"He said he'd kill us if we called the police or tried anything." Julie shivered. "He'll try to find us."

"I know. That's why I brought you so far away. These shelters are used to this kind of thing."

"Will we see you again, Father Jerry?"

"Yes. I'll come visit as often as I can."

Julie smiled for the first time since he had sat down. "You'll come back so you can see Rebecca, right?"

"I'll come back to see you and if it works out, it would be nice to visit with Rebecca, of course."

"I think you're in love with her." Why in the world would she say something like that?

Jerry wondered. He decided to ignore it. "You write to me, or call collect, and let me know how things are going. And if there is anything I can do for you, and I mean anything. Okay?"

"Okay. And, Father, thank you for helping us."

They both stood up and Jerry gave her a hug. "Julie, you're a truly wonderful person, don't ever let anyone tell you otherwise."

Jerry met Sister Claire, a diminutive woman, who exuded kindness and understanding. He shared as much as he could with her about Angela, Julie, and Ralph Kurtz. It took him nearly an hour to tell her the story. He left feeling that maybe it was more than Rebecca and Helene who had led him to St. Louis with Angela and Julie.

Helene and Jerry sat in the foyer of a rustic seafood and steak restaurant somewhere near downtown St. Louis. The walls were covered with weathered boards from an old barn. Rusty farm tools and implements were mounted around the place. After they had unpacked his car and settled Angela and Julie at the shelter, Helene had given him a tour of her 'home' for girls. They were waiting for Rebecca.

Dressed in a rose-colored suit and white blouse, Rebecca looked rushed as she came through the door. She spotted them and headed their way. "I thought you guys would have had a couple of beers by now. Sorry I'm late." She gave Helene a hug and reached out a hand to Jerry. "How do you like this place, Jerry? Remind you of your prairie?"

"A little. I looked at the menu. Hamburgers are six ninety-five. Mabel's are two dollars."

"It probably took a lot of money to transport all this barn wood from Kansas."

After they were seated, Helene said, "Rebecca, I'm impressed with your friend here."

She then turned to Jerry. "Well, Jerry ... okay if I call you 'Jerry'?" He nodded. "Good. It looks like you and I have had a positive effect on Rebecca. Because of your friend, Alice, she is doing an article on the dying. Have you seen the draft?" Jerry shook his head, 'no.' "It's great, at least to my untrained eye."

Rebecca interrupted her. "How is Alice, Jerry? I talked to her on the phone last week and she said she was fine, but she sounded weak. I'm afraid I wore her out a bit. My interview with her was the best I had, even though it was over the phone."

"She told me you called. She enjoyed talking to you. I believe that she is getting weaker." Jerry hesitated a moment and then added, "We spent a couple hours last week picking out readings for her funeral." Both Rebecca and Helene looked a bit shocked. He didn't have to ask why. "There was one particular piece that she wrote." He looked at Rebecca. "She asked if you would read it at her funeral." Jerry didn't add that Alice also said that Rebecca would probably like an excuse to visit him. He asked her why and she just muttered something about a woman knows. "I told her I would ask you."

"Tell her yes. Better yet, I'll call her and tell her it would be a privilege—and tell her that I hope it will be years from now. Did you bring a copy of her piece?"

"No, but I'll send you a copy." Again, he turned to Helene. "Helene, you had more to say about Rebecca's inspiration."

"Yes, I do. She is also doing a piece on at-risk teens. And, of course, you can guess who will be the two central figures."

"Rene and Denise."

"Those two will probably censor half of what I've written. I promised them I'd show it to them before I turned it in."

As they were leaving the restaurant, Helene hugged Jerry and whispered, "Be nice to my best friend. Don't break her heart."

Her words jolted him. "Break her heart?" A chill ran down his spine. What in the world would cause her to say something like that? What had Rebecca said?

He followed Rebecca back to her townhouse. She changed into slacks, blouse, and sweater before showing him around St. Louis. They managed to go to the top of the Gateway Arch and spend an hour at the arboretum before it closed. He enjoyed the time with Rebecca, but he could feel a certain tension between them. Often he would glance her way and catch her studying him. Jerry was a little apprehensive that someone he knew would see them together. He and Wayne had once attended the theater in Kansas City and found themselves seated next to a couple who were parishioners from Aberdeen. He and Rebecca would probably appear as a couple. He shivered slightly at the thought. Rebecca asked him if he was cold. Rather than try to explain, he said, "A little."

They decided that they would go back to Rebecca's condo and eat the leftover lasagna for dinner rather than go to a restaurant. He had two glasses of scotch before dinner and a glass of wine with dinner. Rebecca did not drink scotch but had a glass of wine.

*   *   *

After they finished the dishes, Rebecca poured brandy into glasses and they moved to the living room. She was pleased that Jerry felt comfortable enough to take off his shoes. She had to resist the temptation to move to his end of the couch and snuggle up in his arms. "Well Jerry, what do you do in the evenings when you're home?"

"Two or three evenings a week I visit with parishioners. I watch television a little. More often than not, I read and listen to music. What about you?"

"About the same, I guess, no parishioners though. Do you enjoy living alone?"

"I miss Wayne a lot. We always had something to talk about."

Rebecca curled her feet under her. "How's Wayne

doing? Do you see him much?"

"We get together every other Wednesday. Okay if I put my feet on the coffee table?" It had plastic legs and frame with a heavy glass top. Rebecca nodded and he put his stockinged feet up. He went on to tell her that Wayne enjoyed the smaller parish and the people there. Sometimes they would meet in Aberdeen to play golf or racquetball.

"Has he been to Paris?"

"Once. He said, and I quote, 'Jer, ol' buddy, you've sure got yourself exiled. God, what a hellhole.' No golf or racquetball in Paris. So I do a little more driving."

"Give him my love, next time you see him. What would you like to do tomorrow?"

"Oh, anything you'd like to do." He sounded nervous.

Rebecca looked up at him and smiled mischievously. "Anything?"

He turned red for a moment then laughed self-consciously. "Well, not anything."

"It's too bad you couldn't stay for the weekend. My birthday is Saturday and Helene is having a party for me."

"Well, happy birthday. Which birthday is it? Sorry, I guess one shouldn't ask a woman such a question, huh?

"I don't mind. It's my thirty-third. Tomorrow we could take a riverboat cruise on the Mississippi. How would that be?"

"You know, when I came through St. Louis on my way to Chicago, I often saw those boats and thought it would be interesting to go on one." He held up his empty brandy snifter. "Mind if I get a refill?"

Rebecca noticed he staggered a bit as he headed for the kitchen. What was it Marge said about his drinking? Something about he was worried about it when he first came to Paris. The large glass was filled almost to the top with brandy, she noticed, and made a mental note to make an attempt to get it away from him before he finished it. "So let's take the cruise, okay? Oh, by the way, I've been meaning to tell you all day. I like the shirt and pants on you, blue brings out the color in your eyes."

"Thanks. A friend of mine gave them to me." He slurred his words.

"She has good taste." Rebecca studied Jerry's face. He still looked serious and somewhat nervous. She had enjoyed the afternoon with him but didn't feel connected as she had in Paris. Was it she or something in him? "Jerry, you, uh, seem distant somehow. I felt it this afternoon, too. Are you sorry you brought Angela and Julie to St. Louis?"

Jerry looked at the floor and then into her eyes. "No. I'm very glad that I brought them here. Sister Claire is wonderful. I hope you'll get a chance to meet her. She's just the person to look after Angela and Julie. I was wondering if you would be willing to stop by and see them sometime."

"I was thinking of doing that. Julie looks like Mclanic in that picturc."

Jerry looked sad when he said, "Yes." He didn't say another word but only drank or, more accurately, gulped more brandy.

"Jerry, why are you so uncomfortable? Is it me? Is

it the article?" She hoped he hadn't drunk too much to talk coherently.

"No, it's not you or anything you've done or said. It's me. I'm just uncomfortable, uh, being with you." He took another gulp of brandy and looked at his feet. His speech was slurred as he said, "You know Rebecca, I haven't spent this much time with a woman, other than a family member, uh, ever." He smiled somewhat sheepishly and added, "I've never stayed in an apartment with a ... uh..."

Rebecca laughed and finished his sentence, "Woman. Are you afraid of me?"

"Uh... no, just uncomfortable, I guess." He finished the brandy. He slowly turned his head towards her. His eyes seemed blurry—out of focus. "I think I drank too much. I'm feeling sick." He staggered to his feet and headed for the bathroom.

CHAPTER 12

Do not let your hearts be troubled. Trust in God...
There are many rooms in my Father's house .... I am
going to prepare a place for you.

Gospel of John 14:1-2

The smell of coffee awoke Jerry. It hurt to open his eyes, but he did. Lying on the couch, he saw Rebecca holding a cup of coffee and sitting on a chair only a few feet in front of him. She smiled. "Good morning, sleepy head."

His head hurt in a way he had never experienced before, like a thousand little men with jackhammers running around inside it. He muttered, "What's good about it?"

"I'm alive and thankfully, so are you." She stood and picked up a glass and some pills from the coffee table. "Here's some aspirin and tomato juice. Good for hangovers, I understand."

Jerry leaned on one elbow and chased the aspirin down with the juice. He moved up and put his head down on the arm of the couch. He felt his chest. It was naked. Moving his hand down his body, he realized he was nude. How in hell did he get undressed. He could feel his face flush. "I'm, uh... I don't have anything on."

"I know." Rebecca's smile was almost a laugh.

"Uh, what happened, and why am I n ... don't have

any clothes on?"

"The word is 'naked', you're naked, Jerry. Is that a bad word in your priestly world?"

"No, dammit. Why am I naked? Do you have any more of that coffee?" He couldn't remember ever having such a headache and his mouth felt like it was full of cotton.

"Be right back." Rebecca got up and headed for the kitchen. She placed a cup on the counter; it sounded like she dropped a brick. She reappeared with the coffee and a cold washcloth.

"Thanks." He sipped the coffee and put the cloth on his forehead. It helped. "You haven't answered my question." As his head cleared, he saw that Rebecca was dressed in tight jeans, a blue sweatshirt, and running shoes. He wondered if she had jogged already.

"Tell me how much you remember from last night?" Her voice was soft and soothing.

"I remember we were sitting on this couch and I was drinking brandy. I was feeling uncomfortable. I think the last thing I remember is going into the kitchen and getting some brandy. Uh, I, uh, was thinking that I was pouring too much in the glass and well, that's about it." He wrinkled up his face and added, "I think you said something about my being nervous. So, what happened? Uh, what did I do?"

"You not only poured too much brandy, you drank too much of it. You said you felt sick, and then you staggered toward the bathroom. You would have fallen on your face if I hadn't helped you."

He was puzzled by her smile, as if she knew something terribly amusing. "And why am I, uh, naked?"

"Because you puked all over yourself and I had to clean you up." Now she laughed.

"Why are you laughing? I've had to clean up after a few drunks in my life and I didn't find it funny."

"Well, you were funny, disgusting too, but mostly funny."

"What did I do that was so funny?"

"When I was trying to clean you up and get you undressed, you kept singing, 'Oh Rebecca, Oh Rebecca, Oh Rebecca darling girl, you are lost and gone forever, dreadful sorry, darling girl.'" She had deepened her voice and slurred the words to the tune of "My Darling Clementine."

"You're putting me on, aren't you?"

"I certainly am not! You're heavy! I had a helluva time getting you on the couch, undressing you, and tucking you in."

Jerry looked down at his feet. "I'm sorry, Rebecca. Singing or not, I'd still be angry, if I had to do what you did."

"You know, when I was in Paris, I kept wondering if you were human. Now I know, you are! I like you better, knowing that."

Jerry pulled the blanket around him and said, "I've got to go to the bathroom." He hesitated, then told himself that she wouldn't bite and got up. He clumsily stood and as carefully as possible, draped the blanket around him. He stepped on a corner of it and exposed his rear. He quickly pulled the blanket back around him.

"You've got cute buns, know that?"

He didn't look back nor respond. This, he thought, had to be the most embarrassing moment of his life.

After urinating, he looked at himself in the mirror and muttered, "As my brothers would say, your eyes look like two piss-holes in the snow."

Rebecca knocked on the door and said, "I have some clean clothes for you."

He stood behind the door, took the clothes and said, "Thank you." As he closed the door he wondered what she could possibly mean by saying she now knew he 'was human.' Of course he was human. He took a shower and put on the clothes.

Rebecca fixed him some toast for breakfast; it was all he could imagine keeping down. He wished she'd stop looking at him with that bemused smile.

"Do you remember saying last night that you would like to go on a riverboat cruise today?"

"Sort of." He looked out the window. It was a gray looking day.

"Well, are you up for it or are you too hungover?"

"It seems I'm being a lot of trouble and not being very good company. You still want to spend time with me?"

"Sure. Even more so because you don't make me nervous anymore."

"Why in the world would I make you nervous?"

"You, my dear, are a priest. Or have you forgotten?"

He couldn't figure her out. He had vomited all over the place, forcing her to clean him and everything else up, undress him, see him stark naked and then called him 'my dear' like it was the most natural thing in the world. He felt like Alice in Wonderland. "You didn't seem nervous in Paris."

"I can put on a pretty good act when I have a job to do. What about the boat ride?"

"Okay I'll do it, and I won't drink any more alcohol. If my headache continues, I won't complain because I deserve it."

"That's the way God works, huh, punishes us for our sins by giving us physical pain?"

"I don't think God has anything to do with it. I did it to myself by drinking too much."

Rebecca sat her cup down and looked serious for the first time. "Jerry, you said you were uncomfortable being here with me last night, remember?" He nodded. "What made you so uncomfortable? I guess uncomfortable enough to get drunk."

Jerry looked at her across the table and sipped his coffee. "I'm not sure. Well, that's not entirely true, I am sure. Rebecca, you are, as you know, a very beautiful woman, and as I think I said, I've never stayed in an apartment with a woman before. So I'm nervous."

She got that mischievous smile again. "Are you afraid I'll try to seduce you?"

He pictured the cartoon devil and angel on his shoulders and smiled. "No, not really." That damn devil thinks it would be a marvelous idea, though, he thought.

Rebecca asked, "Why are you smiling?"

He told her about the devil and the angel.

"And, of course, you always listen to the angel, right?" Again, the mischievous smile.

"You know something, Rebecca Brady? When you

225

smile like that you look awfully seductive." He looked at his left shoulder and added, "And you quit leering at her."

"And what is the angel telling you?"

Jerry folded his hands prayerfully in front of him. "She says, control your passions, my son, and you will get to heaven."

"Your head must be getting better, 'cause you are getting your humor back. By the way, are angels always female and devils male?"

"How would I know? I've never seen either one."

Rebecca picked up the dishes. "We better get going if we want to make that cruise. It's the last one of the season, I'm told."

His head had cleared by the time they got to the river. The temperature was in the fifties, cool but not cold. They stood with their hands in their pockets, on the bow of the boat as it pulled away from the dock. The sun was making a valiant effort to disperse the clouds. Except for a few evergreens and some colorful buildings, the shoreline looked very gray. A barge loaded with some kind of cargo and pulled by a tugboat was headed down the middle of the river.

Rebecca brushed her hair from her face and said, "I've only been on a cruise once before. It was spring and everything was brighter and more beautiful. You'll have to come back in the spring and we'll do it again." She leaned against the railing and gazed at the surroundings.

Jerry joined her at the railing. "So how's the mentoring going with Denise and Rene?"

Rebecca told him about her work with them and

how much she was enjoying it. She also talked about the articles she was writing. She then asked him about Kenny Gaffin, Ricky Alexander, and Kathy. Jerry was curious as to why she seemed so interested in Kathy and why she seemed to relax a bit when he told her about Dylan Bradford, Kathy's music major friend.

Rebecca looked up at him and smiled. "I get the impression that you don't like this Dylan fellow. Are you jealous?"

"Of course not!" He said that too quickly and wondered why. He was sure that she noticed the defensiveness. "I'm hungry, how about you?"

"I'm more cold than hungry, but I could eat something. Let's go inside."

The riverboat dining area was quite stark: plain wooden tables bolted to the floor and walls with equally plain benches. It had plank floors that needed varnishing and a white somewhat ornate ceiling. Diners had to order their food at a window. A few other couples were occupying the tables or standing in line for food. Some were holding hands, and Rebecca envied them a little and wondered what Jerry would do if she took his hand. They ordered fish and chips. They seated themselves at a window table a few feet from a couple with a cute little red-haired girl who looked to be about seven years old.

They had taken only a few bites when the girl came over to their table. She held out her hand to Jerry. "My name's April, what's yours?"

"Jerry, and this is Rebecca." He felt a jolt of despair as he thought of the April who appeared on his first day in Paris. He shrugged off the negativity and noticed the cute April in front of them.

April held out her hand to Rebecca and said politely, "Nice to meet you, Rebecca."

Rebecca smiled, wiped her hands on a napkin and took April's hand, "Well, thank you April, she said. "How are you today?"

"Bored." She glanced at her parents and then whispered, "They said this would be a fun day and all they've been doing is arguing about money. May I sit with you?"

Jerry looked at Rebecca. She smiled and he pulled the outside bench closer to their table. "Sure."

April climbed up, straightened her sweater, and looked at Rebecca rather intently. Then she looked at Jerry. Looking back and forth at each of them, she asked, "Are you married?"

Rebecca laughed and shook her head, 'no.' Jerry chuckled but looked embarrassed.

"Why not?" April asked Rebecca.

Without hesitating, Rebecca, still chuckling, answered, "Oh, I want to, but he doesn't."

Jerry almost choked on the bite he'd just taken and wondered why Rebecca would say that.

April studied him for sometime and then turned to Rebecca. "Is he retarded? 'Cause you sure are beautiful." She said it like it was spelled 'bee-you-ti-full'.

Rebecca grabbed a napkin and put it to her mouth and almost fell off the bench laughing. Jerry laughed too, more at Rebecca than the reference to his intelligence. April looked puzzled.

Rebecca composed herself enough to answer, "Yes,

April, in some ways, I think he is." She continued laughing.

At that moment, April's mother yelled, "April, get back over here this minute and stop bothering people."

Jerry said, "She's really not bothering us. You have a lovely daughter."

The woman looked rather sour and responded, "Well, thank you, but we just can't have her running around like this."

April climbed down from the bench, took Rebecca's hand, and said, "Thank you for talking with me." She then took Jerry's hand, smiled, and said, "I really don't think you're retarded; I was just teasing." She scampered back to her folks and waved as they left the dining room.

Jerry looked at Rebecca, who was wiping tears from her eyes with a napkin and still laughing. She stopped laughing long enough to say, "That was fun. Isn't she precious? I don't think her mother appreciates her."

The gentle fun she had with April was a side of Rebecca that Jerry hadn't seen. Somehow, he expected her to be impatient with children. "So, Ms. Brady, would you please tell this somewhat retarded person if you ever wanted to have children?"

"Not really. I've really never given it much thought. What about you?"

"I've thought about it. I like kids and enjoy my sixteen nieces and nephews, but I guess I'll settle for enjoying other people's kids."

"Sixteen nieces and nephews! How many siblings do you have?"

Jerry was surprised that Rebecca didn't know the answer to that question after all the research she had done on him. "Five—two brothers and three sisters. It was like two families when I was growing up. I was the oldest of the younger three. There's eighteen years difference between my oldest sister and my youngest."

"And if I recall, it wasn't the happiest of families. Why did your mother and father divorce?" Rebecca wrinkled her brow as if trying to remember if she had been told about that.

"As I think I told you, my dad was a violent alcoholic. After one particular beating, my mom went to the parish priest and he encouraged her to get a divorce, with the proviso that she couldn't remarry, of course. But, still, that was quite a step for that priest to take. In those days, most priests were telling battered women that they were obliged to stay with their husbands, no matter what. Want to hear something funny?"

"Sure, but I have a hunch that it isn't very funny."

"Probably not, but anyway, I think one of the many reasons I became a priest was because of the way my dad treated my mother. I believed that to love a woman was to hurt her."

Rebecca reached across the table and took Jerry's hand. "Oh, Jerry that is so sad. It's not funny in any way. Do you still believe that's true?" Jerry looked puzzled, and she attempted to clarify her question by saying, "I mean, do you still believe that to love a woman is to hurt her?"

Jerry tried to smile but it looked more like a grimace. "I guess I do or I wouldn't have gotten drunk last night, would I?" Rebecca pursed her lips, pulled her hand away, and looked away. Jerry, feeling heavy and fearing that it was weighing down Rebecca, too, said, "Let's talk about you. Why haven't you given much thought to having children?"

Looking more than a little uncomfortable, Rebecca said, "Oh, I don't know, perhaps, like you, my own background told me that childhood wasn't all that great, maybe to have a child was to hurt her or him." She brightened up for a moment as if she had discovered a new truth. The brightness seemed to turn wistful as she said, "Of course, to have children, I'd have to find a likely father. I haven't found a good prospect yet."

"But I think you said, or indicated, that you've dated quite a few fellows. What about the ACLU guy?" It worried Jerry that he wanted her to say that the lawyer wasn't the one. Even more worrisome, was his wondering if he, Jerry, would be a likely prospect for Rebecca. He tried to get rid of such ridiculous ideas.

"No, he's nice enough but well, there's not that kind of chemistry between us."

"What about the wealthy fellow you mentioned when you were in Paris?"

"That would be Sam Hawkins. Yes, he was wealthy but could think only of himself. If I had married him and we had two children, I would have three children to take care of. Maybe I'm just too picky, or selfish to get married. I don't know. Back to you. The other evening when you and Julie were singing that lovely song, you seemed, oh, kind of disturbed, upset, or something. Why was that? I didn't want to say anything at the time and made a mental note to ask you later."

231

Jerry thought that he probably had the disturbed face on again, as he said: "You remember me telling you about Melanie and how I refused to help her get an abortion?"

Rebecca nodded and Jerry went on, "Well, there was one item I didn't mention. That Sunday evening she called and left a message on my answering machine that said, "What color is your heart now, Father Jerry? I think it's yellow!" If you remember, 'knew the color of the heart' was the line just before 'knew love by its first name.'" He looked away.

"Oh Jerry, that's so sad. Now I can see why you were upset with the song. I'm sorry."

"That's okay. You had no way of knowing. I'm sorry for being so grumpy."

"So we're both sorry. So let's quit being sorry and enjoy the rest of the trip." Rebecca reached over and took his hand in both of hers. Jerry grinned.

They made their conversation a bit lighter for the rest of the trip. As they were leaving the boat, Rebecca took Jerry's hand, but quickly let it go when she felt him get tense. She didn't say anything and neither did he.

Rebecca suggested they eat dinner at a French restaurant near downtown St. Louis. He said he would pay for dinner in exchange for the hospitality she'd shown him, Angela and Julie. When he saw the prices on the menu, he was embarrassed to tell her that he didn't have enough to pay for both of them. Between his nearly maxed-out credit cards and clearing out his checking account for Angela, he would barely have enough to get home. Rebecca insisted on paying for both of them if he would buy her dinner when he returned to St. Louis to visit Julie and Angela.

They returned to Rebecca's place around ten and talked a little longer and turned in early. Ever since the riverboat trip, Rebecca seemed to avoid saying anything too personal and asking questions that would make him uncomfortable. He had done the same and was glad that they had put things on a solid platonic basis. It had been a pleasant day and he had managed only to laugh when she teasingly suggested he join her for a shower. He wasn't about to let her know how arousing that thought was.

CHAPTER 13

We ought, then, to turn our minds more attentively than before to what we have been taught, so that we do not drift away.

Hebrews 2:5

It had started raining soon after he left St. Louis at five thirty in the morning. He had told Rebecca that he would slip out quietly so as not to awaken her. She got up anyway and made coffee for them. He surprised himself by nearly crying when he gave her a hug and said goodbye. A terrible sadness continued deep inside him as he drove through the rain. It was a kind of anguished sadness that was only vaguely familiar, like leaving something behind that he would never find again. It was similar to the sadness he had felt when he left St. Gabriel's, but this was even more personal, it seemed.

He had to talk to someone about what he was experiencing. During the morning, as he was driving somewhere in the middle of Missouri, he stopped to call Wayne Cameron to see if he would be up to a visit. Thankfully, he was.

He turned on the car radio and pushed the button to an 'oldies' station. The Beatles were singing, "Yesterday, all my troubles seemed so far away, now it looks as though they're here to stay. Oh, I believe in yesterday."

"Oh, shit." He turned it off.

He pulled into the driveway between Wayne's two-story red brick rectory and the church. Jerry opened the storm door on the back porch just as Wayne opened the kitchen door. "Hey, Jer, just in time. Lunch is all ready."

They went through the kitchen and into the dining room. Wayne brought a steaming platter of roast beef, potatoes, onions, and carrots from the kitchen. He sat down at the end of the large, maple table covered with a linen tablecloth.

A place was set on the side and Jerry pulled out the chair, sat down, and looked at the matching china cupboard opposite him and thought that it wouldn't even fit in his little bungalow in Paris. "Don't tell me you cooked all this yourself?"

"I'd like to say 'yes' but it would be a lie. One of the ladies of the parish comes in once a week and cleans up. She said I was getting skinny and decided to cook for me a couple of times a week. You've hit a lucky day. Eat hearty because I'll be having the leftovers till Sunday. How're your culinary skills coming along?" Neither of them had ever lived in a parish without a housekeeper and cook.

"I'm getting pretty good at sandwiches, soup, and salad. I get wholesome meal two or three times a week with parish families."

Wayne put down his fork and, looking serious, asked, "Jer, you called collect today from somewhere in Missouri. What were you doing in Missouri?"

Jerry finished the bite he had just put in his mouth, wiped his mouth with his napkin. "Remember Angela and Julie Kurtz?"

Wayne nodded.

"Well they arrived at my place in the middle of the night on Sunday. Monday morning, really. They were badly beaten up."

"It was Ralph, right?"

"Yes. I decided to find a shelter for them far enough away that he couldn't find them. Found one in St. Louis." He went on to tell Wayne the story of Angela, Julie, and Sister Clair. He didn't mention Rebecca.

"Sounds like leaving the car at the airport was a good idea." Wayne glanced at his watch just as the doorbell rang. "Uh, oh, it's two-thirty. As I mentioned I have a young couple coming in for pre-marriage instructions. But I want to hear the rest of the story, especially why you chose St. Louis." He wiped his mouth and got up. When he neared the door, he turned. "St. Louis. Isn't that where your reporter-friend lives?"

"Yeah." Jerry poured himself another cup of coffee and leisurely drank it. He found himself thinking of Julie and Angela and hoping they were adjusting well to the shelter. His thoughts turned to Rebecca and he wondered what he would tell Wayne. When he remembered Rebecca telling little April that she wanted to get married but he didn't, he got up and cleared off the table and put the dishes in the dishwasher. He wandered into the living room and admired the woodwork around the doors, the stairs, and bookshelves flanking the fireplace. The house was nearly a century old but in very good shape. Once, Wayne had informed him, Lakeside had over seven thousand people; and it was the bustling trade center of the area, and the parish had over three hundred families. Now the town was only a little over four thousand and the parish only about a hundred and fifty families. Still, it was quite a bit more than poor old Paris. The Bishop didn't consider Wayne's "sin" of not publicly condemning Jerry's sermon to be as great as his own "sin" of giving it. Wayne really did seem to enjoy the slower pace of the smaller parish.

Although he was quite tired, he felt too restless to sit down. Putting on his jacket, he went over to the church and entered through the side door. Compared to his little church in Paris, it was huge, holding about eight hundred people. The stained glass windows gave a wonderfully mellow glow to the marble statuary and the smell of burning votive candles added to the feeling of peace and solitude.

Slowly making his way across the aisle in front of the sanctuary, he stopped at the votive candles, and wondered when was the last time he had lit one? About two years ago when his sister lost her baby, stillborn. He felt for her and somehow hoped the candle would be a prayer for her and the baby. Does God pay attention to such things? He wondered. He didn't know, but decided to light one for his struggle with temptation. He picked up the matches and lit a large blue candle and put two dollars in the box.

Kneeling in front of the Blessed Virgin's statue next to the candles, he thought of how much peace he had always found inside a church. As a young boy, it had been an escape from the turmoil of his family and the wrath of his father. Serving Mass for old Father Groel was one of the most serene times of his life, especially after his own father had died. While attending the Cathedral High School in Aberdeen, every morning before classes, he had stopped at the Cathedral and prayed before the Virgin. Now, in the solitude of the church in Lakeside, he longed for the peace and harmony he had experienced then. Becoming a priest was his way of finding permanent peace and helping others to find it. His brothers and sisters constantly chided him about his living "in a dream world." Maybe he had been, and now the dream and the peace seemed shattered. He felt little peace since Melanie's death, maybe even before then.

Looking up at the marble statue of Our Lady, Jerry saw her enigmatic smile, flickering by candlelight. She seemed to be taking pity on him. Was she simply being indulgent to another poor mortal? He found himself feeling nostalgic for that time in his life when things seemed so clear, and all powerful, all knowing and loving God who looked down from heaven and gave clear directions, through His Church about how to live life. Then he knew exactly what was good and what was not. It seemed so clear and beautiful then but through the years he realized how stultifying and non-life-giving the messages were. Most people became fearful and shame-filled rather than the loving and creative beings God intended. As he knelt there, he realized that he would have to find a different way to pray, a way that would match what he hoped would reflect a more mature theology.

His stay in the church was longer than he realized. He found Wayne in the kitchen wiping off the counter. They headed for the living room. Jerry sat down on the end of the couch and Wayne sat in a recliner opposite him. "Well, Jer, you sounded a bit down when you called. I got your message about not being able to get together on Wednesday, so we have our get-together on Thursday. Tell me more about your trip. Did you see Rebecca? The last time I saw you, you were quite steamed about her article."

"Yes, I saw her. She arranged, through her friend, for the shelter for Angela and Julie. We stayed at her place the first night." He hesitated a moment, than added, "And I stayed with her the next two nights."

"Jer, you know I met Rebecca?" Jerry nodded. "She's a very attractive woman."

"And you're wondering what I was doing, staying with her, right?" Jerry guessed he would wonder, too, if Wayne told him that he had spent two nights with an eligible gay fellow.

"You didn't say 'Rebecca and her husband.' I'm assuming she's single?" Wayne was on the verge of sounding like he was scolding.

"Yes, Wayne, and you're beginning to sound like a constipated seminary rector." Jerry smiled.

Wayne chuckled. "'Constipated rector', that's good. And I'm beginning to think you're acting like a seminarian who's strayed and it's bothering you. You said you wanted to talk about something. Tell me, old buddy, did you stray?" Wayne's voice was that of the kindly confessor.

"I didn't go to bed with her or even kiss her, if that's what you mean." He was feeling defensive and didn't like it. He knew it wasn't Wayne's intention. "No, Wayne, that's not what's disturbing me. What's bothering me is that I've felt so damn sad ever since I woke up this morning—especially since I left St. Louis." He glanced over at Wayne and saw only compassion on his face. Looking at the floor ashamedly, he added. "You know, when I was leaving St. Louis, I felt like crying, just like I did at my dad's funeral. And like at Melanie Kurtz's funeral ... I felt like I'd lost something. But I don't know what it is."

Jerry sat looking at the floor. Wayne remained silent. After several minutes, he looked at Wayne and broke the silence. "After Melanie killed herself, I think I allowed myself to feel real anguish for the first time in my life. I wanted to shut down my feelings like I did when my dad died, but I just couldn't do it." He smiled a self-deprecating little smile. "For some reason it felt good to just feel the sadness. Now I'm wondering if I can allow myself to feel joy. My second day in St. Louis, I really felt good being with Rebecca. We just toodled around the city. Several times I wanted to put my arm around her or hold her hand, but I didn't. She didn't say anything or do anything to make me uncomfortable, except the way she looked at me several times." He didn't mention that she teasingly asked him if he wanted to take a shower with her. Sitting there thinking about it was enough to feel aroused.

"What kind of look did she give you?" Wayne's tone was that of a wise counselor.

"Oh, warm, kind, like she was interested in me and wanted to really know me, I guess. I felt elated and uncomfortable at the same time. So uncomfortable that I got drunk."

"Jer, I've seen you drink a little too much but I have

a hunch you're talking about seriously drunk. How drunk?"

"Drunk enough to pass out, vomit all over the place, and have to be put to bed." The same half-smile returned.

"Is that what's bothering you, getting drunk?"

"No. Oh, I'm ashamed of it, but that's not it. I think it's what I did yesterday."

"And what's that, my friend?"

"I numbed myself and was nice and polite and dead, all day."

"What's so bad about that?"

Jerry sounded more impatient than he intended when he said, "Wayne, don't you get it? I *numbed* myself! Just like I've done all my life; whenever I begin to feel any strong feelings, I push them away, numb myself and go dead!" Jerry stood up and began to pace. "That's it. I want to let myself feel! Feel joy, sadness, up, down. Hell, maybe even feel sexy and not feel guilty."

"Feel sexy but not feel compelled to act on those feelings, I hope." Wayne sounded a bit alarmed.

"So tell me, Wayne, do you ever allow yourself to feel sexy?"

Wayne leaned forward and seemed to study the carpet for a few moments. He glanced at Jerry and back to the carpet. "I guess it's my turn. Of course I feel sexual urges because I'm human."

"I mean seriously tempted by a particular person?"

"Yes. For instance, there's a minister here in town, about five years younger than me. We met at the

Ministerial Alliance. After the first meeting he came over to welcome me to Lakeside. After we talked a while, he asked me if I was gay. I've heard that gays often know when a person is gay. I never paid much attention. Anyway, I told him I was and he told me he was and wondered if we could be friends. I said 'sure.'"

"And..."

"And we've spent quite a bit of time together. We went to a ballet in Kansas City. He encouraged me to go to a gay bar with him. I told him I wasn't ready for that. He's had two relationships before, consummated, I guess you'd say. And, believe it or not, he tells me he's in love with me."

"You've never mentioned him to me before."

"I guess I thought you'd sound like, what's the phrase you used? Oh, yeah, a constipated rector. I guess we both have a constipated friend." Wayne smiled for the first time since they began the discussion.

"And what are you going to do with him? Would you like to, ah, er--" Jerry couldn't bring himself to say "make love" to a man. It was hard to imagine.

"Have sex with him? Of course I would like to, but I'm not going to. I like being a priest and I've been able to be celibate for over forty years. I guess I can continue with it. My new friend can't understand my thinking, just as I imagine Rebecca can't understand yours. But he's willing to continue being a friend. I hope you will continue too, Jer. I need you and your understanding."

"Of course I'll always be your friend, no matter what. You really think Rebecca would want to, uh, make love with me?"

"How did she take your getting drunk?"

"She thought it was funny, even though she had to clean up after me." He wasn't about to tell Wayne she also had to undress him and clean him up, too. "She said I sang some dumb song to her, but I'm not sure she wasn't putting me on. What's that got to do with anything?"

"If she didn't care about you, she would have written you off. Instead, she found you funny. Yep, I'd bet she'd want to make love with you."

"Okay, I'll take your word for it. So what are you doing about your gay friend, numbing yourself?"

"Maybe a little. Believe it or not, I've thought about that. Here's my conclusion: I'll enjoy my friends, including my minister friend. I will not have sex and I will feel that joy! And I hope you will do the same, Jer. Look around you. How many men do you know, married or not, who really allow themselves to feel? I mean who are vibrant people?"

Jerry looked at the ceiling for an answer. "Not many."

"Not many is right. I'd guess that as many priests are feeling people, percentage-wise, as men in general."

"You're probably right. So I should quit feeling sorry for myself and get on with my wonderful celibate life, right?"

"Right. You've been able to handle a friendship with the beautiful Kathleen Olson, so you'll be able to handle Rebecca. Better, I'd guess, because she's hundreds of miles away."

Jerry began to wonder if maybe Wayne was made

of different stuff, as Jerry was   already shutting himself down.

*   *   *

On the same Thursday, Rebecca sat opposite Dr. Marilyn Fisher. The therapist was dressed in a crimson business suit, softened by a frilly white blouse.

"Thanks for changing the time of our appointment, Marilyn."

"I'm glad it worked out.   You said you had unexpected out-of-town guests. A positive experience, I hope."

"Well, yes and no." Rebecca told her about Jerry's arrival with Angela and Julie and about their ordeal and placement at St. Claire's home. She mentioned that Jerry stayed over for two days. She laughed when she told her about him getting drunk and singing. Rebecca didn't want to tell Dr. Fisher about undressing him and putting him to bed.

"So, except for his getting drunk, it sounds like you had a good time. I got a chance to read your article about him since I saw you last. He sounds like quite a guy." There was a note of concern in her voice as she asked, "Rebecca, is he an alcoholic?"

"I don't think so. He said that this was the first time he'd gotten drunk like that. Yes, he is quite a guy, but hc's so damn uncomfortable around me. Yesterday, we were okay together but both of us tried to sound casual, at least, I did. Whenever we talked about anything personal, we tried to make it impersonal. Does that make sense?" The therapist nodded and Rebecca went on, "He seemed sad when he left this morning. I don't know why. I was afraid to ask." Rebecca looked out the window, sighed and said, "You know, Marilyn, I'm already missing him."

"It sounds to me like he's made it very clear that he enjoys his priesthood and wants to continue to do so. So what are you going to do, Rebecca?"

"I guess I'll settle for being his friend."

CHAPTER 14

*For love is strong... it is a flash of fire, a flame of
Yahweh himself. Love no flood can quench, no
torrents drown.*

Song of Songs 8:6

It was the third weekend of November as Jerry,
preparing for the Saturday evening Mass, reflected on
the previous week. In many ways, it seemed like a
month, the arrival of Angela and Julie, the trip to St.
Louis, the time with Rebecca, and his talk with Wayne.
He was glad that he stopped at Lakeside. Talking with
Wayne was helpful, although the sadness he had felt
had not lifted entirely. He told Alice Peterson of his
trip and the plight of Angela and Julie. As expected,
she was her usual compassionate self. Rebecca had
already called her to tell her she would be happy to
read her poem at her funeral, and hoped it would be
years away. Alice invited her to join the family for
Thanksgiving, and Rebecca had accepted.

He hated to admit it but he was happy to learn that
Kathy had dropped Mr. Dylan Bradford. The news also
helped him to stop thinking of Rebecca so often. Kathy
arrived earlier than usual on this Saturday because she
wanted to talk with him. "Jerry, that jerk told me that
he wanted to break off our relationship unless I loved
him enough to have sex with him. Up until that point
I thought I did love him but when he said that, I went

cold. When I told him I wasn't ready for that, he called me a 'prick-teaser.'" She had put her hand over her mouth and grinned. "You know what I did? I slapped his face!" He resisted the urge to shake her hand.

"Be honest with me. Do I do that?"

"Not around me you don't." He had hesitated and then chuckled as he said, "But I don't know how you acted around him down at the university."

"You want me to slap you too?" Kathy said.

He pulled the chasuble over his head and looked at himself in the sacristy mirror to make sure everything was straight. He pulled the alb up a little on the right and tucked it in the cincture. He grinned at himself. Okay, Haloran, let yourself enjoy Kathy being herself again, even if it is more disturbing than when she seemed to have a beau.

Of all the things he did at the parish, the most enjoyable was the Saturday evening Youth Mass. The numbers had grown each week since September, and he was happy to note that the church was nearly full as he processed down the aisle behind the readers and servers. As usual, a group of adults stood in the back half of the church—probably accompanying their children who insisted on going up front.

The musicians had improved under Kathy's tutelage and had begun selecting popular music that they adapted for the service. He smiled to himself as he began his sermon on the subject of feelings, which primarily aimed at the males in the audience, including himself.

He had just uttered the words, "All feelings are okay, even if they are negative ones, as long as we do not act on those feelings. For instance, we all feel anger at times, maybe even want to hurt someone, but it is not the Christian thing to do, to act on those feelings of anger," when he saw someone burst through the door at the back of the church. The foyer was somewhat dark, so he could not tell who it was.

A man wearing a parka with the hood pulled over his head staggered forward holding something. As he took a few more steps, Jerry saw that it was some kind of automatic pistol. Who was he and what did he want? Jerry wondered, sensing the danger. On shaking knees, Jerry stepped slowly off the sanctuary platform. Everyone in the congregation was fidgeting and looking at the intruder.

The man yelled, "Hey, Holy Man, I wanna know where you took my wife and kid!" His words were slurred as he staggered forward near the back pew.

It was Ralph Kurtz!

How in the world did he find out that they came here? Jerry wondered. He wasn't sure whether the man's drunkenness made him more or less dangerous. The side door opened and he thought he saw someone crawl out. He couldn't remember ever being so scared. His knees continued to shake and he could feel clammy sweat trickle down his back as he slowly walked down the aisle. He definitely was afraid, but the anger that continually boiled inside him kept him moving toward this despicable man.

He stopped about ten feet from Kurtz. "Mr. Kurtz, what makes you think I know where your wife and daughter are? Aren't they home?"

Kurtz unsteadily aimed the gun at the priest. His

finger was on the trigger of the gun. "Don't lie ta me, ya sonofabitch! You know, an' ya better tell me or I'll shoot the shit outta ya!" Several people gasped; most of the people were ducking beneath the pew backs. One man near the back wall crouched down and moved out of his place. Kurtz quickly turned the gun in his direction and pulled the trigger, letting out three rounds against the wall and shattering one window. "Everybody stay where ya are, goddammit! I'm here ta get infermation from this sonofabitch, tha's all."

It seemed as if everyone became frozen in place. Jerry briefly glanced at the people on each side of the aisle. They were petrified. For the first time in his life, Jerry knew what people meant when they said they "smelled fear."

He folded his hands in front of him to hide his own shaking. He slowly took two more steps toward Kurtz. As calmly as he could, he said, "I don't understand why you think I would know where they are."

Kurtz puffed out his chest and declared proudly, "Cause I found the parking guy at the airport the night you took them away. He saw three cars come in and only two went out. One had a Paris County license. He remembered, and cost me a goddamn hunnert dollars. One of th' gals at work gimme a magazine with yer picture on it. An' I put two and two tagether." Kurtz aimed the gun over Jerry's head and pulled the trigger. Jerry could hear the whiz of the bullets. "That's ta let ya know I mean bizness, Holy Man!"

Several people gasped and many screamed as the gun again went off in the small church. Jerry believed that he had to keep Kurtz talking until someone, or maybe he, could figure out how to stop him. "That's pretty flimsy evidence that I might know where they are, Mr. Kurtz." He saw someone trying to slowly open the entry door. Please, God, don't let it squeak, he thought.

Kurtz again pointed the gun at the priest. "There's a li'l girl behind ya. Tell me where they are or I shoot tha li'l snot."

Jerry glanced back. Two pews behind him a mother was struggling to contain a three-year-old attempting to see what all the excitement was about. Is this bastard crazy enough to do something like that? Kenny Gaffin had silently entered the church as Father Jerry said, "Mr. Kurtz, even if I had that information, what good would it do you if you went to jail for murder."

"Let me worry 'bout that, asshole!"

Jerry took two more steps. Kenny was only a few feet behind Kurtz and looked ready to pounce. It would have to be a perfect tackle to keep him from shooting someone.

"Stay back, asshole, and tell me where my wife is!" Kurtz had an unfocused, crazy look in his eyes. The weapon was pointed at Jerry's chest.

Kenny Gaffin caught Jerry's eye and nodded. Kurtz started to turn to see what Jerry was looking at. Kenny made his move toward Kurtz, and Jerry, having a moment as the madman turned, lunged forward and grabbed the arm with the gun. With both hands he struggled to push the gun toward the ceiling. The drunken man kept his finger on the trigger. The gun went off. Jerry felt a searing pain in his left shoulder but he didn't loosen his grip on the madman's arm.

Kurtz's elbow bent when the gun went off and Jerry kept struggling with the arm and the gun. Kenny had both arms around the struggling man, trying to pin his arms to his side. Kurtz was able to keep his right hand free from Kenny. Jerry managed to get Kurtz's free arm pushed flat to the heaving man's chest and the gun pointed at the ceiling. Another blast nearly made Jerry fall backward, but he held on, keeping the gun pointing up. He kept pushing at the gun and the arm. As he worked to pry Kurtz's finger from the trigger, it went off again, this time splattering blood all over himself and Kenny Gaffin. Kurtz, his face twisted and covered with blood, went limp. Kenny dropped him to the floor.

Jerry fell to his knees and put his right hand to his left shoulder. He toppled over on his right. God, it hurts. I can't see out of one eye. Oh, shit, I won't be able to finish celebrating Mass. What's all the screaming and shouting about? The floor is cold.

*   *   *

Rebecca put the open book down on her lap. She was reading Colleen McCollough's *Thornbirds.* Helene had given it to her, saying, "This might help you get a better understanding of priests and the Catholic Church." Rebecca wasn't so sure. The priest reminded her of Jerry in some ways but seemed more ambitious and egotistical. She wondered if Jerry was the same but just hid it well. In the part she had just read, the wealthy and scheming old woman had just given him a challenge and dilemma: Follow his heart and ideals or let her name him the controller of her vast estate, allowing him to have the riches needed to arise to the pinnacle of power in the Church hierarchy. Rebecca thought he had a third choice: drop the stupid priesthood and marry the beautiful Meggie. So, as she saw it, the priest had three choices—leave the priesthood, follow his priestly ideals, or accept the patron's deal and rise in the Church. She guessed he would accept the power trip, like most men. She picked up the book again to find out if she was right.

Her telephone rang and she let the answering machine monitor the call. "Rebecca, this is Marge Woerner in Kansas." Rebecca immediately picked up the phone. "Hi Marge, what a pleasant surprise. What's up?"

Marge's voice sounded very subdued as she said, "I've got some bad news, Rebecca. Father Jerry was shot this evening. He was--"

Rebecca interrupted her. "Oh God, Marge, was he, he, killed?"

"No, I don't think he'll die from the wound. He was shot in the left shoulder. He's lost a lot of blood but I don't think it's affected any vital organs."

"Where is he, I mean, where did they take him?"

"To Mercy Hospital in Aberdeen. I was in the church and it's a good thing, because I was able to bandage him up and stop the bleeding. As you know, there's no doctor here in Paris."

Rebecca couldn't get the near panic out of her voice as she asked, "What happened? Who did it?"

Marge told her about Ralph Kurtz. She included hearing Kurtz say that he learned where Jerry lived

253

from Rebecca's magazine article and ended her recitation, saying, "Ralph Kurtz is dead." Marge waited a moment and then added, "Rebecca, I don't know if this will make the papers but I was wondering if you would break the news to Angela and Julie Kurtz before they hear it from someone else?"

Rebecca sucked in her breath. She had never done anything like this but it was so little to ask under the circumstances. "Of course. You think I need to go over there tonight?"

"I'm sure it can wait until morning. I think it will be a relief to them to know the bastard is dead."

"Uh, Marge, did Jerry kill him?"

"Not directly, I'd say. They were struggling with the gun and it went off. I did talk to Sheriff Gaffin and he said he'd report it as a self-inflicted wound but the district attorney will be obliged to investigate. Gaffin was sure no charges will be filed against his son or Jerry."

Rebecca was trembling as she hung up the phone. Marge didn't sound too sure that his gunshot wound wasn't fatal. She wrung her hands as she paced back and forth in the living room. She had an overwhelming need to get to Aberdeen to see for herself how Jerry was. She muttered aloud, "Why do I need to do this? Hell, I don't know, I just can't sit here and I know damn well I won't be able to sleep."

She called the St. Louis airport. There were no flights to Aberdeen until morning. She muttered to herself, "Okay, dammit, I'll drive there!" She quickly packed a bag and changed clothes. She was about to walk out the door when she thought of Marge's request that she tell Angela and Julie. She dropped her suitcase and called Helene. After she told her about the shooting and her need to go there, Helene asked her why she felt compelled to go. "Maybe guilt. Marge said that Kurtz learned about Jerry's whereabouts through my magazine." But Rebecca really didn't believe that, because Kurtz could have found out some other way. Helene told her to drive safely and that she would call Sister Claire and if the nun was not available, she'd inform Angela and Julie herself in the morning.

It was seven in the morning when a disheveled and tired Rebecca arrived at the hospital. She stopped in a restroom, touched up her make-up, and brushed her hair. When she stopped at the receptionist's desk, she was told only family members could see patients at this hour. "I'm Father Haloran's sister." She hoped they wouldn't ask her for a name.

"In that case, he has been moved from Intensive Care and is in room four-o-eight."

The door was slightly ajar. Rebecca gingerly pushed it open. A woman was sitting at the side of the sleeping man's bed, holding his hand. Rebecca's mouth dropped and an overwhelming feeling of jealously came over her as the woman turned to look at her. It was Kathy Olson. Damn!

Kathy was sure that she looked as resentful as she felt. What the hell is this reporter doing here, looking for another story?

Rebecca took a deep breath and whispered, "Hi, Kathy." She moved closer. "How's he doing?"

Kathy did not feel like showing any kind of warmth and continued to hold the priest's hand, responded,

"All his vital signs are good. They gave him three pints of blood. Luckily the bullet didn't hit his lungs or heart. The doctor said some bones in his shoulder were shattered." She never took her eyes off the sleeping man.

Rebecca moved to the other side of the bed. "May I hold his hand?" That, she told herself, was a dumb thing to say. Kathy looked like she had been crying. Rebecca thought of the look she had given Jerry the night she had sung "The Rose."

Kathy answered curtly, "I don't own them. Be careful, don't move it though, that's the side where he was shot." She wanted to add, "Why do you want to hold his hand? Go away," but didn't.

His hand was positioned on his chest and Rebecca gently placed her hand over his. Quietly, she asked, "Have you been here long, Kathy?"

"I came with him to the hospital last night." Kathy grimaced and added, "It's getting to be a habit, I guess."

"What do you mean?"

"I went with him to the hospital when he was shot last May."

"Oh."

Jerry began to stir. He moved his head a little from one side to the other. He squinted and then opened his eyes, looking at the ceiling and then at Kathy. He smiled and turned toward Rebecca. "Hi." He broke out in an ear-to-ear grin. "God, it's good to see you two. I was afraid I'd wakeup to see the Bishop staring down at me. How'd I get here?"

Kathy smiled. "We, Jim Peterson and I, brought

you here last night in the Peterson's station wagon. What do you remember?"

Before answering, he turned to Rebecca. "Rebecca, I'm surprised to see you. Uh, how'd you know about me?"

"Marge called and told me." She hesitated and then added, "She told me that Kurtz said he found you through my article and ... well, I felt a bit guilty." She couldn't just say she was there just because she cared. Maybe she could say that if Kathy weren't in the room.

He furrowed his brow and turned to Kathy, "Is Kurtz dead?"

"Yes, thank God. I was so afraid he'd kill a bunch of people last night." Kathy squeezed his hand and softly added, "You were really brave, Jerry."

"So was Kenny Gaffin. How is he?"

"The last time I saw him, he was covered with blood. He wasn't hurt, physically, anyway. I saw his dad put his arm around him and take him to the car. What's the last thing you remember, Jerry?"

The priest moved his arm a bit and winced. Rebecca quickly pulled her hand away. "Pain," he said. "And I remember Marge hovering over me and cutting away on my vestments. I wondered where she got the scissors. Isn't that funny?" He smiled at both of them. "I think I passed out when Marge was putting bandages on and I recall hurting as they bundled me into the back of the station wagon. I thought it was an ambulance. And you rode in back with me didn't you, Kathy?" She nodded and he pressed her hand. "Thanks. I hope that's the last time you have to do that." He turned to

257

Rebecca. "Did you know that Kathy accompanied me when I was shot in Aberdeen, too?"

Again, Rebecca had to suppress the jealous feelings. "Yes, she told me about that. So, how are you feeling now?"

He looked to his left shoulder. "That area hurts." He moved his arm again and winced. "And I'm hungry. Kathy, have you been here all night?"

"Yes. I wanted to keep your guardian angel company."

"He hasn't done a very good job lately, has he?"

"Oh, I think she has. I'm sure your angel is female, they're smarter." She smiled at Rebecca for the first time and went on, "If she had not done so well, you would have been dead back in May. If not, then last night. So thank your angel!"

Jerry looked at the ceiling and smiled. "Thanks, angel. If you have a name, give it to me and we'll communicate better." He turned back to Kathy. "Suppose they'd give me breakfast?"

"I don't know. You just got out of intensive care about two hours ago. I think they're feeding you with that." She pointed at the IV bottle filled with clear liquid. "They gave you three pints of blood."

"That much, huh? Rebecca, you say you drove from St. Louis?" She nodded. "Did you have breakfast?"

She was happy that he asked. It made her feel less like an outsider. "No, I haven't. How about you, Kathy, have you been able to get breakfast?"

"A nurse brought me some coffee."

"Well, why don't you two go down to the cafeteria and get breakfast? I'm sure I'll still be here when you get back." He glanced at the IV. "But I don't think that thing will fill my stomach." He let go of Kathy's hand and pressed the call button.

Rebecca looked over at Kathy, who didn't look too excited by the idea. "I am a bit hungry. Want to join me, Kathy?"

At the cafeteria, they both got scrambled eggs, bacon, toast, and coffee. They sat at a table near the back wall, away from the dozen or so nurses and hospital workers.

Rebecca took a sip of coffee. "That must have been quite a scene at the church last night."

Kathy looked at her in a way that Rebecca could only interpret as accusingly. "Are you going to do another article on him now?"

Rebecca dropped her fork. "I hadn't even thought of it! What makes you think that?"

"Then why are you here?"

"I've been thinking about that. When Marge called last night, I just felt the urge to be with him. I'm not sure why."

"You've only seen him that one weekend in Paris. He can't mean that much to you, to drive all night to see him in the hospital." Kathy wanted to shout at this uppity reporter.

Rebecca remembered that Marge said once that Kathy was in love with Jerry, and she was sure that was true at that moment. She wondered where the boyfriend was that Jerry told her about. Kathy definitely did not want the reporter in the hospital, that was obvious. Was Kathy jealous? "I guess Jerry didn't tell you that he brought Angela and Julie Kurtz to St. Louis this past week?"

Kathy looked shocked. "No, he didn't. Last night Kurtz kept jabbering that Jerry knew where his wife and daughter were. Jerry didn't tell him, of course. Why did he take them to St. Louis? In fact, why did they come to him in the first place?"

"According to what Jerry told me, Angela didn't know anyone else to turn to. I don't know how she managed to drive to Paris. She was so banged up when they got to St. Louis, she could hardly walk or see. As to why St. Louis, when I was in Paris, I'd mentioned that my best friend was a social worker. Jerry remembered that. He called in the middle of the night last Sunday and asked me to check to see if Helene, that's my friend, could find a shelter for them. He said he wanted to get them as far away from Aberdeen as possible. Helene found them a wonderful shelter named St. Claire's. I talked to them yesterday. God, it seems a week ago. Anyway, they're doing fine."

"So Marge must know. That's why she called you?"

"Yes, she knows. She bandaged up their wounds as best she could before they left Paris." Kathy's face had softened quite a bit while Rebecca told her the story. "Kathy, Jerry means a lot to you, doesn't he?"

Tears began to form in Kathy's eyes. "Yes, he's the most wonderful man I've ever known. You should have seen him last night. There he was, slowly walking down the aisle while this madman is yelling at him, calling him 'Holy Man' and 'asshole' and threatening him with a big gun. Everybody else is hiding down in the pews and Jerry keeps walking. God, Rebecca, I've never seen anything like that. He was the same at the anti-abortion rally, just jumped right in there and saved that doctor's life. I don't think Jerry fears anything."

"Oh yes he does." Rebecca had to smile.

"Like what?" Kathy looked incredulous.

"Like you, me, Marge and any other attractive woman who tries to get close to him. Remember that Saturday when you sang 'The Rose'?" Kathy nodded. "Well, the look you gave him afterward would have melted an iceberg, and Jerry looked like he was about to run off the altar."

Kathy blushed. She really had no idea that she showed her feelings that evening, or any other time, for that matter. "Well, Rebecca, he's a priest. Was my look really that obvious?"

"To me it was. Ask Marge the next time you see her. I know he's a priest but he's also a man." She thought about telling Kathy about his getting drunk and what he said afterward but decided against it. "Oh, and did you notice how subdued he was around us when we had dinner at Marge's?"

"I just thought he was tired." Kathy studied the middle of the table for sometime, then asked, "Did, uh, Jerry stay at your place when he was in St. Louis?"

Rebecca lied. "He said he could go to a motel but I told him it was a waste of money because I have an extra bedroom. He was a bit uncomfortable but okay, I think."

"How long did he stay?" Kathy was obviously wondering if he stayed long enough for Rebecca to get her claws into him. Rebecca realized that she could lie again, but it could too easily be revealed. "Let's see, he arrived Monday evening and left Thursday morning."

Kathy began counting the hours in her head. "So he stayed with you for three nights." She couldn't help making it sound like an accusation.

Rebecca had to work to keep the defensiveness out of her voice. "Kathy, I hope you are not implying that we did anything wrong, like sleep together. I showed him around St. Louis and we talked, that's all."

Still sounding petulant, Kathy asked, "Then why did you drop everything and drive all night to see him?"

"I guess I'm like you, I think he's the most unusual and admirable man I've ever met. He really touches me, but, uh, not physically. He touched my heart."

Kathy's jaw tightened as she said, "He touches too many hearts, I think."

Rebecca decided to change the subject, or at least re-focus it. "Jerry told me that you had a friend who has been helping you with the kids and their music. Was he there last night?"

"No. He wanted our relationship to be different than it was. He made demands on me and I told him to get lost. End of story."

Rebecca hoped that she didn't show her disappointment. She glanced at her watch. "I think we better get back to our boy."

When they got back to the room, Jerry, detached from the IV, was sitting up and finishing what looked like a bowl of oatmeal. "Just in time. The doctor says I can go home today as long as I take it easy." He wrinkled up his face and looked around the room. "Now I have to figure out how to get dressed. One of the nuns found a new shirt and undershirt for me and washed everything else."

Rebecca grinned and looked at Kathy. "We can dress you, can't we Kathy? If two women dress you, it won't be scandalous, will it?"

Jerry looked startled and then blushed scarlet. "I'm sure I can manage. Just hand me the clothes over there."

Evidently Kathy was feeling rather playful herself as she handed him the pile of clothes and said, "May we watch?"

"No you may not! Wait in the hall and I'll tell you when I'm ready."

Grinning, Rebecca and Kathy went into the corridor. Kathy said, "I don't have a car here."

"We can take mine, if that's okay with you. I'll just plan to go back to St. Louis tomorrow. Did you see the look on his face when I suggested that we dress him?"

Kathy put her hand over her mouth and laughed. "I'll bet it'll take him an hour to dress himself."

They heard a loud thud accompanied by, "Oh shit!" Opening the door they saw Jerry sprawled on the floor. He was lying on his right side with the left shoulder heavily bandaged and his arm in a sling that pressed his forearm and hand against his chest. He had his shorts on and one leg halfway in his pants. He was sweating, red in the face, and obviously in pain.

Kathy rushed to his side and knelt down. "Are you all right?"

"Do I look like I'm all right?" he snapped.

With arms crossed in front of her, Rebecca looked down at him and asked, "Well, Mr. Independent, are you ready to accept a little assistance?"

"Just help me up and stop yapping!"

Rebecca knelt opposite Kathy. Jerry was facing her. "Take my right arm and help me sit up straight."

Rebecca started to lift his arm as Kathy pulled gently on his left side. They got him lying flat on his back and then managed to get him in a sitting position. The two women had their hands on his back and waist when they heard a booming, indigent voice, "And what, may I ask, is going on here?"

Kathy whispered, "It's the Bishop." Jerry groaned.

Rebecca glanced at the pudgy fellow in a black suit, clerical collar, and gold chain and cross over his chest standing in the doorway. She said, "You may ask, but it would be more helpful if you'd get your ass over here and help us get this man up."

Kathy stifled a giggle and Jerry started laughing so hard he fell back toward the floor. If Rebecca and Kathy hadn't caught him, he would have banged his head. He started coughing.

The Bishop called down the hall, "Nurse, nurse, get an orderly in this room immediately." A lot of scurrying seemed to be going on near the nurses' station. The Bishop turned back to the trio on the floor. "And who might you be?" He motioned toward Rebecca.

"I might be Kathy Olson, formerly Sister Kathleen. But I'm not, I'm Rebecca Brady." This time, Kathy did allow herself to giggle.

"And you, the laughing one, who are you?"

"I'm Father Haloran, Bishop." Jerry laughed again.

"I know perfectly well who you are, Father." He

pointed at Kathy.

Kathy managed to control her giggling long enough to say, "I'm the real Kathy Olson, Bishop."

By this time a female nurse, who looked bigger and stronger than her male companion, arrived. The woman motioned Rebecca and Kathy out of the way and expertly placed Jerry back on the bed. "Everybody out, while we help this man get dressed."

Rebecca and Kathy followed the Bishop out in the hall. "Tell me, my good ladies, what was going on in there?"

Kathy started to say, "We were just--."

Rebecca interrupted her. "We were attempting to molest him while he was helpless on the floor." Kathy started to giggle again and Rebecca continued. "What did you think we were doing?"

"Young lady, do you know who you are talking to?"

"Yes. I'm talking to someone who seems too full of himself for his own, or anyone else's, good."

"Well I'll find out what your name is and who your superior is and tell him about your outrageous behavior!"

Rebecca was really hitting her stride now. "Well, fatso, I don't have anyone who is superior to me, and the person I work for is a she. And I'm sure she would agree with me that you are an egotistical ass!" Rebecca turned on her heels and went back in the room.

She heard the Bishop ask Kathy, "Who is that woman?" Kathy responded, "Bishop, I don't think it is any of your business!" She could hear the Bishop's "Hmmmph" and his stomping off down the hall.

As the male nurse pinned Jerry's left shirtsleeve over his chest, the priest said, "Thanks, Rebecca, that's the best laugh I've had in years. It hurt but it was worth it. I've wanted to say things like that for a long time."

"Why haven't you?"

"Because it would get me thrown out of the priesthood on my ear, that's why."

Rebecca looked at Kathy and winked, "What would be so bad about that?"

CHAPTER 15

There is a variety of gifts but the same Spirit...
working in all sorts of ways in various people, it is the
same God who is working in all of them.

1 Corinthians 12: 5-7

On the Wednesday after returning from the hospital, Jerry groaned as he sat down in the recliner. Nearly every movement hurt his shoulder. The physician had told the priest that he could take a pain pill every four hours, but they made him so sleepy he had limited himself to one in the morning and one before bedtime.

As he waited for Sy Peterson to arrive, he thought of Angela and Julie Kurtz. Helene had relayed to him on Monday morning that when she had told them of Ralph Kurtz's death, Julie had immediately said, "Good!" Helene was rather mystified by Angela's question, "Do you think I killed him?" Helene went on to tell him that Angela seemed to be in a state of shock and that, in fact, she appeared to be in very poor health ever since she arrived at St. Clair's. "Jerry, I don't think she has recovered from the beating." Jerry muttered to himself, "That poor woman."

He smiled to himself as he thought of Kathy and Rebecca giggling as they returned from a visit with Alice Peterson the same day they had accompanied him home from the hospital. They never did tell him what they were laughing about. They are both so beautiful in their different ways, he thought. He looked around the room; it was tidy, for a change. Both women had spent several hours Sunday cleaning and dusting the whole house for him. After spending the night at Marge's, they had stopped by the rectory before heading their separate ways. He felt abandoned and terribly lonely after they left.

Hearing a light knock on the door, Jerry yelled out, "Come in, it's unlocked."

Sy Peterson entered and sat down on the couch opposite Jerry. "Well, Father, how's the shoulder?"

Jerry smiled. "Okay, unless I move. I'm glad you came over, Sy. I've been meaning to tell you how much I appreciate Jim helping me out these days. He's a fine boy."

"Yes he is. And thanks to you, I think he's beginning to think so himself. The challenge of setting up and leading the band at Mass has done wonders for him. Oh, and he's got a terrible crush on Kathy Olson."

"I've noticed how he looks at her." Jerry attempted to mimic Jim's face by dropping his jaw and staring wide-eyed across the room.

Sy laughed. "That's it. Anyway, he's coming out of his shell and, finally, getting good grades in school. But that's not what I came to talk about." Sy looked around, coughed, and said, "What I want to ask you is this: You know, Alice and I have been married for thirty-seven years. The first few years she asked me, every once in a while, if I wanted to become a Catholic. I just kinda brushed her off by saying, 'Maybe, sometime I will.' To tell you the truth, I've never been too impressed with most Catholics and definitely not by the priests we've had around here." Sy chuckled a little and added, "Present company excepted, of course. To get to the point, Father, you know Alice only has a little while to live and..." Sy's eyes moistened a bit and he ran the back of his hand over them. "Pardon me. Anyway, I wonder if you'd baptize me? It'll have to be soon, you know, because..."

"Because you're afraid Alice has only a few days left. I'll be happy to baptize you, Sy, whatever your reasons. But, tell me, are you doing it only to please Alice?"

"No, Father Jerry. To me, that would be hypocritical and Alice would know it was. I've always thought of myself as a spiritual person. Not religious, mind you, but spiritual. I've read quite a bit about Eastern religions, Native American practices, and all and liked a lot of what I read. Better'n what I heard your predecessors talk about. But, here you come along and talk about love, relationships, peace, and justice rather than rules. And damned if you don't 'walk the talk' as they say. I like that and can see myself being your kind of Catholic."

"Thanks, Sy. I appreciate that. Almost from the day I met you I felt a certain dignity and spirit about you. And then meeting Alice and seeing the two of you together, I said to myself, 'That Sy is a better Christian than most churchgoers I've known.'"

"Now it's my turn to say thanks."

"When would you like to have the baptism? How about if I have a Mass in your living room on Sunday. That way Alice can attend and you can invite the whole family and whomever else you'd like."

"That sounds like a grand idea. Will you do me one more favor?" Jerry nodded. "Would you have a little talk with Alice about it all, kinda convince her that I'm not just doing this to please her."

"Sure, no problem. Oh, one more thing, Sy, you'll need to have a Godfather and Godmother. Have anyone in mind?"

"Yeah, I do. For Godfather, how about Joe Gaffin, the sheriff. I know he's not Catholic, but—"

"But he's a good man, like you. Good choice and I'd be a hypocrite myself if I didn't say, 'yes.'" Jerry chuckled. "I'll tell him to shoot you in the foot if you stray. How about Godmother?"

Sy blushed a little as he said, "How about Kathy Olson? Always wanted a pretty young mother. My mother was near forty when I was born and jest about as pretty as me."

"Another great choice. You want to ask them or do you want me to?"

"I'll do it, 'cept I don't have Kathy's phone number."

"I'll get it for you." Jerry clumsily got up from the chair accompanied by numerous groans, and went to the office. He handed the paper to Sy. "Welcome to the fold, Sy, my friend." He put his right arm around Sy and gave him a sideways hug.

When Jerry took Communion to Alice on Thursday morning, he could see that her health was failing more each day. She gave him a weak smile and touched him with her cold hand. Jerry took the communion wafer from the small gold container and held it in front of Alice, saying, "The Body of Christ."

In a weak voice, Alice responded, "Amen." He put the wafer on her tongue. Weeks earlier she had decided her hands were too shaky to hold the wafer herself, so she asked him to put it on her tongue.

Jerry covered the locket-like container and gently placed it in his pocket. "I understand that Sy told you that he wants to be baptized a Catholic."

Her voice was weak but the spark in her eyes was as strong as ever. "Yes, indeed, he did. And I suppose he asked you to talk to me so I wouldn't think he was doing it just to please me, huh?"

There's nothing wrong with her thinking or articulation, Jerry thought. "He did say something like that."

"Well, Father Jerry, you needn't bother. That man has never done a single hypocritical thing in his life. If he wants to become a Catholic, it's because he sees some good in it. And, Father Jerry, I want to thank you for that, you've not only helped Sy, you've helped me these past months. I've finally found a priest who has some sense." Alice smiled a weak little smile. "Of course, that means one who agrees with me."

Jerry winked at her and smiled. "As you know, Alice, great minds think alike. So Sunday is okay with you?" She nodded.

"Alice, one more thing, I've been meaning to ask you all week. Kathy and Rebecca were giggling after they visited with you Sunday. What did you say to them?"

Alice bit her lower lip, turned a very noticeable pink, and looked away. After a minute, she turned and looked at him. "Maybe I should go to confession now."

"That bad, huh?" He couldn't imagine Alice doing or saying anything that would be considered sinful.

"Maybe just mischievous. The two of them were laughing and talking about which one was going to run off with you."

Jerry chuckled self-consciously. Of course, they were teasing. They couldn't have those kind of feelings for him...could they? He couldn't bring himself to share with Alice how much the thought bothered him. "And you said…?"

Again Alice blushed. "I said, 'why don't you help him get ready for bed tonight and take a peek. See if his pecker is ... uh….'"

"All shriveled up?" Jerry shook with laughter and then abruptly put his right hand on his left shoulder and hollered, "Ouch!"

Alice put her small hand on his knee. "I'm sorry. That wasn't very nice, was it?"

"Not nice, but funny. I forgive you." He waved his hand in the sign of the cross as if he were giving her absolution.

"May I be serious for a moment?"

Jerry nodded.

"You know, Father Jerry, they were laughing and joking but in some ways, I think they were both serious. You have touched their hearts. I don't know what kind of feelings you may have for either of them, but they are wonderful young women. I've always thought that a person needs to love someone, love someone in a very special way, to become a truly whole person." Alice looked at him questioningly for a long moment and then went on, "I'm going to be bold now. I haven't got much time left but I have been having these thoughts and I want to share them with you." She took a labored breath. "Of course, I think of you as a fine man, better and more whole than most, married or not. But, Father, I often see you as very sad. You cover it up pretty well most of the time. I suppose most people don't notice it, but an old woman like me with nothing to do but sit around all day notices things."

Jerry listened. Reflecting on his feelings, he thought that it was a kind of emptiness he felt so often, not sadness, but concluded that Alice was probably right.

He must have shown something as Alice said, "Now, please don't get defensive with me. Let me tell you something. When I was young, I felt like I was so ugly and stupid. I was so shy I couldn't talk to anyone. Then Sy came along and changed my whole life. "When I fell in love with Sy and he told me he loved me, I felt like I was the most beautiful and wonderful person in the world. Father, you are a wonderful person. Do you believe it?"

Jerry was getting choked up and couldn't for the life of him figure out why. "I don't know, Alice. Sometimes I do, I guess."

"You should feel it all of the time. A good woman could do that for you. Personally, I think this priestly celibacy business is stupid. Now, should I make a good act of contrition?"

"No."

CHAPTER 16

*Charm is deceitful and beauty empty, the woman who
is wise is the one to be praised.*

Proverbs 3:30

On Thanksgiving Day it was not snowing, but snow
was blowing across Interstate 70 as Rebecca drove her
BMW west toward Paris, Kansas. She drove carefully,
not only for safety reasons but also so she would not
awaken her passengers, Rene and Denise. She had
invited them to join her, both for the company and to
give them a break from St. Louis. She had grown fond
of both of them since beginning the tutoring in July.
Helene thought the trip would be good for them.

Thanksgiving was turning out to be very different
than she had expected. Alice Peterson had invited
her and the girls for Thanksgiving with the 'Peterson
clan.' Now they were heading to Paris to attend Alice's
funeral, as well as the funeral of Marge Woerner's
father. Rebecca thought of her last conversation with
the frail and dying woman. Although Alice sounded
weak when Rebecca talked to her the week before, she
was so happy because Sy had just been baptized that
day. "Wasn't it wonderful of Father Jerry to have Mass
right here in our living room and baptize Sy here?"
Because Alice felt it to be so wonderful, Rebecca did,
too, even though she had no idea why baptism would
be such a big deal. She thought that any God who

demanded that you have water poured on your head and the "right" words said over you in order to get to heaven (whatever that was) wasn't worth a second thought.

"Rebecca, dear, are you still willing to read my little poem at my funeral?"

"Of course, Alice. And that's going to be a way off, isn't it?"

Alice coughed a few times, then said, "I'm afraid not, dear. I hope I make it to Thanksgiving, but if I don't, you'll still be able to come to Paris for the funeral, won't you?" She coughed again and Rebecca could almost feel it wracking the poor little woman's body.

"Yes, Alice, I'll be there, don't you worry." Rebecca had never talked to anyone who was dying before she met Alice and then those she interviewed for her article. The only people she had been close to who had died were Tom and Grace Ripkin, her foster parents, but she hadn't even known they were dying until afterward. She had a difficult time understanding how Alice could sound almost cheerful over the phone. She had to ask, "Alice, ah, you sound like you're not afraid of death."

"Oh, I am, Rebecca, a little, anyway. But to be honest, it will be a relief to shed this old body—it's just worn out, you know. Father Jerry and I have been working on the funeral. Lots of people will be there, besides my family. And Rebecca, I'm vain enough to be happy about that. Lots of people have really loved me and that's all that's really important in life, don't you think?"

Rebecca had wandered off on her own reverie at that point and didn't hear what Alice said next. Who would come to her own funeral? Oh, the people from the office, of course, but could she say she loved them or they her? Who really loved her? Helene and her daughter. Rene and Denise are beginning to, she thought. She wondered if Jerry, or someone like him, could learn to love her? Even as Rebecca recalled these thoughts while she drove, she began to get teary-eyed just as she had been on the phone. When she had shared the thought with Alice that very few people loved her, Alice scoffed and said, "Rebecca, you are a very lovable person and a loving one, too. I began to love you that first day we met, remember?" Alice's words meant a lot to her but the feeling of emptiness continued.

Seeing the sign for the county road to Paris, Rebecca exited the Interstate and, as slowly as possible, stopped. Neither Rene nor Denise awoke. They were only a few miles from the freeway and going about forty miles an hour when she hit a big pothole. "Shit!"

Rene immediately woke up, looked around, and seeing no houses, cars, nor trees— only blowing snow, hollered, "Oh, my God woman, where'n hell have you taken us? The moon?"

From the backseat Denise exclaimed, "Rebecca, are we lost?"

"Relax, girls, we are on a country road headed for Paris."

"You're lying, this can't be no road to Paris. Besides Paris is across the ocean. What you got us into, lady?" Rene sounded genuinely frightened.

Rebecca laughed. "Didn't I tell you that the town where Father Jerry is, is called Paris? Paris, Kansas, and you'll see it can't be confused with Paris, France."

"How big is this Paris?"

"About a thousand people, I think."

"A thousand! Hell! Mor'n that live in one block in my neighborhood. I bet it's full of rednecks.

Denise asked, "What's a redneck?"

Rene, sitting shotgun, looked back. "Midget, don't you know nothin'? A red-neck is a stupid asshole who hates everbody who ain't white and stupid, especially black people." She turned to Rebecca. "If someone in this Paris calls me 'nigger,' okay if I punch 'em out?"

"I'm sure no one will, but if they do, punch away. If Father Jerry is around, he'll do it for you."

"A priest ain't gonna punch nobody out!"

"This one would." Rebecca told them about the scuffle with Kenny Gaffin and his fatal encounter with Ralph Kurtz.

Rene sat back on the seat. "Hey, I'm liking this Father dude better already."

When they drove into Paris about four p.m. and didn't see a single car or truck moving or even parked on the main drag, Rene said, "I think ever'body dead aroun' here. Damn, I'd rather be dead, too, than live in a dump like this. Hey, Becky-baby, if anybody does live here, what're they like?"

*   *   *

Jerry glanced at his watch; it was three fifty five. He wasn't sure when Rebecca and the girls would arrive, only that it would be mid-afternoon. When she had told him that she was bringing Rene and Denise, he spent some time finding a place for them. He was thinking of the possibilities he had come up with when he heard a car crunching the gravel near the house. Quickly he put on his black windbreaker and went out the front door. Plato followed him. Rebecca, dressed in a white turtleneck and jeans, was already out of the car.

As he and Plato jumped off the side of the porch, he yelled, "Hi there! How was the trip?" As his left arm was still in a sling, he held out his right hand and arm.

Rebecca, smiling easily, put her arms around him, saying, "The trip was good." They hugged for a brief moment. "Father Jerry, you remember me telling you about Rene and Denise?" Both girls were glued to their seats as they starred at Plato. The dog's tail was wagging furiously.

"Of course. Thanks for keeping this lovely lady company all the way from St. Louis. Don't worry about Plato. He's friendly, he won't bite you but he'll probably sniff you." Denise gingerly stepped to the ground and put a tentative hand on Plato's head. Rene stayed put until she was convinced that Denise wouldn't get eaten, then she got out of the car.

Jerry gave Denise a sideways hug, then turned to Rene. "May I give you a hug, too?"

Rene shrugged and looked around. "Ain't never hugged a honkie dude before."

"Well, I've never hugged a beautiful young black woman before." He held out his right arm. "Let's both have a first." Rene raised her left arm slightly and he put his arm under hers and pulled her close for a moment. He stepped back. "That wasn't so bad, was it?" Rene smiled a little.

"Welcome to beautiful Paris, and to my castle. Come on in and get warm." Jerry led the way and held open the door for them. He took their jackets and hung them up near the door. He offered refreshments. Rebecca declined but Rene and Denise asked for Pepsi. After serving the drinks, Jerry asked Rebecca to go into the office with him.

Just as he was about to close the door, Rene called out, "No smoochin' in there, you two!" Both girls giggled.

Jerry motioned to a chair and sat down. "How is Angela and Julie?"

Rebecca smiled coyly. "What, no smoochin'? Just get right down to business, huh?"

"Rebecca, please don't tease me. I'm having enough trouble these days."

"I'm sorry ... uh ... hmmm, maybe I'm not teasing."

"Rebecca!" He realized that he was sounding too harsh and reminded himself to lighten up.

"Okay, about Julie and Angela. The first thing Julie asked me was if they'd have to go back to Aberdeen. She doesn't want to go back there. And Angela still seems really ill. I talked to the doctor and she thinks it's a combination of things: depression, post-traumatic stress, and even some physical problems she hasn't figured out yet. She's in no condition to live on her own so, at the moment, the plan is for them to continue to stay at St. Claire's. Kurtz didn't leave a will but he had some life insurance. I've got an attorney friend looking into all this for them."

"Thanks, Rebecca. Sorry I snapped at you a minute ago. It's been a rough two weeks. I don't sleep well with this shoulder." Jerry told Rebecca that he had made arrangements for Rene and Denise to stay with the Gaffin family. "Even though Marge has a house full with her sister and her family, she really would like for you to stay with her. She needs an ally."

"An ally? What's happening?"

Jerry relaxed back in the chair and put his fingers under his chin. "It's been a rough week for Marge. Last Friday, the doctor visited her father and said that there was just no way the old man could last much longer. As you know, he had not been fully conscious for some time. He developed a horrible cough and was in a great deal of pain. They couldn't increase the dosage of pain medication. Anyway, Marge called her sister and brother in Aberdeen to tell them that their father had only a short time to live. They came up on Saturday and Marge told them there was no hope. The doctor said he could hospitalize him in Whelan but it wouldn't help, only add to the medical expenses."

Jerry put his hand down and grimaced. "The sister, Mary, who visited her father only three or four times a year, insisted they take him to the hospital immediately. Marge, who has power of attorney, refused, and they spent the rest of the day and Sunday morning arguing."

Jeanne asked, "What about the brother?"

"A complete wimp. He didn't want to take sides.

Anyway, Marge asked me to come out to the house on Sunday to see if I could talk sense to Mary. Mary is the one who's supposed to be the 'good Catholic' who follows all the rules. Marge thought she might listen to a priest. The Church's position is that we are not obliged to continue extraordinary measures to keep a body alive. The doctor had suggested that the merciful thing to do would be to take the old man off the intravenous tube and the ventilator."

Rebecca leaned forward. "So what happened?"

"It took me about two hours to convince Mary that it would not be sinful to let her father die. I had a hard time containing my anger. Here she lets Marge give up her job in Chicago and take care of him for nearly two years, seldom visits, and then calls Marge 'heartless.' So Mary finally gives in, reluctantly and resentfully. The brother, Robert, sits there like a lump. So Robert and Mary went back to Aberdeen and got their kids, they are all over at Marge's now. Marge is feeling like the odd man out. She needs an ally."

A loud blast of Beethoven came from the other room. Rebecca jumped up just as the volume was turned down. "I think my girls are getting restless. What do we do for dinner?"

"Sy Peterson wants us all to come over to his place for Thanksgiving dinner. The whole family's there. I think they are waiting for us."

"Thanksgiving dinner the day before the funeral?"

"Alice asked Sy to promise to have a festive dinner, even if she died before. So he's doing it, for Alice, and the family of course."

"And the girls are welcome?"

"Definitely!"

*   *   *

On Friday morning, Rebecca sat between Rene and Marge in the fourth pew of St. Patrick's newly remodeled church. In front of them were three rows filled with members of the Peterson family. The church, as Alice predicted, was full, standing room only. Both Rebecca and Marge wore black suits. Rene had borrowed Jerry's black windbreaker and wore it over black jeans. Rebecca looked across the aisle at Denise. She was holding the sheriff's oldest daughter's four-year old retarded daughter, Karen, on her lap. Both smiled back at her.

Both Rene and Denise had enjoyed the large Peterson family dinner. Any fears Rebecca had had about Rene's acceptance vanished when she saw, within a few minutes, that the color of Rene's skin did not make any difference to any of them. Alice's grand-daughter, the one who had asked for prayers for her grandmother at the youth Mass, seemed to go out of her way to spend time with Rene and to make her comfortable. Both girls were warmly welcomed by Joe and Kenny Gaffin. Joe's wife, Sharon, was visiting their oldest son in Kansas City over the weekend. Joe's granddaughter, Karen, immediately took to Denise for some unknown reason. Two wounded and helpless children perhaps? Similarly, Rene and Kenny had hit it off and were already talking basketball before Rebecca and Jerry left.

Rebecca went back to the church for the customary rosary for the deceased. It was another first for her, and she was surprised that the church was more than half full for this brief ceremony. She didn't pretend to understand the significance of all these people saying, "Hail Mary, full of grace..." over and over again. But there was something very solemn and sacred about it all. She surprised herself by crying.

After the rosary, Jerry informed the congregation that there would be a final viewing of "our beloved Alice." The mortician, Rebecca guessed, opened the casket and nearly everyone present filed past, paused briefly, seemingly in prayer, and many making the Catholic sign of the cross. She was the last one before the family to approach the casket. Tears were running down her cheeks even before she saw Alice's emaciated but serene and, to Rebecca, beatific countenance. She paused, felt her knees weakening, and unable to keep from sobbing, resisted an urge to turn and run away. Standing very straight for a moment, she did something she was sure she would never have done even a few weeks before. She bent over and kissed Alice on the forehead and whispered, "Thank you."

After the service, she spent more than an hour talking with Jerry. They spent some time discussing Angela and Julie Kurtz and then the relationship between Sy and Alice Peterson. He explained that although Kathy was present for Sy's baptism, she could not be at the Thanksgiving dinner because of her mother's illness. Rebecca was a bit ashamed that she felt more than a bit disappointed when Jerry added that Kathy would be at the funeral. She slept very little that evening because she spent nearly the entire night talking with Marge. She had to admit she didn't care much for Marge's siblings.

Rebecca looked at the paper in her hand and wondered if she would be able to compose herself enough, when her turn came, to read Alice's note and poem. Jerry, wearing a similar snow white chasuble and brightly colored stole he had worn at the Youth Mass, closed the Bible and began the eulogy: "We have all gathered here this morning to celebrate the final journey of our friend and loved one, Alice Peterson. I use the word 'celebrate' deliberately for that is what Alice wants us to do, celebrate her life and our lives with her. I will keep my words brief, as Alice has asked a few others to say, read, or sing some words for you."

"Often I told Alice that she was my spiritual director. She would chuckle that delightful little chuckle of hers and say, 'Get on with you.' But I truly meant it. She was and is one of the most spiritual people I have ever had the good fortune to know. In this morning's scripture, which Alice picked out, we heard that 'No one has ever seen God, but as long as we love one another, God will live in us and his love will be complete in us.' Alice lived in God and God in her; she knew how to love. Sy and Alice Peterson were the first people I met when I came to Paris only a few months ago. The minute I saw the beautiful glow in Alice's eyes that day, I felt I was in the presence of love." He paused, looked down at the coffin in front of the altar and then out over the crowd. He made eye contact with Rebecca and seemed to be speaking only to her, as he said, "and in the presence of God. She has taught me more in only a few short months about the meaning of Jesus' message than all the years of schooling I've had."

"Alice never preached or pretended to teach, she just shared her wisdom and wonder of life and of the world. She was just herself and that was such a gift. I asked Sy if I might share an incident that, to me, was an expression of the deepest and most passionate love I've ever encountered." Jerry choked up before going on. "One day I was a bit early for my visit with Alice. I knocked on the door and I thought I heard Sy say, 'Come in.' But what he had really said was: 'Just a minute.' Anyway, I opened the door and there was Sy gently and lovingly giving Alice a sponge bath while she lay on the hospital bed in their living room. I said, 'Pardon me.' and started to back out when Alice said, 'Don't be an old prude, Father Jerry, come in and sit down. It won't embarrass me but it'll embarrass you, but that'll be good for you. You priests stay too far away from real life, you know.'" A subdued laugh coursed through the congregation. "She's right, of course. I was embarrassed but I stayed. My presence made Sy a little nervous, I think."

Rebecca could see Sy smile a little, nod his head, and cry. She could picture the scene but would never have thought to call it a 'passionate' encounter. She guessed she still had a lot to learn about love.

"But Alice just chatted away as Sy continued to take care of her in such a cherishing way." Jerry gazed at Sy for a long moment. Rebecca could see tears in the eyes of both men. "Sy, my heart and the hearts of all of us here are with you. Thank you for helping this wonderful woman become the great gift she has been to all of us."

Sy mopped his cheeks with his handkerchief as Rebecca wiped away her own tears.

Rebecca stiffened as Jerry said, "Alice has asked Ms. Rebecca Brady to read a note and poem she had composed some weeks ago. Of course, Alice was too weak to write, so she dictated it to me." He looked at Rebecca and extended his hand.

Nervously, she stood, stepped past Marge, and unsteadily made her way to the podium. With trembling hands, she unfolded the paper and smoothed it out on the small platform. She had given many speeches at various gatherings but none of them prepared her for such an emotional experience. She looked out over the congregation, saw Rene and Denise watching her intently, and finally focused on Marge, who was giving her a smile of encouragement.

She began, "I've given talks to groups before but never had to worry about breaking down in tears." Tears were already streaming down her face. "So please be patient with me when I have to pause at times. I am very pleased and honored that Alice asked me to read her words to you. When I said 'yes,' I thought it would be rather easy. I've only known Alice for a few weeks, but had never before met anyone who touched me so deeply. Here are her words for us."

"I have asked Miss Rebecca Brady to read the following to you for two reasons. One is because there are so many wonderful people in and around Paris whom I would be very pleased to have read my poem. But if I choose one, others would be left out. Rebecca lives in St. Louis, so she won't mind if you get upset that she's the one. Secondly, and more important, I have gotten to know and love Rebecca in a very short time and, well, she just seems right for the part. I hope you agree. Thank you all for coming to celebrate my passing on. I do hope that the Good Lord has a nice place for me."

Rebecca wiped tears from her face and looked out at the crowd. Nearly everyone was weeping. In as steady a voice as she could manage, she continued to read.

"God has blessed me in so many ways
To give me the ability to see
The morning sun, the rain, the wheat, and a
    tree
More importantly, to see
The sparkling and loving eyes of my children,
My grandchildren,
My friends,
My beloved Sy.
To hear kind, honest and even sometimes angry
    words
Of the dear people I have loved.
Hearing God's voice in every word
To hear 'I love you'
To touch and be touched
By the breeze, leaves, the earth
By babies, children, friends, life
All is being touched by God
To feel love, joy, sadness, elation,
Even the pain that has allowed me to have
    time

To reflect on the wonders of my life and my
 loves
To be thankful to everyone who has come into
 my life
Old and young, near and far,
Especially to Sy Peterson - my dearest love,
My children and grandchildren
Thank all of you for being with me in this
 world.
I'm looking forward to meeting you in the
 next.

Rebecca looked down at the poem, tears falling, hoping her many pauses didn't destroy the beauty of Alice's words. She raised her eyes and looked at Sy. He raised his eyes to her and she was sure she saw a certain radiance through his tears. She continued to cry as a granddaughter and grandson haltingly, but beautifully, read meaningful poems that Alice had selected. She wondered if she was crying more for herself than for Alice and her family. Alice had never done any of the so-called "glamorous" things that she herself had done, yet Alice seemed to have had a more meaningful life. Rebecca felt a kind of emptiness within herself that was nearly overpowering.

To Rebecca's surprise, Jerry announced that Alice asked Kathy Olson to sing a few words that she, Alice, found meaningful. Kathy approached the sanctuary with her guitar under her arm and turned and faced the congregation. She looked beautiful in a black dress suit with a gleaming white high-collared blouse. Kathy adjusted the guitar strap on her shoulder and addressed the crowd. "As most of you know, I have been visiting St. Patrick's since September to help the young people with their music. Most Saturdays, I have arrived early enough to spend a little time with Alice." Kathy stopped for a moment and took a deep breath. "Three Saturdays ago, she asked me to sing a few songs that I particularly liked and that might be appropriate for her funeral." Kathy again took a deep breath and seemed to be holding back tears as she said, "Alice chose two songs that I truly believe express her. I hope I am able to sing them in a way that captures Alice's wonderful spirit.

As she began, "Who has touched the sky…," Father Jerry nearly fell off his chair.

Knowing the history of that song for him, Rebecca could understand why and was surprised no one had told him of Alice's selections. When Kathy was finished, she said, "I believe that Alice, more than anyone I've ever known, knew love by its first name. And with that love, she was the wind beneath all of our wings." She then began, in her beautiful voice, *You Are The Wind Beneath My Wings.*

* * *

Jerry followed the pallbearers to the small cemetery behind the church. Most of those present in the church came with them. The sun was bright but the day chilly because of a stiff breeze from the north. He kept the graveside service brief. In place of one of the Scripture readings, he inserted a poem Alice had selected.

Do not stand at my grave and weep
I am not there, I do not sleep
I am a thousand winds that blow;
I am the diamond glints on snow;
I am the sunlight on ripened grain;
I am the gentle autumn's rain.
When you awaken in the morning's hush,
I am the swift uplifting rush
Of quiet birds in circled flight.
I am the soft star that shines at night.
Do not stand at my grave and cry.
I am not there...I did not die.

Jerry saw that Rebecca and nearly everyone there had not heeded the poem's words, and he, too, cried, but his tears were internal.

At the buffet dinner served in the church basement, he noticed many people came up to Rebecca and complimented her on her reading of Alice's beautiful poem. He was glad that Rebecca was accepted as a member of the community.

He waited until everyone had been to the buffet before filling his own plate and heading to the table where Rebecca and Kathy were seated with Denise and Rene. The four were seated across from the Gaffin family, and Jerry pulled up a chair at the end and sat between Rene and Kenny. Rene smiled at Kenny and said, "You mean, you let this dude throw you out of the church?"

"I didn't let him, he just did it." Kenny smiled somewhat sheepishly and added, "If I hadn't had a coupla beers, I'd a cleaned his clock." He puffed out his chest and gave the priest a light punch on the arm. He looked back at Rene. "I really deserved it, ya know?"

Joe Gaffin, sitting next to Kenny, added, "You certainly did!" He turned to Rene. "They've become friends since, though." Addressing Rene, Joe asked, "Did Kenny tell you that he helped Father Jerry subdue that guy who was shooting up the church?"

Rene punched Kenny on the arm. "Hey, man, that's awesome!"

Jerry thought he would never see Kenny swell up with so much pride, justified in this case.

Joe went on, "You know, Padre, that has to be most meaningful funeral I've ever attended."

"Thanks Joe, Alice did a wonderful job, just like she lived her life."

"You might make a Catholic out of me yet."

"Just be a good Methodist, Joe, that'll be just fine."

* * *

Rebecca attended Marge's father's funeral on Saturday. Kathy had to hurry back to western Kansas right after Alice's funeral because of her mother. Rebecca felt herself relax a bit when she learned that Kathy was leaving. Although Rene and Denise were very impressed with Alice's funeral, they did not want to attend another. Mr. Woerner had never been the friendly presence in the community that Alice had been, but his funeral was well attended, as was the reception afterward. Marge told Rebecca several times how much she appreciated her support and companionship.

On Sunday morning, before the Spanish Mass, Rebecca and the girls stopped at the rectory to say good-bye. Rebecca had planned to leave on Saturday after Mr. Woerner's funeral, but the girls begged to stay another day.

Kenny had spent Saturday showing Rene around the countryside, even taking her out to Marge's place where she rode a horse for the first time in her life. Denise stayed with little Karen. Sue Gaffin said she would like to have Denise with them all the time— Karen had never seemed so happy. Both teens enjoyed the Youth Mass.

Jerry invited Rebecca into the small rectory office. They stood near the desk and he took both her hands in his. "I'm so glad that you joined us and that you brought the girls. Joe said that they gave a new life to Kenny, Sue, and little Karen. And, of course, you always bring light into my life."

"Thank you, kind sir, it has been a wonderful experience for me, too, "especially Alice's funeral and my time with Marge. I've spent more time with her than with you." She knew she sounded a bit sad as she added, "I guess that's how it has to be, huh?"

Jerry looked at her quizzically and in silence for some time and then said, "I'm going to go over to St. Louis sometime in December as soon as this shoulder gets to feeling better." He seemed to want to say something more but, again after a silent pause, said only, "I'll see you then, okay?"

"Sure, I'd like that. Just let me know when." They gave one another a brief hug and then rejoined the girls in the living room. Rebecca thought Jerry looked sad as he stood in the driveway and waved as they drove off.

* * *

They were a few miles out of town when Rene, again in the front seat, saw tears streaming down Rebecca's face. She looked concerned and in a surprising gentle voice, asked, "Rebecca, the funerals are over. Why are you crying?"

Rebecca was sure she was crying for herself, and had no idea as to why she was feeling so completely empty. She said, "I'm not sure, Rene, I guess I was thinking of Alice and what a wonderful person she was. I'll miss her."

"Ever'body seemed to like her. Ain't never seen so many people at a funeral. What did she do that was so important?"

"She didn't DO much, I guess you'd say. But she knew how to love."

"I think my Grandma down in Mississippi was like that. Ain't known anybody else."

An unexpectedly strong voice came from the back seat, "Rene, you're full of shit. You're sitting next to someone like *that*!"

Rene looked back at Denise and then at Rebecca. "Ya know, Midget, I think fer once, you got somethin' right."

Rebecca got even more choked up as she said, "Thank you both. I ... think... that's the nicest thing anyone has ever said to me."

CHAPTER 17

If we take happiness from God's hand,
must we not take sorrow too?

Book of Job 2:9

The windshield wipers vigorously swept snow from the glass as Jerry drove, below the speed limit, toward Omaha, Nebraska. It was Christmas Day. As had become usual for him over the past eight months, he felt divided between duty and adventure, responsibility and freedom, from what he "should" do and what he wanted to do. One of the "shoulds" was attending the Haloran family reunion. He was not looking forward to it even though it was the first one in twelve years, the last being at his own ordination to the priesthood.

When he visited St. Louis in mid-December, Rebecca was on assignment in New York. He had lengthy talks with Angela and Julie as well as the attorney friend of Rebecca's. They were "okay" temporarily at St. Claire's but Angela's health was not good.

Rebecca had called him the Sunday before Christmas and invited him to join her and Helene in San Francisco at Christmas time. The magazine owner had given Rebecca two airline tickets and four nights at the Hyatt. She said that she had thought of him first but knew he would be committed for Christmas Masses and the family reunion, so she had invited

Helene. Jerry was sure that Rebecca would know that it would have been inappropriate for him to join her alone in California. The very thought of sharing a hotel room with her definitely did bring on a rush of sinful thoughts.

Rebecca had added, "If you get tired of that family of yours, you could join us on Christmas Day." Joining both of them? He wasn't sure. It was tempting but she was probably only kidding anyway. Knowing it was impossibile, he told her he definitely would rather be with them but "being a dutiful and responsible child, I better join the family." He didn't tell her that most of the adults would probably spend the bulk of the days drunk or nearly so.

The Aberdeen radio station began to fade and he fiddled with the knob until he heard a DJ from Omaha announce, "I don't know about you, but I'm tired of all this Christmas music. I'm going to play some of my own nostalgic favorites, starting with *Lara's Song* from *Doctor Zhivago*. I think it's appropriate for this wintry day." Jerry turned the radio up a bit. "Somewhere, my love, there will be songs to sing although the snow covers the hope of spring / Somewhere's a hill covered in green and gold and there are dreams more than your heart can hold..."

He sang along with the tune until he got so choked up, the tears turned his singing to a murmur and then stopped altogether. Damn! He got irritated at himself for feeling self-pity again. He rarely cried before Melanie died, now it seemed he would cry at the drop of a hat. What the hell is wrong with him? His thoughts turned to Rebecca and Helene and what they might be doing right then in San Francisco. He dug into his pocket and retrieved a handkerchief and dabbed at his eyes and face.

The DJ seemed to be reading his mind as he played, and Jerry sang along with "Unchained Melody", and several more nostalgic love songs, all of which he had memorized as a boy. As he sang, he thought of his father. Their happiest times together were the Sunday trips in which dad would sing show tunes and folk songs as they drove through the countryside. Jerry had never figured out why his dad had memorized so many love songs when his life seemed so loveless. He wondered what his life would have been like if his dad hadn't died when he did. A chill ran down his back as the thought that entered his mind said: "If you hadn't killed him." He admonished himself for thinking that thought again. It was an accident, dammit!

As he drove along and accompanied the radio, he reflected on Wayne's comment that not long ago, Jerry had talked like he'd had breakfast with God. No, he didn't have breakfast with God, more like breakfast with Epectitus, the Greek philosopher of Stoicism. Thinking of the family chaos he was headed into, he thought that he had become a natural stoic to survive the turmoil around him as he grew up. Better not to feel anything than to get engulfed in the drunken anger and hysteria of the family. Now, he was afraid of feeling too much. Could he go back to being a stoic after months of finding his nerves on edge? He wasn't sure if he could or even if he wanted to. In many ways, he felt more alive than at any time in his life, even if many of the feelings were of the sad or, maybe worse, sinful variety.

The radio DJ started playing modern, unfamiliar songs. He turned down the volume. His thoughts refocused on his work at the parish. At the Midnight Mass, the church was packed with all segments of the congregation, young people, Hispanic farm workers and their families, along with the older folks. He had divided the music between the youth band and the Mexican mariachi group. Even the old timers commented that St. Patrick's had never been so lively. Even the Mass that morning had been attended by several dozen people. He was most proud of involving the large Hispanic community in the parish. Getting the church repaired and painted, although something to be proud of, was mainly something to keep him busy. In December, the Sunday collection more than covered all the expenses for the first time. It had been a good five months' work. Why, then, didn't he feel better about it? During the Fall, several people asked him about becoming Catholics. When he asked them if they would continue to be Catholics after he left the parish, they hesitated. He encouraged them to think about it and, in the meantime, to feel free to participate in the services and, more importantly, do their best to live Christian lives of love, compassion and justice. He smiled grimly as he thought that the Bishop would be impressed if he brought several families into the Church. But he wasn't interested in impressing the Bishop.

The snow stopped falling by the time he reached Interstate 80 near Lincoln and he made better time into Omaha. Six children were working on a snowman as he pulled into the driveway of his sister Gladys' suburban home. It was a sprawling ranch house on half an acre. The expansive front yard looked like a small army of munchkins had fought a battle there. The kids abandoned their project and rushed to meet him.

"Uncle Gerard, Uncle Gerard, we've been waiting for you!" One freckle-faced ten-year-old hollered. "Will you play football with us?" Jerry had introduced himself as "Jerry" to everyone since he was sixteen but the family persisted on calling him 'Gerard,' the family and the Bishop.

"He can't play football with us, dummy, he's been shot."

Derek asked, "Is that true, Uncle Gerard?"

"I'm afraid so, Derek." Jerry opened his jacket so they could see his arm in a sling. "I might be able to play a little football with you, if I can be quarterback." As they huddled around him, he knelt down and gave sideways hugs all around, calling each by name. The youngest two, a boy and girl, were Gladys' grandchildren. "I better run in and say 'Hi' to the big people first, don't you think?"

Jonathan, twelve, his brother Scott's youngest, looked disgusted. "Go on in but they don't care, they're so drunk that they won't even see you." He hoped Jonathan was wrong, but doubted it.

Nancy, Jonathan's sister, piped up, "Jonathan, don't talk that way, it's not nice."

"Yeah, but it's true."

"Uncle Gewaawd, can I be on your side?" This from Stephen, a grandnephew, age five.

"Sure, Stephen." Jerry untangled himself and stood

up. "I'll go see if anyone is awake in there and then come back out, okay?" As he headed toward the front door, he thought he could enjoy the visit, if most of the adults went away. Only Mary, Kelli, his mother, and Scott's wife had sent him a get-well card when he was in the hospital in May and only Mary and his mother seemed interested in his last hospitalization.

Without knocking, he opened the door and entered. Two brothers and two brothers-in-law were sprawled out in front of the television watching a football game. A fifth, Nathan, Mary's accountant husband, sat solemnly in back of the slouching four. He alone stood and extended his hand in greeting. Nathan was a small, shy man who knew he didn't fit in with the Haloran clan. Jerry was sure his presence was due only to Mary's insistence. Jerry had seen only Gladys and family, Kelli and his mom, all of whom lived in Omaha, and Mary and her family in Kansas City in the past three or four years.

Jack, Gladys' bald and fat husband, looked up and waved. "Welcome to my house, old man." He quickly looked back at the game. John, Jerry's oldest brother, thin and depressed looking, gave him a weak smile and raised a hand. Jerry nodded.

Scott, six years older than Jerry and the third oldest of the siblings, was a little louder. He yelled, "Hey, Holy Man, I hear you were shot. Between the legs, I hope—bein' you never use anything down there anyway." All but Nathan laughed. "Grab yerself a beer and come join us." A chill ran down Jerry's spine and his right hand automatically made a fist. In manner, if not looks, Scott reminded Jerry of Ralph Kurtz. He wondered if his brother physically abused his two boys and one girl when they were home. He had heard him verbally hurt them, but had never seen him hit any of them.

Spade, Shelly's truck-driver husband, smiled and waved without taking his eyes off the television.

Jerry outwardly ignored Scott. Why in hell aren't these guys outside playing with the kids? He wondered. What a pathetic sight.

Nathan stood near Jerry as all this was going on. "Good to see you, Gerard." He lowered his voice to a near-whisper. "You fit in around here about as well as I do, I think. How are things going for you? I understand that you were wounded again."

"Yeah, I guess it's getting to be a habit. Twice in one year is a little much, don't you think?"

"I'd sure think so. I hope you can find time to tell me about it."

Jerry went into the kitchen to greet the women of the family. A Formica counter divided the kitchen from the combination dining room-family room. His mother, four sisters and two sisters-in-law were all present: four in the kitchen working on dinner, two on barstools at the counter, and his mother in a rocker nearby. All but Mary, busy stirring something on the stove, and Mom, had a beer in hand or on the counter. They seemed to be caught up in a conversation about men.

"I tell you, they don't have the brains they were born with." Shelli waved a knife over a head of lettuce.

"I don't think they were born with any!" Gladys added.

No one had noticed Jerry standing in the doorway.

"Awe, come on, you all, all men aren't brainless."

They all looked his way. Mary said, "Oh, hi, Gerard, we didn't hear you come in. The zombies come to life in there every once in a while and make a little noise. We don't pay any attention."

None of the women moved to give him a hug as he made his way over to his mother. The little old lady, seventy-nine, lifted her head to him as he bent over, took her hand, and kissed her lightly on the lips. "Hi, Mom. How are you?"

"Okay, I guess, son. I was worried about you with the snow and all." Her weak voice matched her frail body, which was wrapped up in an old, faded blue sweater. Her gray hair was tied back in a bun. Jerry tried to remember a time when her hair wasn't in a bun or when she didn't look like all the life had gone out of her. Her eyes had none of the sparkle he had found in Alice Peterson's, a sparkle the Paris woman had kept up until the day she died. Jerry's whole family always said that Mom was "just tired out". Several years ago, he realized that it was more than that: his mother was chronically depressed and had been for over twenty years. Kelli, with whom she lived, as well as all the others, strongly resisted the idea that their mother would benefit from therapy. He guessed they believed it would reflect badly on them.

"No need to worry, Mom." He glanced at his watch. "I made pretty good time. No traffic, everyone stayed home except me, I guess." He sniffed the air. "Smells pretty good, what's cookin'?"

Gladys put down her beer. "How about turkey, ham, roast beef, dressing, yams, mashed potatoes, cranberries, salad, oh, and rolls? Except for Mary and Nathan..." She looked down her nose, attempting to look snooty. "Who have gone vegetarian on us. They'll have tofu, whatever that is."

Mary glared at Gladys then smiled at Jerry. He winked back at her and her smiled widened. For years he had thought the vegetarian philosophy made sense, for health, the environment, and even for the animals' sake. He just hadn't been quite willing to entirely wean himself away from meat.

John's wife, Tiffany, piped up, "Can you imagine not eating meat in the meat capital of the world?"

"You gonna go watch football with the couch potatoes?" Kelli asked.

"No. I promised the kids I'd join them in a little football."

Mary said, "You can't play football with an arm in a sling. How bad is it, anyway?"

He was glad someone noticed. There for a while, he felt just like he did as a kid, like there was no one in the world that cared about him. "It still hurts a bit at times. I can take it out of the sling for brief periods. The kids said I could play quarterback and use one hand. If the left side hurts too much, I'll quit. Where are the older ones?"

"Down in the basement playing with the computer or something."

He went down the stairs behind the kitchen and found eight more kids, one boy about fourteen playing some kind of game on the computer and three more waiting a turn. Three girls and another boy were playing pool. Not present were five more nieces and nephews, either married or away at college. The girls rushed over and gave him hugs and asked him how he got wounded and if it hurt. All the boys, true to form, only said "hi," but unlike their elders upstairs, they did shake hands.

"I promised the kids outside I'd join them in a football game. Who else wants to play?"

All three girls immediately said they did. Jason, Scott's fourteen year-old son, pushed one of them aside. "Girls can't play football."

She pushed him back. "I know Uncle Gerard will let us. So come out and see whether or not we can play. I can beat you any time, weirdo."

Jason called out, "Come on, you guys, let's show these dames that they don't know nothin'." All but Nathan's boy, Brian, agreed to come along. Unfortunately, Jerry thought, Brian looked like the stereotypical nerd, he even wore pressed slacks and a tie. It was going to be a long day for him with this crowd.

When they all got together in the front yard, Jerry looked the group over, six girls and eight boys. The girls ranged in age from five to sixteen and the boys, from six to fifteen. They matched up pretty well in size. He shouted, "How about this: Six girls and eight boys. I'll join the girls and we'll beat you macho-men." Only little Stephen objected but agreed when Jerry told him he would do something special with him later.

The girls clapped their gloved hands together and squealed. The boys muttered, "Okay, we'll show ya." "We'll clean yer clocks." "Let's go fellas!" "Cornhuskers against the Pansies."

They played 'tag' football until the sun was only a golden glow on the horizon. Once Jerry had carried the youngest girl over the goal line with one arm, as she clutched the ball. The boys called it cheating but the girls said it was fair. He ran interference for two girls as they scored touchdowns. The score was tied thirty-thirty, when one of the mothers hollered from the door, "Come in and clean up. Dinner'll be ready in fifteen minutes."

They were all covered with snow as they headed to the back porch of the house. Jerry brushed as much snow as possible from the little ones and encouraged everyone to clean their shoes or take their boots off before going in. He realized, too late, that he should have had them all take their shoes off as he saw wet and muddy tracks across the tile floor. Just a he entered the kitchen, he heard Shelly yell, "Hey, you stupid little shits, don't you know how to clean your shoes? Use your brains, if you have any. Damn!"

The kids who had not reached the kitchen huddled in the doorway as Jerry quickly walked over to Shelly just as she was about to slap her six-year-old girl, Kathy. He gently pushed the girl behind him. Struggling to control his voice, he said, "Shelly, it's my fault, I thought I got them cleaned up. I honestly don't think a little mud on the floor warrants calling them such awful names."

Shelly glared at him as if he had accused her of murdering their mother. "What the hell do you know about kids, you've never had any! When you get out of your ivory tower and have some kids, then you can tell me how to talk to mine." She was shouting. Only

Mary seemed to be disturbed by the outburst. Men gathered across the counter near the table piled high with food. Jerry's mother, still in the rocker, wrung her hands and looked agitated.

Spade, Shelly's six-foot, four-inch husband, came around the counter and grabbed Kathy by the hair. Kathy held on to Jerry's pant leg as her father sputtered, "Let go of him, you little snot! I'll show you what happens to kids who mess up."

Jerry immediately freed his left hand and arm from the sling. Using both hands he grabbed the arm holding Kathy's hair and twisted. His left shoulder felt like it was being shot all over again, but he didn't let go of Spade's arm. After a few moments, which felt like hours, the big man let go of the little girl's hair and drunkenly shouted, "Ya sonofabitch!" He made a wild and akward swing at Jerry's head, missed, and sprawled on the floor. Kathy was crying hysterically. Jerry picked her up and cradled her in his right arm and moved quickly to the counter. He sat the girl down on the counter and picked up the telephone and dialed 91 then paused. He was sure that Spade and Shelly had been abusive to Kathy and the others but he had only witnessed what the child protection people would consider a minor hair-pulling incident.

Spade had gotten to his feet and advanced toward Jerry. "Take one more step, Spade, and I complete this 911 call and you'll spend the night in jail." His brother-in-law stopped, rocking unsteadily from side to side. He was bleary-eyed as he looked around for some kind of support. "Ain't no police doing anything to me, asshole," Spade slurred.

"You started this by pickin' on my wife."

Shelly, tears running down her cheeks, looked frightened as she said, "Now look what you've done, Gerard, you've ruined a perfectly good Christmas!" She attempted to take Kathy from his arms. The girl had quietly nestled her head against his shoulder.

Still holding the phone, Jerry turned away from Shelly. "I'll hold her for a while; she's calm now."

Spade again lurched at Jerry. "Gimme my fuckin' daughter, asshole." He made a grab for Kathy. Jerry stepped aside, put his foot out, and tripped the lumbering Spade. The women screamed and cleared the way as the big man nosedived toward the cabinets. His head banged against a cupboard with a resounding thud. Spade lay there without moving.

Jerry's stomach was in knots as he flashed back to his father's death. He put an arm around Kathy as he stared at the fallen man. Relief flooded over him as he saw Spade begin to breathe heavily.

Shelly knelt down by her husband. "Spade, are you okay? Should we call an ambulance?"

She helped him to a sitting position. "Naw, I'm okay." Spade looked up at the worried faces around him and then at Jerry. "Better get that sonofabitch outta here 'fore I kill him!"

Gladys, as hostess of the gathering, seemed compelled to speak. "Gerard, you have really ruined everything."

Mary went to Jerry's defense. "He hasn't done anything except try to protect that precious little girl."

"Protect, my ass!" Scott interjected. "He butted in on something that was none of his business." He turned to Jerry. "We all knew you thought you were better'en the rest of us, now we know fer sure. Yer so damn high 'n mighty!"

Jerry looked around at the group. Several of the children were crying, and of the adults, only Nathan and Mary seemed not to agree with Scott. He turned toward the living room. "Mary and Nathan, could I speak to you for a moment?" Still holding Kathy in his arms, he walked through the door. The couple followed him through the living room and outside. When they got to the small front porch, Jerry said, "I think it best that I leave." He handed Kathy to Mary.

With tears flowing down her cheeks, Mary took Kathy and held her close. "Gerard, I fear for this little girl, and for her brothers, too. I wish you would have made that call. The children are not safe."

"I know, but we didn't have enough to go on, only the hair pulling. Child Protective Services won't arrest on that; they'll only give a warning. I was afraid the police coming would only make things worse. I'm sorry if I spoiled everything."

Nathan put his hand on Jerry right shoulder. "You didn't make things worse." He hesitated a moment, then added, "I hate to say this, but your family has more than its share of nutcases."

"I'm afraid you're right." Jerry gave Mary and Kathy a hug. "I hope you can find a way for her to be safe, at least for today."

Mary held Jerry's hand. "I'll do my best. I don't think we can stay here very much longer, either. I'll talk to Shelly when things calm down."

"Please tell Mom that I'll call her soon." Jerry

shook Nathan's hand.

Several of the children had gone out the backdoor and were standing at the bottom of the porch steps. "You're not leaving are you, Uncle Gerard?" one of them asked.

"I think it's better if I leave. I'm sorry. I really enjoyed our game."

Stephen threw his arms around Jerry's legs. "I wish you were my daddy. My daddy's mean." Tears were running down his cheeks.

Jerry knelt down and gave Stephen a hug. "I'm sorry, Stephen." The other kids took turns with the hugs, saying, "I wish you wouldn't leave." "You're our favorite uncle." One of the older ones said, "You were right to help Kathy out."

He held back tears and waved to the kids as he drove away.

Lost in thought, he automatically headed south. He was tense, his shoulder hurt like hell, and he was getting a headache as he ruminated about his family. Maybe he should have stayed. No, it would just have made things worse.

CHAPTER 18

*....there was no one to support me...Then I
remembered your mercy
Lord and your deeds from earliest times...*
Ecclesiasticus 5: 10-11

Looking around him, Jerry began to wonder where he would go. He had planned to stay in Omaha until Saturday morning; it was Wednesday. He couldn't stand the idea of going back to Paris because it seemed so bleak and lonely on Christmas Day. He needed to talk to someone. If Alice were still alive, Paris would be more inviting at the moment. Marge Woerner was visiting friends in Chicago. Wayne was off to his own family gathering. Alice, Wayne, Marge, and to a lesser degree, Kathy and Rebecca were his only confidants for the past several months.

Kathy had invited him to join her family in Ashland, Kansas, but that would be too awkward and besides it was too late. Could he get in touch with Rebecca? Was she really serious about his joining them in San Francisco, or was she just being nice? He probably should go to a Trappist monastery he once visited in Missouri, have a quiet retreat, and straighten himself out. But he didn't want to be alone in a monastery, or anyplace else.

He glanced at his watch; it was seven-fifteen. That would be five-fifteen in San Francisco. Spotting a

Denny's near the next exit, he pulled off the freeway. He found a phone near the restrooms, looked up the area code for San Francisco, and asked for the number for the Hyatt Hotel. Cradling the phone on his shoulder, he wrote down the number. His hand shook as he dialed the number and then his long-distance card number. The hotel operator told him she would ring Ms. Brady's room.

His fingers were crossed as the room phone rang three times. Rebecca picked up the phone and answered, "Hello."

Jerry wanted to ask her if he could join them but something stopped him and he remained silent.

Rebecca repeated her "Hello" and added, "Who is this?"

Jerry began, "Re…" but could not bring himself to say her name or anything else and remained silent.

He heard Helene ask, "Who is it?" Rebecca must have turned from the phone as her voice was somewhat muffled as she said, "Some kind or weirdo, I guess. For a moment there, I thought it was J." She was hanging up.

Jerry's hand was shaking as he hung up the phone. He muttered, "Yeah, Rebecca, it is some kind of weirdo." He really didn't feel like eating, but he felt hungry. Looking around the restaurant, he noticed a rumpled and poorly dressed fellow at the counter, an old man sitting alone at a table reading a paper as he sipped coffee and a fairly young couple dressed in matching black leather jackets sitting in one booth. That was the entire population of the restaurant on this Christmas Day. The "Please Wait To Be Seated" sign was turned around, so Jerry slowly made his way over to a window booth and sat down. An unsmiling waitress promptly brought him a menu and poured him a cup of coffee. He ordered a cheeseburger and fries. It didn't take long to arrive and the only positive thing about the meal was that it filled him up. Only ten miles away was a pile of deliciously cooked food that would mostly go uneaten because the adults were too drunk to eat.

He decided to go to the Trappist monastery. He needed to just spend some quiet time and try to get his head on straight. Although he had spent a lot of quiet and alone time in Paris, he had deliberately avoided deeper contemplation of himself, his priesthood, and his faith. It was more than a "perhaps" that he thought he needed to quit distracting himself with busy-ness and take a deeper look. Because he really did not want to, was a good reason to do it.

On Christmas Day it would be highly unlikely the monastery's guest rooms would be full but, because it would be quite late when he arrived, he called to make sure he was welcome. He was.

It was ten in the evening as he drove up the country road lined with four-foot snow banks on each side. He had visited the Prince of Peace Abbey when he was in the seminary, some fifteen or so years earlier. At the time he had been quite taken by the writings of Thomas Merton and wanted to experience at least a weekend at a Trappist monastery. Ringing the doorbell, he was quickly greeted by a thin, serene-looking middle-aged monk dressed in the traditional white habit covered in front and back with a black, head-to-foot scapular.

He felt he could literally inhale the peace and quiet even though nearly every bone in his body ached as he followed the silent monk down the hall to his room. The only decoration on the walls was a plain wooden cross. Jerry had forgotten how austere the place was.

The monk informed him that Matins would be chanted at two a.m., if he cared to join them. Jerry was sure that he would not. Maybe, he told himself, he would be more rested and able on Thursday night. The monks called their rooms 'cells,' and the guests used the same, a six-by-ten foot room with only a small cot, table, and chair. It made his bedroom in Paris look luxurious. It took him only about ten minutes to fall asleep on the uncomfortable cot.

In the morning, he borrowed a cassock from the monks as he had not brought one for his trip to Omaha. He guessed he was not the first as the monk handed him a black cassock similar to his own back in Paris. He was surprised as he entered the chapel to chant the office of Prime, that it was less than half-full, about two-thirds the number of fifteen years earlier. He guessed that the Trappists were having the same problem with religious vocations as the rest of the Church world. Even with the relatively small group of monks, the chanting was magnificent and Jerry found himself feeling lighter than he had in months. Or years? A period of silent meditation followed Prime and then the celebration of Mass by three of the monks.

After wandering around the abbey's snow-cleared walks and pathways many times and often visiting the chapel, Jerry decided to make an appointment with the monk who was appointed spiritual director for guests.

Maybe the priest could help him sort out his jumbled thoughts. Every time he attempted to pray or meditate, his thoughts tumbled around like clothes in a clothes dryer—the family, Kathy, Bishop Mazurski, Rebecca, the parish, the nature of God, faith, death and back again. What was most maddening and disturbing were the recurring images of Rebecca or Kathy in some kind of pose that he found provocative. Both women had been careful to be modest around him but he could "see" Kathy in shorts with her legs curled up under her as she sat on the couch. Or Rebecca, sitting at her glass-topped table and her robe slipping in a way that revealed her knee and part of her thigh. Or simply either of them smiling and teasing him as they did in the hospital or with Alice Peterson.

The time for meeting the spiritual director was set for Friday morning at nine. Jerry chided himself for feeling like Thursday would never end and wanting and needing to do something other than think, pray, chant, and silently walk around. How did the monks stand it? Was he that far removed from the kind of spirituality they seemed to practice with such serenity? Several times he looked at one of the monks to see if he was unhappy or dissatisfied with the life at the abbey. He saw smiles and serenity. That was all. Was it simply that these men had more faith than he did? When he visited the monastery years ago, he remembered having a similar question but just thought that they were taking the contemplative path while he was taking the "active" path of a parish priest. At the time, he believed his faith and commitment would match the most devout monk. Just wishful or boastful thinking? He wondered.

Well, he definitely had taken the active path. Had he let that path lead him away from the Catholic faith and into doubt? He was sure that he hadn't yet fallen into despair, the complete hopelessness that kept a person from reaching God. Or had he?

On Friday morning, Jerry walked down the hall to the counseling room. Heading toward him was a thin, pleasant-looking, gray-haired man dressed in the white and black habit. Jerry guessed that he was in his mid-sixties. As they met at the door, the priest held out his hand and said, "I'm Father Augustine. You must be Father Gerard Haloran."

Jerry took his surprisingly calloused hand and remembered that the Trappists, from the Abbot down, spent many hours a week doing manual work. "Yes, I'm Father Jerry. I'm happy to meet you, Father Augustine."

The door was open to a small office, about the same size as the cell where he slept.

Father Augustine motioned toward one of the two hard-backed chairs next to a table with only a Bible as ornament. "Well, Father Jerry, let me first say that everything you say to me is confidential, just as if we were in the confessional. Also, I would like to ask that you keep confidential everything I say to you. Okay?"

"Definitely!" Jerry was relieved that the priest had so quickly said this. He, himself, had never asked anyone to keep his remarks confidential and wished he had, for at least on two occasions he had told penitents that birth control was a matter of their own consciences and they in turn told Bishop Mazurski. Both times he had been called in on the Bishop's carpet. Each time he remained silent and listened to the Bishop's harangue.

Jerry wanted to ask the priest about his own background and theology before saying what was troubling him, but decided to just take a kind of leap of faith. He guessed that part of the reason for his 'faith' was Father Augustine's eyes, which reminded him of Father Groel, the pastor of the small parish in Henning, Nebraska. They also reminded him of the eyes of Father Teilhard de Chardin, who had written many books that had been his inspiration for years. "I suppose, Father Augustine, that you do not read the daily papers?"

Father Augustine smiled and shook his head. "Have you made the news lately?"

"I guess last May would be 'lately,' wouldn't it?" Father Augustine nodded and Jerry went on to tell him all the events of his life since May, starting with Melanie Kurtz's confession and subsequent suicide. The monk did not say a word but Jerry could tell that he was listening carefully. Father Augustine made such wonderfully compassionate contact with his eyes. He didn't even flicker when Jerry mentioned Melanie's confession. Jerry hoped that he himself demonstrated such good listening skills when others were attempting to unburden themselves to him. He continued to tell him of Wayne Cameron's burden of shame over his homosexuality. Jerry was quiet a moment and then leaned forward and said, "After the girl's suicide and Father Wayne's confession, I found myself fed up with the seemingly thousands of confessions about masturbation and birth control and, well, the Church's entire position on sex. So, three weeks after I was shot, I gave a sermon contradicting the Church on masturbation, birth control, homosexuality, and abortion." Jerry leaned back in the chair and looked defiantly at Father Augustine.

The monk simply asked, "And what was your Bishop's reaction?"

Jerry could not detect any kind of astonishment, surprise, or condemnation from the old man's face. He chuckled self-consciously and answered, "He asked me to give a sermon taking back all that I had said. I refused. When he said that he would expel me from the priesthood, I told him that I would sue the Church."

With this, Father Augustine did raise an eyebrow and quietly said, "Please go on."

"I knew a lawsuit wouldn't work because it had been tried before. But I had received a great deal of publicity about the so-called saving of the abortion doctor. I knew a press conference would be well attended. Bishop Mazurski is publicity-shy so he assigned me to a very small parish in western Kansas with the agreement that I would not teach or preach anything about sex nor talk with the media about the sermon."

"So you have been at the small parish for several months and are, what is it?— disappointed, dissatisfied, dispirited? Please tell me."

"No. Honestly, I really enjoy the small parish. I do get lonely at times but the people there have been great." Jerry went on to tell of his work, of Alice Peterson, Kathy Olson, Julie and Angela Kurtz's escape and his trip to St. Louis, Rebecca's article, and his second run-in with the Bishop.

Father Augustine looked at his left arm, still kept

in a sling except when he needed it for some brief task. "And what happened to your arm?"

"And that's another long story but I'll keep it short." Jerry told him of Ralph Kurtz's unexpected arrival at Paris, his death, and Jerry's own gunshot wound. Lastly, he told the monk of the Christmas Day fiasco with his family. He did not mention his attempt to call Rebecca in San Francisco. He did share his too-frequent uncomfortable feelings when he was around Kathy and Rebecca. He was sure that would be the area that Father Augustine would pick up on and ask him about.

And, so he was surprised when the priest said, "Please tell me more about your family. But first, I must use the bathroom. At eighty-two, that is a more frequent exercise." He chuckled a bit as he left the room.

Jerry nearly fell off the chair. Eighty-two! Surely he's jesting. "I'll take a break, too." As they walked down the hall, he asked, "Are you really eighty-two, Father?"

The older priest, five inches shorter than Jerry, looked up and said, "I'm afraid so."

When they returned to the room, Father Augustine again asked Jerry to tell him more about the family. Jerry told him about his father's drinking, the poverty, and lack of education among all the family members. When he described the death of his father, the monk leaned forward with increased interest. "And after your father died, who became the breadwinner of the family? Did your older brothers and sisters help out?"

"No, they were struggling, too. I was fourteen and

my dad had taught me a lot of carpentry and handyman skills. The townspeople gave me a lot of work, so I guess you could say I was the breadwinner. When I was sixteen, we moved to Aberdeen, Kansas, where we lived with my older sister for a while, and then when I graduated from high school. I bought a house from the construction company I was working for."

Father Augustine asked, "You mean after you worked a few years?"

"No, only one month after graduation, I was eighteen. I had worked for the company since I was sixteen—they let me build cabinets and all after school. Usually I worked about thirty hours a week."

"When did you decide to become a priest?"

"Right after my father died. We had a wonderful priest there in Henning. Uh, ah, Father Augustine, you remind me of him."

"I'll take that as a compliment. I'm wondering, Father Jerry, you worked to take care of your mother and two sisters, bought a house for them. How did they treat you? I mean, you were a son and brother, but acted more like a father."

Jerry was completely surprised at his emotional reaction to the monk's question.

His eyes filled with tears and he looked away. He found himself on the verge of bawling. As best he could, he choked back the tears and blurted out, "Oh, shit! Ah, sorry Father." He glanced over at the priest.

Father Augustine grinned. "My, my, I've never heard that word in my entire life. Father Jerry, I'm going to venture a guess. One of the reasons you find the attention—I'm going to call it 'love'—you have received from the two women, Kathy and Rebecca, is because it's so much more expressive, accepting, and well, even wonderful than anything you ever received from your family, and you really don't know what to do with it. Or I should say, 'with them.' Is that making any sense to you?"

Jerry's jaw dropped. That's it! He thought. It explains so much. It wasn't just lust that attracted him to them. It was their compassion, patience, caring, things he never got from his own family. "Father Augustine, how do you know all this? I've never thought of it that way, but yes, it's true. You know, I think I became a priest to get some of that love. I worked hard to get it, but I still felt empty. Like I had a big hollow place inside me, a hollow place I've had since I was a boy." Jerry looked at the floor and then out the small window. "You know, Father, I thought God would fill that hollow place but, well, I still feel hollow. I've always felt it. Maybe it's smaller now but it's still there. It's not just since I've been sort of isolated in that small town of Paris. But I have always escaped into work, into activity, all of my life. Since that girl's suicide, I've let myself feel, for the first time. Feel everything. Take Kathy Olson, for instance. She says that she has always loved me." Jerry immediately turned red when he uttered these words and stopped what he was saying.

"You needn't feel ashamed for feeling anything, Father. Sometimes it is the actions that follow the feelings that we need to be ashamed of. Anyway, please continue."

Jerry wondered how this man had become so wise. "Kathy Olson says that she always loved me, but that I ignored her or never took her seriously. I do know that I was afraid of the lustful feelings that would sometimes come over me when I thought of her. I have to admit that I never thought of her love as being something that could help me."

"As you know, my son, our wonderful religion has often been more than a little misogynistic. It is a wonder that the faithful Catholics have managed to enjoy deep intimate love after all the fear so many priests have instilled in them. And with that, I'm afraid, not only of women but of sex, too. Otherwise, you wouldn't have felt compelled to give that sermon and you would not have been exiled because of it."

Jerry smiled. He couldn't believe this man. What an unexpected surprise!

"May I ask, Father, why you are smiling?" Father Augustine asked.

"I wandered around the monastery nearly all day yesterday before making the appointment to see you. I was afraid I would find some stuffy old monk who would have no idea what I was talking about."

Father Augustine smiled back at him. "I am an old monk"

"But you're not stuffy, and you understand. Please tell me, Father Augustine, where did you get all this uh...worldly wisdom?"

"All wisdom is worldly and all wisdom is of God, if it is true wisdom. I suppose some of my understanding of your predicament comes from my own experience. It may help you to know that I was married for twenty-six years to a wonderful woman before I became a Trappist twenty-eight years ago."

Jerry suddenly remembered reading about a Trappist who had been widowed and then entered the order. "And you have four children, if I remember correctly."

"That is correct. And tomorrow is a banner day. My two sons, two daughters, and their spouses, my seven grandchildren, and three great grandchildren will visit me here at the abbey." The monk smiled radiantly as if seeing the family in his mind.

Jerry thought he could detect tears in Father Augustine's eyes. "How often do they get to visit?"

"Twice a year. One day in the summer and always on Saturday after Christmas."

"I suppose you miss them all?" Jerry thought of the warm Peterson family gatherings in Paris.

"Oh, yes. But I am with them in spirit or perhaps, I should capitalize the 'S' in 'Spirit.' I somehow believe that I am closer to each of them than if I had stayed on the outside. Father Jerry, I would like to move back to you. I am a better monk because I have had this rich family life and this deep love of a woman. Not all men need that to become deeply loving and spiritual. I would like for you to contemplate this thought. You, if you choose, may become a better priest because of your experience of love of the two women you have told me about. Or perhaps you will find that you need to experience the daily love that marriage can bring in order to find the spiritual fulfillment you need. About that hollow place, that is part of your history. It may not go away. But it definitely will not go away if you continue to escape into work. God can fill it, but only if you let Him. Nor will the love of a woman fill that hollow place. It would be unfair to expect any woman, no matter how compassionate and loving, to fill such a void. Please let that hollow place, present or absent, become less burdensome and help you to understand others in a more compassionate way."

"Father, I hate to admit this, but I'm more worried about my ability to love deeply and intimately than I am about leaving the priesthood, although that bothers me a great deal, too."

"You doubt your ability to love intimately because you never received that kind of love and trust as a child. You can learn, however, if that turns out to be your choice. You must be open to learning how to love. It is not an automatic thing."

"I would like to ask a personal question. You need not answer it if you do not want to." Father Augustine nodded and Jerry went on, "Father, were you ever bothered by, uh, sexual thoughts after you entered the order?"

The old priest seemed offended as he said, "I resent that!" He then chuckled. "What do you mean 'was I ever' in the past tense? No, I am not bothered by them…" He used the quotes gesture when he said 'bothered.' "I just accept them as being human, natural. For example, last summer one of my granddaughters brought a friend of hers along for our meeting. The friend was in her late twenties, I'd guess. Anyway, she was a real knockout. Do they still use that word for a beautiful woman?"

"I'm kinda out of the loop myself but I think they still use it, but not as much."

"Anyway, I had several rather racy dreams after

that young woman left."

"Night dreams or day dreams?"

Father Augustine chuckled. "Some day dreams, I think. I didn't dwell on them but I did kind of enjoy them for a few days. You know, Father Jerry, back in the early days here at the abbey, I would fight myself whenever I would have what you call 'sexy thoughts,' but then I just realized that was part of being human and let them be. So I quit being bothered by what some priests still call 'impure' thoughts. Of course, when I stopped fighting myself, those thoughts were less frequent and less, ah, forceful, I guess would be a good word."

In only a little over one hour, he had received more spiritual direction than he could have imagined. He glanced at his watch and realized it was time for the chanting of None. "One last question, Father. Please tell me, what did you do out in the secular world?"

Father Augustine grinned as he said, "I was a stockbroker."

*   *   *

On Saturday morning as Jerry was pulling out of the abbey parking lot, he saw several families walking toward the monastery. They were all smiling and waving as they approached the guesthouse. He saw Father Augustine smiling and waving as he walked toward them in his white-and-black habit. Jerry stopped the car and watched the group encircle the old priest. Tears formed in Jerry's eyes as he turned down the road leading to the highway.

CHAPTER 19

Happy you who weep now; you shall laugh.
Gospel of Luke 6:2

Jerry looked out of the window at St. Claire's parking area. It was ten fifty-five and Wayne Cameron still had not arrived. The rain had turned to sleet and he was sure the roads were treacherous on this February morning. He and Wayne were to concelebrate the funeral Mass for Angela Kurtz. She had not been well since November and went rapidly downhill when she contracted pneumonia just after Christmas.

Wearing his black cassock, he stepped out of the closet-sized sacristy attached to the little chapel at St. Claire's. Sister Claire was standing near the back, he approached her and whispered, "Father Cameron hasn't arrived yet. Okay if we wait another fifteen minutes? If he isn't here by then, I'll begin the Mass." She nodded and he went up to the front and standing between the coffin and the small altar, he announced the need for a few minutes' delay. The chapel held about forty people in two rows of three-person pews that had been resurrected from some old church. All of St. Claire's staff and residents were present. In the right front pew were Kathy and Rebecca with Julie Kurtz nestled in between them, her head resting on Rebecca's shoulder.

Rebecca had called him on Thursday to tell him

that Angela had been taken to the hospital. Julie, she said, was so distraught that Rebecca had brought her back to the condo with her. Jerry had promised to drive to St. Louis on Sunday, right after the Masses were over. Early Sunday, Rebecca called again to let him know that Angela had died during the night. He called Kathy to tell her the news; after all, she had known Angela, Melanie and Julie for nearly five years at St. Gabriel's. Kathy came to Paris only once a month since Christmas and he missed her. She wanted to go with him to St. Louis and arrived in Paris just as he was planning to leave. They had an okay visit as they drove to St. Louis, but there was some kind of distance between them that he did not want to ask about. He hadn't taken time to call Rebecca and immediately regretted it when he saw the cold look on her face when Kathy arrived at the condo with him. He was puzzled because they had seemed so friendly when they were in Paris together after he came home from the hospital in November. They seemed polite and cordial toward one another then.

Something had changed between himself and Rebecca since around Christmas. She called at least once a week until his visit in late January. She was always warm and friendly but he attempted to stay aloof by joking and being impersonal. When he visited Julie and Angela in January, she seemed to be miffed at him for staying in the rectory of a priest-friend rather than with her. He didn't know how to tell her that he was fearful of getting too close to her and that he continually had difficulty keeping her out of his mind. He knew he had not reached the level of detachment and enlightenment that Father Augustine had talked about. He didn't want to tempt himself too much.

In the left front pew were Ralph Kurtz's sister, Marie, and adult niece, Sandra. They easily filled up the pew by themselves. The two had arrived that morning from Dallas and Jerry had just met them briefly before they waddled into the chapel. Why they were present at all was puzzling in itself, they were not blood relatives of either Angela or Julie. Ralph Kurtz had been Melanie and Julie's stepfather. The sister and niece sat with their arms crossed in front of their well-padded bosoms and appeared to be bored nearly to death. To Jerry they had the same detached and smug look that Ralph Kurtz had at Melanie's funeral.

Julie said that she had met them only once in her life and that was several years ago. Before they went into the chapel, Julie nervously said, "Father Jerry, they are the only relatives I have, I think. I don't have to live with them, do I?" He was quite sure that they could make other arrangements for her even though she was only fourteen and he told her so.

Jerry announced to the small group that they would have to wait a few minutes, because Father Cameron had not yet arrived. He heard one of the over-stuffed women in the front pew murmur to her partner, "Well, if that doesn't beat all. Here, we fly all this way and then have to wait on some preacher."

Sister Claire ushered Wayne into the sacristy from the outside door, just as Jerry entered from the chapel. They gave each other a hug as Wayne apologized for being late. "The roads were terrible." As they were putting on their vestments, Wayne stunned Jerry by saying. "I heard on the radio, driving over here, that Bishop Mazurski has been appointed Archbishop of New Orleans."

Jerry almost dropped the chasuble he was about to put over his head. He quickly closed the door to the chapel. "You've got to be kidding!"

"Nope, it was repeated twice as I was driving. You should be happy!"

"Depends on who replaces him in Aberdeen. Any rumors?"

"Too early, I'd say. There's an Auxiliary Bishop here in St. Louis who, I hear, is a real, authentic human being. Name's David Scalleti. I hope he's our man."

"Poor New Orleans, our gain is their loss. I didn't think even our current Pope would do something like that."

"Life is full of surprises, huh?"

Wayne and Jerry each gave part of the eulogy. Wayne compared Angela's life to that of many valiant women who had suffered much but managed to continue to love others. Jerry heard a distinct 'hmmmph' from the front pew and saw Julie glare at her aunt. Jerry emphasized Angela's courage, patience, stamina, and love for Julie the night they left Aberdeen. In deference to the Kurtz women, he did not emphasize Ralph Kurtz's abuse, but focused instead on Angela's virtue.

At the end of the funeral Mass, Jerry announced that Angela would be buried in the same cemetery as her grandparents and eldest daughter, Melanie, in Lawrence, Kansas. Wayne followed the mortuary attendants as they rolled the coffin out of the chapel. Jerry, following Wayne, put his hand out to Julie. She took it and he put his arm around her from one side as Rebecca did from the other. In the hallway outside the chapel, the residents and staff gave Julie their condolences.

The Kurtz women stood several feet away. When only Julie, Kathy, Rebecca, Jerry, and Wayne were left near the chapel door, Julie's Aunt Marie came up to them. She rudely asked Rebecca, "And who are you?"

Rebecca kept her right arm around Julie. "I'm Rebecca Brady."

Marie evidently assumed Rebecca was somehow responsible for Julie as she said, "Well, Ms. Brady, I hope you have made arrangements for my niece, here."

Fearful that they might have some ideas about taking Julie with them, Jerry jumped in, "Arrangements have been made for her."

Julie looked visibly relieved.

Marie glared at Jerry and said, "I wouldn't think that you, Reverend Haloran, would have anything to say about it, being you're the one who killed my brother!"

Julie jumped out in front of the woman, spread her feet, and put her hands on her hips. "He most certainly did not! Your stupid brother killed himself."

Marie's daughter, chucked Julie under the chin, and said in a mock-sweet voice, "Were you there, sweetie?"

Kathy moved between Julie and the two plump women. Jerry had never seen her so angry. "I was there! And what Julie says is true. Your brother would probably have killed dozens of people if Father Haloran had not tried to get the gun from him. He was drunk and shot himself with his own gun!"

Marie again glared at Jerry. "I talked to the sheriff and he says the same thing. I suppose you're in cahoots with the sheriff."

Jerry attempted to be diplomatic, "I can understand your grief at your brother's death, Mrs. Cowell. I have to admit that I'm puzzled as to why you are here at Angela's funeral."

She puffed herself up importantly. "I felt it was the Christian thing to do, bein' my brother was married to her for twelve years. I also understand that he left a sizable estate. I want to make sure it has been properly settled. I might add, that my brother had twelve miserable years with that woman you...," She motioned toward Wayne and Jerry. "...raved about in there," She leaned her head in the direction of the chapel. "He worked his butt off to support that lazy woman and her two brats."

Julie again jumped in front of the women. "She wasn't lazy and your brother didn't have to do anything. He was an asshole and raped my sister and tried to rape me."

The two women recoiled at the girl's angry outburst. Marie responded. "Well, I'm glad that we came and to be certain that we don't have to take care of you, you ungrateful, lying little brat!" They turned and began to walk down the hall.

Jerry called out cheerily, "And God bless you! By the way, his sizable estate amounted to a little over eighteen hundred dollars." The two women didn't look back but he thought he heard a "humph" from one of them. He was sure the 'estate' was the reason they came to the funeral and to make sure they did not have to take care of Julie.

*　　*　　*

Jerry, Wayne and the others joined Sister Claire and the hospital staff and residents at the luncheon following the funeral. Although Helene could not make it to the funeral, she did arrive soon after they began eating. After lunch, Sister Claire asked to see Rebecca, Helene and Jerry privately. She told them that Julie could stay at the home for another few days but then other arrangements would have to be made. Helene said that her own home for adolescent girls was already full and had a waiting list. She added that it would be very difficult for her to keep Julie with her and Melissa at their apartment.

Rebecca looked at Jerry and then, very hesitantly, said, "I guess she could stay with me for a while." She really liked Julie and enjoyed her company the past few days, but being responsible for her for an indeterminate amount of time? She looked over at Jerry who was studying her. She wondered what he was thinking. He had complicated her life more than she could ever have imagined possible. It wasn't just caring for Julie, it was her relationship with the priest that bothered her. She desperately wanted to know what he felt about her. She wanted him to tell her that he loved her in some special way even though he knew he would remain a priest. She knew wanting his love was stupid but she couldn't help it. She didn't think she was taking Julie in just to win his love.

Jerry seemed to want to give her a chance to change her mind as he said, "I'm sure I could find a foster home for her in Aberdeen, but you know how she hates everything about Aberdeen. What about the foster-home system here in St. Louis, Helene?"

"It's a crapshoot. It can be very good or it can be horrible, especially for teens. I would hate to see Julie in that system, to be honest."

Rebecca put a stop to the speculation. "I said I'd take her for now. Let's see how it works out, okay?" She didn't know why she sounded so defensive.

The four of them rejoined Wayne, Kathy, and Julie in the dining room. Rebecca sat down next to Julie and said, "Julie, if it's okay with you, you can stay with me. How's that?"

Julie looked down at the table and then turned to Rebecca. She looked both sad and pleading. There were tears in her eyes as she said, "Do you really want me, Rebecca?"

The girl looked so forlorn, Rebecca's eyes moistened and she put her arms around her. "Yes, Julie, I want you to stay with me." She didn't have the heart to say, "but only for a little while." The girl had been through too much already.

Julie squeezed her so hard Rebecca found it hard to breathe. "I won't be too much trouble, Rebecca, I promise."

They talked a little while longer and then Wayne informed them that he had to get back to his parish that evening. He would take Kathy back to Kansas with him as Jerry planned to stay another day to help Julie get settled at Rebecca's. Rebecca did not let on how relieved she was that Kathy was leaving so soon. Maybe she would get some alone time with Jerry after all. Julie sounded so adult when she thanked Wayne and Kathy for being present at her mother's funeral. Kathy seemed to give Rebecca a "be careful what you do" kind of look as she left. It seemed that the look she gave Jerry was the same.

Rebecca, Jerry and Julie spent most of the afternoon taking Julie and her mother's meager belongings out of St. Claire's home and putting them away in Rebecca's spare room. They decided to eat dinner out.

While Julie was taking a shower and changing her clothes, Rebecca had her first moment alone with Jerry. She had been concerned about Julie all afternoon. The girl had been laughing and giggling and it seemed to Rebecca to be so inappropriate on the day of her mother's funeral. "Jerry, I'm worried about Julie. Have you noticed how jovial she's been since the funeral? That isn't normal, is it?"

"Yes it is, Rebecca. The giggling and all is in itself a release of some of the grief and tension she's feeling. I wouldn't worry about it. I've seen it many times. I remember being scolded before my dad's funeral when I was laughing and carrying on at the mortuary. I pretended to climb into the coffins on display and talking about which ones were the most comfortable and all. The scolding made me ashamed of myself and I carried that shame for years until I learned it was a normal response. Enjoy it, in a few days, she'll be terribly depressed, I'm sure."

335

Rebecca chose a nice restaurant not too far from her home and was surprised when Julie ordered a cheeseburger and fries. She had a lot to learn about kids. Halfway through the meal, Julie, with a big smile and mischievous eyes, said, "Rebecca! Jerry! I've got a wonderful idea!"

They both looked at her questioningly and asked, simultaneously, "What's your wonderful idea?" They looked at each other and laughed.

Julie put her cheeseburger on her plate and solemnly said, "I think you two should get married and adopt me!"

Jerry had just taken a sip of his beer. He coughed it up and turned scarlet. He put his napkin to his mouth and swallowed hard. He took a sip of water.

Rebecca also choked up a bit but her reaction wasn't quite as severe as his. She glanced at the priest who had the look of someone who had just been told he was going to be on the first flight to Mars, but had not been in training as an astronaut. "Well, Jerry Haloran, that does sound like a wonderful idea. What do you think?" How will he react to that? She wondered. What if he said it was a good idea, how would she respond to that? Somehow the idea seemed more serious than the time when the little girl said something similar on the riverboat.

He did the seemingly impossible. He turned even redder. "I, uh ... well ... I ... uh... thank you, Julie, for thinking I would be a good dad but, well, I doubt if I would be, even if I were available. And besides that, Rebecca wouldn't even think of marrying me. She was just teasing." He turned from Julie to glance at

Rebecca and quickly looked back at Julie. "Isn't that right, Rebecca?"

She grinned and winked at Julie. "Oh, I don't know. It sounds like a very interesting idea."

By this time, Julie was laughing almost hysterically. She stopped long enough to say, "Father Jerry, you sure look funny when you're embarrassed!"

When they got back to Rebecca's place, they talked about the funeral and made fun of Ralph Kurtz' Dallas relatives. Julie went to bed before nine. As she ascended the stairs, Rebecca whispered, "She's a precious child."

"I think she's one of those miracle survivor children. From all that has happened to her, she should be a basket case, but I'm amazed at how well she's doing."

Rebecca got up from the chair. "I'm going to have a brandy. I'll offer you one if you promise to stop at one."

"I promise! No repeat of last time I stayed here."

When Rebecca returned with their drinks, she handed one to Jerry and sat down on the end of the couch. "Who says you are going to stay here?" She wasn't smiling as she looked at her brandy snifter. "I thought you'd go back to your friend's rectory just as you have the last three nights." There was no invitation in her voice to indicate she thought otherwise.

"Well, sure, I can do that. I just thought that now that Kathy has left, well…"

"You know something, Jerry Haloran, you've assumed a helluva lot. You assumed that I would welcome Kathy Olson with open arms, and I'm sure you assumed I would take Julie in. Do you ever stop and think that I might have other ideas?" She was angrier than she realized, now that she was saying what was really on her mind. "Did you call me and ask if it was okay if Kathy could stay with me? No! Back in November, you practically demanded that I look after Angela and Julie."

"Rebecca, I'm sorry I didn't call about Kathy. I was wrong. But I did not demand that you look after Angela and Julie."

"Not in so many words, but you sure let it be known that if I didn't I would be an inconsiderate and selfish person." Rebecca had only begun to realize that she really was an inconsiderate and selfish person a few weeks ago, but she wasn't about to reveal that to anyone, especially to this priest sitting in front of her.

"Rebecca, that wasn't my intention at all. I wouldn't think of you as a selfish person if you didn't help them out. I appreciate it and, of course, you know that Angela did and that Julie does."

"Yes, I know that. What I'm objecting to is your paternalism. You know, I've been reading about your Catholic Church, it's so damn paternalistic and I think you're infected by it, too. The priest always knows best, right? That's why they call you 'Father.'"

Jerry slumped lower on the couch and looked at the floor. His face was wrinkled into a deep grimace, as if he had just heard some horrible news. Or maybe he was trying to hold back tears. "I'm not sure what to say, Rebecca. I'm sorry if I've hurt you or taken you for granted. I guess I have been inconsiderate and paternalistic." He continued to look at the floor and, after a moment, added, "I'll go now, if that will make you feel better."

She had never known a man who so quickly admitted his faults. Was it a strength or a weakness? He isn't defending himself at all. She had hit him where it hurts. She felt a little remorseful as she knew he worked hard not to tell people how to live their lives. "No, it wouldn't make me feel better. Now it looks like I've hurt your feelings. I'm just upset with you, Jerry."

He looked puzzled as he turned toward her. "Because I didn't call you about Kathy? You've always been so generous and seemingly easy-going, I guess I didn't think you'd mind. I'm sorry."

"Quit saying you're sorry, Jerry." It was as good a time as any to tell him what was really bothering her. "I don't think it's about your bringing Kathy along with you to St. Louis. It's my fear that Kathy means more to you than I do." He definitely perked up with this remark. He raised that one eyebrow and continued to look puzzled. "Okay, here's my problem: I felt hurt with the way you've talked to me on the phone since Christmas. And then you came in January and didn't even ask if you could stay with me. I wanted you to, but you had made arrangements to stay in that rectory. Jerry, I've grown to really like you." Rebecca bit her lower lip and hesitated a moment before adding, "No that's not strong enough. Jerry, I really love you and want to spend as much time as possible with you. It really hurts when you act impersonal and stay away from me, especially when you could easily spend time with me, like in January." She let out a deep breath as if to say, "There, I've said it."

He looked at her for some moments, trying to figure out how to respond. "Thank you, Rebecca, for saying you love me. That means a lot to me." He looked away a moment and then went on, "It also scares me. I've been thinking of you too much. I thought if I put some distance, emotionally I mean, between us, then I wouldn't be bothered so much. I didn't mean to hurt you. I spend too much time alone out there in Paris. When I think of you, I feel I'm drifting away from the priesthood, in my thoughts and feelings anyway."

"Do you have to push thoughts of Kathy away, too?"

"Uh, yes, in some way. It's different."

"How?"

"I'm not sure. I guess I think about her kind of like she was a daughter." He chuckled a little. "I'm sure you'd say I'm, ah, I'm paternalistic toward her."

Rebecca was sure he was not telling her all of his thoughts but decided to check that out later. "I'm sure she doesn't think of you as her father. Jerry, she's in love with you."

"I believe you said that once before."

"Yes, I did. Then it was a guess, but now I'm sure. Are you saying that you don't feel the same way toward her?" You're really pushing it, Rebecca told herself. Watch it.

"I don't think so. I really don't know. I kind of miss her now that she's coming to Paris only once a month. But that also helps a bit because I don't think about her as much."

Rebecca was sure that he was lying. He was as

confused about his feelings for Kathy as he was about his feelings for her. She decided to focus on how he felt toward her. "And you are afraid you might allow yourself to fall in love with me if you don't keep it impersonal, is that right?"

He again looked away, then turned her way and reached out and touched her hand and softly said, "Yes."

*   *   *

Rebecca returned home late after staying at the office to finish an article that was due the next day—March first. Julie was staying the night with Helene and her daughter. The condo felt empty without her. She reached down and picked up the letters, flyers, and all that had been pushed through the mail slot.

Quickly glancing through the little pile, she felt both excited and apprehensive when she saw Jerry's scrawl on one envelope. Their telephone conversations had been more cordial, if not as personal as she would like, since his stay in St. Louis for Angela Kurtz's funeral. Her apprehension, she knew, came from a constant nagging feeling that at anytime Jerry would tell her that he had to distance himself from her to save his priesthood. She sometimes wondered if, even now, he was staying in touch with her because of Julie.

She kicked off her shoes, sat down on the couch, tore open the envelope, and began reading the typewritten letter:

Dear Rebecca:

It's two in the morning and since I can't sleep, I thought I'd write you a letter. One time you mentioned that you do like to receive letters, right? I'm quite sure you wouldn't want me to call this time of night. I haven't been sleeping all that well in recent weeks. Sometimes I read and other times I write to myself –kind of like keeping a journal

I really appreciate what you're doing for Julie. I think the idea of a teen hospice group is great. And I'm glad that she's not too much trouble (or are you just shining me on?). I think she's a remarkable child to keep up the spirit she has with all that she's been through. Of course being with you helps enormously. You'd pick up anyone's spirit!

Things are going pretty well here. A friend from Aberdeen rounded up two used pool tables for our teen center. A bunch of kids helped paint inside and out and put down floor tile. Our one big setback was the second week after it opened—a kid from Whelan (forty miles west) was caught selling crystal-meth. Joe Gaffin and one of the deputies have volunteered to patrol the place in the evening. I've gotten the owners of the chicken and egg ranch to come up with $200,000 for housing for the farm workers. We'll need to double that and I've got pledges for about $100,000. Should break ground on the first three this month (March).

I've been thinking a lot about you as usual. Suppose that's the reason I'm having a hard time sleeping? Rebecca, I apologize for not saying anything that evening at your home when you said 'I love you.' It really meant a lot to me for you to say that. No-one in my family ever said that to me, nor did I ever hear my mom or dad say it to one another. A few people have said it to me—like Alice Peterson but the closest anyone has come to saying it like you said it was Kathy Olson and that was on a card. I'm still trying to figure out how real, personal love, as you call it, can fit into my life. It worries me a bit (that's an understatement—It worries me a lot).

The night I returned from St. Louis, I was dead tired but couldn't sleep so I watched a movie: WILD STRAWBERRIES, directed by Ingmar Bergman. Maybe you've seen it. Anyway, it's about an old physician who is on his way to Stockholm to receive some kind of humanitarian award. His daughter-in-law tells him he's a phony (not in those words, of course) because, although he does a lot for people, he doesn't allow himself to be close to anyone. I identify with the old doctor.

I'm getting sleepy, so will sign off.

Love, (or better - I love you!)
Jerry

Rebecca stared at the "I love you." She murmured, "Yes, it was better but I'd still rather hear you say it out loud, Jerry. And yes, I was disappointed and hurt that evening when you didn't say much after I told you I love you." She reread the letter and then folded it and set it on the end table. She had talked to him three or four times since Angela's funeral and he hadn't said "I love you" once. She wondered if he found it easier and less threatening to write it. When Kathy put it in her card, she probably did it for the same reason, afraid of saying it out loud.

Rebecca thought about the impact of knowing Jerry and how he had changed her life. Introducing her to Alice Peterson was probably the biggest thing, other than her falling in love with the big jerk. Every time she found herself feeling cold or judgmental toward someone or sounding harsh, she thought of Alice's comment on her "hardness." She picked up the letter again and after reading the part about the movie and the old doctor she whispered, "Well, Jerry, my friend, maybe I've been a phony, too. You've pushed me into loving Angela and Julie and even loving Helene, Denise and Rene more than I thought possible. Have I helped you?" She looked forward to talking to Helene about Jerry's letter. When she went to pick up Julie, they made a date for lunch.

On Tuesday, Rebecca looked across the table at Helene, casually dressed as usual, in a faded aqua sweatshirt and jeans. Helene was excited to tell her that both Rene and Denise were talking about college for the first time. She asked if Julie enjoyed her stay with her and Melissa. When they finished their meal, she asked, "Well, what do you hear from your noble knight of the prairie?"

Rebecca smiled. "Well, I do want to talk with you about him. I'm not sure what I hear from him. Maybe you can help me." She opened her purse and took out Jerry's letter.

Helene wiped her hands on a napkin and picked up the typed page. She alternately frowned, smiled, and nodded as she slowly read it. When she was finished she looked up at Rebecca. "Hmmm, 'I love you.' Sounds pretty serious, Rebecca. What do you make of it?"

"I don't know really. That's the first time he has put it in words. I've talked to him nearly every week on the phone and he never, even once, ended the conversation with the shortened version: 'Love ya.'."

"But you did tell him how you felt when he was here for the funeral?"

"Yes. And he said for the first time, in that letter, it meant a lot to him."

"How about the movie *Wild Strawberries*. Have you seen it?"

"I rented it last night. Like Jerry said, it's about this old physician who is heading to Stockholm with his daughter-in-law to receive some kind of humanitarian award. The daughter-in-law doesn't like him very much and tells him that he's done a lot of good for people but as a person he's a cold, aloof , and closed individual. They do manage to connect as the old man opens up to her."

Helene looked thoughtful as she said, "Somehow

345

the movie really touched Jerry. He said he identified with the old doctor." Helene put the paper down on the table. "You know what I think?"

"No, what do you think?" Rebecca hoped Helene's answer was one she wanted to hear.

"I think he's struggling with all kinds of mixed emotions, maybe even feeling some for the first time. Like love and passion." Helene looked intently at her for a moment and then smiled. "I asked you a few months ago if you were in love with him and you said 'no.' Remember?"

"Yes. So...?"

"Maybe he has begun to be in touch with his feelings just as you are. Remember I was with you two at Angela's funeral. The energy between you was so strong I wanted to run away." Helene tapped the letter. "I see here the depiction of a very human man struggling to love, have courage, and develop faith."

Rebecca only heard the energy part. "Why didn't you say something before about the energy between us?"

"Rebecca. Why do you think?"

Rebecca tapped the table with her fingers and thought for a moment, then said, "One, if you said it when Jerry was present, he probably would have run away. If you had said it to me, I probably would have gotten angry with you. So, seriously Helene, you don't think I should end our relationship?"

"End it? No. First, unless you're keeping something from me, it's still platonic. Secondly, he's brought a lot to your life and I think it's a pretty good guess that you brought more to his life than just confusion. Didn't you tell me that his favorite passage from the Bible is 'God is love?'"

"Yes, but I think it was a more sedate..." Rebecca giggled. "I guess 'spiritual' would be better word to describe it, than the kind of love I'm looking for. Helene let me tell you about another movie that bothered me."

"Okay. I suppose it involves our prairie friend?"

"Indirectly, but yes. The title is *Molokai*, it's an island in Hawaii. It's about this nineteenth-century priest named Father Damien who takes care of lepers who are quarantined on the island. He volunteers to be there and stays for years among these poor, wretched people. He finally contracts leprosy himself and dies. It's a true story."

"I remember hearing about Father Damien when I was in school. Please go on."

"There was this one scene where this beautiful woman, in the early stages of leprosy I'd guess, comes into his bungalow. She is obviously in love with Damien and begins to caress him. He looks very disturbed and then orders her to go home. Jerry is kind of like that when he is with me. He isn't quite as blunt as in the movie but I think his feelings are the same."

"I imagine that if we were living in the nineteenth-century, Jerry would be more like Damien and wouldn't even think about being alone with you. I think that there are a lot of priests today who feel the same way. As I said before, I think Jerry is searching and is not entirely satisfied with his Church."

"So, I'm still competing with God, huh?"

"I don't think your Jerry would put it that way. I

think he would say that he is confused as to the best route to take to find God." Helene glanced at her watch. "I better get back to my little colony of 'lepers.'"

As Rebecca gave her friend a hug, she said, "I really love you, Helene!"

"Thank you, Rebecca! I love you, too."

Rebecca was sure that she had never said "I love you" to Helene before. Jerry's influence?

CHAPTER 20

*Wake up from your sleep, rise from the dead,
and Christ will shine on you.*

Ephesians 4: 14

Jerry visited St. Louis again in March, after Angela's funeral. This time he did stay with Rebecca and again he was nervous and more than a bit worried about his too frequent sexual thoughts and feelings. Remembering Father Augustine's comment that they were natural and just to let them 'be' helped him be more comfortable and humorous than on the previous occasions. The week after he returned to Paris, Jerry sat down in his recliner and opened the large manila envelope Sy Peterson had given him. Sy had invited him over for dinner, a well-prepared meal that the man had cooked himself. After they had eaten, Sy had handed Jerry the envelope, saying, "Before Alice died, I started keeping a journal. Last week I put my scribbles on the computer. I've been wondering if I should share it with the kids. Father Jerry, would you mind looking it over and telling me what you think?" Jerry said he'd be happy to read the material. Just before he left, Sy said, "Those last ten pages or so are different. They reflect a lot of what I've picked up from you. Thanks for helping me."

Curious as to what the last pages would be, Jerry turned past the first twenty or so pages and looked at the page entitled, "Love, Death, and Gratitude." He began to read:

Moments before Alice drew her final breath, I moved to her side and took her hand in mine. I placed a cheek to hers and with my lips brushing an ear, whispered one more word of love.

Already, Jerry was in tears. He could easily picture the scene and wondered how Sy could think that he, the priest, could have inspired such expression of feelings. He longed to have such an experience but had never even come close nor had he ever witnessed it in his family. He continued reading Sy's manuscript:

Her hand suddenly arched, then relaxed slowly. I could hear the last of her life drain away in a long steady sigh. When it was over, I said, "Thank God."
I meant it!
That may sound callous to some; not the words of a lifelong husband and friend to a faithful love. Yet they may be the most selfless ever spoken between us.
For Alice was now free of the pain, discomfort, and indignity imposed for over three years by that rapacious predator, cancer.
No longer need she avoid gazing into a mirror seeing, but not wanting to see, her beautiful figure fade and give way to a skeletal imposter. No longer need she seek a stronger

dose of the drug that masked her ever-growing pain, a pain she didn't want to believe was worse today than it was yesterday. No longer need she make believe that she is in control of her own body, nor need she seek the aid of another when nature makes one more surprise call. No longer need she face the moment-to-moment struggle to live while in her heart she fears the awesome unknown drawing ever near.

Since Alice died, there have been many moments when my sadness for her plight has slipped dangerously close to self-pity. There are times when cancer's victory stirs anger in my soul, breeding a resentment that threatens to consume me. While I know I did all I could to help Alice, something called pride tells me lies and tries to make me feel like a failure--the fear-filled product of an ego run wild.

I am human. Yet I cannot let ingratitude and fear mask reality. Yes, I do miss Alice. But do I want her back? The answer must be NO! The cost would be too dear. Her life was over. Her work in this world is done. God recalled the body she'd no longer need; a prelude to the spiritual hereafter. Yes, there are moments when I hurt. But when that happens, I pray to regain the truth: my hurt is nothing compared to what that courageous lady endured without complaint at the end of her days. That is enough!

I still have the love we bred and shared. That can never wither or die. For that I am grateful. That I will never forget!

Jerry sat there and let the tears flow. He mumbled to himself, "Sy, thank you! I don't know how I could have inspired you to feel or write like that; I've never allowed myself to be that close to anyone."

After he read more of the pages and managed to compose himself, he called Sy to thank him and tell him the writings were extremely inspiring and that definitely he should share them with his children. He then asked if he could share some of the pages with Rebecca and Kathy. Sy said, "Sure, please do, if you think they are helpful."

Jerry dialed Rebecca's number. As usual, she picked it up as soon as she heard his voice. After exchanging greetings, he asked about Julie and thanked Rebecca for being so supportive of him over the months since they met. He then said, "I'd like to share something with you." He started reading Sy's Love, Death, and Gratitude section. He only got as far as "Moments before Alice drew her final breath...", before he broke down in tears. "I'm sorry, Rebecca, I guess I won't be able to read this to you. You have a fax machine don't you?"

"Yes. It sounds wonderful. Sy wrote it didn't he?"

"Yes, he did. After you read it, give me a call, okay?"

While he waited for Rebecca's call, he made a copy of the section to send to Kathy. He knew she didn't have a fax.

He sat back in the desk chair and knew, perhaps for the first time, what was meant by the words: "God is love." And he knew he wanted to participate in that kind of intense love.

CHAPTER 21

"You are a priest forever..."
Ordination Ceremony

Jerry looked over at Ricky Alexander as they approached the city of Aberdeen. Ricky was dressed in clean khaki trousers and a blue plaid, short-sleeved shirt. His arms were quite muscular from years of pushing himself around in his cart. It was not benevolence that prompted Jerry to bring Ricky along with him to Aberdeen. He needed the company and the distraction. He had been more depressed, anxious, and confused than he could ever remember. As he thought about it, he could trace the depression back to around Christmas time. Or maybe Alice Peterson's funeral or even earlier, to Melanie Kurtz's suicide. Hell. He really didn't know, because he'd spent so many years completely unaware of his feelings.

He only knew that he had been feeling almost low enough to see a psychiatrist but whomever he saw would probably only give him a bunch of pills. Several times he thought of going back to the monastery and visiting Father Augustine. But he hadn't. He had gone back to anethesizing his pain with scotch almost every evening. Just last week, he told himself, "Haloran, old buddy, you just have to quit living a lie. What you really want is the kind of love you've witnessed between Sy and Alice. You are afraid and that's okay. You can still learn to love like that." He quit the scotch that evening, but the depression and anxiety continued.

He had not told anyone know how torn up he was inside, managing, he thought, to put on a good front even with Kathy and Rebecca. He couldn't remember the last time he had a full night's sleep. Marge had finally confronted him about it three weeks ago, saying, "Jerry Haloran, you look like shit!" After she had prodded him to admit some of his confusion and feelings, she said, "A feeling has to grab you by the throat before you recognize it, doesn't it? And I'll bet you're drinking again like you did when you first came to Paris." He hadn't responded.

Singing along with Ricky the past two hours helped lift the depressed feelings and definitely helped reduce the anxiety he felt as he anticipated his talk with the Bishop.

Ricky's head moved in his usual fashion as he looked around. "It...it...it sure is... is...is a big city."

"A little bigger than Paris, huh?"

Ricky smiled and spit a little as he stuttered, "Ye... ye... yeah."

The young man had never been outside of Paris County until a few weeks ago, when Jerry took him to Manhattan, Kansas. Kathy had arranged for Ricky to meet with the Academic Dean about the possibility of enrolling at Kansas State University. Kathy had taken him back a week later so he could take the SAT exam. Jerry was afraid Ricky would hurt himself when he gave him the news that he had aced the test with a score above 1400. It seemed that every muscle in the boy's body had gone into spasm, but he couldn't stop grinning.

As Jerry thought about Kathy, a flood of feelings overcame him. He hit the steering wheel with his right hand, nearly bruising it.

"Wh ... wh ... what's th...th... the matter, Fa... fa.. father?"

"Oh, nothing." He lied, "I just remembered that I was supposed to call someone this morning." He wasn't about to tell Ricky about his confusion and anguish whenever he thought of Kathy Olson. He and Ricky were going to stop by Kansas State and visit with her after his meeting with the Bishop.

As they approached the diocesan chancery office and the church next to it, Ricky exclaimed, "Is th..th.. that the ca..ca..cathed..d..d..dral?"

"Yes. I'll park around in back and then give you a tour. We have about a half hour before I meet with the Bishop." Jerry had called the new Bishop, David Scalleti, the previous Thursday to make an appointment. He was surprised when the Bishop himself came on the line and cheerily said, "Father Haloran, I'm glad you called. I was planning to give you a ring soon. I have some ideas I would like to discuss with you." He didn't sound like he was ready to kick him out of the priesthood. Jerry wondered if he had read his file. Well, he'd listen to the Bishop's ideas before telling him his own.

He got out of the Pontiac, opened the trunk, and picked up the collapsible wheelchair.

Marge Woerner had managed to obtain both the smaller model and an electric one through the state's program for the disabled. Ricky's mother thanked

Marge with a loud "hmmmph", but Ricky was overjoyed and tooled around Paris like he owned the town.

Jerry held the wheelchair steady as Ricky awkwardly seated himself.

As they entered through the huge doors, Jerry thought of his ordination day that May, one month shy of twelve years ago. He had been the only one ordained that year and he was treated as if he were king for a day. And, in a way, he did feel like a king that day.

Ordination was the crowning achievement after eight years of college work. He had been anxious to get into a parish and begin saving souls, as they say. He smiled to himself as he thought of his own naivete' at the time. He had endured the many rules of the seminary and had tolerated being treated as a child for eight years because, he believed, after ordination he would be his own man. That illusion ended four months after ordination when he was called into the Bishop's office for making a comment to a small group of parishioners that he "had trouble with the Church's position on birthcontrol." The Bishop had said, "Father, that was a very indiscreet and immature statement you made to your parishioners." Bishop Gilsennen, Jerry thought, is probably still spinning in his grave after Jerry's sermon on sex. Now he realized that he had been 'discreet' too long and had substituted obedience for maturity and courage.

He slowly pushed Ricky up the center aisle as the boy gawked at the ornate Romanesque interior. Ricky repeatedly made 'oh, oh, oh' sounds as he looked around. As he wheeled the lad over to the Blessed

Virgin altar, Jerry said, "You know, Rick, when I was in high school, I would come here and say a prayer every day before classes."

Ricky gazed up at the marble statue of the Virgin. The exquisite form made the plaster image in Paris look so pitiful. "Sh..sh..she's very be..be..beautiful. You kn .kn..know what, Fa..fa..father?"

Jerry shook his head.

"I ca..ca..can't de..de..decide if sh..she re..re.. reminds me of Ka..ka..kathy or Re..re..rebecca. Wh.. wh..what do you th..th..think?"

Jerry was glad Ricky didn't know he was touching a sensitive area. He glanced up at the serene marble face. Rebecca could have been the sculptor's model with her thin Semitic nose and high cheekbones. The look on the Virgin's face, the innocence and softness, would more aptly fit Kathy. Kathy would be flattered and Rebecca flabbergasted at being compared to the image of the Mother of God.

Glancing at his watch, Jerry said, "Well, Rick, we have eight minutes to get to the chancery building." He wheeled him quickly back to the entrance. Leaving the relative darkness of the cathedral, the bright April sun nearly blinded them both.

As he pushed the wheelchair up the ramp of the chancery building, Jerry wondered how, only one year ago, he could possibly have been proud to have an office in the place. The exterior of beige brick had a certain charm but the white-walled interior appeared cold and sterile. He stopped the wheelchair in front of the receptionist's desk.

A pretty young woman with honey-blond hair

falling to red-jacketed shoulders sat behind the desk. Her outfit and smile certainly warmed up the place. When she saw Jerry, she jumped up and came around the desk and took his extended hand in both of hers. "Father Haloran, it's so good to see you! We've missed you around here. Are you coming back?"

"No, Paula, I'm sure that I am not. I'd like you to meet a friend of mine: Ricky Alexander. Ricky, this is Paula Evans. She runs this place."

Paula graciously bent down and took Ricky's hand. "I'm pleased to meet you, Ricky. Do you live in Paris?"

Ricky turned pink the moment Paula took his hand. "Ye..ye..yes." Embarrassed, he put his left hand over his forehead. He grinned and looked up at Jerry. "Do..do..does sh..sh..she re..re..really run this pl..pl.. place?"

Jerry winked at Paula. "Sure she does."

"Don't pay any attention to him, Ricky, he's always teasing. Are you here to see the Bishop, Father?"

He glanced at his watch. "Yes, I'm due to meet him two minutes ago. Uh, Paula, do you suppose the Bishop's secretary would mind if Ricky waited in her office?" The old battle-ax Bishop Mazurski had employed wouldn't have even considered it; and Jerry hoped Bishop Scalleti had the good sense to get rid of her.

"Father Haloran, you'd know better than I would, she's Sarah Johnson, your old secretary."

"Sarah! Hey, that's great. Thanks, Paula. See you soon." He quickly wheeled Ricky down the hall toward the Bishop's office. This new man must be okay if he re-hired Sarah, Jerry thought. For five years she was the only African-American employee in the building and, in his sometimes humble opinion, the best secretary.

Sarah immediately stood up at her desk and ran around the side and gave Jerry a hug. She even bent down and embraced Ricky. She was in her mid-fifties and the widowed mother of three boys—all college graduates. Sarah was nearly as tall as Jerry and had a beautiful dark complexion that made her look ten years younger. She wore a nicely tailored cream-colored suit and beautifully embroidered red blouse. She looked elegant, as usual. As she stood in front of Ricky, Bishop David Scalleti, emerged from his office. Jerry guessed him to be in his late forties or early fifties, thin, athletic-looking, and about six feet tall. Salt and pepper hair, more pepper than salt. He had an open, confident, and handsome face. He extended his hand. "Father Jerry Haloran, good to see you. I'm sorry we didn't get to talk much at my installation."

Jerry returned the Bishop's firm handshake and was glad he didn't extend his hand in a way that indicated he expected his ring to be kissed, as had his predecessor on their first meeting. "Nice to see you again, Bishop. I'd like you to meet a friend and parishioner from Paris: Ricky Alexander. This is Ricky's first visit to Aberdeen."

Scalletti took Ricky's shaky right hand in both of his. "Welcome, Ricky. I haven't been here long myself."

Ricky seemed to be awe-struck as he said, "N.. n..n..nice to m..m..meet you, B..b..bishop."

Jerry addressed the secretary, "Sarah, would it be okay with you if Ricky waited out here while I talk with the Bishop? He'll not be any trouble, right Rick?"

Ricky smiled and nodded.

The Bishop said, "Would you like something to drink while you're waiting, Ricky?"

Ricky looked a bit confused as he glanced at Jerry. Jerry nodded and Ricky said, "Co..co..Coke, pl..pl.. please."

His excellency, Bishop Scalletti, glanced at Sarah. "Sarah, would you mind getting this young man a Coke, or would you rather I did?" Jerry's mouth dropped open. This man wasn't kidding, he'd do it himself if Sarah hesitated just a bit.

"No, Bishop, I'll run and get it—no problem. You want one too, Father Jerry? Bishop?"

"I'd prefer coffee, Sarah, if it's not too much trouble."

"No trouble. Black with a little sugar, right?"

Bishop Scalleti smiled. "That's right! You two know each other. Well, Father Haloran, one thing I do know about you is that you know how to pick good secretaries. I'll have a coffee too, Sarah, if you don't mind."

Sarah blushed as she raised her hand in a dismissing way and left to get the drinks. Jerry was willing to bet that she had given Scalleti some ideas about the kind of priest she thought he was. He had often felt that she was his greatest fan and supporter.

The Bishop invited him into his office. Before closing the door, Jerry smiled at Ricky and gave him a little wave. The Bishop seems to be the kind of fellow

I could work with. The office looked warmer and more inviting but it couldn't just be the Bishop's personality, surely. Jerry looked around. The window blinds were open, and the maroon drapes had been replaced with a pleasant and warmer off-white. He was sure the two potted plants on each side of the walnut bookshelves were new. Scallleti had a rather worn manila file about an inch thick on the left side of his desk. Jerry could just barely make out his name on the tab.

"Well, Father Haloran, you called for this appointment and I told you I had some ideas I wanted to discuss with you. So do you want to start, or would you prefer I started?"

Just then Sarah lightly knocked on the door and Bishop Scaletti got up and opened the door for her. She sat the coffee down on the edge of the desk and each man picked up his cup. Scaletti thanked Sarah and then said, "Now where were we?"

"You were asking which of us would start sharing his ideas. I would like to hear your ideas first, Bishop." He noticed that Scalleti didn't wear the traditional Bishop's gold cross across his chest. Wayne Cameron once joked that Mazurski probably wore it to bed.

The Bishop folded his hands on top of the desk. In a relaxed and conversational tone of voice, he began, "Okay. I've read through your file and am quite impressed with your record as a priest. You've shown dedication, hard work, leadership, and original thinking. Perhaps too original, considering the sermon you gave that apparently landed you in the small parish in Paris." He smiled a little, as if what he was saying was somewhat amusing. He seemed to await some

361

kind of response.

Jerry did not know what to say, so he didn't say anything.

"Well, as you know, Father, we have a shortage of priests, like every other diocese in the world. I personally think that your talent is wasted there in that small parish. The people could easily be served from Whalen, I understand."

Although he was sure that whatever the Bishop had in mind would not change his own ideas, he asked, "So what are you considering, Bishop?"

Scalleti sat back in his chair and studied a pen he had been holding. Looking at his hands and then at Jerry, he said, "Father O'Brien has been at the diocese-sponsored parish in Guatemala for five years. His health is not good and he needs to return to the States. I understand you have learned some Spanish since you've been in Paris." He hesitated a moment and Jerry could guess what he was going to say next. "I would like for you to take over the parish in Guatemala for at least three years. One thing Father O'Brien suggested is that we send down a priest who has some knowledge of construction. I understand that that, too, is one of your skills. What do you say?"

Jerry was more than a little stunned. The parish in Guatemala had over two thousand families, about ten thousand people. More than the entire population of Paris County. At one time, the Diocese of Aberdeen had sent three priests down there. Twelve years ago it was reduced it to two and four years ago to one. It would be a big challenge. He had volunteered right after he was ordained and again five years later but Bishop

Gilsennan, Mazurski's predecessor, said he needed and wanted him in Aberdeen. Over the years he had re-evaluated the entire mission system and decided that it was a kind of spiritual and intellectual colonialism. It only continued the paternalism of the Church that he increasingly detested. Perhaps he could do some good but they could do well for themselves without him. Rebecca called his work in Paris "paternalistic," but to him it was nothing compared to the built-in paternalism of the mission system.

Bishop Scalleti, aware of his hesitancy, said, "I honestly thought of asking you to become the director of Catholic Charities but, well, as I'm sure you know, there would be a bit of resentment among some of the priests because of your sermon and subsequent exile."

Bit of resentment? That is quite an understatement, about half the priests of the diocese would be enraged and another fourth would be disapproving at least. Very few would be co-operative with him in that position. If he went to Guatemala, he would be his own boss, maybe. He had met a Maryknoll priest who had been ousted from Guatemala for attempting to set up co-ops for the farmers there. He had been labeled a 'communist' and sent back to the States. "Thank you, Bishop, for the offer and the confidence." Jerry did not let the Bishop know how much his offer bolstered his confidence at the moment. How could he tell this good man that he no longer believed in the missions? He honestly believed that the people of the United States and other developed countries should help the people of the developing world. But they should go down there with aid only if they were asked for some kind of specific assistance. David Scalleti seemed like a very sincere and kind man and Jerry decided to keep his ideas to himself.

"A few years ago, Bishop, I would have jumped at the chance to go to Central America. In fact, I volunteered to do so twice. I definitely appreciate your offer." Jerry smiled. "It would be a good way to get me out of sight without raising too many eyebrows." Scalleti shook his head and started to say something, but Jerry went on, "I don't think you intended that, Bishop, but, of course, it is true. I think it's time I tell you why I wanted this appointment."

Bishop Scalleti relaxed back in his chair. "Please do."

Jerry folded his hands on his lap, unfolded them, and put them on the arms of the chair. He took a deep breath. There was no easy way to begin. "Bishop, I want you to be the first to know that I am resigning from the priesthood."

Scalleti immediately leaned forward and put his hands on the desk. "I have to admit that I am surprised. From what I've heard, you have done some marvelous work in Paris, and you seemed to enjoy it."

Jerry wondered where he could have gotten that information. Except for simple greetings at various gatherings, Wayne Cameron was the only priest he had really talked to over the past year. "I don't know how marvelous it has been, but I have enjoyed the people and the work there. I will miss them a great deal." He didn't know how to explain to this sincere man his reason for leaving the priesthood. He couldn't even explain it to himself in any logical terms. It was just the right thing to do.

The Bishop hesitated a moment and then slid the manila folder over in front of him and leafed through it quickly. "Are you planning to marry, Father? Is that your reason for leaving the priesthood?"

Jerry took a deep and quiet breath to calm his rising anger. What in hell could be in that file about his relationship with Rebecca or anyone else? he wondered "Is there something in my file indicating that may be the case?"

The Bishop looked serious and, Jerry thought, disapproving, as he looked at the papers in the file. "Yes, there is. It looks like Bishop Mazurski kept pretty scrupulous notes about your activities in Paris, and before. Here's one that is particularly interesting." He held up a yellow sheet with neat handwriting on the top half and in large bold print on the bottom half were the words: "FREE THINKER."

Jerry leaned forward. "I take it, Bishop, that you aren't so uncomfortable with free thinking among the priests."

"Not for the most part, however I would have disapproved of that sermon of yours. I've known Bishop Mazurski for several years and he has to be one of the most conservative bishops in the country. After looking over your file, I wondered why he didn't kick you out of the priesthood."

"He threatened to and I told him I would hold a press conference and give the whole thing as much publicity as possible. He hated any kind of public uproar and I had quite a press following after being shot at the pro-life rally."

"I've noticed. I read about it in St. Louis. So you blackmailed him?"

Jerry couldn't tell if the Bishop's expression was one of approval or scorn. He wondered if the man played poker? "I guess you could say that. The Paris assignment was a compromise."

"So only a year ago you went to great lengths to stay in the priesthood and now you want to leave. You still haven't told me if you are leaving the priesthood because of a woman."

"You asked that question after looking at my file. I asked if there was something in there to indicate that I was involved with a woman and you said yes. Would you mind telling me what it is?" Somehow Jerry's anger had dissipated; he was now simply curious.

The Bishop looked down at the file. "I'll read the notes to you. 'According to a source in Paris, Father Haloran appears to be unseemingly close to two women there. One is a divorcee named Marge Woerner with whom Father Haloran often goes horseback riding. The two of them have been seen together all over the county. The second woman is a former nun with whom Father Haloran worked in Aberdeen. Her name is Kathleen Olson and she spends each Saturday at the church or in the rectory.' Bishop Mazurski seems to be quoting someone else as he wrote: 'Is this not a great scandal to all of the faithful?' So, Father, I was wondering if one of these women was the reason for your wanting to leave the priesthood."

"No they are not, Bishop." For some reason he could not fathom, Jerry was relieved that Rebecca was not mentioned in the file. Could it be because, despite

Father Augustine's talk, he felt he had more 'sinful' thoughts about Rebecca than about Kathy or Marge? "Both women are very attractive and I have to admit I have been very tempted by them. I'm not sure it has been virtue that has held me back from pursueing them romantically. More than likely I'm just afraid of being rejected. Besides, I do not have the kind of feelings for either of them that would make me want to marry."

"Thank you for being so candid, Father. Somehow I'm still under the impression that there is a woman in your life."

"There is, but I'm not sure whether or not she is interested in marrying me. I haven't asked. I am not leaving the priesthood only to marry her."

"Have you lost the faith, Father?"

Jerry did not expect this question. He had decided earlier that if the Bishop was in any way antagonistic, he would tell him that the biggest reason for leaving the priesthood was that he had lost faith in the organization of the Church—its paternalism, legalism, dogmatism, and moralism. He did not want to lay this on the man sitting in front of him. This Bishop would have enough trouble with the Neanderthals of the diocese anyway. "No, Bishop, I think I gained faith, faith in myself and a new faith in God. I don't know if you can understand this, but I have come to the realization that all these years I have been ignoring my feelings, escaping into my head, so to speak. Getting to know people in a deep and intimate way in Paris has made me aware that it is a different kind of love that I want in my life. It is not the distant, careful kind of love that I have to live as a priest. I have gotten to know a couple in Paris who have taught me more about love this year than all the education and retreats I've made in my life. They have led a simple life running a country store and raising children. They have five grown children now whom they love very much and who love them in return. The wife and mother died of cancer last November. She is a saint but will never be in any book. I want to be like that couple and not like most of the priests I've known." Jerry then relaxed, although he felt like he had shared or, perhaps, preached too much. He thought of adding that he wanted to know love by its first name, but knew that would entail a long explanation.

The Bishop again leaned forward and put his hands on the desk. "Believe it not, Father, I do understand. I've often had those same thoughts. The thoughts and feelings were so intense that I took a sabbatical around my twelfth year of the priesthood." He flipped a few pages from the folder and added, "Hmmm, you are in your twelfth year. How about taking a year off, Father Haloran, and then decide?"

"I've thought of that also, Bishop. I have not told another soul of my plans." The next person he planned to tell was Kathy Olson. Jerry was amazed at the level of anxiety that arose in him as he thought of telling Kathy.

Bishop Scalleti surprised him by saying, "What if that woman you are thinking of, tells you to go to hell?" He had a bit of anger in his voice.

Jerry sat silently for a few moments and then said, "I don't know what she'll say. If she doesn't want to marry me, I plan to spend the next year convincing her that it would be a good idea. If she continues to say 'no' after a year, then I will search elsewhere." Jerry felt good about what he had just said even though he had not thought about it that clearly before. Kathy probably wouldn't be available in a year if Rebecca rejected him, he thought egotistically.

"So when do you plan to make this public?"

"I thought I would explain it to the people in Paris next Sunday."

"And I suppose you do not plan to go through the proper channels to be reduced to the lay state."

"I know that this will sound heretical to you Bishop, but I have never thought of myself as having been elevated above the lay state." Scalleti smiled and shook his head knowingly. Jerry went on, "I believe that the only one who can excommunicate me from God is myself."

The Bishop chuckled, "As our friend Bishop Mazurski said, you definitely are a free thinker." He rose from the desk and walked around the desk. He extended his hand and said, "Well, Jerry Haloran, I guess that is more appropriate now, I hate to lose a good man. Good luck to you and I hope you will continue to bring love into the world no matter what you will be doing."

Jerry took the Bishop's hand, held it tightly for a moment and looked into the man's eyes. They were steady, sensitive, and compassionate eyes. He hoped he was not making a mistake. "Thank you." He chuckled. "Now that I've told you of my plans, I guess I can give myself permission to call you 'David.' Thanks, David, you will be a great blessing to the people of the diocese."

Jerry turned toward the door and then stopped himself. "Oh, I almost forgot, I have an idea for you that might help people. I've thought about it for years but never brought it up to Mazurski because I was sure he was so entrenched in the thirteenth century that he wouldn't be interested."

The Bishop chuckled and looked interested. "The twelfth century would be closer. What's your idea?"

"When most of the religious orders were founded, life expectancy was between thirty-five and forty and life itself, for the ordinary person, quite bleak. So a vow for life in a relatively secure and comfortable religious order was often a good deal. Now that life expectancy is close to eighty and there are many wonderful choices and lifestyles for people, I think a religious order with five- or six-year vows is in order. I believe that there are many college students who would devote some years to teaching, nursing, and social work, if they didn't have to think of it as a lifetime committment. Think about it."

"I will. Want to stay around and implement it?"

"No thank you, David. It has been good to know you, even if it is such a brief knowing."

"Your choice, not mine."

"I know. Goodbye, Bishop, and good luck. You'll need it."

As Jerry left Aberdeen he felt like a heavy burden had been lifted off his shoulders. He began singing, "Born free, as free as the grass grows, as free as the wind blows, born free to follow your heart..."

When he finished, Ricky was grinning from ear to ear. "S, s, sing it again. I, I, I like it."

Jerry sang it several more times until Ricky had it down. They sang several more songs. At one point Ricky said, "You m, m, must ha, ha, have had a g, g, good m, m, meeting with the Bishop."

"Yes, I did Ricky. At least it was good for me." He didn't tell him that the singing also helped reduce the anxiety when he thought of his upcoming meeting with Kathy.

"Ca, ca, can you te, te, tell me about it?"

"I'll tell you on Sunday."

It was three-thirty when Jerry drove up to the apartment complex where Kathy lived in Manhattan, Kansas. Kathy had a first-floor apartment and he wheeled Ricky up to the door and rang the bell. She was expecting them and almost immediately opened the door. She was dressed in khaki shorts and a white blouse. It had been months since Jerry had seen her in shorts and he took a deep breath.

"Well, hi, you two. Welcome." She bent over and gave Ricky a kiss on the cheek and then gave Jerry a hug. Interestingly, he felt the shape of her breasts for the first time even though he had hugged her dozens of times. He guessed that he had finally given himself permission to feel another new feeling and wondered what else was in store for him. As they went into the living room, Kathy asked, "Have you had lunch?"

"Yes, but we are thirsty." Jerry sat down on the sofa that Kathy called 'early Goodwill' when he visited earlier. She handed each of them a Pepsi and asked, "Well, Jerry, how'd the meeting with the Bishop go. Are you being reassigned?"

Again Jerry's anxiety reached a peak and his hand

shook as he put the glass of Pepsi down on an end table. "Well, yes, in a way but not by the Bishop."

Kathy looked puzzled. "What do you mean?"

"Kathy, is there some place we could talk? I mean just you and me?" He knew it was a one bedroom apartment and it wouldn't be appropriate for him to talk with her in the bedroom, not with Ricky present. "You wouldn't mind if we left you alone Ricky?"

Ricky looked confused but shook his head. Kathy said, "I guess we could go out by the pool."

Jerry wished he had brought along a change of clothes but hadn't thought of it until then. He had left his suit coat in the car but was still wearing his short-sleeved clerical shirt. He pulled the white collar out and put it in his shirt pocked and folded the top of the shirt in so that it just looked like an ordinary black shirt. While he was doing this, Kathy turned on the small television and showed Ricky how to use the remote.

As they went out the door, she smiled and said, "Anyone seeing you will still think you're a priest."

Jerry winced and wondered if that were true. She led them to an area near the pool where there were a number of lawn chairs and lounges. As they sat down on two of the chairs near the water and facing each other, Jerry remarked, "I'm surprised they have water in the pool so early."

"They just filled it over the weekend. The solar panels take two or three weeks to heat it enough to use. They said it would be ready for swimming by May. So, Jerry Haloran, tell me about the reassignment that isn't the Bishop's idea."

Jerry took a deep breath, looked at the pool, and then

into Kathy's eyes. "Kathy, I'm leaving the priesthood. After the Bishop, you're the first to know. I'm planning to announce it at the Masses on Sunday."

Kathy put a hand to her throat, looked away and then back at Jerry. "You're not kidding are you?"

"No, Kathy, I'm not. As I'm sure you can guess, I've been giving it a lot of thought."

"What are you going to do?"

"I hope to get into a doctoral program in psychology."

Kathy crossed and uncrossed and re-crossed her legs. "Jerry, I don't know what to say. Even though you've given it a lot of thought, it's a real surprise to me. All these months, you've been saying that you like Paris. Was that a lie?"

"No, Kathy, that wasn't a lie. I've enjoyed it as much as any assignment I've had as a priest. And your visits helped make it a real joy."

This time, Kathy took a deep breath, was silent for a moment, and then asked, "And this new assignment has nothing to do with me, does it?"

Jerry could see tears forming in her eyes, "No, Kathy, it doesn't, except I just wanted you to be one of the first to know."

"It's Rebecca, isn't it?" Her jaw was tight and, if it were anyone else, he would swear that he saw hatred in her eyes.

Jerry couldn't remember when he felt so awkward. "Well, yes and no, I haven't told her yet and I do plan to ask her to marry me. I don't know whether or not she'll accept."

"Oh, she'll accept, all right. She's had her sights

set on you since that first weekend in Paris last fall."
Kathy stood up. "Well, I guess our private discussion
is over, isn't it?" She stood, turned and began to walk
back toward the apartment.

Jerry jumped up and moved toward her. He didn't
know what more he could say but hated to see her
so angry and unhappy. He put his hand on her arm.
Kathy spun around and shouted, "Don't touch me, you
bastard!" She pushed Jerry away as hard as she could.
She caught him off balance and he fell backward into
the cold swimming pool.

Jerry went under and then surfaced, sputtering,
flailing his arms, and shaking his head. The water
was like ice and he could feel his muscles tighten. He
quickly swam to the edge of the pool. He seemed to
turn blue in the few seconds he was in the cold water.
Hand over hand, he reached the ladder and climbed
out. He lay on the deck for a moment and then got up
on all fours and stood. He put his arms around himself
and shook. Kathy was nowhere in sight.

Kathy paused a moment and saw Jerry flailing
away in the cold pool. She sursprised herself by
mumbling, "I hope he drowns." She was pretty sure he
could swim and she almost ran to her apartment. Ricky
was startled as she burst through the door. She almost
shouted at him, "I'm sorry Ricky, but I'm going to ask
you to leave." She grabbed his wheelchair and almost
dumped him out as she pushed him over the threshold
and down the single step landing. She knew that Jerry
would be wet and cold when he got out of the pool but
it served him right.

Ricky asked, "Wh, wh, wh, what ha, ha, happened,

Ka, Ka, Ka, Kathy?"

"Jerry will tell you. I'm sorry. I'm sure he'll be here shortly." Kathy went back inside and locked the door. She heard Jerry speak to Ricky and then knock on her door.. She peeked through a drape and saw a wet and shivering Jerry begin to push Ricky toward the parking area. She wasn't about to let that snake-in-the-grass in her apartment. She flopped down on the bed and bawled.

"Wh, wh, what happened ? Ka, ka, Kathy said 'so, so, sorry' and pu, pu, pushed m, m, me o, o, out the d, d, door."

"She pushed me into the swimming pool." Jerry had already knocked on Kathy's door several times and got no response. "Well, Rick, I'm soaked. Let's go find me some dry clothes."

They found a Wal-Mart at the edge of town and Jerry bought himself a pair of jeans, shirt, socks, and underwear. He changed in the men's dressing room. As he dressed, he started laughing at how suitable Kathy's response had been. He then began to feel sad about hurting her. He told Ricky why she was so angry and asked him to not tell anyone about his decision. Ricky said he would not tell but added that he felt sorry for Kathy. He ended by saying, "I, I, al, al, always thought ya, ya, you were all wet. Nn, n, now I know." Jerry couldn't help but chuckle but it disappeared immediately when he saw tears streaming down Ricky's face..

As he drove into Paris, Jerry was surprised at how dreary it looked, even worse, it seemed, than his first sighting last August. He dropped Ricky off at home and went to the rectory.

The light was blinking on the answering machine. The first message was a request to set a time for a baptism. The second was a short message from Rebecca, "Hi Jerry. It's Monday at eleven, please call as soon as possible. It's important, call me at home!"

If she's home, it must be important, he thought. A cold chill ran down his spine as he thought of Rebecca calling him to say that she was getting married to someone and wanted him to perform the ceremony. The thought made his hands shake. He nervously punched in Rebecca's number.

She picked it up after the first ring and sounded very business-like as she said, "This is Rebecca."

"Hi, Rebecca, what's up? You sounded a bit upset when you left the message."

"Thanks for calling back, Jerry. I need to ask a favor."

"Sure, what can I do for you?"

"Jerry, I just got word that I have been nominated for a literary award in New York. I would like to attend the ceremony on Thursday and I'm wondering if you would go to New York with me? I'll pay your way. I just can't go by myself. I thought of asking Helene but I would really rather have you with me. Could you do it, Jerry? Please?"

It was the first time she had really asked for anything since the first interview. "Of course I will. Rebecca, I'm happy to do it." Jerry had debated about when to ask her to marry him. It couldn't be over the phone. On the way home, he decided to drive to St. Louis on Tuesday, if Rebecca was available. Maybe after they arrived in New York, the Statue of Liberty would be symbolic. "When is this shindig?"

"On Thursday at eleven. I've checked out flights and, believe it or not, there's a flight from Aberdeen to New York tomorrow morning. And it stops in St. Louis! How about that? Oh, Jerry, thank you. I'll reserve your ticket in Aberdeen as soon as I hang up."

"Thank you for asking. It will be great to see you. Have I told you lately that I love you?" Jerry felt wonderful.

"No, as a matter of fact, you haven't. Jerry, you aren't drinking, are you?"

"No. And I do love you. I'll see you tomorrow." That is the first truly *"I love you,"* he had ever said to anyone and with shaking hands he quickly hung up before Rebecca could respond.

About the Author

Don Hanley is the ninth of ten children and was born in Nebraska. He grew up mostly in Kansas and South Dakota. He decided to become a priest at the age of twelve but worked in a lumber yard and remodeled houses before entering the seminary. He was a priest in Kansas for six years and then married and moved to Southern California where he received a Ph.D. in Human Behavior. For the last many years he has been a Marriage and Family Therapist, University and College Administrator and Professor of Psychology and, with his wife Anne, has written two non-fiction books for parents and teachers. He has two daughters and one grandson. This is his first work of fiction and he is currently writing his second novel.